MY SPANISH ROMANCE

FALLING FOR MY BROTHER'S BEST FRIEND

OLIVIA SPRING

To my amazing friend Jas

PROLOGUE

'Dinner's ready!' Mum shouted.

I closed my textbook and sighed. My parents and elder sisters, Cassie and Flo, were already downstairs, and normally, I was first at the table. But this evening I had to study for my maths exam. And if you asked me, that was more important than meeting another one of my big brother Nate's frosty friends from uni, who wouldn't even bother to acknowledge me.

Well, that was what I'd thought, until I saw *him*.

After scraping my thick, dark curly hair into a bun, I left the bedroom clutching my huge textbook, with every intention of continuing to revise whilst I ate. But as I entered the brightly lit dining room, Nate's friend stood up from the large rectangular table and flashed me a warm smile, and I lost the ability to do anything.

To think. To function. To speak.

My mouth fell to the floor and I wouldn't have been surprised if a little dribble rolled down my chin.

He. Was. A. Vision.

Six foot tall, jet-black cropped hair, flawless olive skin and those eyes. What colour were they? Brown? Green? After staring for longer than was socially acceptable, I settled on light brown with a hint of green.

The sleeves of his navy top were rolled up, exposing his muscular forearms, and those dark blue jeans fitted his body in all the right places.

And OMG. Look at those eyelashes. Why did men always have such long ones? I'd have to use a whole tube of mascara to get mine like that.

I was so entranced that I didn't even notice when Mr Pretty Eyes stepped in front of me. My body temperature rocketed by about twenty degrees.

'You must be Lily,' he said in a strong accent. I couldn't work out whether he was Italian, Spanish or French, but his voice sounded like honey. Thick, delicious and sweet. I wondered how he knew my name, then guessed that Mum had probably pointed me out in one of the many embarrassing childhood photos within the gold-rimmed picture frames that lined the burgundy-painted walls. 'I am Carlos.' He smiled, causing my stomach to flip-flop like a hundred happy dolphins were swimming around inside.

And then he kissed me.

Okay. That came out wrong. Let me rephrase: he kissed me, but not on the lips like I would've liked. Just the friendly greeting thing.

As his warm lips brushed against one cheek and then the other, fireworks exploded inside me. I'd never been this close to a boy before. Unless you counted the time when the bus had stopped suddenly and the captain of the school football team had accidentally fallen on me. But being kissed by this god was too much for my poor body to bear. I dropped my textbook on the floor. At least I *thought* that was where it had fallen, until I heard a loud 'ooof' shoot from Carlos's lips.

I glanced at the burgundy carpet and saw it on his foot.

'Oh my God! I'm so sorry.' I bent down to pick it up at the same time that he did and our heads collided. 'Ouch, shit!' I shouted. 'I mean, crap!'

'Language!' Mum scolded in her St Lucian accent, resting her cutlery on the fancy red-and-white china plates. She was wearing the purple chiffon blouse that only came out of her wardrobe on special occasions.

Gosh, I hadn't realised until now that not only was Mum dressed up, but the table had been laid with the special white lace tablecloth and crockery that normally only saw the light of day at Christmas. The gold-rimmed wine glasses were still locked away in the oak cabinet, though. She was probably saving them for when the king came to visit.

'Sorry!' It was always so hard to remember not to swear around my parents. 'Are you okay?' I winced, looking up at Carlos.

'*Tranquila*.' He smiled.

'Tran-what-now?' I frowned.

'It's Spanish, sis. It means *chill*, or no worries,' Nate explained, running his hand through his short curly hair.

'No worries. I am a big boy,' Carlos said.

I bet you are… I thought to myself before dragging my mind out of the gutter.

Carlos scooped up the textbook, and my mouth dropped open again as I watched his huge bicep flex. 'It will take more than a book on my foot or a crash of heads to make me cry.' He smiled again.

'I-er… um…' I couldn't move. It was as if I'd been struck by lightning.

And it wasn't just his accent. His body was divine too. He wasn't wrong in saying he was a big boy. Those arms and, God, his chest and…

'Yo, Lily!' Nate shouted, snapping me out of my thoughts. 'Stop drooling and take your damn book.'

Heat flooded my cheeks. Clearly I hadn't hidden how smitten I was.

'Here.' As Carlos handed it to me, his fingers brushed against mine and it was like someone had set my skin on fire.

'Th-thank you,' I stuttered before reaching for a serviette to dab my forehead. I could tell I was sweating. How could I not? The hottest man I'd ever laid eyes on had kissed my cheeks.

'When is your test?' Carlos asked. Even if I hadn't already been floored by his looks, him asking when my test was would've shocked me. Apart from his mate Jack, Nate's friends rarely gave me the time of day. They'd usually just nod, grunt or, on a good day, say 'alright?' But *this* guy…

And he didn't seem loud like the others either. His voice was soft. Gentle. Soothing.

'Next Thursday,' I said.

'But today is Saturday?'

'That's Lily.' Nate rolled his eyes. 'She revises for exams weeks in advance.'

Nate was one of those annoying people who didn't have to study a lot to get good grades.

'That is sensible,' Carlos replied, and my stomach somersaulted for the hundredth time.

Somehow I made it through the meal, but as soon as I swallowed the last spoonful of curry and rice, I made my excuses and said I had to get back to studying.

'It was nice to meet you,' Carlos said.

My eyes bulged from the shock that he'd acknowledged me, again. I grunted an awkward 'yeah' before bolting out of the room like my feet were on fire.

So embarrassing.

'Someone's got it *bad*!' Cassie teased as she joined me in our bedroom.

'Stop!' I winced. 'I'm trying to study!'

'My arse!' she laughed. 'I think the only thing you want to study right now is a certain Spaniard's body!'

'No, I don't!'

I totally did.

'It's okay, sis. It's good for you to show an interest in something else other than your school work.'

As Cassie switched on the tiny TV, I tried to focus but couldn't. All I could see was Carlos. I quickly pushed the thought out of my mind. Thinking that anything could ever happen was stupid.

A twenty-year-old man would never be interested in a sixteen-year-old who was still at school and lived at home with her parents.

He was way out of my league. A guy like him could have a supermodel. So why would he choose a spotty teenager like me?

And of course, there was the biggest taboo of all: I was Nate's little sister. I remembered when one of Nate's friends had been interested in Cassie and he'd told him to back off. Everyone understood the bro code: friends did *not* get involved with his sisters.

So that was that.

Carlos was like the fancy wine glasses my parents kept in the dining room cabinet: something that you could look at but not touch.

If only things could be different…

CHAPTER ONE

Sixteen years later
13 February

Valentine's Day.
Normally I'd dismiss it as a load of commercialised nonsense, but not anymore.

This year, I was actually looking forward to it. I wouldn't be spending tomorrow night alone with a tub of Häagen-Daaz, a bottle of wine and pizza like I'd done for the last three years. Instead I'd be with my boyfriend, River, enjoying a romantic evening together. A flutter of excitement filled my belly.

As I continued walking down bustling Oxford Street, weaving through the crowds whilst taking in the romantic red window displays, I pictured how happy River would be when he saw his gifts.

I'd bought him a bottle of designer aftershave and I'd

just collected the pair of silver cufflinks which I'd had engraved with his initials. I was all set. Tomorrow was going to be the best Valentine's Day ever.

The loud sound of a double-decker bus tooting its horn at a lorry in the thick central London traffic snapped me out of my thoughts. I looked at my watch. I'd met my older sister Cassie briefly for lunch, so now there was only ten minutes before my break was over. I quickly walked back to work and headed straight for the loo.

After washing my hands, straightening my grey trouser suit and tightening my hair bun, I checked my face in the mirror.

Great. Another one.

I touched the angry spot that had appeared on my cheek. It was bad enough that there were several others along my jawline. I also had the dark scars from previous pimples, which were so visible on my light brown skin and took months to fade. Hopefully if I put some anti-blemish cream on it tonight, it'd go down a bit by tomorrow. I pulled some concealer from my make-up bag and covered it up.

That's better.

After pushing the heavy mahogany door, I stepped into the main office. It was a functional space. No bells or whistles, just rows of rectangular wooden desks and one large window on the right-hand side of the white wall. There wasn't much of a view—just the tall brown building across the road.

The buzz of colleagues chatting and phones ringing rippled through the air. I waved to my workmate Ayo whilst walking towards my desk. My mobile chimed. It was River. An excited squeal flew from my lips.

River
Hey babe
River
Typing…
Me
Hi!

I quickly typed out a reply to let him know I was online.

'Lily? Lily!'

I span around and saw Ruth, my boss at Fairchild & Keen Chartered Accountants. She was dressed in her signature smart structured black dress, and her razor-sharp bob didn't have a hair out of place.

I'd been so focused on River's message that I hadn't heard her come up right behind me. Ruth towered over my five-foot-four frame. I hoped she hadn't seen my phone screen.

River was one of our clients, and to say Ruth wasn't a fan of mixing business with pleasure was putting it mildly. Even though I didn't work on his account directly, if she found out we were dating, it would still land me in hot water.

'You still okay to send over that financial report for Wilkes & Sons?'

'Course!' I smiled, sliding my phone into my handbag, then placing it on the dark grey carpet beneath my desk. 'It's almost done.'

I had to finish yet another tax return and chase a client for the invoices and receipts I needed to submit their VAT return, but I could do both with my eyes closed.

I'd pretty much worked with the same clients for the

past seven years, which I supposed was a compliment because it meant they were happy with my work, but it would be nice to switch things up a bit.

It wasn't that I didn't enjoy my job. I liked helping clients manage their finances, and advising them how to minimise their tax payments. Not that dodgy offshore accounts stuff, of course. Our work was always above board. But I'd been asking Ruth for ages to let me do something more challenging with bigger clients.

A promotion would be nice too. But apart from that, I couldn't complain. It was a nice steady role. People would always need accountants, so I knew I had a job for life.

'Great! If you can send it over by end of play, I'd appreciate it.'

'No problem.'

Once Ruth had left, I took my phone out of my bag and my stomach flipped with excitement when I saw that River had sent two more messages.

River

Sorry, can't meet tomorrow night. Not feeling well.

River

Let's speak in a few days. I'll come to yours on Fri night after work around 11.

WTF?

Not again.

My heart crashed through the floor.

I was really looking forward to tomorrow. But I didn't want to sound unsympathetic.

Me

What's wrong? Anything I can do to help?

. . .

I stared at the screen, waiting for his response. After several minutes without a reply, I rested my phone on my desk and continued working.

The more I thought about it, the more it didn't make sense. If we were meeting this evening, I'd understand why he'd cancel if he wasn't feeling well this afternoon. But how did he know today that he wouldn't be feeling better tomorrow night?

If it were anyone else, I wouldn't have questioned it. But River had been falling mysteriously ill and working late a lot recently. Like on my birthday last month when I'd suggested he meet my family for dinner. He'd messaged at the last minute to say he wouldn't be able to make it but would come to my place around eleven.

Nate said it sounded like a booty call. And now River had suggested meeting late at my place this Friday night again instead of going out for our Valentine's Day dinner, the alarm bells were ringing louder than ever.

Maybe I was overthinking. River always had his phone attached to his hip, so he'd probably reply soon and we could speak properly.

By five o'clock, I'd sent the report to Ruth but still hadn't heard from River, and my message was still on one grey tick.

I tried calling again, but his phone was switched off.

Something wasn't right. I could feel it in my gut.

I needed to see him. If River really *was* ill, I'd do whatever I could to help him. But if he wasn't, well, we'd need to have a serious talk. I'd have to do what I'd wanted for weeks: ask him outright how he really felt about me.

Once I got home, I jumped in the car and drove to his place.

Even though we'd been dating for six months, I'd only been here a couple of times, which also bothered me. He'd said it was because his neighbours were loud, so he preferred coming to my house because it was peaceful. And when I'd suggested visiting again a few weeks ago, he'd said he was getting some work done, so the place was a mess. Which was strange, as he'd never mentioned it was being refurbished before.

There were no spaces directly outside his house, so I parked across the road, then rang his doorbell three times. No answer. The same when I tried his phone.

Something told me to try his office line. I rarely called him at work, just as a precaution—you know, with the whole dating a client thing—but if he was really that ill or had been rushed to hospital, they might know something. The phone was answered after a few rings.

'Hello, River's phone!' a bubbly woman announced.

'Oh, hi, it's er…' I paused. 'Is River around?'

'No, sorry, he's left for the day.'

'Was he feeling okay when he left?'

'I'm sorry, who am I speaking to, please?'

'It's, er, his… sister.' I hated lying, but my Spidey-senses were tingling like crazy.

'Oh! Hello! Yes, yes. He was in good spirits. Left around five. I think he had another hot date, judging by the tie he was wearing. He thinks I don't notice, but he always wears that sparkly blue tie when he's going out on the town. I'm sure you already know this, but your brother is *very* popular with the ladies!'

I dropped the phone on my lap.

On a date?

Popular with the ladies?

Yes, River was handsome. With his dark blonde hair and sharp suits, I didn't doubt he attracted female attention, but he was my boyfriend, so why would he be going on a date tonight? Especially when he told me he was too ill to meet me tomorrow?

I had no idea who this woman was and I couldn't take her speculation about River as gospel, but I wasn't going to dismiss it outright either. Like the saying goes, there's no smoke without fire.

After abruptly ending the call, I took a deep breath and thought about what to do next. As much as I hated the idea of camping outside his house, I had to go with my gut and find out what was going on.

A distraction would calm my nerves. I reached for my phone to text Cassie. She'd messaged earlier to say that after we'd met for lunch, she'd quit her job, so I wanted to check she was okay. But when I looked up, I saw River strutting towards his house. And he wasn't alone. Two women had their arms linked in his.

I swallowed hard.

It wasn't illegal to link arms with the opposite sex, but something told me this wasn't innocent.

They stopped under a street lamp outside River's gate, giving me a better look. Not that I wanted one. Both women looked so glamorous. Legs as long as a giraffe's, skyscraper heels and beautiful blow-dried hair. One was wearing a short vibrant pink skirt and the other a thigh-skimming lime-green dress. If someone told me they'd stepped straight off a catwalk, I'd believe them.

Suddenly River pulled Ms Pink Skirt towards him and

started kissing her passionately. Then lime-green dress lady ran her hands down his arm whilst her friend stepped aside, giving her full access to grab River's dick.

WTF?

I blinked several times. I couldn't believe what I was seeing.

They stumbled through the gate, hands and mouths everywhere.

When that woman said River was popular with the ladies, she wasn't joking. River couldn't just cheat on me with one woman. He had to have two.

I opened the window. I needed air. I was going to be sick.

My mind raced. My heart pounded. I had no idea what to do. Confront him? Or just drive away and never look back?

I grabbed my phone and messaged Cassie.

Me

I'm outside River's house. He messaged earlier to say he wasn't well, so wouldn't be able to see me tomorrow— on Valentine's Day. I didn't believe him and I was right not to!

After a few minutes, Cassie started typing. I was frozen. Everything felt fuzzy and my whole body was wobbly. I was still in shock. I wanted to look, but I was worried what else I'd see if I did. I wanted to go and say something, but if I got up now, I wasn't sure I'd be able to stand up.

Cassie

Why? What did you find out?

·   ·   ·

Me

It's not good, Cass. It's definitely over between us.

Cassie

What happened?

I started typing, but then my eyes darted back to River's front door. They were still there. Why hadn't they gone inside yet? Did he know I was there? Was this his sick way of ending things?

Rage ripped through me. My blood was so hot I could feel it scalding my skin. I'd given him the benefit of the doubt so many times. I was kind to him. And yet he lied. Over and over.

I flung the car door open and stormed towards him.

'You bastard!' I screamed. River jumped, and when he saw me, his eyes bulged. 'You fucking bastard! Don't ever call me again!'

'Babe!' he called out. 'It's not what you think! I can explain!'

I ran to the car and drove away but then pulled over shortly afterwards, tears streaming down my face. If I drove in this state, I'd have an accident. My phone pinged. Better not be that arsehole.

Cassie

Are you okay?

Me

No, I'm not, but can't talk now.

Cassie

Sorry to hear that… Text me when you're home so I know you're back safely, okay?

. . .

Me

Will do.

After blocking River, I switched off my phone.

So much for having a romantic Valentine's Day tomorrow.

I'd given River my heart and he'd pissed all over it.

I was done with men.

I was done with romance.

I was never falling in love ever again.

CHAPTER TWO

Two months later

As the credits rolled for *The Martin Lewis Money Show*, I reached for the remote control, then switched off the TV. It was time for my Saturday afternoon visit to see Doris at the residential home.

Since breaking up with *the arsehole who won't be named*, I'd been doing some volunteering there and it had been a real tonic.

After making a quick stop at the florist's, I arrived and found Doris sat in the big canary-yellow armchair by the window with a china teacup beside her.

Doris always looked like she was dressed for a special occasion. Whilst I was wearing a pair of grey trousers and matching baggy jumper, Doris wore a sparkly, fitted electric-blue blouse. Her chic, short silver hair was neatly styled, and as always she sported dark smoky eyes, with matte red lipstick. It was as if I'd come to visit a glamorous Hollywood film star.

'Lily!' she beamed as I handed her a bouquet, pulled up a wooden chair beside her and placed one of her red velvet cushions behind me. 'My favourites!' she gushed as she brought the sweet red roses to her nose. 'Thank you so much, dear. I was starting to wonder if you were coming. Thought maybe you'd been swept away by some tall, dark and handsome stranger and forgotten all about me!'

'Pff!' I rolled my eyes. 'I told you—I'm over all that dating bollocks. I have about as much interest in finding a man as having a root canal without anaesthetic.'

'Come, come, now.' Doris shook her head. 'Don't tell me you're still moping over that ex. What was his name again? Ocean? Stream? Puddle?'

'*River*,' I spat, feeling like I'd just uttered the rudest swear word. A shiver ran down my spine. We'd avoided talking about him for the past couple of weeks, but hearing his name still made me wince.

'I knew it had something to do with water. My next guess was going to be sewage. That's a more accurate description, don't you think?'

'Too right!' I chuckled.

'There we go!' Doris rested her hand on mine. 'So much better to see you smile.' I didn't know how she did it, but it was impossible to be around Doris and not feel joy.

Cassie used to chat about her all the time when she volunteered here, and I always thought she sounded like a hoot, but even Cassie's animated stories hadn't prepared me for how fun she was in real life.

When Cassie had moved to Paris to live with the love of her life, Frenchman Nico, she'd asked if I wanted to continue volunteering in her place. Although I'd been reluctant at first, eventually I'd come around to the idea. So after I'd been interviewed and passed all the checks, I'd gone for it. I knew it'd be a good distraction from my arse of an ex.

'Thanks.' I squeezed Doris's hand.

'So what's new in Lily-land? It's been over two months since you caught Mr Sewage playing away, so that's more than enough time to jump back into the dating pool. Plenty more fish in the sea and all that. Goodness! Look at how many water references I included in those few sentences. Despite what my son may think, I've still got my marbles!' She chuckled.

'Cassie and I reckon you're eighty-seven going on seventeen! Nothing new to report,' I sighed. 'Same old, same old. Just working and trying my best to get on with things, but it's not easy. It's not that I miss him—it's more the humiliation, you know? That was stupid enough to get involved in the first place and ignored all the red flags.'

My stomach twisted. Thankfully, since that awful night, I'd managed to avoid speaking to and seeing him. I was glad he'd stayed away from me and that Ruth hadn't found out. I couldn't believe I'd jeopardised the career I'd worked so hard for by dating a piece of shit like him.

'It's happened to us all, darling. You can't change the past. But you *can* control your future. Whenever one of my husbands cheated, I didn't sit around moping. I got out there. After filing the divorce papers and cutting up their favourite suits.'

'You didn't!' I gasped.

'Oh yes, I did. I was sick of it. It had already happened twice before.'

'Your husband cheated on you three times?'

'No, dear. It happened with husband number two and four. I was calmer with those. I just dyed my hair and went shopping, using their money, *of course*.' It was hard to keep up with Doris's stories about her husbands. She'd been married seven times. 'The third time it happened, with husband number five, I'd had enough. That's when I keyed his Bentley and weed in his coffee. Then I took myself off on a long holiday and found someone else to get under to help me forget…' Her mouth twitched and her eyes twinkled.

'Are you serious?' My eyes widened.

'Absolutely! I had the time of my life! I'm not recommending that you resort to those extreme measures—these days you'd probably get arrested, and I enjoy your visits, so I wouldn't want that. But there's nothing stopping you from going on holiday. Maybe you'll find yourself husband number one.'

I knew Doris was trying to cheer me up, but that was a hard no on both counts.

First up, like I'd told her a billion times, I had no interest in another relationship. Clearly I had piss-poor judgement when it came to men and wasn't able to attract anyone decent, so it was best to steer clear of them completely. And I needed time to *heal*.

Secondly, I didn't do holidays. My idea of long-haul travel was taking the Tube to the end of the Northern Line. It was a family thing. Cassie was the same. Up until she'd met Nico, she'd rarely travelled abroad. Same with Flo. The only sibling who ventured overseas was Nate.

'I don't like to travel abroad.'

'What?' Doris frowned. 'Remind me how old you are?'

'Thirty-two.'

'My goodness. Lily, you are in your prime! Do you want to settle down and have kids?'

'I'd love kids. One day.' Admittedly, it would be harder without a man, but with sperm banks and all the scientific advances, I didn't need one.

'Well, you should be having the time of your life! You'll never be this free again! When you have kids, it's a lifelong commitment. Right now you only have to focus on you. If I was your age again, I'd be living it up. Where have you travelled before?'

'Dad's mum is from Scotland, so we used to go there, and once we went to St Lucia to see Mum's family.'

'And that's it?'

'Pretty much.'

'Didn't you travel when you went to university? I thought backpacking around India was a rite of passage for students of your generation.'

'No. I went straight to work after I graduated. I wanted to start building my career.'

'Oh, *good Lord*. Well, it's not too late. You can still have an adventure. Look at Cassie! Why don't you go and see her, then travel around France and find yourself a hot *monsieur* like she did?'

Cassie constantly invited me to stay with her and Nico. Paris did sound nice, and I would go at some point. Just not right now.

'Maybe…'

'Or better yet, go to Spain. The weather is wonderful. So are the men!' She sat up straighter in her chair. '*Ah…* I remember my first trip to Spain. That's where I met my husband.'

'Which one?'

'Number six. We made love on the beach that night. It was such an adventure.'

That did sound cool. Not the sex on the beach part. Getting sand up my lady parts would be uncomfortable. I meant going to Spain. Apart from Paris, that was somewhere I might consider visiting. One day.

'I've always wanted to go to Spain. My brother's best friend is from there, and whenever he spoke about it, it always sounded cool…'

My thoughts turned to Nate's bestie, Carlos. I used to have a stupid crush on him when I was my late teens. And, okay, in my twenties too. Anyway, he'd moved back to Spain. I hadn't seen him in the flesh for ages.

'Oh *really*?' Doris grinned. 'And what does this best friend look like? Is he muff?'

'*Muff*?' My face crumpled.

'Isn't that what you youngsters call handsome men with big muscles?'

'Oh wait! You mean *buff*?'

'Yes, dear, that's what I said.'

'Right…' I stifled a giggle. Doris was so funny when she tried to be *down with the kids*. I wasn't even sure if people still used *buff*, but I was hardly a youth lingo expert. 'Sorry, I must have misheard you.' I didn't want to make her feel bad for getting her words muddled, but at the same time, it wouldn't be right to let her walk around saying the wrong thing. 'It's just that *muff* has a completely different meaning. It can mean vagina, sooo…'

'Goodness!' Doris blushed. 'Of course it does!'

'Anyway, why did you ask if he's handsome?'

'It's just that your face has gone all flushed and your eyes are sparkling. What happened with him?'

'Nothing!'

'Because he wasn't *buff*?' she said, this time emphasising the letter B.

'No… he was very *buff*.' Heat flooded my cheeks as I pictured him. Carlos was tall, dark and handsome personified. 'But like I said, nothing happened.'

He bought me a really cool maths book once to help me revise, which was sweet. Generally, though, when Carlos came round we were rarely alone. Nate never liked leaving his friends with me and my sisters, but if he went to the bathroom, Carlos and I would chat and he'd ask how my studies were going. That was as far as it ever went, though: talking.

'But I can tell by the twinkle in your eyes that you wanted it to.' The corner of Doris's mouth twitched mischievously.

'Doesn't matter.' I waved my hand dismissively. 'It was a stupid crush. That's all.'

'Well, you never know. Maybe if you went to Spain you could arrange to meet him. It's never too late. Reminds me of John.'

'John?'

'My seventh husband.'

I think that was the first time I'd heard Doris refer to one of her husbands by name.

'What happened with him?'

'We liked each other when we were teenagers. I had the biggest crush on him, but, hard to believe it now, but back then I was too shy to tell him how I felt and, well, he was too much of a gentleman to make the first move. Then he joined the army and we lost touch. Anyway, long story short, our paths crossed again six years ago and we got married five weeks later.'

'After five weeks? Wow!'

'It sounds fast, but we'd loved each other for a life-time. Those were the happiest and best two years of my life. After six practice runs, I finally got the marriage thing right and then the bugger only bloody went and died on me. I wish we hadn't left it so late to find each other.'

Doris had tears in her eyes. She'd clearly loved John deeply. I'd never seen her so sombre.

'Sorry to hear about John.'

'Thanks. But if you're really sorry, don't waste another second worrying about your silly ex. Go and have an adventure somewhere.'

Doris was lucky. She'd grown up with money, so it had been easier for her to just up and leave and travel on a whim for months at a time. But people like me had to work.

'It's not that simple.'

'Ah, yes. I can hear that brain of yours whirring away. Worrying about work and bills. I know a sensible woman like you must have savings stashed away, so put them to good use. And as for that job of yours, ask for a sabbatical. Take it from me, a woman who could kick the bucket at any moment: no one ever went to their grave saying they wished they'd spent more time at work or watching TV at home. Live your life, Lily. *Now*.'

I did more than just work and watch TV. I went to the cinema sometimes and for walks in the park… well, I hadn't recently, but I'd been going through a break-up. Plus it'd been cold and rainy, so going straight home after work was more comfortable.

Doris took a sip of her tea. I opened my mouth to tell her I was trying to do more at the weekends and coming to see her every Saturday proved that, but she was on a roll and continued her speech.

'By the sounds of it, you've got a lot of years to make up for. Relive your twenties. Go travelling like you should've done after uni. And if you're still worried about money, get a job when you travel. Somewhere where you can soak up the culture and the sunshine. I always loved doing bar work. I'm sure you'll find something. Just think, this time next month you could be on a beach, the sand between your toes, the sun kissing your skin and a hot Spaniard kissing your lips—and not just the ones on your face!' She winked.

'Doris!'

As shocked as I was at hearing a pensioner talking about getting oral, my traitorous body tingled at the idea. I quickly told it to behave. A few minutes of pleasure wasn't worth the months of heartbreak afterwards.

I know Cassie's life had been transformed thanks to a holiday. But the chances of the same thing happening to me must be close to zero. Lightning didn't strike in the same place twice.

Although my company offered sabbaticals, I wasn't interested in taking one. I was trying to convince Ruth to give me bigger clients, so swanning off on an extended break wouldn't exactly help my cause.

No. Maybe I'd speak to Cassie about visiting her, but I wasn't about to abandon my stable job to go travelling. I was thirty-two, not twenty-two.

And as for kissing a hot Spaniard, although years ago I would have loved nothing more than locking lips with a hot guy like Carlos, that ship had sailed. In fact, it was never in the dock to begin with.

I knew Doris meant well, but I wasn't interested in any *buff* guys, English, Spanish or otherwise. It was safer to be single.

Me, my *muff* and I were fine just the way we were.

CHAPTER THREE

The sharp screech of the kitchen smoke alarm made me jump. I was so engrossed watching *Bridgerton*, I'd completely forgotten about the rice I'd left cooking on the hob.

After turning off the smoke alarm, I opened the window. Not ideal, considering it was pouring with rain, but it was the only way to clear the smoke.

Once I'd tossed the pot in the sink, I took a packet of microwave rice from the cupboard, warmed it up with the chicken curry Mum had dropped off last night, then returned to the living room.

My two-bed house was pretty modest. When I'd bought it a few years ago, I couldn't decide what colour to paint it, so I'd gone for magnolia. It was a safe choice. Most of the furniture, like my comfy sofa, was grey, but the TV and bookcase were black. Nice practical colours that would never go out of style.

I'd been giving what Doris said yesterday some more thought. It wasn't travelling or a new man that I needed. I reckoned that if I kept working hard, sooner or later I'd get bigger clients and *that* was what would make me happier. Work was where I spent most of my time, so it made perfect sense to focus on that.

But I wasn't all about work, so now that Cassie was living in Paris and we couldn't hang out as much as we used to, I just needed to reconnect with my friends and socialise with them more instead.

I fired off texts to Ashanti, Rita and Chanel to see if we could set something up for next weekend, like girly drinks or a trip to the cinema. Sorted. I didn't need to jet off to Europe to have fun.

My phone rang. It was Cassie.

'Hey, sis!' I answered. 'Or should I say *bonjour*?'

'*Oui*! I saw you were online, so thought I'd give you a quick call. How's it going?'

'All good, thanks.' I quickly swallowed a spoonful of rice. 'You?'

'I'm great! So, did you visit Doris yesterday? I miss our catch-ups.'

'So you miss Doris, but not your favourite sister?' I teased.

'*Please*.' I could tell from the tone of her voice she was rolling her eyes. 'You know I do. That's why you *need* to come over! You'll love Paris!'

'Yeah,' I sighed. 'Doris was saying the same. She spent most of the afternoon banging on about me taking a sabbatical and going travelling.'

I filled Cassie in on everything Doris had said. Except the stupid part about going to Spain and calling Carlos, of course.

'She's spot on! Travelling is amazing! Nico and I are

going to Marbella tomorrow to check out a cool new hotel that's interested in stocking his tools in their fancy salon and gym changing rooms. Can't wait!'

'Marbella's where the rich people go, right?'

'Yeah.'

Cassie's boyfriend Nico was a billionaire, so she was probably getting used to mixing in those circles. A few of the clients we represented at work were millionaires, but apart from Nico, I'd never met a *billionaire* before. Must be nice to never have to worry about money.

The irony was that despite being an accountant, I always seemed to attract guys that were terrible with money. Not because they didn't earn enough, but because they handled it badly or had poor judgement. My arsehole ex used to blow through his salary a few days after it hit his bank account, splashing out on designer clothes to keep up appearances or buying strangers drinks at the bar, before he'd even paid his rent.

In approximately five to ten years' time, which was when I *might* consider dating again, I'd definitely need to find a guy who a) wasn't a ladies' man and b) was financially secure. Cassie was lucky to find Nico.

'I kinda like Doris's idea about working behind a bar to fund your travels. Sounds fun! If you want, I can ask the hotel if they're looking for temp staff?'

'Thanks, but there's no point. With all the new Brexit and employment laws, it's probably super complicated,' I said, thinking that sounded like a better excuse than just telling her I wasn't interested.

'It's not as easy as it used to be, but it's possible. I'm a Brit working in France. Nico's lawyer knows about all this stuff. I know you're not used to travelling, I was the same, but I wish I'd done it sooner. And everything's changed because of it! Paris is amazing. Travelling literally changed my life. I'm in love with my dream man, I have my dream career and I'm living in a cool new city. You never know, travel could change your life too! Think about it, yeah? I'll send a link to the hotel now.' My phone chimed as the message came through. 'Anyway, just wanted to say hi and check you're okay. Better go and pack for tomorrow.'

We blew each other kisses down the phone. I finished the last of my lunch, then flopped back on the sofa.

It was kind of Cassie to think of me and send me a link, but there was no point looking at it when I had no intention of swanning off to Spain.

When I looked at my phone, there were two replies.

Ashanti

So sorry, Lily, but the kids have a b'day party on Sat and then play dates on Sun. Xx

Chanel

I'd love to, but hubby is away next weekend, so I need to stay at home with the kids. Chat soon, hon.

My stomach sank. It had been hard to meet up with them since they'd had children. They were always off to kids' parties or doing other family stuff. Maybe Rita would be free, though. She was single, so hopefully she'd be up for going out.

Rita

Lily! Long time no speak! I've been meaning to

message to tell you the news! I'm engaged! It's all been a bit of a whirlwind. I'm away with my fiancé (still can't get used to saying that!!) and my in-laws for ten days, but let's video call once I'm back. Xx

It was official. I was the last single friend standing.

But it was okay. I'd make new friends. Find new activities. And anyway, I thought, glancing out at the dark gloomy sky, staying in wasn't so bad. I had food, central heating and Netflix. There were at least two documentaries with my name on them.

CHAPTER FOUR

I squeezed into the packed Tube carriage. My head was wedged underneath a guy's armpit and, judging by the aroma, he hadn't showered this morning. *Nice.*

I felt someone's rucksack dig into me. The Tube made a sudden stop and a woman's stiletto went right in the middle of my foot.

'Ouch!'

'Sorry!' she said.

The tinny sound of someone's music blaring from their headphones was so irritating. This was the reality of commuting in rush hour. It was times like these that I wished I didn't work in central London.

After arriving at the office, tackling my emails and finishing off a set of accounts, I went to the kitchen. Whilst the kettle boiled, I checked my phone. There were loads of messages from Cassie. I clicked on WhatsApp.

Cassie

Arrived in Marbella! Xxx

. . .

I opened up the first photo, which showed her standing on a gorgeous beach.

A loud crash of thunder made me jump. I glared out the office window at the dark, gloomy London sky. A bolt of lightning flashed through it. Clearly the weather was a *lot* better in Marbella. I continued scrolling through the messages.

Cassie

This place is A-MAZING! I asked one of the managers and they're definitely looking for temp summer staff. They're doing a big recruitment drive at the moment, trying to attract British speakers.

Cassie

You should definitely do it! Did you look at the website?

I definitely hadn't. I couldn't tell Cassie that, though. She seemed so enthusiastic.

Me

Something came up, but I'll take a look soon. Thanks for asking about the job. Enjoy the rest of your trip!

I took my tea to my desk and sat down. The thunder and lightning had stopped, but the sky was still so depressing.

Lucky Cassie. She'd only been in Marbella a few hours and already seemed like she was having the time of her life. I supposed it wouldn't hurt to take a little peek at the hotel's website.

Wow. As much as it pained me to admit it, Cassie was right. It was out of this world. The hotel had a gorgeous white stone exterior and fancy swimming pool, and the stunning sandy beach was just metres away.

Once I'd started looking, I went down a rabbit hole: reading over every page and looking at every photo in the gallery.

Then I googled Marbella. No wonder the rich and famous flocked there. With its golden sand and sparkling blue sea, it looked like paradise.

Next, I moved on to Tripadvisor. The hotel had only been open a few months, so there weren't lots of reviews, but the ones they had were glowing.

And when I did a quick search (forty-five minutes qualifies as quick, right?), I spotted more rave reviews from different travel websites.

This hotel definitely seemed like the place to be. But looking at a hotel you'd love to stay in (although with those prices, I'd need to win the lottery first) for a dream holiday was one thing. Working there was a whole different story.

I had a steady job, so would it really be a good idea to swap working in an office to serve rich, possibly demanding and potentially drunk people?

It wasn't because I was being snooty. My parents had had loads of jobs over the years. Mum had done cleaning alongside her nursing and Dad was a builder. They'd always taught us that we were never above anyone else. But the idea seemed so topsy-turvy. Like, I should've travelled and done bar work for the first time in my early twenties, not be looking to break from my stable job to go travelling in my *thirties*.

I could only imagine what my parents would say, and Nate would definitely hate the idea. Even though I was a grown woman, he was still the overprotective big brother.

I closed down the web pages. My eyes were stinging and I was starting to get a headache. I'd probably tied my bun too tight. I removed my hairband and my curls fell to my shoulders. Couldn't believe I'd spent almost two hours looking up this hotel when I was supposed to be working.

The sky had cleared. In fact, the sun was even peeking through. The London weather wasn't so bad. We occasionally had sunshine too. Okay, we didn't have a beach and the sea, but we had lots of other great things, like… well, I couldn't think of anything right now, but…

Time for lunch. Normally I ate a sandwich at my desk, but I needed to drop off a jacket at the dry cleaners.

'Want anything from Pret?' I poked my head into Ruth's office.

'Oooh, yes, please. A salad would be great. And when you come back from lunch, I'd like to have a chat.'

'Oh.' I swallowed hard. 'Okay, sure.' I hoped she hadn't noticed that I'd spent so much time skiving.

'Don't worry!' Ruth must have read the nervous expression on my face. 'I just want to have a chat about giving you more responsibility…'

'Oh!' A flash of excitement raced through me. 'Okay! I won't be long.'

Finally.

I knew my hard work would pay off. I couldn't wait to hear all about what she had in mind.

After buying lunch, I was about to pick up a ready meal from M&S for tonight's dinner, but then I heard the sky rumble. No. Don't tell me…

I glanced up. The sky, which had been bright when I'd

left, had now reverted to an angry grey. And who had been so fooled by the glimpse of sunshine that she'd left her coat at the office and hadn't thought to take an umbrella? Yep. Me.

Maybe if I hurried, I could make it back to the office in time.

The sky rumbled again like it was belly laughing at me and saying *as if*. Seconds later, the heavens opened and the rain began to pour down.

Within minutes, the paper bag with my sandwich and Ruth's salad was sodden. I clutched it to my chest to avoid the contents crashing to the ground.

And God, my hair. It wasn't that I was vain and wanted to keep it looking glam. A storm like this would make it explode into a ball of frizz and I'd have to spend ages trying to untangle my curls. I should've left it tied up in a bun like I always did, or at least brought a hairband.

A plastic bag blew across my path and I had a brainwave. I'd look like a plonker, but needs must and all that. I whipped it up from the floor. It had Bargain Basement, the discount store name, written over it, but the important thing was it could act like a makeshift rain cap and keep my head dry. It wasn't stylish, but it'd be better than having to wrestle with my hair later.

I checked that the inside was clean—well, as clean as a bag blowing about on the street can be—then whacked it on my head.

The rain streamed down my face. I could barely see. I grabbed a tissue from my bag and wiped it.

I sprinted to the office, crashing through the glass doors, then doubling over, desperately trying to catch my breath. I hadn't run for ages.

'Lily?' A deep voice called my name. 'Is that you?'

Oh no. Don't tell me…

I lifted my head slowly, hoping that I was wrong. Shit.

'H-hi,' I stuttered.

It was River.

Why, God? Why?

'What are you doing here?' I snapped.

As one of our clients, River visiting our office wasn't totally weird. But in the whole two years that we'd done the accounts for the company he worked for, he'd only visited three times and that was at the beginning. He hadn't been here for several months. So why did he have to rock up here now?

'I came to see Ruth. Oooh.' River grimaced, glaring at my cheek. 'That's a nasty one. You should cover that up.'

My stomach twisted. Shit. I must have wiped my make-up off when I was drying my face. I quickly hung my head and touched my cheek nervously, trying to shield the giant spot.

I knew I should've left it alone this morning, but every time I looked in the mirror it taunted me, shouting, 'Pick me! Pick me!' It was like scratching an insect bite. I couldn't help it. As soon as I got upstairs, I needed to go to the bathroom to fix my face before anyone else saw how bad my skin was.

'Ruth?' I added quickly, keen to change the subject. 'I didn't see any client meetings scheduled in the calendar today.'

'I didn't come to see her about the accounts. I came to talk about something else.'

Oh God.

'About what?' I hoped he hadn't told her that we'd dated.

'Good news!' River beamed. 'Our company will be renting the fifth floor. In a couple of months, we'll be working in the same building!'

'What?' I gasped. 'You-you're moving your office, *here*?'

'Yeah! It'll be great!'

Bile rose in my throat. He was moving into my building? So I'd have to see his face every single day?

No. This couldn't be happening.

I'd worked so hard to get over River. The last thing I needed was a daily reminder of what a fool I'd been to date him in the first place.

'What's wrong, babe?' He placed his hand on my shoulder. I batted it away like I was swatting a mosquito. Actually, that comparison was unfair to the mosquito population. The idea of having one of the most hated insects on the planet on me was more appealing than being anywhere near *Mr Sewage*. 'Just think, when we get the urge, we can just use my office here.'

Did he just…?

Unbelievable.

'Is there something wrong with your memory?' I hissed. 'You remember that we're not together anymore, right? I made that clear when I caught you with those women.'

'I told you, babe, it wasn't what you think. They were my cousins.'

'And you kiss your *cousins* like *that*? On the lips?'

'What can I say?' He smirked. 'We're a close family. Come on, babe.' He tilted his face, giving me his doe eyes.

It was a move he used a lot and I was annoyed when I realised I was about to fall for it again. 'Don't be like that. I'm sorry you saw whatever you saw, but it doesn't have to be the end. Blocking me was immature, but I forgive you. Let's forget about the past and try again, yeah? I've got some time before my next meeting. Maybe we could go somewhere…' He winked.

Oh. My. God.

'No!'

'Come on, don't be such a bore!'

I opened my mouth, then closed it again. I wished I could've given him a piece of my mind, but my brain was racing so much I couldn't think straight. Instead I ran towards the lift and bashed the buttons repeatedly to quickly close the doors behind me.

There I was thinking wet hair was the worst of my problems today. Little did I know that the news of my sleazy ex moving into my office building would blow that out of the water.

Shit.

CHAPTER FIVE

M y heart thundered and my cheeks were so hot you
could fry eggs on them.

The audacity of that man.

How could I be so stupid? How had I ever fallen for a
cretin like him? I didn't know how or why I'd managed to
stay with him for so long.

Actually, that was a lie. If I was honest, I knew why. I
was just too embarrassed to admit it. I was lonely.

When River had asked me out, I'd been flattered. He
was handsome and charming and I was surprised he'd be
interested in someone like me. I liked having someone to
hang out with in the evenings.

The sex was okay too. Most of the time, it was all
about him, but I'd reasoned something was better than
nothing. Before River, I'd been single for a while and
missed that physical contact. And the more I got used to
him being around, the harder it was to leave.

Deep down, I knew things weren't right, but most of
my friends were coupled up and I didn't want to feel like

the odd one out. So I'd stayed. Hoping that he'd change. But now I realised I'd lost my self-respect in the process.

Lesson learned. The next time a guy paid me attention, particularly if he was good-looking, I'd know to avoid him like the plague.

As the lift doors opened, my phone chimed.

Cassie

You've got the job! Congrats! Call me when you're free and I'll fill you in. Xxx

What? How was that possible when I hadn't even applied? And anyway, despite the bombshell River had just dropped, at least I was minutes away from getting good news from Ruth.

Me

Thanks, sis, but Ruth told me before lunch that she's going to give me some more responsibility, so I might be getting a promotion! FINALLY! Which means I can't go travelling. Will tell you more later. Xxx

'Lily.' Ruth stood at her office door, then frowned as her eyes jumped up to my head. 'Can we have that chat now, please? Maybe take the plastic bag off first, though…'

'Oh… yeah. Sure. Give me two secs.'

I'd forgotten about that. Which meant I'd had it on when I was downstairs speaking to that loser. I winced. Of all the times to bump into my ex, I had to see him when I looked like a drowned rat, with a giant zit and a bloody Bargain Basement plastic bag on my head.

I rushed to my desk, whipped off the bag, tossed it in

the bin, dabbed some concealer over my spot as discreetly as I could, grabbed my coat to sit on so I didn't get Ruth's chair wet, then returned to her office.

'Take a seat.' Ruth gestured to the chair in front of her. I sat down, my heart still thudding from the run-in with River. After she'd told me about my new role, I'd ask her about him moving here. It had to be a mistake.

'So we're making a few changes with day-to-day client management. Ian will be moving to the Hodgson Global account because they're giving us more business, which means we'll need someone to oversee Manson Electronics, and we think you'd be perfect for it.'

I froze.

The blood that had previously boiled hotter than a kettle when I'd run into that arsehole downstairs had dropped to minus ten degrees.

Manson Electronics was the company River worked for.

And Ruth wanted *me* to head up his account.

Shit.

I'd thought seeing him in the building every day would be bad enough, but working on his account full-time? It didn't even bear thinking about.

During the whole time we'd dated, I'd only ever worked with him once when Ian was off sick, which was ideal as it made it easier to keep our relationship a secret. But there was no way I could work with him now.

'Um, er, thank you for thinking of me, but I-I'm happy with my current clients, so I'd, erm, really prefer it if I could just stick to that, please?'

'I don't understand.' Ruth's eyes narrowed. 'I thought

MY SPANISH ROMANCE 43

that you'd be delighted. Manson Electronics is becoming a huge client for us. Especially now they'll be renting one of our offices to give them another central London base.' So it *was* true. 'And River requested you, personally. He was very impressed when you stepped in before to help out, and I know you've always wanted to work on bigger accounts.'

Fuck.

For years I'd been telling Ruth I was ready for more responsibility and now she'd given it to me on a silver platter, I was rejecting it. What a mess. For about the hundredth time today, I regretted getting involved with a client. *Dammit.*

'I did, and I still *do*, it's just that…'

I wracked my brain, trying to think of a plausible excuse. What reason could I possibly have to turn down what was, on paper, a golden opportunity?

If River and I worked together, I wouldn't be able to hide my anger. Ruth would guess that something had gone on, and she'd be so annoyed that I'd crossed the professional boundaries that she felt so strongly about.

Two years ago, her now ex-husband had become the biggest cliché when he'd slept with his secretary, and Ruth had understandably been cut up about it for months. Their divorce was not pretty.

And four months ago, when one of our team members had left the company to work in-house at a client that he'd secretly been dating, taking their business and revenue with him, Ruth had been furious. She'd ranted for weeks about how unethical it was for employees to use sex to climb up the career ladder and said people should earn their positions fair and square. So I wasn't about to tell her that *I'd* also been sleeping with a client for months. Especially now that same client had asked me to head up his accounts team. Imagine how that would look.

Ruth had always championed me and my career. She was my mentor. She respected me. Considered me trustworthy, hard-working and smart. I didn't want to disappoint her by telling her I'd fallen for River's charms and was now struggling to get over him. She'd think less of me. And even though, strictly speaking, what I did in my personal life was my own business, she'd treat me differently. She'd question my ability to be professional, and she'd be spot on. There was no way I could work with River with a clear head. It was still too raw.

Think. Think. Think.

'It's just that I...' Cassie's text flashed into my head. She'd said I had the job, right? Still didn't understand how, but having a chance to work abroad might be my only escape route right now. 'Sabbatical!' The words flew out of my mouth. 'I'd like to take a sabbatical...'

'What?' Ruth's eyes widened.

WTF indeed.

Now that I'd said it, I wasn't even sure myself if it was a good idea. A sabbatical was only temporary. It'd get me out of the office for a month or two, but how would running away solve anything long-term? And what the hell was I going to do when I got back and River was still here?

Ruth's mouth was now on the floor. I couldn't back out now, though. I had to run with it...

'Yeah... I want to... I'd like to go travelling for a bit. So it's probably not a good idea to start working with a new client, especially one that's so important, if I'm planning on taking some time away, right? I know how important stability and continuity are to clients, so…'

'Yes, of course. I didn't know you were thinking of taking time off.'

Ruth was clearly shocked. *That makes two of us.* This was not how I'd seen the conversation going when I'd stepped into her office.

Doris and Cassie had been banging on about it for the past few days, so I'd given it some thought, but thinking about going away was one thing. Actually doing it was another.

'Sorry. I was trying to find the right time to ask. It's just, I've had a bit of a bad break-up…' *Oh God.* I was supposed to be staying off the subject of *him*. I didn't have to mention any names, though. 'He cheated, and it's left me feeling… raw. And I feel like I need to get away. To *heal*.' Yes. *Heal* was a good word. It sounded deep. 'To reset and get a new perspective.'

'Oh, Lily!' Ruth jumped up from her desk and knelt down beside me, resting her hands on mine. 'You poor thing! I'm sorry. I know *exactly* how you're feeling right now.'

As much as Ruth and I got on, we didn't really talk about our personal lives much. Well, with the exception of her messy divorce. She'd shared that story with me when we'd gone out for drinks after a conference and got a bit tipsy. The day after, she was mortified.

'Break-ups can be hard, particularly when there's a third party involved. *Bloody men*. Why can't they just keep it in their pants? Anyway, it's been a while since you took a holiday. Maybe you could take a couple of weeks off? I wish I'd done that.'

Two weeks wouldn't change anything. I'd be back before River even moved in. But a sabbatical, on the other hand, would take a while to arrange, and if I was working abroad, I'd need time to sort out getting a visa. So with any luck, I'd be out of here before that twat arrived, then I'd be away for at least a month after that. I'd worry about what to do about the situation when I got back, later. I could only jump one hurdle at a time.

'Um, I think I need something longer. I recently turned thirty-two, and without sounding like an overdramatic thirty-something going through a pre-midlife crisis, I've been thinking more and more about my life choices and what I have, or in my case, *haven't* done.' As Ruth went back to her chair, I thought about the things Doris had said. 'And, well, I've never really travelled, and the older I get, the more responsibilities I'll have and I kind of feel like it's something I need to do now. Before it's too late.'

'I see.' Ruth nodded. 'And aside from that, you're still happy working here?'

'Yes, of course!' I said quickly. I didn't jump out of bed every morning bursting with excitement, but who did? I would've loved to have the challenge of a new client, but even without that, I still liked what I did.

'Right. Good.' I could tell she was turning everything over in her head. The silence was deafening. I desperately wanted to hear what she thought. Was it an outright no or something she'd consider?

'So, could I take a sabbatical? I wouldn't ask unless it was *really* important.'

'I understand. I'll have a think and speak to HR. Leave it with me.'

'Okay, thanks.' I got up and closed the door.

Well, *that* was an unexpected meeting. Now I'd mentioned the sabbatical, there was a chance that it could happen. Which meant I'd better speak to Cassie about this job I supposedly had. Just in case…

CHAPTER SIX

After leaving Ruth's office, I went to the filing room to call Cassie. Luckily, she hadn't seen my earlier text, so confirmed that the position working at the hotel was mine. I was still trying to understand how.

When she told me it was at the hotel's beach bar, my throat went dry and my heart raced. How the hell was I going to cope with working abroad—in a country where they spoke *Spanish*? The only Spanish I knew was that '*un, dos, tres*' bit in Ricky Martin's 'Maria' song, and something told me that counting to three wouldn't get me very far.

Plus, I'd be away from my home, my family and everything that was familiar. I hadn't had a new job in seven years, and I knew as much about serving drinks and working in the hospitality industry as a tortoise knew about winning a 100m race at the Olympics.

I'd asked Cassie if they had any office jobs, prefer-ably in accounts, as that'd be better suited to my skills. But she said the idea of travelling was to get out of my comfort zone, not just do the same thing in a different location.

She also insisted that working in the bar would be more social and fun than staring at a computer screen full of figures all day. I was going to remind her that I enjoyed that, but decided against it.

'So, that's it? I've just got the job? No interview or anything?'

'Yep. Me and Nico vouched for you. The HR manager said if we give you the thumbs up, that's good enough for them.'

'*Seriously?*'

'Is there something wrong with your hearing, Lil? I said you've got the bloody job!'

'Sorry, I heard you, but it just seems too easy, y'know?'

'This is how things work when you have connections. I'm still getting used to this stuff too. Nico's name carries a lot of weight. It's amazing how many doors instantly open because of it.'

Never in my life had I got a job so easily. I'd been interviewed three times for my current position, so I was surprised that this posh hotel didn't even want a five-minute phone conversation.

'Don't get me wrong, Cass, I'm super grateful and everything—it's just, it kind of feels like cheating. Like jumping the queue. I didn't get it because of my abilities, but just because I know someone rich.'

'I hear you. And ordinarily, I'd agree. But this isn't a long-term career. It's not like you're applying to become a heart surgeon or a teacher and people's lives or futures will be affected if you're not up to it. The worst you can do is spill your drink over someone or put too little rum in their cocktail. Yeah, the customer would be pissed about it, but I'm sure they'd forgive you if you gave them a free drink or something.'

I still wasn't sure…

But now that I'd asked for it, *if* Ruth gave me the sabbatical, I couldn't just sit at home for two months. That would be irresponsible. Plus people would ask to see photos of my travels when I got back.

And the more I thought about it, the more I was convinced that being around River every day would be a disaster. He'd push my buttons with some smarmy comment, I'd scream at him and end up getting fired.

Or what if he laid on his charms and caught me at a weak moment and I ended up sleeping with him again? A shiver ran down my spine.

No. The best thing to do would be to create some distance. And going to Spain would definitely do that.

It'd be nice to feel the sand between my toes and the hot sun on my skin. And I supposed having a change of scenery, visiting different places and meeting new people would be good. Especially seeing as my current friendship group didn't have time to hang out anymore.

If I didn't do this now, when would I? What was I waiting for? Like Doris said, no one went to their grave wishing that they'd worked more.

After all these years, taking a couple of months off wouldn't make a big difference. I trusted Ruth, and my position would still be here when I came back. And hopefully the possibility of more responsibility with a different client would come up again soon too.

I couldn't remember the last time I'd taken a risk.

Done something exciting. Maybe it was time I did.

'Okay…'

'Okay, as in you'll do it? You'll go to Spain and take the job?'

'Yeah,' I replied quickly before I changed my mind. 'I'll give it a go.' My heart thundered against my chest.

Part of me said that it was a mistake. That I was crazy. That it was irresponsible to run away because of a man. That I should stick around and try to ignore him. But it wasn't all about River. Something told me that I needed this.

My stomach fluttered. I wasn't sure whether it was nerves or excitement. Probably ninety-eight per cent fear and two per cent excitement. But two per cent was better than nothing.

'Yay!' Cassie screamed. 'It's going to be great. And even if you hate it, at least you would've tried.'

I really hoped I didn't hate it…

'Can you send me the details of who you spoke to?'

'Will do. And don't worry about the visa and stuff. We'll sort all of that for you.'

'Wow, really? Thanks.' At least that was one less thing to worry about. Which only left about nine hundred and ninety-nine other concerns…

'That's what big sisters are for! I'm so happy and I just want you to be happy too. I know I sound like Bella, by talking about all this "the universe" stuff, but I really think this will be great for you, Lil. I can feel it in my waters.'

'In your waters?'

'Okay,' she laughed. 'I took it a bit too far with that part, but you know what I mean!'

Our cousin Bella was a big believer in things

happening for a reason, stars aligning and how, if we believed in something and wished for it hard enough, the universe would bring it our way.

Cassie had been sceptical too until she'd literally bumped into Nico on a crowded London street at Christmas and they'd ended up falling in love.

Carlos's face flashed in my mind and I quickly pushed it out again. I wasn't going away to meet him or another hot Spaniard. From what I'd gathered from Nate's stories of their wild nights out, Carlos was an eternal playboy. Guys like him were just looking for an easy one-night stand, and I could get that kind of disposable sex in London, minus the white sandy beaches. *No, thanks.*

The fact that Doris had mentioned travelling to Spain and then a few days later I ended up landing a job there was just a coincidence. That was more realistic than thinking it was some sort of fate nonsense.

'Yeah, I get what you're saying. So when do they need me to start?'

'Well, they wanted you to start at the end of May…'

'What?' I gasped. 'But that's just over a month away!'

'Don't worry. I said it was too soon, because we'll need to organise your visa, you'll have to sort things with work, etc.' I exhaled. That was a relief. 'But they do want you to start asap.'

'I have to see if I can get the sabbatical first, though.'

'I'm sure you will. At least your boss is nice, not like my old one.'

'Yeah. Ruth's great.'

'If I were you, I'd start looking up flights and buy a suitcase. If things pan out how I think they will, pretty soon you'll be jetting off to Spain!'

CHAPTER SEVEN

Mid-June
Seven weeks later…

I stepped off the plane and squinted as the sun shone in my eyes. My skin tingled under the blazing heat. Wow. It was *hot*. I switched on the mini electric fan and pointed it at my face. It'd take a lot more than the tickle of a breeze it was generating to keep me cool, but every little bit helped.

It was hard to believe that I was really here, in Spain.

Ever since that meeting with Ruth, everything been a whirlwind. She'd got back to me a week later to say she could give me a five-and-a-half-week unpaid sabbatical, which I was happy to accept.

Cassie arranged everything with the hotel's HR department, and I've no idea how, but as promised, Nico's lawyer had sorted out my work visa.

The bar job didn't pay much, especially compared to my London salary, but once I did the calculations, I knew I'd be fine. My savings could cover my mortgage, and as long as I was careful, my Spanish wages should pay for my rent, food and some basic travel.

My neighbour would keep an eye on my house, and in Marbella I'd found a small apartment that wasn't too far from the hotel. So, the practical things were sorted, but I was still trying to manage my emotions...

As I walked through to passport control, my stomach tensed.

Shit's getting real...

It still hadn't quite sunk in that I'd come to a foreign country to do a job I had zero experience in, to live in a flat that I hadn't seen in real life, in a city where I knew not a single soul. On a crazy scale of one to ten, with ten being the highest, I was topping the scale at nine point five.

I only shaved off that half a point because I'd read that there were a lot of Brits living and holidaying in Marbella, so maybe the language barrier wouldn't be as bad as I'd first feared.

Here's hoping...

Once I'd collected my suitcase, I found an English-speaking taxi driver and slid onto the back seat. Ordinarily I'd get the bus, but the hotel induction started in a few hours and I didn't want to risk arriving late because I couldn't find my flat. This way, I'd arrive nice and calm.

My face was glued to the window, taking in the views along the motorway. The sky was ridiculously blue, like someone had taken a paintbrush and coloured it in perfectly. There wasn't even the teeniest cloud.

The landscape was so different to the greenery I'd seen beneath me when the plane had taken off from Gatwick airport. Instead, hay-coloured fields stretched along the roadside.

It wasn't all burnt grass, though. There were also fields with rows of olive trees, and I even saw a scattering of cypress trees in the distance.

This was going to be a totally different experience to what I was used to. I knew that was the point, but it was also so scary.

These past few weeks, there'd been more knots in my stomach than in a dozen heads of tangled hair. As well as worrying about the trip, because River's company was due to move in next week, I'd also worried about whether I'd avoid seeing him before I left. Thank God I had.

To make it on the plane, I kept telling myself that this trip was for the best and that stepping out of my comfort zone meant I'd meet new people and travel to exciting places around Spain.

Obviously I wanted to check out Marbella and visit some of the other towns in the Costa del Sol. And I had to visit the capital. That was the only reason I'd be going to Madrid. Not to get in touch with a certain Spaniard I'd crushed on years ago.

I got two days off a week, so hopefully that'd give me enough time to travel to a new place and spend the night there at least once a week.

As we approached Marbella, the views became even more attractive. Strips of pretty pink flowers and large palm trees lined the roads and we approached a round-about with *Marbella* written in big bronze letters.

Soon afterwards, the driver pulled up outside a white

stone apartment block and announced that we'd arrived. After paying him, collecting the key to my flat from the maintenance man and going to the fourth floor, I opened the door to my new Spanish home.

Ahhh...

As I stepped onto the dark wooden floors of the studio apartment, I breathed a sigh of relief. It looked just like the photos online.

To the left was a double bed with a light green duvet cover. There were two small pine bedside tables on either side and a built-in wardrobe.

Then in the centre of the room was a long white cupboard, which acted as a kind of divider. There was an orange sofa with several colourful cushions, a coffee table and a little flat-screen TV in the corner. Brightly painted art lined the wall above the sofa, and a small glass dining table faced a large window which gave the whole apartment a bright and airy feel.

When I looked outside, as well as seeing the bright blue sky and the street in front of the apartment block, in the distance I also saw a glimpse of the sea, which I wasn't expecting. It definitely beat the dreary views from my house in London.

To the right of the apartment were two sliding white doors.

The first one was the bathroom. The decor was minimalist with white marble-style tiles and a pure white sink, toilet and shower.

The second door led to a small kitchen with plain white kitchen units. It was barely big enough to move in, but I wasn't fussed. I was hardly a culinary goddess, so I doubted I'd be doing much gourmet cooking while I was here. It was perfect. Clean, comfortable, compact and just what I needed.

I showered, then opened my suitcase. There was no way that accountant Lily's wardrobe would fit into a cool place like Marbella. A new country called for a new Lily.

Although coming to Marbella was scary, not knowing anyone meant it was also an opportunity to reinvent myself. Start afresh.

People liked people who looked stylish and fun, right? Like those women River was with. If I wanted to make friends in this new town, I had to do things that I wouldn't normally do and project a more exciting image. River thought I was a *bore*, but not anymore. It was out with the grey trouser suits I normally wore and in with a selection of bright shorts, colourful T-shirts and knee-skimming skirts.

Because I'd be wearing a uniform most of the time at work, I had to think of other ways to look cool. So I'd got a three-week mani-pedi in a bright red shade. There was a new red lipstick in my make-up bag too, but I wasn't sure I'd be brave enough to wear it. It might bring too much attention to my face. Or it could make people focus on my lips rather than my skin. *We'll see…*

After settling on a white T-shirt and fitted purple skirt, I touched up my make-up, then took the bus to the hotel.

Cassie said they'd mainly need me to work the evening shift, which meant the buses wouldn't be running by the time I'd finished in the early hours of the morning, so I'd allocated enough in my budget for taking a taxi home each night. It wasn't ideal, but it was the safest option.

As the bus pulled up near the Playa Élite hotel, my

eyes widened. The photos on their website didn't do it justice.

It was a grand whitewashed building with an elaborate bronze crest on the front, surrounded by tall, lush palm trees, manicured gardens and more pretty pink flowers like the ones I'd seen lining the roads.

This was the kind of place that cool rich people hung out in. Not someone like me.

But then I remembered my revamped image. Right now, my clothes and nails didn't say boring accountant. They said outgoing and fun. Yes. Whilst I was here, that was exactly what I was going to try to be.

I took a deep breath, smiled at the doorman and walked to reception.

After introducing myself, I was escorted through to a staff area, where I was given an in-depth briefing with a few other new recruits on the hotel's practices and policies. We were then shown around the building and handed a thick manual, which I was told I'd need to study thoroughly.

'Now, let me take you to the bar,' announced Pandora, my British manager. I had no idea how she hadn't passed out wearing that blouse and navy suit jacket. Even in my short-sleeved T-shirt and skirt, I still felt like I had my head in an oven. 'You come highly recommended, so I'm looking forward to seeing what you can do!'

She sounded a bit too excited about my bar skills and I wanted to tell her to manage her expectations, but I was sure it'd be fine. I reckoned the first week here would be various light-training days where they'd teach me how to mix different cocktails step-by-step before letting me loose on the customers. Once I'd completed the training programme, it'd be plain sailing. If I could manage clients' finances, I'd be able to mix a cosmo, right?

Now I was here and saw first-hand that a lot of people did speak English like I'd heard, I was starting to feel a bit more relaxed.

We walked across the immaculately polished white tiled flooring and stepped outside.

The scent of the fresh sea air immediately hit me. My head spun from left to right as I took in my surroundings. Wow.

On one side, there was a rectangular pool surrounded by large and luxurious-looking four-poster daybeds and oversized circular white sunloungers shaded by white parasols. Then on the other, there was a decked area with a stage and *Playa Élite, Marbella* sign in front. It looked like they used that space for different performances.

Behind the pool and decked area there was a gorgeous stretch of white sandy beach. And the azure-coloured sea was spectacular.

Chill summery music played softly in the background. The sound of splashing water from the pool and the chitter-chatter of the beautiful guests with expensive-looking bikinis, toned bodies and chiselled abs mingling with friends or relaxing on the loungers with colourful cocktails filled the air.

'Here we are.' Pandora led me along the decked section to a circular beach bar. It had a thatched roof, which I hoped would provide some shade on hot days like this, and a wooden bar area with tall white stools surrounding it. 'Zachary'—she gestured to a clean-shaven short guy with wavy, shoulder-length bleach-blonde hair and brown eyes—'this is Lillian, your new colleague.'

'Nice to meet you.' I smiled.

'Hiya!' He also sounded British. He had a slight accent, possibly from Essex, but I couldn't be sure. Zachary was dressed in the bar staff uniform, which was a short-sleeved white shirt with the hotel's logo on the left pocket and a pair of smart dark blue shorts. From what they'd said in the briefing, I'd be wearing the same, or I could choose to wear their branded dark blue skirt.

'Lillian, make me a drink,' Pandora demanded.

'Course! What would you like?'

'Let's start with a gin and tonic.'

I exhaled. Now *that* I could do. I knew a lot of people who loved G&Ts, so at least I'd mixed a few at home before. Pandora was clearly checking my entry-level skills to see how many weeks of training I needed.

I went behind the bar and washed my hands. First things first: the glass. I picked up a tall one. Next, ice. I plunged the glass into the ice bin, thinking that this bar stuff wasn't as hard as I feared. But as I looked up, Zachary's eyes were like saucers.

'Nooo!' Pandora shouted. 'What are you doing? For God's sake, use the scoop! If there's a crack in the glass, when it hits the ice, that crack could turn into a full-blown break. And can you imagine how much time it'd take to clean up when it gets busy? You'd have to throw the whole lot away! Or risk the hotel getting sued for serving customers a massive shard of glass in their drink!'

'Sorry.' I hung my head. I could've sworn I'd seen bartenders doing that before.

After mixing the G&T, I handed it over. Pandora took a sip and winced like she'd just sucked on a bitter lemon.

'Too much gin! Get me a beer.'

'Okay.' I opened the fridge and plucked out a tall green bottle. 'Would you like a glass?'

'The first thing you ask me is whether I'd like a glass? You haven't even asked what type of beer I'd like! How do you know I want a bottle rather than draught beer from the tap? Or what brand?'

Doh. I resisted the temptation to slap my forehead.

'Sorry,' I muttered again, seriously considering whether I should order a T-shirt with *sorry* printed on it. If the last ten minutes of this pitiful practical session were anything to go by, I'd be apologising a *lot*.

I was right. From that moment, things went from bad to worse. When I served the beer from the tap, there was more white froth in the glass than in a bubble bath.

Next, when I attempted to shake a cocktail, I hadn't checked that the lid was on properly, so the red liquid sprayed my face and all down the front of my white T-shirt.

And when I went to give Pandora a glass of sangria, somehow it slipped out of my hand and smashed on the floor, so I spent ages sweeping and mopping up the sticky mess. No mean feat in the blazing heat.

Pandora grew angrier by the second. Her cheeks were now bright pink and she was scowling so hard she'd give a grizzly bear a run for its money.

'I will need to rethink your position, Lillian. Your performance today was diabolical, to say the least. I was told by HR that you had bar experience and you'd be able to hit the ground running. But clearly that's not the case. Nepotism at its finest.' She sneered.

Wait, what?

She'd been told I had *experience*? What the hell had

Cassie said? I thought I'd be fully trained and be given time to get up to speed. If I'd known I'd be thrown in at the deep end, there was no way I would've come. And Cassie knew that… *I'll bloody kill her.*

My stomach sank. This was what I was afraid of. Being called out for not earning the position here.

I hadn't even been here a day and I was already getting the boot. Despite what nonsense Cassie must've told them to get me the job, I hated the thought of letting her and Nico down when they'd vouched for me. And I didn't want to go back to London with my tail between my legs.

'I'm sorry. It's my first day and I'm a bit nervous.'

'You're not nervous. You're a disaster! I'm afraid that I have no choice but to—'

'Wait!' I jumped in. 'I know I haven't got off to the best start, but I promise, I'll get better. I know I'm not due to start until Monday, but I'll work an extra shift. *Tonight.* So I can shadow Zachary. Learn the ropes. It might not seem that way right now, but I'm a fast learner. I'll pick it up. You don't mind, do you?' I turned to face him.

He looked like he'd rather eat a plate of live cock-roaches for dinner, but he nodded reluctantly.

'Fine,' Pandora snapped. 'Put on a uniform and sort yourself out. If I don't see an improvement tonight or if I receive *one* complaint from a customer about you, you're out. I don't care if your sister is the Queen of Sheba, I will not have you bringing down the reputation of this hotel. Are we clear?'

'*Crystal,*' my heart thumped against my chest.

I had one night to become a cocktail-making, perfect-beer-pouring queen. It was a tall order, but somehow, I had to make it happen.

CHAPTER EIGHT

I walked along the beach, marvelling at the blue-and-orange sky in front of me. The sun was setting and it was like staring at the pages of a glossy travel brochure. I loved my new surroundings.

Zachary had told me to take a break, probably to give himself an hour off from my constant questions and questionable serving skills.

On a scale of one to ten, I'd rank my bartending abilities as a solid two. Considering I had easily been at minus twenty when I'd started a few hours ago, that was decent progress. And as I kept telling myself, it was my first day. I'd get better. Who knows? In a week, maybe I'd be able to serve a drink without spilling half of it down my top.

A thumping bassline filled the air. There went the tranquillity of listening to the waves crashing against the sand. Seeing as it was past nine in the evening and guests were ready to kick off their Saturday night partying, it was to be expected. *Time to get back to work.*

As I walked towards the hotel's beach, my jaw

dropped. Anyone would think I'd been gone for three hours rather than just one. It was packed. There was a crowd of people dancing, waving their hands in the air, having a great time and the bar was two rows deep with people eager to get a drink.

I rushed over.

'Thank God!' Zachary wiped his forehead. He actually looked happy to see me. 'Clara should've started half an hour ago, but she's running late. Can you grab me five Alhambras?'

'*Al-what-as*?' I frowned.

'The green bottles of beer.' Zachary rolled his eyes.

I reached for the fridge and pulled them out, grateful that he was taking care of the cocktail a woman had just requested.

Two men at the other end of the bar shouted their orders. I had no idea who was next in the queue, so headed over to them.

'What can I get you?' I asked, crossing my fingers that they didn't want anything too complicated. Thankfully, they only asked for four Jack Daniels and Cokes, which I could manage.

For the next hour, we didn't stop, even when Clara turned up. She was another Brit, with a short dark pixie cut and a permanent frown. So far, I didn't take to her, but maybe I needed to get to know her better. Just as the queue started to die down, Pandora came over.

'The glasses need to be collected.'

'No problem!' I said enthusiastically. 'It's just been so busy we—'

'Just get it done. And I need someone to take the DJ his beer.'

'I'll do it!' Zachary and Clara replied in unison.

'No!' Zachary snapped. 'It's *my* turn.'

'But it's my last proper shift here, so *I* should go!' Clara shouted.

'I don't care who does it!' Pandora turned on her heel. 'Just get it done!'

'You're fighting about who will take the DJ a beer? Do you get paid extra for doing that or something?' I frowned. I'd never seen someone so enthusiastic about pushing through a sweaty crowd of dancing people to give a beer to someone who was perfectly capable of getting it himself.

'Depends on how you define getting paid extra.' Zachary smirked.

'I don't get it…'

'The DJ is *hot*, so, you know, if he's interested, he can pay me with a night in his bed. Or his car. I'm not fussy.' His cheeks flushed and he fanned himself with a serviette.

'He's not interested in *you,*' Clara snapped.

'What, and you think *you* have a chance?' he retorted.

Jeez. They were making a lot of fuss about this guy. It'd been so busy that I hadn't even had a chance to step out from the bar and check him out. I stood on my tiptoes, but there was no one in the DJ box.

'I can't see him.'

'That's a shame. I'm telling you: he is the hottest guy *ever*.'

'That's a *big* statement,' I scoffed. I hadn't known Zachary long, but I'd already noticed that he exaggerated a lot. Earlier, he'd encouraged me to try a cocktail, which he said was the best cocktail *ever*. If you asked me, it was a bit sickly. And this evening he'd said a song was the biggest track of the summer, but I'd never even heard it before.

Admittedly, my knowledge of dance tunes was limited, but even so.

'Trust me. It's true.'

'I bet he's just ordinary. It's just because he's a DJ that you think he's more attractive than he actually is. Falling for a DJ is *such* a cliché. Take away the silly stage and headphones and it's just some average bloke pushing a few buttons and pretending to be cool, just to pick up women.'

Zachary's eyes widened and he froze.

Okay, I admit, that was a bit harsh seeing as I didn't even know the guy, but what could I say? I was still scarred by my ex, and ladies' men like River who had women hanging off their arms weren't my favourite right now.

Zachary was still glued to the spot, but now his eyes were doing some sort of weird movement. My brow furrowed. He was signalling me to do something, but I couldn't work it out. Now he was tilting his head. What was with the facial expressions and miming? If he wanted something, why didn't he just tell me?

'*Oh, Lily!* You really do know how to put your foot in it!' Clara laughed.

'Pandora said she will get me a beer, but I think she forgot, so I have come to get it myself.'

Oh no.

I had a horrible feeling that the DJ was standing right behind me. Which meant he'd just heard me calling him an average-looking, womanising slimeball. *Cringe*.

Wait.

That voice.

It sounded familiar.

I didn't see how it could be possible, but even though I hadn't heard it in years, the tone and accent were something I couldn't forget.

I'd recognise that deep, delicious, velvety-smooth voice anywhere.

My heart raced.

I turned around slowly and…

Oh. My. God.

It was *him*.

Zachary was right.

The DJ really was the hottest guy ever.

I'd thought the same thing when I'd first seen him.

That was because the DJ wasn't a stranger.

The DJ was Carlos.

My brother's best friend.

Fuck.

CHAPTER NINE

Good Lord.

As well as apologising for my catty comments about DJs, I also made another silent apology for accusing Zachary of exaggerating. Carlos really *was* a vision.

He was wearing a white vest, which showed off his huge, muscular arms, and khaki shorts. And my God. Those pretty greeny-brown eyes sparkled under the fairy lights. I could get lost in those for days.

'Carlos?' I gulped as if I'd just swallowed a whole pineapple. My pulse raced and the temperature felt like it had raised a hundred degrees.

'Lily?' He blinked rapidly. Carlos's mouth fell open, then he flashed his megawatt smile. '*Hombre! Cuanto tiempo!*'

My brain and whole body froze. I had no idea what he'd just said, and before I had time to attempt to work it out, Carlos had leant forward and kissed me on both cheeks.

I swear my heart stopped beating. In fact, was I still

breathing? The butterflies that fluttered in my stomach told me that I was, but if that was true, why had I lost the ability to move? To talk? To think clearly?

Carlos smelt all fresh and woody, like he'd just stepped out of a shower. The sensation of his cheek against mine was divine. Even though it was just for the briefest of seconds, his skin felt so soft. I'd kill for skin like that. Mine was probably all sticky and sweaty.

Oh God. Was I drooling? Although so many years had passed, it was like the first time we'd met all over again.

Get a grip, Lily, my brain finally commanded.

I came to my senses, and when I looked up, Carlos was just staring. Our eyes locked. Time froze and everything around us went quiet. It was as if somebody had turned off the music, everyone had left and all that remained was me and Carlos. On a beach. In Spain. Alone.

'What are you doing here?' Carlos broke the silence.

'I-I'm working…,' I stuttered.

'I see, but… I thought…? You are an accountant, no?'

He remembered. My stomach flipped.

'Yeah, I'm on a sabbatical. But how come you're DJing here? I thought you were based in Madrid?'

Doh. I wasn't thinking straight. Everyone knew that DJs travelled. I remembered Nate had said Carlos DJ'd in Barcelona at Christmas or New Year, so he was probably doing a guest spot for the evening. It was a Saturday night after all.

'No…' He paused. 'I need to get back now, but we can speak later, *si*?'

'Yes! I mean, *si*!' I nodded like a lust-struck teenager.

'Nice to see you.' He flashed his smile again.

'Same,' I said, watching him head back through the

crowd. My stomach flipped again. I turned to see both Zachary and Clara with their mouths wide open.

'You know *him*?' Zachary gasped. '*How? When?* Spill! I told you she was a dark horse!' he said to Clara.

'He's my brother's best friend.'

'Wait: so… don't you speak to your brother anymore?'

'Yeah, course I do!'

'Well how did you not know that his hot friend would be working here?'

The truth was, only a handful of people knew that I was in Marbella: Cassie, Nico and Doris. My boss thought I was travelling around Europe, and I'd told my friends and the rest of my family that I was going on holiday.

I'd kept the details vague because I didn't need the headache. Even though I was a thirty-two-year-old woman, sometimes my parents and elder siblings, especially Nate, still treated me like I was a teenager.

My parents would never understand why I'd want to take unpaid time away from an office job, which they saw as the holy grail of employment, to work in a bar.

If Nate knew, he'd be here right now, babysitting me. I'd only just arrived and I was already struggling to get the hang of the bar work, so the last thing I needed was my overprotective brother breathing down my neck.

It was better to just live my life the way I wanted. Once I was settled in a few weeks, I'd tell them, but right now, I didn't need their doubts clouding my judgement.

'My brother kind of doesn't know that I'm working here, so…' Which reminded me: I'd have to ask Carlos not to mention it.

'Right.'

'Anyway, he wouldn't necessarily have known that

Carlos was playing here tonight. DJs do different gigs all the time,' I said, trying to rescue the comment I'd made earlier, 'and even though they're best friends, I'm sure he doesn't keep track of all the places Carlos is at.'

'But he's not just here for tonight,' Zachary said. 'Carlos is the hotel's *resident* DJ. He'll be playing here for the whole summer.'

'What?' My stomach dropped.

No way.

The crowd had cleared a little, so now I had a better view of the DJ box. There was a group of women standing in front of it, giggling and playing with their hair. Carlos was also smiling.

Now he'd come to the front and bent down whilst one of them whispered something in his ear. She giggled again, then reached into her handbag. I wasn't sure what she took out, something gold. Ah, it was a lipstick. She swiped it over her lips seductively, then started doing something with it on a tissue. Huh? After folding it, she handed it to Carlos.

Oh.

She'd written her number on the tissue in lipstick and given it to him.

'Happens every night,' Zachary sighed.

The realisation hit me like a truck.

Carlos was going to be working here this summer. And so was I. Which meant that every night, I'd have to watch the guy I'd had a crush on for years flirt with different women.

This was going to be a long five weeks.

CHAPTER TEN

As I helped Zachary and Clara clear up the bar, I glanced over again at Carlos. One of his hands was resting on his headphones, making his huge bicep curl. I swallowed hard.

The dance track boomed around the beach, and he announced on the mic that this would be the last song of the night. The crowd groaned in unison. I wasn't into dance music myself, but what he'd played this evening had me tapping my feet a few times.

I'd given the whole working in such close proximity thing some more thought, and I'd overreacted. So what if I saw different women crowded around him constantly? It didn't matter. I had zero interest in men, including Carlos, so he could do whatever he wanted. It was none of my business.

Yeah, he was bloody gorgeous. That was obvious. And yeah, my body had gone all tingly when I saw him, but it didn't mean anything. It was just the shock. It was like the quote from that *Casablanca* film. *Of all the bars in all the world, he had to walk into mine.* I couldn't remember the exact quote, but that was the gist of it.

I knew that Carlos lived in Spain, but Spain was a big country. The chances of bumping into him like this were crazy.

I could imagine what nonsense Doris and Cassie would say when I told them. Doris would harp on about it being fate and Cassie would start channelling her inner Bella and talk about the universe working its magic or some rubbish. But it was just a coincidence. A huge one, admittedly…

So yeah, although Carlos was clearly attractive, I was professional enough not to let him working here get to me. He could kiss a hundred women every night for all I cared.

No big deal. I'd be fine. All good.

The song ended and the crowd started to disperse. Well, most of them. Another group of women had gathered around Carlos. *Honestly.* I rolled my eyes. It was as if Ryan Gosling *and* Regé-Jean Page, the duke hero from *Bridgerton*, had both come to town.

Pandora came to check the bar, then nodded with approval.

'You can go home. Lily, you weren't a complete disaster tonight, but you still have a long way to go. Do better on Monday.'

'I will,' I exhaled. That was as close as I could get to a compliment, so I'd take it.

'Laters!' said Zachary. Clara left without saying good-bye, which, judging by how cold she'd been towards me all night, was no surprise. I was glad that I wouldn't have to work with her every day. She'd be starting at the restaurant next week, so I'd replace her position at the beach bar.

I looked over at Carlos. Although everyone was

supposed to be leaving, the crowd around him had grown even bigger.

He'd said we'd catch up later, but at this rate, it would be seven in the morning by the time he'd finished chatting to his groupies.

Like I said earlier, what Carlos did was his business, but I needed to make sure he didn't text Nate to say he'd seen me. I didn't have his number or know whether he'd be working on Monday, and he spoke to Nate a lot, so if I waited until then, I might be too late.

No. As much as the thought of interrupting his flirt-fest made me cringe, I had to ask him to keep quiet. I couldn't risk it. I took a deep breath and strode over.

'Oh my God, you were, like, *so* good tonight!' a woman gushed.

'*Gracias*.' Carlos smiled.

'Your accent is *so* hot!' Another lady touched his arm. I bet he loved having these women fawning over him. *Just like River.*

It took every ounce of willpower not to turn and leave. My feet were killing me and I'd stifled about ten yawns in the last two minutes, so crawling into bed was a more attractive prospect than joining the Carlos fan club. But then Nate's face flashed in my head and I knew what had to be done.

I stood to the side of the crowd, thinking of how best to politely get Carlos's attention. A megaphone would come in handy right now. Just as I debated what to say, Carlos looked up. His eyes brightened.

'Lily! Hey! Excuse me one moment, please, ladies.'

Oh. I wasn't expecting that.

As Carlos walked through the crowd towards me, the

women's faces fell. If looks could kill, I'd be six feet under by now and they'd be merrily tossing dirt on my coffin.

'H-hi!' I stuttered. *So embarrassing.* I'd always acted so nervous around him. I had to remind myself that I wasn't a teenager anymore, and even though he looked— well, like *that*, he was just a man. A very gorgeous one, but still a man. And those kinds of men were trouble.

'Sorry I did not come over again. I got held up.'

'Yeah. I can see…' I raised my eyebrow. 'Anyway, I needed to speak to you because Nate doesn't know I'm working here and I'd prefer to keep it that way.'

'What?' His eyes widened. 'Why?'

'It's a long story, and I can see you're busy…' I nodded towards his groupies. 'Just, please. I'd rather tell him myself.'

'I am not sure if I feel comfortable lying to him.' Carlos rubbed his neck. 'He is my best friend. We do not keep secrets.'

'I'm not asking you to lie. Just pretend you didn't see me. *Please.*'

Carlos paused.

'Okay. I will not mention it. But only for a few days.'

'Thanks! Enjoy your night.' I turned and headed to the staff lockers.

'Wait!' Carlos called out. I span back around. 'Where are you staying and how will you get home?'

'It's fine.' I waved my hand dismissively. 'I'm getting a taxi back.'

'No,' he said firmly. 'It is past two in the morning. It is one thing to pretend I did not see you, but Nate would never forgive me if he knew I had let his little sister go home alone at this time.'

Hearing the words *little sister* was like a punch in the stomach. Even though of course it was true, to me, it meant that even after all this time, despite the four year age gap, Carlos still saw me as being so much younger than him. He must be thirty-six now, but in his eyes, I was still a sixteen-year-old girl and not a woman. Anyway, *whatever*.

'I have my car.' Carlos stepped towards me. 'I will take you.'

'Haven't you got better things to do with the rest of your night?' I nodded again in the direction of the women. Nate had always said that Carlos attracted women like bees to honey, which now I could see for myself was true, so maybe he was planning to take some of his *fans* back to his place. My stomach twisted as the memory of River and those women all over him flashed into my mind again.

'You are family.' Carlos touched my arm, sending shockwaves around my body, which I quickly suppressed. 'And family must always take priority.'

First I was Nate's *little sister* and now he called me *family*. It was a good thing that I *wasn't* interested in him because those words would've just poured cold water all over whatever fantasies I might have been having. No guy wanted to get involved with his best friend's *baby sister* or with a member of his *family*. Ugh. I supposed it was sweet that he wanted to make sure I was okay, though.

'Haven't you been drinking?'

'No. I drink only alcohol-free beer when I am working.'

Even though I'd made a note of the cab numbers, I wasn't really looking forward to waiting for a taxi to arrive, and my limbs grew heavier with every second. I was so tired. Getting a lift would be helpful.

'Okay, that's really kind of you. Thanks.' I hadn't learnt the address off by heart yet, so I showed him the street name for my building on my phone.

'I know where that is. Just give me ten minutes to pack up my things and I will be with you, *vale*?'

'You want me to wait at the car valet?' I frowned. I didn't know the hotel offered valet parking for staff, but it was so fancy here, it made sense.

'No.' Carlos flashed his smile and my stomach flipped again. I warned it to behave. '*Vale* means *okay* in Spanish.'

'Oh…' I winced, feeling like a plonker. 'Okay. *Vale*,' I repeated. It actually sounded like he was saying *ballet* rather than *valet*. I remembered reading that sometimes Spanish pronounce words starting with a *v* like they began with a *b*. 'I'll just go to the loo and meet you back here.'

As I walked away, for some reason, my heart hammered against my chest. Carlos had left that whole crowd of women to speak to *me*. And now he was giving me a lift home. If they hadn't already killed me with their dirty looks, they'd be chasing me with pitchforks when they discovered I was about to be alone in a car with him.

And even though I knew nothing would come from it and had absolutely no romantic interest in him whatsoever, I had to admit, I was also intrigued to find out what would happen next…

CHAPTER ELEVEN

After I'd gone to the loo and washed my hands, I glanced at myself in the mirror. My mascara had smudged, my foundation was streaky and my forehead and nose were so oily. It wasn't the best time to bump into God's gift to women. Not that I was worried about what he thought—I just wanted to not look like crap, that was all.

Once I'd touched up my face as best I could, I headed back to the beach. The waves crashed in the distance and the air was a lot cooler. Still couldn't believe I was here.

As I approached the bar, Carlos was leaning against it, clutching a big bag.

Nope. Seeing his face glowing under the fairy lights did absolutely nothing for me. And my stomach definitely was *not* flipping right now. Why would it? He was just giving me a lift home. No biggie.

'*Lista?*' he said. I frowned. This time I wasn't going to make a fool of myself by trying to guess what he'd said.

'I asked if you are ready. Nate likes when I say things

in Spanish because it helps him to learn, but I will remember to speak English with you.'

'No, no! Don't stop—I like it.' *Oh God.* That sounded so sexual. 'I mean, I want to learn too.'

'*Muy bien!*' His face brightened.

We walked to the car park, then he opened the door of a white four-by-four.

'Where are you going?' he said as I stood on the opposite side.

'Wait, how come…?' I slapped my forehead. 'Sorry. I still haven't got used to the fact that the steering wheel is on the wrong side here.' I walked to the other side, realising that Carlos was holding the door open for me. *So sweet.* 'Thank you.' I slid onto the seat.

'I must correct you.' Carlos put on his seat belt. 'You said that the steering wheel is on the *wrong* side.'

'Yeah! You guys drive on the wrong side of the road.'

'Who says that it is wrong?' He smirked, reversing the car and pulling out onto the main road. 'About three-quarters of roads in the world drive on the right like we do in Spain, so it is the British that drive on the wrong side.'

'Well, smarty pants,' I teased, 'unlike *some* people, I don't have random road facts engrained in my brain, so when I have nothing better to do, I'll ask Google or Wikipedia if you're right. Haha. *Right*. Get it?'

'Was that supposed to be a joke?' Carlos turned to face me.

'Yeah…' I winced. 'Kind of.' I'd just embarrassed myself. *Again.* So much for being the cool girl in Spain. It was like I'd reverted to being sixteen. 'You know—you were talking about driving on the *right* and I said I'd Google it to see if you were *right*, so…'

'I understand, but you know that if you have to explain the joke, then it is not really funny, *right*?' He chuckled.

'I see what you did there.'

'I am just joking with you.'

'Thanks for trying to make me feel better.' I smiled. 'Note to self not to attempt a career in stand-up comedy. It'll probably be as disastrous as my bar skills.'

'Really?'

'Yeah. Let's just say, after working in an office for most of my life, bar work is not coming naturally for me.'

'Do not worry. Like anything new, it is difficult at first, but you will get used to it. You just need practice.'

A warm sensation flooded my body. After Pandora telling me earlier that I needed to do better, it was nice to hear some encouraging words.

'We are here,' Carlos indicated. Already? My stomach sank. Apart from my terrible attempt at a joke, I was enjoying his company. 'This is the road. What number is your place?'

'Don't worry. I can walk it from here.'

'No.' He shook his head. 'If I take you home, I need to see you go inside. I told you. You are Nate's little sister, so I need to take care of you.'

Take care of me. What was I, like five years old?

'Okay,' I sighed. 'It's just a bit further, on the right. That white building there.' Carlos drove up. 'Thank you,' I said as he parked.

'*De nada.* You are welcome.'

'Goodnight.' After undoing my seat belt, I went to open the car door.

'Wait.' He grabbed my arm and I wondered if he was going to give me a goodnight kiss. Not *that* kind of kiss, *obviously*. Just the two cheek kisses that Spanish people gave to everyone. 'Take my number, just in case you need something. You can call me anytime. Day or night. *Vale?*'

I pulled out my phone and let him type in his number. Then he asked me to send a WhatsApp message so that he had my number too.

'Got it,' he said. '*Descansa*, Lily—have a good sleep.'

'*Gracias*.' I opened the car door.

After I put the key in the front door, I turned back and Carlos was still there, waiting for me to go inside, just like he'd said he would.

On the one hand, it was sweet that he wanted to make sure I got in safely, but on the other, I felt like I'd swapped one big brother for another.

The important thing was that I'd survived my first day in Spain. It had already been full of surprises. I wondered what tomorrow would bring…

CHAPTER TWELVE

I opened my eyes slowly. Annoyingly, I'd spent the night thinking about Carlos. Not the *whole* night, obviously. I'd just replayed the moment we saw each other again once or twice. When our eyes locked, his smile and when his lips gently brushed against my cheek. My stomach fluttered. It was hunger pangs, that was all. I needed breakfast.

Just as I was about to get out of bed, my phone rang.

'Hello, Pinocchio!'

'Hey!' said Cassie. 'How's Marbella? All set for your first day at work tomorrow? Wait—what's with the Pinocchio nickname?'

'I had to do my first shift *yesterday*.' I propped a pillow behind my head. 'My new boss got the shock of her life because she thought the hotel had hired London Bartender of the Year, but she got Little Miss Zero Bar Experience instead! Why did you lie?'

'You worked at McDonald's during uni, didn't you?'

'Only for, like, two weeks!'

'Exactly! That still counts as having experience in the *hospitality sector*!' Cassie burst out laughing. 'Come on, Lil! Everyone tells a little porky or two when they're applying for jobs. Of course I didn't tell a posh hotel that you'd worked in a fast-food chain for five minutes, but if I said you didn't have experience, they wouldn't have hired you, so I had to be *creative*.'

'But if you were honest, they could've given me more training.'

'That's the thing. Normally people work there for the whole summer, so they have a longer training period, but you'd missed that. And you're only there for five weeks, so you can't expect them to spend half that time training you up. I'm sure you did just fine!'

'I didn't! She called me a *disaster*!' I winced, replaying my piss-poor performance. 'She was going to sack me! I literally had to beg her to keep me on.'

'See! Told you you'll be fine. And don't worry. Even if you're crap right now, you'll pick it up soon.'

'I hope so!' I blew out a breath. I couldn't stay mad at her. If it wasn't for Cassie, I wouldn't even be here.

'Other than that, how was it?'

'Well, the biggest surprise of the night wasn't related to my shitty bar skills. You'll never guess who I saw!'

'Who?'

'Carlos!'

I *had* to tell someone about the crazy coincidence, and as Cassie was one of the few people who knew Carlos and knew that I was working here, it made sense to spill the beans to her.

'Carlos, as in Nate's hot Spanish bestie, Carlos?'

'Yep.'

'Oh my God, Lil!' She gasped so loudly you'd think I just told her I'd won the lottery. 'This is *amazing*! What are the chances, eh?'

'I know, right? Actually…' I paused. 'You and Nico didn't have anything to do with this, did you?'

'What?'

'Well, you organised this job and you really want me to meet someone, and with Nico's billions he can make anything happen. Like track down Carlos and arrange for him to work at the hotel at the same time.'

'Wow. That's actually a genius idea! I wish I'd thought about that, but nope, sorry. This was all Lady Luck and the universe's handiwork. Even you have to admit it must be fate!'

This was exactly how I'd expected Cassie to react.

'Call it whatever you want, but we're just working in the same hotel, that's all.'

After filling her in on the fact that Carlos had dropped me home because he'd felt guilty about not telling Nate, my phone chimed.

'No way…' I looked at the screen.

'What's happened?'

'Carlos has just messaged.'

What the actual hell was going on? First we met yesterday and now just as I'm talking about him, he messages me? If I read about this, I wouldn't believe it.

'What does it say?'

He would've already seen that I was online, so there was no point trying to play it cool by waiting before replying. I clicked on the message.

Carlos
Are you awake?

. . .

'Well?'

'He just asked if I was awake.'

'Message back, then!' I could hear the excitement in Cassie's voice.

Me
Yep.
Carlos
Typing…

'Maybe he's going to ask you out!'

'He's not going to ask me out,' I scoffed. 'He's probably just checking that I've eaten my breakfast and have my clothes ready for work tomorrow like a good little girl. I told you—it's like he's taken on Nate's big brother role.'

My phone pinged again as his message came through.
Carlos
Are you working today?
Me
No. You?
Carlos
No.
Carlos
What are your plans?

'Hello?' Cassie shouted. 'You've gone quiet. Are you replying?'

'Yeah. He's asked if I'm working and… if I'm doing

anything today.' My heart raced. Even though I knew it was totally innocent, I couldn't deny I was a bit intrigued.

'Woohoo! Told you he'd ask you out! Hurry up and reply!'

Me

No plans so far…

Carlos

Have you visited the centre of Marbella yet?

Me

No. I wanted to yesterday, but then I offered to work, so didn't get a chance.

Carlos

I can take you if you want?

My pulse quickened. I definitely hadn't been expecting that.

'He's just asked if I want him to take me around the city centre…'

'That's amazing, sis! It's happening!' Cassie practically screamed down the phone.

'You're such a sappy romantic! *Nothing* is happening! He's just being nice.' I rolled my eyes again, even though I knew she couldn't see me.

'Yes, I'm a sappy romantic and proud of it! Falling in love will do that to you. You'll see soon enough.'

'*Purlease!*' I shook my head whilst typing out my reply.

Me

That's really kind, thanks.

Carlos

Pick you up in twenty minutes.

· · ·

'Bloody hell!'

'What?'

'He's coming in *twenty minutes*! I need to shower, get dressed and eat. Better go!'

'Good luck! And let me know how your first date goes.'

'It's *not* a date!'

'*Whatever!*' Cassie laughed before ending the call.

CHAPTER THIRTEEN

I pulled up the cream metal shutters and peered out of the window. I could see Carlos's car parked right outside, but I wasn't ready. So far, I'd showered, put my hair up in a bun and covered up my spots the best I could in such limited time, but I hadn't got dressed or eaten.

Most of my clothes were still in my suitcase. And I hadn't even found the nearest supermarket, let alone had a chance to go food shopping. Thankfully, I still had a little cereal bar in my handbag which I'd packed for the flight here but never got around to eating, so I was trying to wolf that down as quickly as possible whilst chucking different outfit options on the bed.

Me

I'm so sorry. I'm running a bit behind. I'll be down asap.

Carlos

Tranquila

Carlos

No worries

.   .   .

Phew. I shoved the last of the cereal bar in my mouth, brushed my teeth, then settled on wearing some jean shorts and a T-shirt. I picked up my cardigan and umbrella too, just in case, then rushed out the door.

Carlos was leaning against the car wearing a white vest, exposing his huge muscles and light blue shorts. I swallowed hard. Had it suddenly got hotter outside? I quickly pulled my fan out of my handbag to cool me down.

'*Cómo estás?*'

'You're asking how I am, right?'

'*Sí*. You are learning!'

'That's pretty much all I remember from Spanish lessons at school! So sorry I'm late.'

'*No pasa nada*—no problem. Why do you have this?' He pointed at the umbrella.

'In case it rains.' I'd learned my lesson. I didn't want to have to scurry around for a plastic bag to cover my head ever again.

'You will not need it.' He smiled. 'Or the cardigan. This is Spain, not England. You will see. How did you sleep?'

'Not bad,' I replied quickly, embarrassed that I'd spent some of it thinking about him. Not mushy, romantic thoughts. Just, you know, the surprise of seeing him. 'My shift definitely tired me out. I'm not used to spending hours on my feet.'

'I am sure you will get used to it soon. Today I will show you the popular areas and my favourite places in the centre, *vale*?'

'*Vale*,' I repeated.

Carlos set off and I took in the views. I loved that tall palm trees literally lined every single road we passed. Beautiful.

'So how long have you been here? I mean, working at the hotel?'

'About three weeks. I worked at another place in Puerto Banús before this, but the manager at Playa Élite asked if I wanted to come and work there because they want more younger customers.'

'So you were headhunted! Shows you're doing a great job.'

'I try. Did you like the music last night?'

'Yeah!' I said quickly. 'It was cool. I was busy most of the night, but everyone seemed to be enjoying it,' I said diplomatically. I couldn't tell him that I wasn't really a big fan of dance. He'd be offended, or ask what kind of music I was into… yeah. Best to leave that for now.

Carlos drove into an underground car park. After finding a space, we climbed the stairs.

'This is Avenida del Mar,' he said as we emerged in a cute square.

I took in the rows of palm trees on either side and the calming sound of water from the mini fountains behind the wooden benches filled the air. I remembered reading about this place. It was described online as a kind of open museum because it had multiple bronze Salvador Dalí sculptures.

'It's pretty.'

'*Sí.*' He pointed towards a big street and the sea that was in the distance. 'I will show you the beach and the port later, but I think the Old Town is the nicest part of the city, so let us go there first.'

He led me through Alameda Park, where there was a cute carousel, a circular fountain and lots of lush greenery. Then we crossed the road to the Old Town.

The narrow cobbled streets were so cute. My head swivelled, taking in all the little boutiques selling everything from beachwear to sandals, jewellery, clothes and tourist bits and bobs.

'So, how are things? I think the last time that I saw you, it was maybe six or seven years ago and you had started a new job in accounts, no?'

'Yeah!' My eyes widened. I'd been shocked last night that he remembered that I worked in accounts, but knowing when I started my job was an even bigger surprise. 'I'm still with the same company. I bought a house a few years ago and, well, nothing much else to report.'

Being able to summarise seven years in a sentence was embarrassing. My life really was dull. But now I was here, I hoped that'd change.

'And what made you want to take the sabbatical and work here?'

'I just wanted to try something different...' My voice trailed off. He didn't need to know that escaping my ex was a catalyst. 'I haven't travelled much and Nate and Cassie make it sound so cool. And then Cassie found me a job at the hotel and, well, the rest as they say is history.'

My stomach rumbled. Clearly the cereal bar hadn't been enough.

'This is so pretty,' I said as we reached a square framed

with historic-looking buildings and classic white Andalusian houses.

'Yes, this is Plaza de los Naranjos: the Orange Square. Because of the orange trees.'

Of course it was. I remembered seeing it online. As I looked around at the people sat at restaurant tables under large white-and-orange sun umbrellas, my stomach growled again.

'Sorry.' I winced.

'Did you have breakfast?'

'Not really. I haven't had a chance to go food shopping yet.'

'You should have said. If I know this, I would bring you some food. Come. I will take you to a good *churrería*.'

'Chur-what?'

'A place that makes churros.'

'Cool! I've always wanted to try churros.' My face lit up.

'You have never tried churros?' Carlos raised an eyebrow. 'We will change that straight away.'

He led me down another narrow street with brown square paving tiles with a thick border of pebbles surrounding it. Rows of light blue flowerpots were fixed to a brilliant white wall. It all looked so pretty. No wonder there was a queue of tourists and Instagrammers waiting to take photos in front of it.

After walking a bit further, we stopped outside the *churrería*. The scent of freshly ground coffee, chocolate and batter flooded my nostrils. It smelt amazing.

Carlos pulled out a chair for me at a table outside, then placed our order. Soon afterwards the waitress arrived with the plate of churros, which were dusted with sugar and came with a pot of thick chocolate sauce.

As she put them in front of Carlos, she grinned and fluttered her eyelashes. Looked like he had another fan. Carlos pulled out some cash.

'I'll pay!' I reached for my handbag.

'No. I invite you.' He handed the money to the waitress, who was still undressing him with her eyes. Once she'd left, I picked up a churro and bit into the deep-fried piped dough.

'So?' Carlos asked.

'This is… *divine*!' I squeezed my eyes shut, groaning with pleasure.

'I am glad you like it.'

'Like it? I want to have it for breakfast, lunch and dinner every day!'

Time to try it with some chocolate. I dipped it into the bowl and took another bite. Carlos smiled.

'What?'

'You—you have chocolate on your face.'

'Oh God, really?' I groaned. *What a way to look sexy*. Not that I was trying to, of course, but I at least didn't want to look like a pig shovelling down its food. 'Where?'

He touched the tip of his nose. I grabbed a napkin and dabbed my nose. Once I was satisfied that it had gone, I dipped the churros in more chocolate, then took another bite. Carlos smiled again.

'What? Don't tell me I have *more* chocolate on my face?'

He nodded.

'Now it is on your mouth. Lick your lips.' I ran my tongue around my mouth. 'No. Higher. Like this.' Carlos licked his lips slowly, then flicked his tongue repeatedly at the corner.

My eyes were now transfixed on his mouth, imagining how it would feel to have his lips on my… I quickly caught myself and remembered that I was supposed to be removing the chocolate, not having indecent thoughts.

'It is still there!' Carlos grinned and my stomach fluttered.

'You know you *could* just wipe it off for me…' I teased.

'Maybe I should…'

Our eyes locked and Carlos licked his lips again.

My breath caught in my throat. Just as I was waiting for him to remove the chocolate, he jumped and reached down to his pocket, pulling out his phone. Carlos looked down at the screen, and his face fell.

'What's up?'

'It's Nate.' He stared at the screen for several seconds and I froze. Shit. 'Hey.' Carlos turned to the side, holding the phone against his ear. '*Gracias por los cascos, tío!* Thanks again for the headphones. I love them!' He nodded. '*Sí.* I-I am out. In the centre—eating churros,' Carlos stuttered. I could tell he was choosing his words carefully. '*Hombre, no. Todo bien.* I am just tired from last night.'

I could hear Nate laughing. Carlos blushed. 'No, I went home. Alone.'

Ah. Nate must have asked him if he was tired because he took a woman back with him.

OMG. *What the hell was I thinking?*

I couldn't believe I'd just flirted and asked Carlos to wipe the chocolate from my mouth. That was way too intimate. Would I never learn? River had already put my heart through an industrial shredder. I didn't need any more heartache, which meant no flirting or having X-rated thoughts about men. Especially not Casanovas like Carlos.

I grabbed a serviette and dabbed it around my mouth, then pulled out my powder compact discreetly under the table to check in the mirror that the chocolate had all gone.

'Anyway, I have to do something. Can we talk later? *Sí*. I will call you. *Vale. Hablamos luego.*'

As Carlos ended the call, I blew out a breath.

'Thank you.'

'I do not like keeping secrets from him.' He shook his head and sighed. 'Why do you not want me to tell Nate that you are here?'

'You know what he's like. If I told him I was working in a bar, he'd start his whole overprotective stuff, and I just wanted to come work and travel around Spain without him breathing down my neck.'

'But you know he only does this because he cares.'

'I know, I know, but sometimes it can be too much.'

'We should go now.'

'Oh.' My shoulders slumped. 'Already?'

'*Sí*, I need to…' His voice trailed off. 'I should take you home.'

Before Nate had called, Carlos was going to give me a tour around the city, but now, he was suddenly busy. Message received, loud and clear.

'No.' He looked at his watch and for a second I hoped he'd changed his mind and we could spend more time together in the centre after all. 'First, we will go shopping. You need food.'

'It's okay. If there's somewhere you need to be, go. I'll

be fine. I'll find the supermarket. I was going to go shopping today anyway.'

'It will be easier with a car. Finish your churros and I will take you.'

See?

I told Cassie nothing would happen and I was absolutely right.

CHAPTER FOURTEEN

'That'll be seventy-eight euros, please.' I lined the drinks up on the bar.

'What?' the customer barked, whipping off his designer sunglasses. 'You just made that up!'

'No, I didn't!' My mouth fell open.

There's always one.

Most customers were okay, but at least once a day we'd encounter an annoying one.

'How could you know how much it is without putting it in the till?'

'I added it up myself.' *Duh.*

'Don't be ridiculous!'

Ever since I was a child I'd added up simple calculations in my head. It was fun. I'd memorised all the bar prices the day after I'd started. But I supposed he didn't know that. I took a deep breath and went to the till.

'You asked for two Alhambra beers, which are eleven euros each.' I pressed the buttons on the till as I read his order out loud. 'A glass of sangria, that's sixteen euros, a frozen strawberry daiquiri is eighteen, and the gin was twenty-two euros.'

The prices at this hotel were eye-watering. I could buy a whole bottle of gin at the supermarket for the price of one serving here. But most guests knew that being at a place like this didn't come cheap.

'Yeah.' He folded his arms across his T-shirt, which had a huge logo in the middle. Bet it cost more than I earned in a week.

'Which, like I said, comes to a grand total of seventy-eight euros, *sir*.' I raised my eyebrow, resisting the temptation to say I told you so.

He threw his credit card down on the bar and I picked it up, biting my tongue so hard I'm surprised it didn't fall out. After huffing like a spoilt child, he and his friend picked up the drinks and turned to leave.

'Enjoy!' I flashed my best fake smile before muttering *wanker* under my breath.

'You handled that better than I would've,' said Zachary.

'I was tempted to say something rude.' I wouldn't have, though. There was no way I was giving Pandora any more ammunition to fire me.

'What are you, some sort of genius? My uncle was an accountant and he couldn't have added all that up so quickly.'

'Just practice.'

I glanced over to the empty DJ box. I was doing the early shift today, so if Carlos was working this evening, I wouldn't be here. It was now Tuesday and I hadn't seen or heard from him since Sunday.

After I'd finished my churros, Carlos took me to the

supermarket. He'd had phone calls to make, so thankfully he'd waited outside. I didn't want him to see what I put in my basket. Imagine if I'd needed laxatives?

Turned out Spanish supermarkets didn't sell medicinal products anyway. If you wanted paracetamol, you had to go to the chemist. I wondered whether it was the same for condoms. Not that I'd need any. I wouldn't be getting jiggy with anyone whilst I was here. It was just out of curiosity, that was all.

Anyway, he'd dropped me home. I'd said he could just leave me at the door, but he'd said, '*En serio?*'—which, judging from his eye roll, I guessed meant something like *are you having a laugh?* Or as that tennis player John McEnroe used to say, *you cannot be serious*—so I let him help.

I was glad I did. Not because carrying the bags gave me another glimpse of him flexing his biceps, but because the lift wasn't working and I'd done enough shopping to last at least a fortnight, so it was heavy. It would've been a nightmare lugging that home on the bus.

'Thanks so much for today—for the churros, taking me shopping and carrying the bags,' I'd said when we'd arrived at my front door.

'You do not want me to bring them inside?'

'No, it's okay, thanks. You've done more than enough and I know you have stuff to do this afternoon.'

'Okay,' he'd said and then we just looked at each other, neither of us seeming to know what to say.

Actually, that was a lie. There was plenty I'd wanted to say, like *how is it that every time I see you, your eyes are a different shade of greeny brown?* But instead I just said: 'Well, see you at work, then.'

'*Sí. Adiós*,' he'd said before heading back downstairs. And that was that.

'So are you feeling a bit more confident with the drinks now?' Zachary wiped up a spill on the bar.

'A bit.' I nodded. 'But still a *long* way to go.'

'I know it's hard to believe, because I'm so *awesome* now'—he winked—'but it took me a while to get the hang of it too when I had my first bar job.'

'How many bars have you worked in?'

'At least a dozen. I've been travelling a lot the past couple of years and I always enjoy bar work. You get to meet lots of people. But now, I'm getting old—I'm almost twenty-five and I've decided that I want an easy life, so I'm hoping to land myself a rich husband.'

'Seriously?' I folded my arms. 'You think that *twenty-five* is old?'

'*Totally*. Last month there was this gorgeous billionaire visiting and oh my God, he was *lush*. Think he was French or Italian and he owned some hair company or something.'

'Did he have dark hair? Was he tall?'

'Yes and yes. Tall, dark and handsome. He ticked *all* the boxes.'

I reached in my pocket and pulled out my phone.

'Is this him?'

'Yes!' His eyes bulged. 'How did you know?'

'Didn't I tell you? I have a side hustle where I work as a clairvoyant. I know everything you're thinking and I can see the future.' I stifled a giggle.

'Shut the front door! That's ace! So what's in my future?' He jumped up and down, giddy with excitement. 'Will I meet a hot rich guy soon?'

'I'm afraid I can't tell you that.' I put on my best serious face.

'Why not? Is it because you need your crystal ball or something, or a pack of cards? Or no, tea? Should I run and get teabags from the restaurant so you can put some leaves in a cup?'

I'd been trying really hard, but I couldn't hold it in any longer. I burst out laughing.

'Sorry! I was joking. I'm not a clairvoyant. If I was, I would've seen into the future and known that I'd be so rubbish working behind a bar!'

His eyes widened again and then he broke out into a fit of giggles.

'You little shit!' He tapped me gently on my shoulder. 'You really had me going there! Well, if you're not a clairvoyant, how did you know who I was talking about?'

'Because he's my sister's boyfriend, Nico.' He must have returned to the hotel last month.

'Wait, your sister has a boyfriend who's a *billionaire*? Can she hook me up?'

'Yes, she does, and no, she can't. If he had any eligible bachelor friends, I'd be on the waiting list.' I was sure it would take several years to find a guy on Nico's level, which might be around the time I'd be ready to dip my toe back in the dating waters again.

'Looks like I need to start hanging out with you more, girl. You know everyone. Billionaires, hot DJs…'

As he spoke, I glanced over to the box. For some reason, my stomach felt a bit empty. I wondered where Carlos was. Silly, really. I'd gone years without seeing him, so it didn't make sense to be thinking about him after less than forty-eight hours. Maybe I was hungry. That would explain why my mind and belly were feeling weird.

'Lily?'

'What?' I snapped out of my thoughts.

'Go anywhere nice?' Zachary smiled.

'Huh?'

'You were miles away. Doesn't matter. We're low on tonic. Could you grab a few bottles from the stockroom?'

'Course.'

I stepped out from the bar and took in my surroundings. The sky was bright blue again. Customers were lounging on the beach and beautiful people in bikinis were emerging from the sea.

It was crazy that I'd been here for four days and I still hadn't had a chance to go and chill on the beach or go for a swim. That would change in a few hours, though. After my shift, I planned to go for a long walk and find a nice spot. Somewhere away from here, though. I definitely didn't fit in. Not just because of the whole money thing. I meant aesthetically.

Everyone here was perfect. Beautiful toned bodies, smooth clear skin and bikinis that probably cost more than my salary.

I wouldn't be surprised if they hadn't endured months of training to get a *beach body*. I hated that phrase. It implied that you were only *allowed* on the beach if you fitted a certain mould, which I did not.

My bottom was definitely not made for one of those thong bikinis that seemed to be so popular these days, and I couldn't lie—I wasn't too fussed. Each to their own and people could wear whatever they wanted, but thongs were uncomfortable at the best of times, so I had no desire to wear one at the beach. Plus, they must make it easier for sand to disappear up your bum crack, and that couldn't be comfortable, surely?

Then again, comfort probably wasn't the point. From what I gathered, this hotel and therefore this beach was a place where you came to be seen and look cool. And as much as I was trying to be the new, improved version of Lily here, cool had never been a word that was used to describe me.

So, no. I wouldn't be hanging out on this beach later. I had my swimming costume packed, so as soon as I clocked off, I'd be good to go. I just needed to ask Zachary if he knew of another beach nearby that was better suited to people without chiselled bodies.

After getting the tonic and some more straws, which I'd seen we were running low on too, I headed back to the bar, then put everything down on the counter.

Zachary was staring into the distance with a huge grin plastered on his face.

'What I wouldn't give to be *her* right now.'

'Who?'

I followed his gaze over to the beach. There were people sunbathing and lounging around the pool, but that was nothing out of the ordinary.

I scanned the horizon again and then my eyes stopped as I clocked the massage table that was set up under a white canopy. It had been empty when I'd left, but now there was a woman lying down and…

Carlos?

Carlos was giving a woman a massage?

'Such a shame we're not allowed to get one. Customers have all the luck.'

'But why is he doing that?' My heart thudded. 'When he's a DJ?'

'He does massages too. Apparently, the woman who did it before quit suddenly a couple of weeks ago and hero Carlos, who's also a masseur pro, stepped in. During the day he works in the spa and sometimes on the beach. I reckon him being well fit helped him get the job too. He's brought in a shitload of clients. I thought you knew.'

Nope. I knew he'd done physiotherapy at uni like Nate, but I hadn't had a clue he did massages.

So as well as seeing him surrounded by women after his set every night, now I had to watch him run his hands all over their bodies during the day too?

My stomach twisted and I instantly told it to get a grip. He was just doing his job.

Anyway, even if he massaged women all afternoon, it was no skin off my nose. I wasn't interested in him romantically and I was a hundred per cent sure that the feeling was mutual.

CHAPTER FIFTEEN

fter getting off the bus, I strolled down a pretty
wooden walkway towards a beach outside of
Marbella, which Zachary said would be *more my style*.

I took off my flip-flops and stepped onto the warm
sand. In the distance people were sitting under umbrellas
or sunbathing and there was only the faintest sound of
chatter. It was much quieter here than at the hotel.

This is the life. Sand beneath my feet, beautiful sea air
caressing my skin.

Once I'd found the perfect spot, I pulled out my beach
blanket. I was about to sit down, but paused, then blushed.
Oops. The man a few feet away must be changing into his
trunks because he was butt naked. I looked away quickly
and continued walking.

A woman in a bikini passed me and smiled. I smiled
back and took a sip from my water, but then I almost
choked. Coming towards me was a man in his birthday
suit, with his cock happily flapping up and down underneath his beer belly. I looked away, only to see another

man in his sixties who also had his meat and two veg on display as he emerged from the sea.

Hold on.

Was this…?

I took in my surroundings. There was a woman lying topless on a sunlounger with a naked man beside her. Then I spotted another, and another.

Bloody Zachary.

He'd sent me to a nudist beach. Some people were wearing swimwear, but it was definitely optional, because they were in the minority.

I quickly headed back to the walkway. Nothing wrong with people enjoying the sun in the buff if that was what tickled their fancy, but I wasn't ready to join them anytime soon.

As I got to the top, a white four-by-four pulled into the car park.

'Carlos?' I frowned, quickly putting a sarong over my back and shoulders. He shut the door and came towards me. 'How did you know I was here?'

'I looked for you after I finished my shift and the man at the bar told me you were here, so I had to come. It looks like I arrived just in time.'

'What do you mean?'

'You still have your clothes on.' He ran his eyes over me and even though it was almost thirty degrees, goose bumps spread across my skin.

'You sound relieved.'

'I am.'

'Thanks very much!' I folded my arms.

'No… I do not mean because I would not want to see you naked…'

'So you *would*?' My eyes bulged and an involuntary tingle raced between my legs.

'Ye—n—*madre mía*!' he sighed. 'This is a conversation that I cannot win, so I will not answer. I will only say that I am happy you are not naked on the beach where everybody can see you.'

'But what if I *want* them to?' I teased. I didn't, but he didn't know that. Carlos was always so calm, so seeing him flustered was funny.

'Of course it is your choice. I-I—' He saw me smiling. 'Lily, stop joking with me.' The corner of his mouth twitched.

'You deserve it! I know you met me when I was sixteen, but in case you haven't realised, that was a long time ago and I'm all grown up now.'

'So I see…' His eyes darkened and for a split second, I wondered if he'd ever thought about me in that way. Of course he hadn't. I quickly dismissed it.

'Well, then, please don't treat me like a child.'

'I am sorry.' He touched my arm gently, sending more fireworks rippling across my skin. 'I do not mean to. It is just… I feel responsible. Knowing you are Nate's sister and you have not travelled a lot before. I do not want something bad to happen to you. Nate would never forgive me.'

'Nothing bad will happen.' I rolled my eyes. 'I can take care of myself. What if you weren't here?'

'But I am.'

'Just forget that I'm Nate's sister and treat me like you would treat any other woman you've just met.'

'I cannot.' He shook his head.

'Why?'

'Because you are not like other women.'

'Why?' I repeated.

'Because you are… because you have always been spe… *look*. Let me take you to a different beach. Come.'

Was he about to say that I was *special*?

As he led me in the opposite direction, I thought of what other adjectives started with *spec*. *Spectacular*? No. He wouldn't think that. *Speckless*? That wasn't a common word. I supposed I'd never know.

After a few minutes we arrived at another area, which was busier than the semi-nudist beach, but still much quieter than the ones in Marbella. A group of teenagers played volleyball, children sat with their families building sandcastles and other people were chilling or reading books. And they were all fully clothed.

'Here's good.' I pointed to a small empty stretch of sand a few metres from the sea. I laid down my beach blanket and unpacked my sun cream. Carlos towered above me.

'You can sit down, you know.'

'I-I should get back.'

'More women to massage?' The words slipped out before I could stop them. 'I thought you said your shift had ended. I didn't even know you did massages,' I added quickly to soften the tone and avoid sounding jealous.

'There is a lot you do not know about me.'

'So tell me.'

'Maybe one day.'

He could be so infuriatingly mysterious sometimes.

'Are you DJing tonight?'

'*Sí*.' Carlos sat down at the edge of the blanket. 'I start in a few hours. Are you going to take a bath?'

'What?' I turned my head to the side and gave my armpit a little sniff. It seemed fine, but now he'd suggested I wash, I wondered if that was why he was sitting so far away from me. 'Why, do you think I need one?'

'That is why you come to the beach, to go into the water, no?' He frowned.

'*Ohhh…*' I slapped my forehead. 'You mean if I'm going to *bathe* in the sea. When you said to have a bath, I thought you meant, to wash, you know, like take a shower.'

'No!' Carlos smiled. 'Sorry, it is my English.'

'Your English is amazing.'

'Thank you. Living in London helped, but clearly I am rusty. So you will go in the sea?'

'Yeah. I might just sit here for a bit first.' I squeezed a blob of sun cream onto my hands and rubbed it over my legs.

I remembered how surprised some of my friends had been when we'd gone to Brighton Beach on a really hot day and they'd seen me using it. I'd reminded them that even brown skin like mine needed to be protected.

My back and shoulders needed to be done, but then I'd have to remove my sarong and Carlos would see how bad my skin was there too. I normally wore T-shirts to hide it and obviously hadn't expected that I'd see him on the beach.

The sun was blazing, though, and I really wanted to go for a swim, so there was no way around it. In any case, Carlos wouldn't be able to see my back from that position. It'd be fine.

After removing my sarong, I squeezed more cream on

my palms, then awkwardly lifted my right hand behind my back and attempted to rub it in.

'Would you like me to do your back for you?'

My heart raced. I remembered how it had felt when Carlos's lips had grazed my cheeks for just a few seconds and when he'd touched my arm earlier, so him running his hands over me wasn't a good idea.

And I didn't want him to feel my bumpy skin. River had always avoided touching my back and used to wince whenever I had a breakout. He wouldn't even kiss me if I had spots on my chin because he'd say he didn't want to catch them.

When I'd told him that acne wasn't contagious, he'd said it was best to be careful, just in case. Yet he hadn't seemed to have a problem with asking to have sex without a condom. Thank God I'd never agreed. I'd hate to think what I could've caught from his dodgy communal dick.

'It's okay. I can do it. Thanks.'

I continued trying to rub it in, knowing I was doing a terrible job. It was so hard to reach that bit in the middle where my swimming costume dipped. Before I had a chance to turn away, Carlos got up and stood behind me.

'Are you *sure* you do not want help? Unless you are going to grow eyes in the back of your head, it will be difficult to do it properly yourself. Let me help you.'

I froze. Wait. He'd seen my back and he still wanted to touch it?

Oh.

He was right. I was doing a piss-poor job.

'Okay,' I said quickly, taking away the opportunity to overthink.

Carlos knelt behind me and I instantly felt his warm breath on my neck.

OMG.

I sucked in a breath, mentally preparing my body for the impact of his hands. My body had already started sparking and he hadn't even touched me yet.

He squeezed the sun cream onto his palms before rubbing them together. As his hands skimmed my skin, I jumped a little.

'Sorry. Is it cold?' The sunscreen had been next to my cold water bottle, but it wasn't that.

'N-no,' I stuttered. The total opposite. My skin felt like it had been set on fire. 'C-carry on.'

Carlos ran his hands over my back, moving his palms inwards, then outwards, slowly up, then down to the base of the back of my swimming costume. My body temperature rose with every stroke.

As he repeated the movements, I closed my eyes. This was heavenly. Although he'd probably massaged in enough cream to protect my skin, I didn't want him to stop. I wanted him to keep going until he'd used up the whole bottle. No wonder there was always a queue for his massages.

'It will be better if you move your straps, no? If you feel comfortable? So I can do your shoulders properly. It is up to you.'

A thousand times yes! my body screamed before I told it to pipe down.

'Okay,' I managed to say calmly. If I was going to use sun cream, it made sense to make sure I was fully covered, right?

I slid the straps down with one hand, clutching the

front of my costume with the other to make sure it didn't fall down. Whilst they wouldn't have minded me going topless on the other beach, the rules on this one could be different.

Without saying another word, Carlos rested his hands at the top of my shoulders and massaged the sunscreen onto my skin.

Holy shit.

His touch was so gentle yet powerful. Like the lightest feathers being traced along my skin. As he moved his hands down the centre of my back, the tingles in between my legs intensified and before I could help myself, a groan of pleasure escaped my lips.

Shit.

I didn't mean for that to happen. I winced with embarrassment, thankful that he couldn't see my facial expression.

'Sorry if I hurt you,' Carlos whispered, his warm, sweet breath tickling the back of my neck. 'It is just that you have a lot of tension. *Here.*' He gently squeezed. 'In your shoulders.'

As much as I hated to admit it, shoulder tension was the least of my worries right now. It was the *sexual tension* building within me that was the problem. It'd been almost five months since I'd slept with anyone. It wasn't even like that was my longest dry spell. And it hadn't bothered me much. Until now…

'There. You should be protected now. But it would be good for you to come for a massage with me. To help with your shoulders.'

'Oh… I don't know.' I paused. The way my body had

just reacted told me that I was wandering down a slippery slope. 'Zachary said staff can't book massages.'

'That is true, but I am sure we can arrange something. You really need it.'

'Yeah. I do…'

Carlos was referring to the massage, but my traitorous body was thinking about something completely different.

Yep. A massage definitely *wasn't* a good idea. Carlos's hands were dangerous. They had my mind and body thinking all kinds of bad thoughts, and I needed to be good.

Agreeing to a massage would be like going into a bakery minutes after committing to a healthy eating regime.

Nope. I was on a dating detox. A strict no-man diet. And no matter how good they felt, I couldn't let Carlos and his magic hands make me fall off the wagon.

CHAPTER SIXTEEN

'Can I get a G&T, please? Excuse me? Hello?'

'Sorry! Yes, of course,' I said quickly. 'I'll be with you in a sec.'

Whilst dragging my gaze away from the DJ box, I knocked over an empty glass, catching it just before it fell to the floor. Shit. I'd already spilt two drinks because I wasn't concentrating properly.

'Which gin would you like?'

After pouring the gin over the ice and topping it up with tonic, I took the customer's card, swiped it, then handed it back with his drink. A loud sigh escaped my lips as I looked over at Carlos.

His biceps were bulging in a navy vest. I know it was hot, but I really wished he'd cover them up sometimes. They were very distracting and some of us needed to focus on work so that we didn't get fired.

I chastised myself. Of course, the guy could wear whatever he wanted. *I* was the problem. I had to learn to keep my eyes on the job.

Before even realising it, my gaze moved to him again. It wasn't just his body that occasionally made me lose focus. He just kind of radiated happiness. It was his smile. The way he bopped his head when he played a song that he loved. And how he interacted with the crowd and got them hyped up in that delicious accent.

Carlos was nice too. *Genuine*. Nate's sister or not, he hadn't had to drop me home that first night. Or take me to the supermarket. And coming to find me yesterday because he knew Zachary had sent me to the nudist beach was also sweet.

'Jeez, you really like him!' said Zachary.

'Who?' I feigned ignorance. I knew what he was thinking, but he was wrong. I just thought Carlos was a nice guy, that was all.

'*Come on!*' He rolled his eyes. 'I'm not even going to bother answering that ridiculous question. If you're going to drool over him all night, at least wipe up your dribble from the bar.'

Dammit. Had I really been dribbling? I looked down in horror.

The bar was dry as a bone. Just like when I'd wiped it down two minutes ago. Zachary was pulling my leg. Again.

'You are so bad! First sending me to a bloody nudist beach and now this!'

'What? I told you earlier. You asked me to recommend a beach with normal people who were more your age, so that's what I did!'

'But most of them were over fifty!'

'Aren't you in your fifties too? *My bad!*' he laughed. 'And for God's sake, please drop the whole *Zachary* thing and call me Zach. Zachary's what Mum calls me when she's telling me off. Actually, my mum's also in her fifties, so you two have something in common!'

'I'm not in my fifties! Not that there's anything wrong with being that age. I'd kill to look half as good as J.Lo or Halle Berry, but I felt just as out of place on that beach as I would be parading around on this one. The one Carlos took me to was *much* better.'

After he'd massaged in the sun cream, Carlos said he had to go. It was for the best. I'd already caught myself in a daze too many times, reliving the sensation of his hands over me. God knows what state I'd be in if he'd stayed longer. I had to get a grip.

'*The one Carlos took me to was much better!*' Zach mimicked.

'Stop!'

'Why don't you just hook up with him and be done with it?'

'I told you. I'm on a dating detox.'

'Yeah, yeah, yeah. Your dickhead, womaniser ex couldn't keep it in his pants, you don't want to get hurt again, blah, blah, blah.' I wished I hadn't told him about River now. But our shifts were long and I was making conversation. 'Who said anything about *dating*? Just have a bit of fun between the sheets. It'll do you good!'

'No! He's my brother's bestie. And anyway, even if I wanted to, which I don't, he's not interested in me. Have you seen the women that throw themselves at him every night? They're in another league.'

'You're alright.'

'Thanks!' I huffed. 'The words every woman dreams of hearing: *you're alright*.'

'Well, it's better than telling you that you look like the back end of a bus! You're not my type, obvs, but you're pretty and sweet. Señor Hot Stuff might like that. *Tune!*' Zach shouted and started dancing behind the bar.

He did that a lot. Zach said working here when Carlos was playing was like gaining free entry to his favourite club *and* getting paid.

I tapped my toes. It was another dance track with a thumping bassline. I had no idea what the song was, but I had to admit, it was catchy.

'What can I get you?' I said to the lady who'd just approached the bar. Thankfully, she only wanted a vodka and orange and not a complicated cocktail. My dream customer.

After handing her the drink, I looked up and my stomach crashed to the floor when I saw Carlos standing in front of me.

'H-hi!' I swallowed hard.

'Hey, Carlos!' Zach said, still shimmying around the bar. 'Amazing tunes tonight, as always. I'm having a great time!'

'*Gracias*. Dancing when you work, I like it! You are not dancing, Lily?'

'No…'

'So you are not enjoying the music?'

'No, no.' I shook my head. 'It's not that. It's just that dancing isn't really my thing. I've got two left feet.'

'I do not believe that. *Everyone* has the potential to dance.'

'Not me!'

Well, it depended on your definition of *dancing*. If not keeping in time to the beat or looking stiffer than a corpse was classified as dancing, then I was outstanding. I knew I looked like a plonker, so I'd learnt that it was best not to bother.

Everyone always assumed I'd be a good dancer. There was the stereotype that anyone with black heritage was automatically blessed with rhythm. Mum, Nate and Cassie were amazing dancers, so in their case it was true. But my father was a half Scottish and half English white man who had some cool moves too. I had no idea how, but despite having two very rhythmic parents, the dancing gene had completely skipped me.

I remembered dating a guy in my twenties who invited me to his cousin's wedding reception. As the night progressed, everyone including him was up on the dance floor, gyrating to the reggae music whilst I sat in the corner. After repeatedly asking me to join him, eventually he dragged me up to shake a leg. And shaking a leg was an accurate description.

I tried my best to move to the music and didn't think I was doing too badly, but when I looked at him, his eyes were wide with horror.

'What are you doing?' he'd asked.

'Dancing?'

'It looks like you're having a fit. Your legs are out of control. Maybe it's better if you sit back down. Everyone's staring.'

I was mortified. Unsurprisingly, that was probably the last time I'd danced in public again. Yeah, occasionally I jigged around my flat if I heard a song I liked, but those few minutes of humiliation had put me off for life.

Needless to say, we broke up soon after. I couldn't be sure if my lack of rhythm was a contributing factor to him dumping me, but it can't have helped. *Whatever*. I didn't like him that much anyway.

'Hmmm.' Carlos stroked his chin. 'Do you finish your shift at the end of the night?'

'Yeah.'

'*Vale*. Wait for me and I will give you a lift home.'

My heart skipped. The polite part of me wanted to insist it wasn't necessary, but I resisted.

'Okay, thanks, but only if you're sure.'

'I would not offer if I was not. I want to make sure you get home safely. I must get back now, but I will see you later.'

'Yeah! C-cool! *Hasta l-luego!*' My insides cringed. Just once I'd like to be around him and not stutter like a bloody fool.

Carlos smiled, then left.

'Oooh! Tonight could be the night!' Zach said.

'For God's sake! For the millionth time, nothing is going to happen! He's just giving me a lift home! End of.'

'If you say so. I was going to tell him that you could go home with me, but I thought you didn't want me to kill your night of passion.'

'It's not a…' I looked at Zach smirking and realised I was playing right into his hands. He liked winding me up and my protests made it more satisfying. 'Whatever, *Zachary.*' I deliberately used his full name. 'I know what you're doing.'

'It's all love, honey. If I was getting a lift home with Señor Hottie, a night of passion would be what I was hoping for, so I'm just channelling my desires through you.'

Despite his constant teasing, I liked Zach. He was fun

to be around. I'd only known him a few days, but I already preferred his company to a lot of people I'd worked with.

Thankfully, the last few hours of our shift went quickly. After clearing up and loading the dishwasher, I went to the loo and fixed my face before returning to the bar.

As usual, Carlos was surrounded by women. Just as I wondered whether or not to go over like last time or wait, my phone pinged.

Carlos

Can you ask your colleague if he will walk you to my car? It is better if we are not seen together. I will be there in a minute.

My heart sank as I wondered if now he'd regretted offering me a lift. The paranoid part of my brain started to think he wanted to go home with one of his groupies and I was cramping his style.

I caught Zach just in time and he walked me over.

'*Gracias.*' He patted Zach on the back, then unlocked the door. I waved goodbye to Zach as he turned and left. 'Sorry about that,' Carlos said as we both slid onto our seats. 'It is just that people talk… the management, they do not like when staff get involved with customers or other staff.'

'Yeah.' I remembered they'd said that during training. That was another reason why we should keep our distance. Although this was a sabbatical for me, it was Carlos's livelihood. He was already going out of his way to help me and I didn't want to cause him any hassle.

'So tell me about the dancing.' He pulled out of the car park.

'Not much to tell. I'm just not very good at it.'

'But you like music, right?'

'I *love* it. As you know, growing up, there was always music playing at my parents' house. I think if we didn't like it, Mum and Dad would've taken us to the doctors to check that we were related! I just don't have *the moves*.'

'I know you do not like the dance music that I play, so what do you listen to?'

I paused. Answering this question wasn't a good idea. Some people didn't bat an eyelid, but *cool* people like Carlos would. I knew it wasn't what people would expect. Although we knew we shouldn't, we all made assumptions about what people liked based on how they looked.

So for me, like I'd said earlier, as someone with mixed heritage and brown skin, the assumption was that I could dance and that I'd love certain types of music—like soul, R&B, reggae, calypso and soca, that kind of thing.

Don't get me wrong. I enjoyed listening to those genres. Especially because some of them reminded me of when Mum used to play music and dance around the kitchen whilst she cooked or the warm summer days when we'd all eat as a family in the garden. But the fact was, I really loved pop. And not the 'cool' pop that crossed over from other genres into the charts. *No*. I loved nineties and noughties pop. Like Kylie Minogue, NSYNC and Britney. Definitely not the kind of songs that would be on any of Carlos's playlists.

'Lily?'

'Sorry, I drifted off.'

'Nice to know that you find my conversation so stimulating!'

'No, it's not that, I—'

'*Tranquila.* I am joking! I asked what type of music you like?'

'I like…' I paused again. 'Nineties pop,' I finally said, as if confessing to murder.

I waited for the inevitable laughter and comments about how cheesy it was. It wouldn't be the first time.

My thoughts turned to the time I was home alone and had Britney blaring from the speakers. I was singing into my hairbrush with my back to the bedroom door when my cousins who were visiting London from the Caribbean walked into the room and were speechless. I wish Mum had told me she was bringing them over. Seeing me in my Kylie T-shirt with my NSYNC duvet cover and posters of JC Chasez didn't help. They thought I was a total weirdo.

But I liked pop. It was happy. To me it offered escapism and a good time. A lot of people I knew didn't share the same view, though.

Carlos was still silent and when I turned to see his reaction, he was just smiling. But not in an evil way. I didn't get it.

'So aren't you going to take the piss?'

'Why?'

'Because you think it's cheesy!'

'Not at all.' He shook his head. 'Everyone has different tastes, no? If you like it and it moves you, then that is what is important.'

Oh. I wasn't expecting that.

'We are here.' He pulled over.

The journey home always seemed to be so quick. I

considered inviting him up for coffee so we could continue talking, but then immediately dismissed the idea. Drinking coffee at three in the morning after working all night made no sense, so he'd think I was suggesting something else, which I wasn't. Like I'd said to Zach, he didn't see me like that, so I'd rather dance naked on that nudist beach than face the whole 'I'm not interested in you' pity look.

'Thanks again for the lift.'

'*De nada.*' Just as I was about to reach for the door handle, Carlos leant forward and kissed me on both cheeks. 'Goodnight.' He pulled back and looked me in the eyes.

I wasn't even sure if I was still conscious. My body was floating somewhere, savouring the sensation of his lips against my skin.

He kissed me. Again.

And God, he smelt so good. How was that possible when he'd been dancing all night in the heat?

'G-goodnight.' I stepped outside in a trance.

Dammit.

Right now, my mind was supposed to be a place of pure, innocent and non-sexual thoughts. But every day, Carlos was making that increasingly difficult...

CHAPTER SEVENTEEN

After grabbing a coffee, I climbed back in bed, picked up my iPad and scrolled through my notes.

It was hard to believe I'd already been in Spain for a week. The time was flying by. If this week had gone quickly, the others would too, so I needed to start planning some city breaks during my days off.

As I thought about how important it was that I went to Madrid, my mind drifted to Carlos. Picturing his face just inches from mine when he leant in for that kiss after dropping me off made my whole body tingle. For a split second, I wished his lips had touched mine rather than my cheeks.

Never gonna happen.

So, back to Madrid. In an ideal world, I'd like Carlos to take me, but he'd done a lot for me already. That would be asking too much. Perhaps he could recommend some places to visit and I'd get the train there instead.

Just as I was about to check the timetables, a message flashed up.

Nate

Sup, sis?

My fingers froze on the screen. It was fine. If Nate knew I was here, he wouldn't ask me what was up. He'd say: *WTF*.

Me

All good, bro. Just travelling.

Nate

Where?

Me

I told you—around Europe. I'm planning to visit Cassie in Paris and maybe go around Italy and Spain too.

That wasn't a total lie. I was currently 'going around' Spain and I was planning to visit Cassie at some point in the future…

Me

Don't worry. I'm fine.

Nate

I just worry about you, that's all.

Nate

Believe it or not, I think it's good that you're travelling. I like that you're seeing more of the world.

Nate

But I'd just feel better if I knew where you were. As great as the world is, it can also be a dangerous place.

Me

Seriously, bro, stop worrying! I've got this!

. . .

Nate

Okay, I'll try. Just remember to take the pepper spray I gave you everywhere, don't take drinks from strangers and never let your drink out of your sight.

I rolled my eyes. Sometimes he was a bigger worrywart mother hen than our own bloody mum. He worried about Cassie and Flo too, but I think because I was the youngest, he was extra protective of me.

When we were growing up, it was hard for my voice to be heard amongst my older and louder siblings. But Nate would always make a point to shush them and say, 'What do you think, Lil?' And I loved him for that.

Me

Will do.

I knew, of course, that he was right about the whole being careful with drinks and things, but it got a bit tiring hearing it all the time. He'd harped on and on about the same thing ever since I was seventeen.

Me

I'll make sure I look both ways when crossing the road and eat all my greens at dinner too so I can grow up nice and strong!

I added a row of laughing emojis.

Me

Anyway, how are you?

.   .   .

Nate

All good. Got a sweet gig working for a woman in Canada starting tomorrow, so just keep the time difference in mind if you need to contact me.

Nate worked as a freelance personal trainer and was also a qualified physiotherapist. He was known as one of the best in London and over the years had built up contacts with some very influential people, so he was able to cherry-pick the jobs he did. And he often preferred the ones that allowed him to enjoy his favourite hobbies: travelling and clubbing.

Clients would book him for weeks or sometimes months at a time. The fact that he was good-looking was probably why the majority of his customers were female.

Me

Canada! That sounds cool. How long for?

Nate

Couple months. She's a divorcee who's going to her ex's wedding and wants a killer bod to show him what he's missing.

Me

And are you part of the package deal?

Nate

Nah. I always keep it professional, sis…

He added a winking emoji.

Nate

Never shit where you eat. That's my motto.

.   .   .

He was right. Getting involved with colleagues was never a good idea. Shame I hadn't remembered that when River had turned on the charm. And another reason why it was good that Carlos and I were just friends.

A flash of guilt ran through me. Partly because I was keeping the fact that I was working with Nate's bestie from him, but mainly that Carlos was withholding it from Nate, because I'd asked him to. Still, if he was away in Canada whilst I was here, that made things easier.

Me

Safe flight and good luck with the job.

Nate

Cheers. Stay safe and if you need me, just shout, okay? Love you.

Me

Will do. Love you too.

My heart fluttered a little. That was the thing. As much as I complained about Nate's overprotectiveness, I knew that he really loved me. He'd always been there for me. Especially during those dark days at school, when I used to get bullied about my skin.

Back then, it was even worse than it was now and there were a group of girls that were so mean. They used to call me *pepperoni pizza*, *scar face* and *dot to dot*—after that activity where you joined the dots to make a picture.

I tried everything to get rid of my spots. Most days I walked to and from school so I could use my bus fare money to buy every lotion and potion I could find in the chemist that promised to give me clearer skin.

Every time I took a new bottle home, a rush of excitement would flood through me, hoping that maybe *this* would be the miracle cure. But it never was.

My parents said that it was normal. That I was going through puberty and would grow out of it. But as the years went on, I grew more and more desperate.

In the end it was Nate that helped me. He still kept in contact with the PE teacher at my school who'd heard some people teasing me. When Nate took me aside and asked me if it was true, I broke down in tears. Nate had wrapped his big arms around me and said he'd sort it.

The next thing I knew, he'd spoken to Mum and Dad and organised an appointment with the doctor. She referred me to a dermatologist, who gave me some stronger creams to try.

And I don't know how he did it or what he said, but those bullies didn't bother me again.

The creams didn't work, so after trying one thing after another, when I was sixteen the dermatologist put me on a course of super-strong pills. That *did* work whilst I took them and for a while afterwards, but still throughout my twenties and even now in my thirties, my skin was never blemish-free. Every time I got a spot, no matter what I did, it always left a mark and I still had a lot of scars. Some of my exes, especially River, had commented on it, which is why I always wore make-up and covered my upper body as much as possible. It was the only way I could feel confident and normal. Having spots in your teens was one thing, but in your thirties? That was just embarrassing.

Anyway, I'd never forget what Nate had done to help me during those times. And ever since, he'd always had my back.

The chime of my phone jolted me out of my thoughts.

Carlos's name flashed on the screen and my heart skipped a beat.

I'd be lying if I said I wasn't hoping he wanted to invite me somewhere. At this rate, if Carlos asked whether I fancied shovelling pig shit at a local farm, I'd have said yes. I seriously needed to get a grip.

Carlos

What are you doing today?

Me

Hola! Working tonight, but apart from that, I'm free.

Carlos

Be ready in half an hour. I will take you somewhere.

My body lit up like the Eiffel Tower at night. Then I pulled the power plug and reminded myself yet again that I should not be interested in any men. Showing me around town or wherever he had in mind was just Carlos being kind.

Me

Great! Do I need to wear anything in particular?

Carlos

T-shirt, leggings and sneakers will be good. Whatever will make you feel comfortable.

Me

Okay. See you soon!

I wondered where we were going. Even though getting ready so quickly would be a challenge, I'd make it work.

I had another non-date with Carlos and as much as I wanted to deny it, I couldn't bloody wait.

CHAPTER EIGHTEEN

I got into the car and did a double take.

Rather than wearing the vest and shorts I'd become so used to, Carlos was dressed in a black T-shirt and trousers. As he reached up to adjust the rear-view mirror, his bicep strained under the fabric. I swallowed hard, then looked away quickly. Nope. Turned out that whether he wore a vest or not it made no difference. The man could put on a potato sack and still look good.

When Carlos had said to wear comfortable clothes, I'd thought we'd be going for a walk, but now I wasn't so sure.

'So, where are we off to?' I asked, focusing on the road ahead to avoid meeting his gaze.

'It is a surprise.'

'A *good* surprise?'

'That is for you to decide.'

'Are you always so mysterious?'

'Why do you think I am mysterious?'

'You ask me a lot of questions, but I don't know much

about you.'

'What do you want to know?'

'I don't know. Normal stuff like where you live, what you like doing when you're not working, whether you have a girlfriend…'

Oops. Yeah, I was curious, but I hadn't meant to ask him outright.

'Why do you want to know if I have a girlfriend?' The corner of his mouth twitched.

'I don't…' My cheeks burned with embarrassment. 'I mean, it doesn't matter. According to Nate, you have women in every city.'

Carlos stayed silent. No denial, then, so it must be true.

'And *you*? Do you have someone back in London?'

'Nope. Bad break-up.' I wasn't in the mood to elaborate. 'I've just realised—you did it again! I asked questions about you and didn't answer—you just turned them back on me. Like I said, you're mysterious.'

'It is not intentional. I just do not like talking about myself. I find other people more interesting. But you will find out more about me today.'

We pulled in front of a building. A boy who looked around ten walked inside with a woman I assumed was his mother.

Carlos led me into a hall. About a dozen other kids stood around the edges. They were an even-ish split of girls and boys.

When they saw him, their faces lit up. He greeted them, speaking at a million miles an hour in Spanish, then moved to the centre of the hall. Carlos returned to me and pulled out a chair.

'Sit here. First you will watch.'

'Watch what?' I frowned.

He walked back to the front of the hall, then took his laptop from his bag and connected it to some equipment.

Seconds later, music boomed from the speakers. Carlos put his hand above his head, struck a pose, then shouted some instructions.

Suddenly the children started dancing.

WTF.

Carlos was teaching them to dance, and man, he was *good*.

I watched in awe as he flicked his hips to the left, then the right, the tip-tapping of his black shoes hitting the floor in time to the beat and the kids doing their best to follow his lead.

A DJ, a masseur *and* a children's dance teacher? How many jobs and talents did this man have?

The music was all in Spanish. I could picture women and men dancing in flamboyant red-and-black clothing as the woman's striking vocal cords hit a high crescendo. I was sure they called this music flamenco.

I watched on, eyes wide, lips parted as Carlos guided them through the steps. Most of the children had the moves down to a T, but when he spotted someone who didn't, he'd go over and help.

It was then that the words he'd mentioned when we'd arrived replayed in my head. *First, you will watch.*

Surely he wasn't suggesting that *I*, Señorita Two Left Feet, should attempt to copy those moves?

No way, José.

About forty minutes later, the class ended. The parents collected their children and thanked Carlos enthusiastically.

'What did you think?' he said once the hall cleared. 'You like it?'

'It was amazing! I didn't know you taught dance.'

'I told you that you would learn something new about me today.'

He plucked a towel from his bag, then wiped the sweat from his forehead and the back of his neck. I bit my lip. Was it weird that for a split second I had the urge to grab the towel, bury my face in it, then take it home to have his scent close to me? Yep. Thought so. Thank God no one knew what I was thinking. Maybe it was just me, but there was something sexy about watching a hot man wipe away his sweat.

'You did! How long have you done this?'

'About eight years. Whenever I know I will be in an area for a while, I try and set something up. I love teaching children. When they first come, they know nothing, and watching them learn and find the joy is very satisfying.'

'I bet.'

'So now that you have watched, I would like you to try.'

'No!' My eyes widened with horror. 'I told you before. I'm rubbish.'

'You can do it. Let me help you.'

'I'm only here for four more weeks. It'd take four *years* to help me.'

'Lily.' Carlos reached forward and placed his hand on my shoulder. The heat from his palm sent electricity racing through me. 'You tell me before that you like cheese pop from the nineties, *si*?' I smirked at that fact he'd called it *cheese pop* instead of *cheesy* pop, then folded my arms, pretending to be offended. He held his hands up. 'Your words, not mine.'

'Yes, that's what I like.'

'Tell me who. Which singer or group?'

'Britney, NSYNC, those kinds of people.'

'Okay. So do you ever go to a club and dance to these songs?'

'No way!'

'Why?'

'Well, first, I don't voluntarily go to clubs or parties, but if I did, I wouldn't attempt to dance because I'd look ridiculous.'

'But you would *like* to?'

'Well, yeah. I'd like to dance to *anything* and not look stupid.'

'So imagine how it will feel to hear a Britney song and to dance instead of just sit in the corner. This would be amazing, no?'

'Course!'

'Then let me help you. I want to teach you how to dance. It will make me happy. Will you try? *For me?*'

Dammit. It was hard to say no when he asked me in that honey-coated accent.

'Okay…'

'*Genial!*' His face brightened. 'We will start with something simple.'

He went to his laptop and put on a new song.

'First, close your eyes. Listen to the music. To the beat. Do not move yet. Just count. One, two, one, two.'

It was nice that he wanted to teach me how to dance, but what if I couldn't do it? My stomach twisted and even though the room was air-conditioned, beads of sweat formed below my hairline. This was why I avoided dancing. The feeling of knowing I was going to embarrass myself was too stressful.

I attempted to do as he'd instructed.

'*Bien*. Now you have the rhythm, move your head.'

As I bobbed my head, I couldn't shake the feeling that I looked like one of those nodding toy dogs people stuck to the rear car window.

'Continue counting, but also tap your foot in time, so tap, one, two, one, two.'

I attempted to focus. To most people it would come naturally, but Carlos might as well have told me to pat my head and rub my stomach at the same time.

I tried to move but ended up stepping on his feet. Then I missed a beat and it was hard to find my place again.

'Sorry, I can't—'

'*Tranquila*,' he said. 'I will stand behind you and touch your shoulders, is this okay?'

'Um.' I held my breath. It was hard enough for me to concentrate without him touching me, but he was trying to help. 'Okay.'

Carlos gently rested his hands over my shoulders and the heat from his palms shot through me like fireworks. Before he touched me, I'd at least managed to count from one to two, but right now my head was all over the place, jumping from one to ten thousand, then to five million, mirroring my soaring heart rate.

'I can tell you are tense. When you dance, it is good to *feel* the emotion, in your heart. Forget about everything else. Just let go and focus on the beat and how the music makes you feel. There is no one here except us. Nobody is watching. It is just me and you. You are safe, okay?'

Just me and you.

I wasn't supposed to be affected by him. My heart was supposed to be locked away in a maximum-security vault. But somehow I felt my defences weakening. Hearing those words instantly made it flutter.

'I am going to move closer now.'

'O-okay.' I swallowed hard, trying to think about how best to keep it together. Carlos pressed his chest against my back.

Holy shit. If he wanted me to be calm, that definitely *wasn't* the best way to go about it. My heart thundered. Carlos's gorgeous woody scent wafted past my nostrils. His chest felt firm, yet comforting. It was true. He made me feel safe. But also very horny, which was a big problem.

Here he was, innocently trying to teach me how to dance, and my body had wrongly assumed that his proximity meant something sexual was about to happen, which was ridiculous.

Despite my sending an emergency message to my hormones to calm the fuck down, they ignored me. Tingles erupted between my legs.

'Can you feel my heartbeat?'

'Y-yes,' I stuttered again. That was the only thing I felt behind me, which confirmed what I'd always believed: Carlos wasn't even the slightest bit attracted to me. If he was, being this close, I'd definitely know.

'Keep your eyes closed and feel my heartbeat. One, two, one, two. Put all of your weight on your left foot, so lift the right foot from the ground a little, so you have all of the weight on the left. *Muy bien.* Now repeat the same with the right foot.'

After a few false starts, my pulse slowed and I tuned into the beat of Carlos's heart. It was so calming that I drifted away for several seconds.

'Keep going.'

I continued to sway from left to right and found my back relaxing into Carlos's chest as my weight shifted from one foot to the other.

'Now start moving your feet even more.' Carlos stepped out from behind and stood in front of me. My body instantly missed his presence behind me. It was like the room temperature had dropped twenty degrees. 'Watch me. So before you move your weight to the left foot, move your foot a little so it's in a different place than where it was before. And try to keep it close to the ground. *Bien.* Remember to *feel* the beat.'

My eyes dropped to his feet. I'd never looked at them before, but now I did, I saw that they were very big.

I worked in a shoe shop when I was a teenager, measuring people's feet. I'd guess that Carlos was at least a size eleven. Maybe even twelve. I wondered if what they said about men with big feet was true...

'Focus, Lily.'

I snapped out of my illicit thoughts and mirrored his actions. My shoulders loosened and I continued moving one foot and then the other, over and over. The more I did it, the more my confidence grew.

'How does it feel?' he asked.

He's talking about the dancing, not how it felt to have his body pressed against you, my subconscious screamed.

'Okay, I think?'

'You are doing great.' A flash of pride raced through

me. Nobody had ever used that word to describe my dancing before.

As the song changed, Carlos returned behind me. He placed his hands on my hips and my body jolted. '*Perdón*. Is this okay?'

'Y-yes, it's fine.' *Jesus*. His touch. Every time he laid his hands on me I felt like I was going to erupt into a ball of flames.

'Now you have the rhythm in your feet, I want you to move your body. So when you move your weight on your left foot, try to move your hips in the same direction. *Vale?*'

'I'll try.'

I gently moved my hips to the left, squeezed my eyes shut and tipped my head back. Without realising, I began circling my hips and pushing back against him.

'That is good. *Feel* the music. Move your body.'

I continued, my body growing lighter with every flick of my hips.

I could feel Carlos's heart beating faster, his warm breath on my neck, and it felt glorious. Warm sensations flooded my veins. The friction of my bum rubbing against him made my hips move even faster. It was like I'd lost control. Once I started grinding against him, I couldn't stop.

He wrapped his arms around my waist and pulled me in closer. As our bodies moved to the beat, I felt something solid press against me.

OMG.

He was hard.

The floodgates had opened in my knickers ages ago. Literally as soon as Carlos put his hands on my shoulders.

But the last thing I'd expected was that *he* would get any kind of pleasure from being this close to *me*.

I pushed my bum back into him a little more. I wanted to feel his hardness. I wanted him to know that I liked feeling him.

'I-I think we should stop now.' Carlos pulled back, then walked over to his laptop, his back facing me. 'You have done very well today, but we… I need to take you back home so you can rest before your shift this evening. We can continue to practise another time.'

'Oh.' My shoulders slumped. 'Yeah. Course.'

Obviously his boner had happened by accident and *not* because he liked me. Like when men wake up with morning wood. And there I was, grinding on him like I was auditioning for a nineties hip-hop video. *Cringe.*

Clearly Carlos was so horrified that he wanted to get away asap so he didn't give me the wrong idea.

He stopped the music and slid his laptop into his bag. But as he turned around, I noticed that rather than slinging it over his shoulder like he'd done when we'd arrived, he was holding his bag up in front of him.

Was he still…? *No.* For a second I wondered if he was also recovering from the after-effects of our close-up hip action, but then I scolded myself for even thinking it.

One thing was clear, though. As embarrassed as I was about what had just happened, I had to start being honest with myself.

Ever since I'd seen him on my first Saturday night here, I'd been trying to suppress my feelings, but after this afternoon, I knew it was pointless. I was attracted to Carlos. Big time.

And I didn't know what the hell to do about it.

CHAPTER NINETEEN

I wandered down the hotel corridor in a daze. I was relieved to be on a break, not just because it gave me a chance to escape making a mojito (mashing up the fresh mint and dealing with the sticky sugar and fresh lime juice was a pain), but also because every time I looked at Carlos in the DJ box, I cringed about my shameless grinding during the dance lesson earlier.

After I'd gone to the toilet to try and sort out my, ahem, damp knickers situation, he'd been waiting for me in the car, his bag resting on his lap. He'd removed it just before we'd set off, but something was different. He seemed quieter. In a way I was just relieved that he hadn't brought up the whole boner-gate thing, which would've been so awkward.

This evening, when he'd started work, he'd nodded and smiled to acknowledge me, but hadn't come over. I didn't want things to be weird between us. I needed him to know how grateful I was. Once again he'd gone out of his way to help me. And these sweet things he was doing had put a bit of a spanner in my strictly no-romance plan.

I'd come to Marbella to clear my head and mend my heart. It was working to a point because I was definitely over River. But although I'd moved on, I wasn't supposed to be thinking about getting jiggy with someone else. Yet every day, sticking to that became harder.

Carlos being hot was one thing, but adding kindness to the mix was becoming a dangerous combination. Was it any wonder I'd made a fool of myself by rubbing up against him? The man looked like a Spanish god and I was only human.

Anyway, lesson learned. I'd had a moment of weakness earlier, but I was back on track. I'd read the room. He wasn't interested. There would be no more illicit thoughts or actions. I was going to keep my badly behaved bottom to myself. Yep. My mind was so pure right now that a hygiene inspector would give it a five-star rating for cleanliness.

As I walked past the kitchen, the scent of chocolate filled the air. I cracked the door and poked my head around it.

'Hey, Eva.'

'Lily! *Cómo estás?*'

'*Bien, gracias.*' I smiled. Eva was one of the chefs. We'd spoken a few times and she'd been really nice. 'You?'

'I am good. Just preparing something for tomorrow. Want to try?'

I glanced at a tray filled with chocolate-covered treats shaped like big swirly hearts resting on one of the large chrome worktops.

'Yes, please! How can I say no to chocolate?'

She plucked one from the tray and handed it to me. I sunk my teeth into the sweet delight.

'This is amazing!' Outside it looked like a hard biscuit, but inside was soft pastry dough. 'What is it?'

'*Gracias*. This is *palmera de chocolate*.'

'Oh my God. I don't know how you make all of this stuff and then give it to the guests. If I'd made these, I'd lock myself in a cupboard and stay there until I'd finished the whole lot. They are *so* good!'

'Take another.'

'Oh no, I shouldn't. And I have to get back to the bar. Actually…' I paused. I had an idea. 'Would you mind if I took one, to give to… someone?'

'Sure. But only if you give it to someone special.' She smiled and wrapped one large one in greaseproof paper.

'I will.'

I headed back to the bar with a spring in my step.

'You're back early.' Zach frowned. 'You still have five minutes left.'

'I know. But I thought I'd make a special delivery.' I took a cold non-alcoholic beer from the fridge.

'Doesn't take a genius to guess who you're taking that to!' He raised an eyebrow. 'What you got there?'

'I got this from Eva.' I unwrapped the paper to show him. 'I would've got you one too, but earlier you said you'd eaten a whole packet of Haribos and if you had anything else sweet, your teeth would fall out, so…'

'Yep. Thanks, honey. I have to stay strong. And anyway, if you're going to give someone your heart, it makes sense to give it to the man you're crazy about. Don't waste it on me.'

'It's just a pastry, not my heart!'

Zach raised his eyebrow again. I was about to protest, then stopped. Before, I'd convinced myself that I wasn't interested in Carlos, but now…

Anyway. No more thinking. I rewrapped the pastry, plucked the beer from the bar top, then headed over to the DJ box.

Carlos's face lit up as he saw me approaching. My traitorous stomach flipped. After he pressed some buttons on his black DJ equipment, the track changed. He removed his headphones, then stepped away from the decks.

'Hey!'

'Hey.' I smiled. 'I thought you might be thirsty, so I brought you a beer. And I also got you this. Just a little thank-you for earlier.'

Carlos unwrapped the paper and his eyes widened.

'*Madre mía!* How did you know? This is my favourite!' He leant forward as if he was going to give me a thank-you kiss but paused and pulled back. After shameless-grind-gate, he probably wanted to make sure he didn't lead me on. '*Muchas gracias*, but it was not necessary.'

'No big deal.' I shrugged my shoulders. 'I'd love to say I knew it was your favourite, but Eva was making them and I just thought you might need some energy. And seriously, I really am grateful. Even though I'm a long way away from getting a call from the *Strictly Come Dancing* production team, I feel like I made some progress this afternoon.'

'Does that mean you are going to dance tonight?' Carlos smirked.

'Let's not get carried away. Like I said, I've still got a

long way to go before I'll be doing NSYNC dance routines. Not that you'd ever play songs like that here.'

'*Nunca digas nunca!*'

'What does that mean?'

'*Never say never*. I must get back now, but wait for me later. I want to take you home.' Carlos's eyes darkened and he licked his lips.

Wait. I swallowed hard, our gazes still locked on one another. *Did he just…?*

'*Vale*,' I said, breaking the silence, then turned and walked towards the bar.

For a second, I could've sworn Carlos looked at me with *desire*.

No. When he said he wanted to *take me home*, he meant just giving me a lift. Like he always did.

Didn't he?

CHAPTER TWENTY

I cleared the cushions off the sofa and pushed the coffee table to one side.

My heart thudded. In less than ten minutes, Carlos would be here. In my flat, and I'd be getting naked.

That came out wrong. Let me rephrase: Carlos would be coming to my flat to give me a massage, which would mean I'd have to remove my top and *that* was why I'd be *half*-naked.

It wasn't like I planned to lie on the sofa with my boobs out and look at him with come-hither eyes inviting him to ravish me. No. It would all be above board.

When Carlos had dropped me off after work, my mind and body had raced, wondering if by some miracle something might happen. Of course, nothing had. But, he'd asked if I still wanted the massage he'd offered before.

Because staff weren't allowed to have massages on the beach at the hotel, he'd suggested he might be able to sneak me into one of the treatment rooms when it was quiet, but it was too risky. So instead of getting caught and landing Carlos in hot water, I'd suggested that he come here.

I'd laid a spare bed sheet over the sofa and had a few towels to hand so that I could cover up in the right places. All I had to work out now was how to control my racing heart rate.

The buzzer sounded. I took a deep breath, then walked to the intercom.

'*Hola?*'

'*Soy yo*. It is me.'

'Hi!' I buzzed him in.

I stood by the door, crossing my arms, then uncrossing them. I leant my elbow against the door frame, attempting to appear relaxed and not like I was so nervous I could pass out, but then it slipped.

In the end, I gave up trying to look cool and just left the door ajar and returned to sit on the sofa.

Carlos stepped inside seconds later.

'*Qué tal?*' he asked, clutching a large bag.

'Fine, thanks.' I twisted a stray curl around my finger. 'You?'

'*Todo bien*. So where do you want it?'

'Huh?' I swallowed hard. *Ohhh…* I dragged my mind out of the gutter. 'I was thinking we could do it here. On the sofa.'

The corner of Carlos's mouth twitched. It sounded like we were talking about something else…

He came closer, towering over me, and I couldn't help but notice that my eyes were now level with his waist. His crotch was just inches away from me and the temptation to reach out and touch it was overwhelming. *Jesus.* I'd turned into a raving nympho.

I bit my lip and stood up quickly.

'Hmmm.' Carlos frowned, resting his knuckle beneath his chin. 'Lie down,' he commanded, and I swear I felt the elastic ping in my knickers.

'Do you want me to, um, take my top off?' My body tingled.

'Not yet.'

'Okay.'

'No.' He shook his head. 'It is like I thought. It is too small. We cannot do it here.'

'Oh,' I sighed.

'Unless…' He paused.

'What?' I perked up.

'The only other place would be the *bed*, but I am not sure if you will feel comfortable with this.'

'The bed is f-fine!' I squeaked. *Wow, excited much?* 'I mean, you use a bed on the beach for massages, right?' I lowered my voice, attempting to sound cool about the whole thing. 'So is it really that different?'

Yeah, on the beach where there are dozens of other people around. Not on a bed, in a private apartment where it's just the two of us. Not on a bed where we could quite easily have sex.

It was totally *not* the same, but, whatever.

Carlos stood in silence. He looked at the bed, then back at the sofa, then back at the bed.

'The bed *is* bigger, so it would be better, but…'

'Like I said'—I shrugged my shoulders—'I'm cool with it if you are?'

'*Vale.* We will do it on the bed,' Carlos said. My cheeks heated. 'I will do *the massage* on the bed,' he clarified. 'First, I will prepare the area. While I do this, please change into a towel. I will let you know when I am ready.'

I left Carlos in the bedroom area, went to the bathroom and took off my bra and T-shirt. I'd showered an hour ago, so I'd be nice and fresh.

Even though Carlos had massaged sun cream into my skin before, I still felt a little self-conscious about the spots across my back and shoulders, so I'd suggest we dimmed the lights before he started.

A few minutes later, there was a knock at the bathroom door.

'*Lista?*'

'Yep. Ready.'

I unlocked the door and gasped as I stepped out and glanced towards the bed.

The shutters were down and the lights were off, but there were candles on the bedside tables, giving the room a warm, relaxing glow.

Thick, dark fluffy towels had been draped over the bed, including one over a pillow for me to rest my head.

Soft music played in the background, just like in a professional spa, and as the candlelight flickered, I noticed there were several bottles of oils lined up on the bedside table too.

'I will wash my hands. Lie face down. I will return in a moment.'

I climbed onto the bed, anticipation racing through me. Carlos hadn't even laid his hands on me yet, but my body was already aching for his touch.

When he'd offered me a massage, I hadn't been expecting him to go to all this effort to create such a beautiful relaxing setting.

I had to admit, given his reputation with the ladies, part of me wondered whether this was one of his *moves*. Y'know, offering to give a woman a private massage at home, saying the sofa was too small and then conveniently suggesting that it be done on the bed instead.

But then I pushed those thoughts out of my mind. *I'd* invited *him* here and *I'd* agreed to do it on the bed. And in all honesty, even if this *was* part of a well-oiled seduction routine, I'd be lying if I said I didn't want it. If he offered me some added massage extras and a *happy ending*, I'd say yes faster than you could say *ravage me*.

I buried my face in the pillow and heard Carlos's footsteps approaching until they stopped at the side of the bed.

'I am going to move the towel down, *vale*?'

'*Vale.*' I sucked in a breath.

He gently lifted the towel and moved it to my waist.

'Now, I am going to touch you.'

My heart leapt in my mouth and I held my breath. I didn't think I'd be able to exhale again until I felt his hands on me.

I heard him pick up a bottle of oil, then rub his hands together.

Any. Minute. Now.

As his hands made contact with my skin, it was like I'd been struck by lightning. Sparks pulsed through every inch of me. I bit down on the pillow to stifle a moan.

Jesus. He hadn't even begun the massage yet. How the hell was I going to cope when he did?

'How do you like it?' he whispered. 'Hard or gentle?'

My eyes pinged open. I was glad he couldn't see the expression of shock spread across my face. The truth was,

I was past the point of denying my feelings. I'd take it any way Carlos wanted to give it to me.

Carlos cleared his throat, snapping me out of my fantasy of him flipping me over and burying himself inside me.

'The massage pressure,' he clarified. My cheeks burned with embarrassment.

'Oh, er, medium, I suppose?' My voice went up several octaves. Of course he was talking about the massage. I knew that.

'Is this pressure okay?' His soft hands squeezed my shoulders.

'Y-yes,' I stuttered, trying to control the sensations of delicious pleasure that were flooding through me.

'*Bien*. But sometimes I may need to do it harder to really get in there, *vale*?'

'U-um…'

Oh boy. If only he knew how much I wanted him *to really get in there.*

'Your back and shoulders… there is a lot of tension.'

'Do whatever you want to me. I mean, whatever you think is best. For my back.' I groaned internally. I'd lost the ability to string a clear sentence together. Could you blame me? I challenged anyone to have Carlos's hands all over them and still be able to think straight.

'If it is too much, then just shout.'

Shout? More like *scream*. The way he was running his hands over my body, he was about to tip me over the edge.

Perhaps I should've used the travel vibrator I'd brought with me to release myself before he came. Ha. *Came*. Every word was loaded with sexual innuendo right now, but it was true. After months without feeling a man's touch, I was ready to explode.

Carlos continued with deep, kneading strokes, lifting and squeezing my muscles along my shoulders and upper back, to loosen the knots and muscles. If anyone else was doing it, I might have found it uncomfortable, but every movement sent a delicious sensation around my body.

After working in circles, moving his hands out from my spine, he switched to long, slow, sensual gliding strokes, all over my back, and this time, the sensations weren't just flowing around my body. They were firing straight between my thighs.

As his soft hands travelled across my skin, another moan escaped my lips. I couldn't help it.

'*Perdón*,' Carlos whispered. 'Sorry if I hurt you.'

'You didn't,' I replied, almost breathless. 'Don't stop.'

As he followed the contours of my body, sweeping from my shoulders, down the centre of my back and out towards the side I secretly begged for his hands to slip and brush along the edge of my breasts. But they didn't.

When his hands reached my lower back, just above my bum, my body jerked into the bed.

Fuck.

If he touched me for much longer, I was going to burst into a ball of flames. I just knew it. There was no way I could risk erupting into an orgasm in front of him. I'd never be able to look him in the eye again.

'Lily, I…' Carlos lifted his hands from my skin, then pulled the towel up to cover my back. 'I-er. You feel good —I mean, your shoulders. There is less tension.'

Maybe in my shoulders, but definitely not between my legs.

'Yeah,' I moaned. *Jesus*. I couldn't even speak without it sounding sexual. 'I feel, sooo…'—*horny, sexually frustrated, like I want to jump you*—'sooo relaxed.'

'That is good. So, I will go now.'

'Oh…' I went to sit up.

'No.' Carlos turned his back quickly. 'Do not get up. Stay and relax. I will let myself out.'

Before I even had the chance to ask if he was going to take his oils and stuff, the door slammed shut. He couldn't get out of here quickly enough.

That was weird. I wondered if he sensed that I was getting turned on and thought he'd better leave before I jumped him?

Unless he'd felt it too…

It was crazy to even think it. I mean, him being interested in me seemed so unlikely. And then there was the whole Nate, bro code thing.

In any case, even if there was the slightest possibility that he'd done all these nice things because he *did* like me, I couldn't go there. Going from one ladies' man to another had disaster written all over it. Nope.

As I sat up, I felt the wetness pooling between my legs. *Damn*. My mind might have good intentions, but my body was saying otherwise. I didn't know if I'd ever felt so turned on in my life from something that wasn't even supposed to be sexual.

Carlos was off limits, but I needed to release, so I'd have to settle for the next best thing.

I reached inside my bottom drawer, lay on my back, pulled down my knickers and spread my legs. It was time to get some electrical assistance and finish what Carlos probably hadn't even realised he'd started…

CHAPTER TWENTY-ONE

Carlos pulled up outside my building. As always, the journey home was over too quickly. Like most people, I hated gridlocked roads, but whenever I was in a car with him, I wished that we'd have to spend hours sitting in traffic, just so we could spend more time together.

It was just after three a.m. on Sunday morning, which meant it'd been a week since the massage, and as much as I'd been trying to suppress it, my attraction to him had only intensified.

I'd used my vibrator more in the last seven days than I had in the last seven weeks. Every time I thought about his hands caressing my skin, my body ached with need.

Each night that he'd dropped me home, I'd wished that he could come upstairs, but so far, no such luck.

'So…' He turned off the engine. 'You have plans later?'

My stomach fluttered. Whenever he asked me if I was

free, I felt like I'd been offered a lifetime pass to an all-you-can-eat dessert buffet.

'No, I'm free!' *Whoa*. I really needed to tone down my enthusiasm.

'You told me before that you come to Spain to travel, yes?'

'Yeah. Although, I haven't really gone anywhere yet. Unless you count that little trip to the nudist beach!' I grinned. 'But I hope to soon.'

I had an early shift this week, so after work I'd also taken a little trip to Puerto Banús, which wasn't too far away from our hotel.

As well as lots of restaurants, there were huge yachts, fancy designer boutiques and people driving Bentleys and Ferraris. I was glad I had a chance to visit, but it was definitely a case of how the other half lived.

'I would like to take you to one of my favourite cities: Granada. We can visit Alhambra, eat tapas and explore the city.'

'Oh my God! I have no idea what Alhambra is—I thought it was just the green bottled beer we serve at the bar—but it sounds great and I definitely won't say no to eating tapas.'

'Alhambra is an ancient palace. It has beautiful Islamic architecture. It is impossible not to love it. It will not take long to drive there, but it is better if we leave early. Can you be ready by nine?'

'Yep!' I didn't care if I only got a few hours' sleep. I'd stay up all night if it meant I'd get to go on a trip with Carlos. Fuck. I had it *bad*.

'Okay. Goodnight.'

Carlos leant forward and kissed me on the cheek. I

held my breath as I waited for him to lift his lips and move them to my other cheek, but he didn't. He kept his mouth pressed against my skin for what felt like seconds and minutes at the same time.

He pulled back and looked me in the eyes. I swallowed hard. His face was right in front of mine, our lips just inches apart.

I might be a little rusty on the whole romance, flirty stuff, but there was something between us. I could *feel* it. Just like I'd felt something when we'd had that first dance lesson. And no, I didn't just mean his hard-on.

Speaking of which, I'd been thinking about that and I was starting to wonder whether it *was* a stray boner. The way he'd been looking at me lately was different. He held my gaze longer. When he said goodnight, his lips lingered on my cheek. Like they had just now.

I wasn't imagining it. There was a connection.

I knew Carlos felt responsible for me because I was Nate's sister. But making sure I got home safely after work every night was one thing. Spending time with me outside of work, giving me a massage at home and voluntarily taking me to visit his favourite city had to mean more, right?

If that was true, maybe it was better that nothing happened. I'd be going home soon and I didn't need any more man drama or heartbreak.

'You should get some sleep.' Carlos broke the silence.

'Yeah. Thanks again for today, and see you in a few hours!'

I held Carlos's gaze, then opened the car door and stepped outside. He waited until I was inside before waving and driving off.

∽

I checked myself in the mirror. I'd woken up early to have more time to perfect my make-up. I wanted to feel extra confident, so I decided to wear the red lipstick that had been lurking in my make-up bag since I'd arrived.

After slipping into an orange knee-length skirt and putting on my sandals, I grabbed my handbag and headed downstairs.

'*Buenos días!*' I said enthusiastically as I got into his car. Carlos was wearing another one of his sexy vests. Today it was green and it matched his eyes perfectly.

As I looked at him, he smiled and my stomach flipped. Whenever I saw Carlos it was like stepping from the cold into beautiful warm sunshine.

'*Buenas. Has dormido bien?*'

'Whoa. Easy with the Spanish! I still only know the basics!' I fastened my seat belt as Carlos indicated, then pulled off.

'I asked if you had a good sleep.'

'So-so,' I replied. I'd spent much longer than I should've wondering whether my gut feelings about Carlos could be right, dismissing them, then pondering again.

'How about you?'

'Not much. So it will take about two, maybe two and a half hours to get there. You can sleep if you want, or we can listen to music.'

'I definitely won't be sleeping.' I enjoyed talking to Carlos. It always felt so effortless somehow. Even when I embarrassed myself, he didn't make me feel bad. Plus I liked to stay awake on long journeys to keep the driver company. It seemed rude to nod off whilst they did all the hard work.

'Okay, my phone is connected. Just press play.'

I touched his phone screen and I gasped as I heard the first few bars of the song.

Britney's '…Baby One More Time' blasted through the speakers.

'What the…? You have a playlist with *Britney*?' My mouth fell to the floor. 'How long have you had this? Who are you and what have you done with the cool DJ Carlos?'

He flashed his smile and my stomach fluttered again.

'I could not sleep, so I made a playlist f-for you,' he stuttered. 'Well, and for the journey.'

'I can't believe you made a *pop* playlist! For *me*.' My heart swelled. 'And you stayed up to do it. Thank you! You must be knackered. Can I have a look?'

'Sure.'

I held his phone up to his face to unlock the screen.

OMG.

I glanced down the list. I recognised every single song. There were more tracks from Britney, NSYNC, Backstreet Boys and S Club 7—the list was endless.

'This is amazing! Are you sure you'll be able to suffer listening to so much cheese? I don't want you to crash!'

'Do not worry. I have put some *good* popular songs on the list too, so there is some Destiny's Child, TLC and Blackstreet.'

'I love them too!'

My brain whirred, trying to process everything. No one had ever made a playlist for me before. I remembered that Ayesha, one of the girls at uni, once dated a guy who made a CD with her favourite songs and everyone in our class thought it was the most romantic thing ever.

The fact that Carlos had made a playlist for a two-hour car journey with a lot of music that he didn't really like meant so much.

'There's just one problem, though…' I turned to face him.

'Problem?'

'Whenever I hear this song, it just makes me want to grab a hairbrush and sing.' It was true. This was the perfect karaoke track.

'Do it!' Carlos shouted enthusiastically.

'I don't have a brush!'

'So use this bottle.' He tilted his head in the direction of the water resting in the holder in the centre of the car console. 'But first, I must ask, will my windows be okay?'

'Your windows?'

'*Sí*. If you sing, will they break?'

'Rude!' I grabbed his arm and squeezed it playfully. *Any excuse to touch him*. It was just as firm and delicious as I'd imagined. I was tempted to do it again but told myself to get a grip. Of my hormones. Not his arm.

'It is a joke. I know you have a good voice. I remember hearing you sing when you were in your room once. I liked it.' Wow. His memory was incredible. He was right. I did use to like singing along to music. It annoyed most of my family because they thought my taste in music was terrible. 'Come on, *queso*. Sing your pop song to me.'

'*Queso*? That's cheese, isn't it?'

'*Sí!* Just like this music!'

I squeezed his arm again, then grabbed the bottle and happily started singing Britney from the top of my lungs.

CHAPTER TWENTY-TWO

The journey to Alhambra felt like two minutes rather than two hours. Carlos would've enthusiastically listened to me croon my way through half of Britney's back catalogue, but after about a dozen pop songs, I suggested we switch the playlist to something he liked. It was only fair.

The playlist he asked me to select was very eclectic. Like I would've predicted, it had some dance songs from artists I'd heard of, like Calvin Harris, Kygo and David Guetta, but there was also some Spanish music, and reggaeton too. All of it was upbeat and happy and I found myself tapping my feet and bopping my head a lot more than I would've done ordinarily. Listening to music with him beside me just made things different somehow.

After parking up, we stopped for a late breakfast and Carlos led me up a street and through a grand medieval stone gateway with three arched entrances—one large one and two smaller ones at either side.

'This is Puerta de las Granadas—the gate of the Pomegranates. It is a big walk to the entrance of Alhambra, but it is good exercise, no?'

Once we passed the gate, we found ourselves in the forest. It wasn't your typical wild forest, though. Just three very steep paths lined with tall trees and lush greenery.

'I suppose we have to burn off those churros some-how.' I could think of other ways, but I was trying to keep my mind a smut-free zone. Well, at least during daylight hours.

Compared to the busy streets we'd walked through to get here, this was so peaceful. And thanks to all the trees, it was nice and cool. Even after living here for two weeks, I still wasn't used to the blazing heat.

'Would you like me to carry you? It might be faster.' He smirked. I trailed behind Carlos as his solid legs carried him easily uphill.

'Very funny! I'm okay, thanks,' I said, despite the protests from my body. 'I just haven't found somewhere to work out locally yet, so I'm a bit out of breath, but I'll be fine.'

Not that I'd go to classes if I did find a gym. I'd had an exercise bike at home for two years and I could count on one hand the number of times I'd used it. It was really useful for hanging my clothes on, though.

'You do not need a gym to have a good workout…'

'Yeah?' My body tingled. 'What do you suggest I do instead?'

The corner of Carlos's mouth twitched mischievously.

'There are many ways… dancing is good.' The devil popped up on my shoulder and wanted to ask whether he meant horizontal or vertical. 'And swimming. The sea is very close. Something that is not typical in London, so it is good to take advantage. I have weights at home, but I also go to a gym. And I like to run on the beach.'

I wasn't surprised. I knew he'd have to work out a lot to get a body like that. So much for keeping my mind smut-free…

'I'd imagine you'd have to go early, though, at this time of year, because of all the tourists.'

'Not really. I go to a small beach outside of Marbella that I discovered. It is very quiet there because not many people know about it. Whenever I want to think or be alone, this is where I go. It is my special place.'

'Maybe one day you can take me there. You know, if it's not too private. I promise not to blast the location all over Insta.'

'*Vale*. I would like that.'

'What, for me to post about it on social media?' I teased. I knew that wasn't what he meant, but I wanted to hear him invite me properly.

'No.' He turned his gaze to me. 'I mean, I would like to take you to my beach. Come.' He took my hand and a zing of excitement ripped through me. 'If you will not let me carry you, then I will need to pull you up this road—otherwise we will miss the next entry time to the palace.'

Carlos's hands were so soft. It was like he slept with them dipped in the creamiest moisturiser. Made sense, seeing as he was a masseur. But holding his hand was a different sensation to the massage. Somehow it seemed more intimate. And his hands were so big… if holding them was the reward for walking slowly, I planned to move at a snail's pace all day.

When we reached the top of the hill, we walked

through a large red stone gate with two arches, which led us to the walled Alhambra complex.

It was a large medieval red-stone-coloured city, with tall cypress trees dotted around and a backdrop of hills, mountains and what looked like the whole of Granada. *So pretty.*

Even though we were no longer climbing up a steep path, Carlos still held my hand and I sent a silent prayer that he wouldn't let go.

'This is the main complex which anyone can walk around, but I would like to buy tickets to go inside the Alcazaba, the Nasrid Palaces and other parts of Alhambra.'

Carlos went to the ticket office, once again refusing to let me pay. The next viewing session was in forty-five minutes, so after queuing to gain entry to another section, he led me up a very narrow staircase.

'This is Alcazaba—all that is left of this castle is the walls and the towers.' The red bricks on the ground looked like a maze.

We went to the top of the tower and took in the breath-taking surroundings. As well as seeing the grounds beneath, it was like every inch of Granada was laid out in front of us.

'The views are amazing!'

'I am glad you like it.'

'Look over there.' He pointed. 'That is Mirador de San Nicolás. I will take you there later. It is very famous for the views of Granada. We can watch the sunset together.'

A buzz of excitement rippled through me. Watching the sunset with Carlos from a breathtaking viewpoint sounded like a dream. I never wished away my time with him, but right now I wanted to skip to being there.

After walking around and admiring the views, we joined the queue to visit the palaces. Once we were inside, I was like a child who'd discovered sweets for the first time. With every corner we turned, my eyes grew wider.

From the striking honeycomb domed ceilings to the marble fountains and intricate and colourful tiling, the architecture and level of detail were incredible. I had no idea how they'd created such beauty all those years ago, but it looked amazing. No wonder Carlos loved this place.

We continued walking along hand in hand like it was the most natural thing in the world. At times, I wondered if Carlos even realised his fingers were interlaced with mine. I definitely did. The heat from his palm made my whole body light up. It wasn't a sweaty, clammy kind of heat, though. It was like the warm feeling you got in your stomach when drinking a cup of hot chocolate on a cold winter's night.

We stepped out on to a grand patio with a pond in the centre, which was like a mirror, reflecting the buildings and everything around it. Perfectly trimmed vibrant green hedges lined either side, as well as pretty semicircular stone arches and columns.

'This is the famous Court of the Myrtles or Patio de los Arrayanes. I am sure you have seen this in many photos.'

'It does look familiar.' I nodded. Now that I thought about it, I had seen photos of Alhambra but hadn't remembered the name.

I looked on as people queued by the fountain at one end to pose for pictures.

'You want a photo?'

'Definitely!'

Carlos released his hand from mine. My heart sank. I supposed he had to let go at some point.

'Give me your phone.'

'Oh no.' I shook my head. 'I don't need to be in it. I'll just take a photo of the monument on its own.' I didn't really like photos of myself. They were just reminders of the flaws I had and the things I couldn't fix.

'Everyone can find photos of this online. What will make it special is to have *you* in the picture.'

My chest tightened.

'I'm not very photogenic.' It was true. When I used to post photos on social media, a few unkind strangers wasted no time in pointing that out to me. What was it one of them had said? 'Try using better filters or buy some spot cream.' Even though it was three years ago, those words still stung like I'd just read them five minutes ago.

'*No te creo.*' Carlos shook his head. 'I do not believe you. You have beautiful eyes. I love your hair and when you smile everything becomes brighter. It is like the moment when someone shows you the light after you have lived in darkness.' He leant forward and brushed his thumb gently across my cheek.

Normally, if someone touched my face, I'd be paranoid about my make-up coming off onto their hand or my blemishes being exposed and watching them recoil in horror, but right now I was frozen. Carlos's eyes were fixated on mine and I couldn't look away.

'It is impossible for you not to look good in a photograph. If you do not take one on your phone, then I will take one of you on mine.'

My mouth fell open and every atom in my body came

alive. No one had ever said something so nice about me before. I was stunned.

Carlos said I had beautiful eyes. He didn't just like my hair. He said he *loved* it. And what he said about my smile. Wow. I wanted to write it down and have it printed on a poster and on a T-shirt.

I was still in a trance, taking in his beautiful words, when I felt Carlos slip his arm around my waist and hold up his phone.

I thought him holding my hand was incredible, but feeling his strong arm around my waist was even better. I felt like I was wrapped in a warm blanket with a steaming cup of tea and a hot water bottle.

'Time for my *Queso* to say *queso*. Look at the camera and say cheese, *cariño*.'

'So first you call my music cheese and now me?' I smirked. 'If you were going to give me a nickname, shouldn't it be something nice? There are lots of very smelly cheeses!'

'*Queso* is one of my favourite things in the world, so believe me when I say it is a compliment...' Carlos's eyes darkened and it felt like champagne bubbles were popping in my stomach. 'Look at the camera.'

I did as instructed, trying to ignore the fireworks that were sparking around my body.

Carlos took several shots of the two of us before a group of rowdy children blocked our view.

'I will send these to you later. Come.' He took my hand again. 'There is so much more to see.'

～

For the next few hours we wandered around Alhambra hand in hand. As well as the palaces, we visited the beautifully landscaped Generalife Gardens, taking a billion photos.

Earlier I'd thought Carlos was just holding my hand without realising it, but now I knew that it was definitely intentional.

When I'd reluctantly released my palm from his to take a sip of water or to snap a photo of the scenery, as soon as I'd finished, Carlos would take my hand again.

My stomach was fluttering so much it was like someone had let off a hundred party poppers inside it. I couldn't believe this was happening. Here I was, the eternal non-traveller, walking around a historic monument in Spain, holding hands with the guy I'd had a crush on for nearly two decades.

Maybe I was a novelty to him. I doubted he'd ever been with a nerdy good girl before, so he liked the idea of trying something different. Either that, or it was the red lipstick. *Yeah*. That must be it. My make-up looked extra good today, and the woman at the beauty counter said wearing red lippy would make me look more confident, glamorous and passionate and make my teeth look whiter. That was why Carlos had complimented my smile and seemed more interested. If he saw the real me with my bare skin, there was no way someone like him would give me a second look.

'How are your feet?' Carlos turned to face me as we headed towards the exit.

'Um, pretty tired, but I'm still up for anything you want.' As soon as those words escaped my mouth, I realised how that sounded.

'*Anything?*' The corner of his mouth twitched. 'Good to know, Quesito.'

'Quesito? What happened to *queso*?'

'I like Quesito better. It means *little cheese*. In Spanish, when we add *-ito* or *-ita* to a word, it means that it is small or we add it to show affection when we are close to someone.' My cheeks warmed.

'So that's why Nate calls you Carlitos?'

'*Exacto*. So for your name in this way you would be Lilita. But I prefer Quesito.' He smiled.

Lilita, Quesito: Carlos could call me whatever he wanted if it meant he felt close to me.

'I like it. So where do you want to go now?'

'When we get to the bottom, we will stop for a drink and tapas and then I will take you to Mirador de San Nicolás.'

We found a bar and Carlos ordered a glass of wine for me and a beer for him. The waiter brought out a plate of meatballs for free. Carlos explained that in Spain you usually got some sort of free food with every drink, even if it was olives or some crisps, but Granada was known for providing amazing tapas. I could see why.

I offered to pay, but like always, Carlos pulled out his cash and settled the bill. He was probably the only person I knew who paid cash for everything. It was so old-school, but I kind of liked it.

After sitting down, getting up again was hard, but Carlos taking my hand was the only motivation I needed. We made our way up the steep cobbled streets and eventually came to a big square.

The sound of loud chatter filled the air. There were big

groups of people who'd come as part of a tour, so it was hard to get a proper look.

'Come.' Carlos led me to a less congested spot. '*Mira!* Look!'

As I took in the views, I gasped. Alhambra was there directly opposite us in all its glory.

A couple of teenagers pushed up beside me and I almost lost my balance. Carlos said something to them in Spanish, and from his tone, it sounded like he was telling them to be careful.

'Stand here.' He stepped back and signalled for me to stand in front of him. I did as he asked and just as I was marvelling at the view again, he wrapped his arms around my waist.

I sucked in a breath.

OMG.

He likes me. Carlos really likes me.

A warm feeling flooded my belly and every internal organ pulsed with excitement.

'So you like?'

'Like? I bloody love it! Thanks for bringing me here. I'm having an amazing time.' I turned my head to face him. He was looking down at me, his lips above my head. I completely lost my train of thought as I imagined how it would feel to kiss him. He was taller, so I'd need to stand on tiptoe to reach, but I didn't care.

'I enjoy it too. I like to spend time with you, Quesito.'

I turned around fully and luckily, Carlos kept his arms wrapped around me.

Our eyes locked and we stared at each other in silence. Carlos licked his lips, then stroked my cheek. Just like when he'd touched my skin earlier, I didn't flinch. My heart fluttered. The way he looked at me somehow made me feel comfortable.

I leant forward an inch. Carlos did the same. I moved forward again. His eyes darkened. He looked at me like he hadn't eaten for days and I was a plate of his favourite chocolate palmeras that he couldn't wait to devour.

Our lips were now so close I could feel his hot minty breath on my skin. My body hummed with anticipation.

There were so many reasons why we shouldn't kiss: Nate, my vow to avoid men and the risk of getting my heart broken. Plus I was leaving in a few weeks, which Carlos knew. But maybe that suited him better because then I'd just be an easy lay. Another notch to add to his bedpost.

Logic told me I shouldn't even consider taking things further. But I wasn't thinking logically right now. There was a magnetic force drawing me to him. Willing me to throw caution to the wind and do it anyway.

I'd dreamt about this moment so much when I was a teenager. And in my twenties and, let's be honest, since I'd first laid eyes on him again in Marbella. I didn't dare believe that the feeling could ever be mutual, but by some miracle, here we were with our mouths in touching distance. I'd tried to deny my feelings, but I was tired of fighting.

Screw it. This trip was all about pushing myself out of my comfort zone, so I was going in. It was now or never.

I stood on tiptoe to reach him, closing in on those last millimetres, and pressed my lips on his.

Oh. My. God.

As soon as I made contact, my knees buckled. Carlos's arms were still wrapped around my waist, so he caught me.

He crushed his mouth harder onto mine and as I parted my lips, he slid his hot, hungry tongue inside.

Fireworks exploded within me. This is what I'd wanted for years. *Decades*. And it was a billion times better than every fantasy I'd ever had.

As the kiss deepened, Carlos's mouth became greedier. He pulled me closer to him, and the moment I felt his hard-on press against my body, I moaned.

Fuck.

That was exactly what I wanted to do with him. Get a room and feel him on top of me. But for now, I was happy to just enjoy his lips on mine.

I'd always been conservative about public displays of affection, but not today. I was kissing Carlos and I didn't care who saw us.

I ran my hands across his firm back.

'Lilita…' Carlos pulled away slowly, his eyes dark with desire. '*Madre mía*. How do you do this to me? I want you so much. But…'

'I know.' My stomach sank. 'You're worried about Nate.'

'*Sí*—that is one of the reasons.'

'He also made me promise to never get involved with any of his friends,' I added. 'And I agreed. Mainly because most of his friends back then were twats—except you, of course. But anyway, that was, what? Sixteen years ago? I was just a teenager. We're adults now. It's different.'

Carlos rubbed his jaw.

'I am not sure that Nate will see it that way.'

My nostrils flared and my chest tightened. I loved my brother dearly, but there was no way I was going to let him stop me from enjoying something I'd wanted for so long.

'Nate isn't here, he's in Canada. Do you really want him to get in the way of *this*?' I wrapped my arms around his neck and pressed my mouth onto his again. It was addictive. Carlos groaned and slipped his tongue between my lips, kissing me as if he was struggling to breathe and I was oxygen.

He gripped my hip with one hand, then ran the other down my back and over my bum. My whole body felt like it had burst into flames.

Carlos pulled away and whispered in my ear.

'I want you, Lilita. But not here. If I break my promise, I must do things properly. Come.'

He led me through the crowds and back down the first set of steep steps.

I could barely concentrate. Carlos said he wanted me. We were going to have sex. I'd already been wet for him, but just the idea of having Carlos inside me tonight made me feel like a dam had burst in my knickers.

As we turned the corner, I pulled him into me for another long, slow kiss. Carlos picked up the pace, pushing his body into mine. His hand trailed along my thigh, then slowly upwards, skimming the edge of my breast.

'Is this okay?' he asked.

'Fuck yes.'

Carlos continued kissing me, his fingers gently flicking over my nipple, and arousal ripped through me.

OMG.

His touch was almost too much to handle. It was like I'd drunk several bottles of wine. I was dizzy with desire. My head was light and my knees wobbled. As I stepped back, I lost my footing and slipped, tumbling down multiple steps before Carlos caught my arm.

'Are you okay?' He pulled me up, concern etched on his face.

'Ouch!' I cried out, resting against him whilst attempting to straighten my foot. A sharp pain shot through me. 'I hurt my ankle.'

'*Mierda*. Sit down.' We sat on the step. 'Put your leg here, slowly.' Carlos patted his lap. 'Let me take a look. Does this hurt?' He prodded my ankle gently.

'Y—ouch!'

'I am sorry.' He moved his hands around, touching my foot and ankle in different areas. 'I do not think it is broken. But it is not good for you to walk on it.' He helped me up, instructing me to keep the weight on my left foot rather than the injured right one. 'I will carry you.'

'What? You can't…' Before I had a chance to finish my sentence, Carlos picked me up and threw me over his shoulder.

I felt like a damsel in distress cliché, falling over like that. But in my defence, Carlos's touch would make the strongest woman go weak at the knees.

Although I knew it was coming, I wasn't prepared for the impact. I expected it would feel amazing, but if I'd known it'd be that intense, I would've made sure I was sitting down. Or better still, lying down. Talking of lying down, I hoped this incident wouldn't get in the way of our sexy time.

Feeling his warm body against me shut down all thoughts of protesting. This was bliss. I wrapped my arms around his neck and let him do his thing.

After a few minutes, I started to worry about whether I was too much for him. There were a lot of steps.

'I can try and walk for a bit now if you want?' I spoke into his back.

'This is what I train for.'

'You train so you can rescue women when they fall over?'

'No!' I felt his chest expand as he laughed. 'To be strong. *Tranquila*. It is not that far to the car now.'

'Okay, *gracias*.'

He wasn't going to get any arguments from me.

I rested my head on his shoulder and closed my eyes.

If we weren't far from the car, that meant we were only a couple of hours away from Marbella and Carlos finally taking me to bed.

CHAPTER TWENTY-THREE

Once we'd reached the car, Carlos insisted on stopping off at a pharmacy so he could get me some painkillers for my ankle.

It was hurting, but the adrenaline racing through my veins that came from knowing we were finally going to do the deed must have taken the edge off. Yeah, I wasn't feeling a hundred per cent, but no pain, no gain, right? I was sure that once we were in the throes of passion, I wouldn't feel a thing: except the ecstasy of him being inside me. Just thinking about it made my body tingle.

I took a large glug of water and swallowed the pills. I must've dosed off soon afterwards because the next thing I knew, Carlos was tapping my shoulder to let me know that I was home.

I blinked several times as my eyes adjusted to the darkness. After turning off the engine, he got out and opened my door.

'Spin around so that your feet are outside.' After I did

what he'd asked, Carlos leant into the car, slid his hands underneath me, then lifted me out of the seat.

Luckily someone was leaving as we reached the door. 'The lift still isn't fixed.' I winced as he entered my building. 'Sorry.'

'*No pasa nada.*'

He carried me up the stairs like I was as light as a bag of sugar.

Once we'd reached my floor, I rummaged around in my bag for my keys and gave them to him. Carlos carried me inside. Clothes were scattered over the bed. Before I'd left, I'd tried on every outfit I'd brought to Spain to look as good as possible. Except, I hadn't had time to put everything back in my wardrobe before I'd left.

Even if I'd secretly hoped something would happen between us, I'd never expected that he'd be coming home with me tonight.

'Sorry about the mess,' I said as he pushed several dresses to the other side of the bed with one hand, then rested me down on the edge.

Carlos shook his head and smiled.

'What?'

'You say *sorry* and *thank you*. A lot.'

'It's polite!'

'I understand. And it is okay to say it once, but you say *sorry* for the lift not working, even though it is not your fault, *sorry* for not having your keys ready to open the door, *sorry* that you have clothes on the bed… it is not a big deal, Quesito. *Tranquila.*'

He had a point. Sometimes when someone bumped into me, somehow my natural reaction was to say sorry to *them*.

'Okay. My flat is a mess, so ignore it. Better?'

'*Sí*. How is your ankle?'

'Still hurting, but I'll survive. I know what will make me feel better.' I held his hands and pulled him towards me onto the bed. 'You on top of me.' I blushed. I didn't think I'd ever been so forward. But I'd waited so long for this. Now wasn't the time to be shy.

Carlos landed beside me.

'What are you doing?' He frowned.

'I thought that was obvious.' I stroked his chest and leant forward to kiss him.

He pecked me on the lips, then pulled away.

'Quesito, you know that I want you, but not like this. You are not well.'

'It's just a sprained ankle, I'll be fine.'

'No.' He shook his head. 'I told you earlier. If I break my promise, I will do things properly. I will not sleep with you when you are injured. It is not right.'

'Don't be such a goody two shoes! I thought you were supposed to be a Casanova, sleeping with different women every night.'

'I am going to make something for you to eat.' Carlos jumped off the bed, ignoring my comment. 'We did a lot of walking today and you need to keep up your strength.'

After all of these years of waiting, I was hoping that things were finally going to happen. Properly.

Looked like tonight wasn't going to be the night after all.

CHAPTER TWENTY-FOUR

I felt around on the bedside table for my phone to check the time. Once the window shutters were closed, they plunged the room into complete darkness, so you had no idea whether it was seven in the morning or seven at night until you opened them.

I found my handbag on the floor, reached inside and grabbed my phone. Bloody hell. It was almost nine in the morning. I didn't even remember falling asleep. There was a missed call from Cassie half an hour ago too, and I hadn't even heard the phone ring.

After lifting up the thin bed sheet and running my hand down my body, I realised that I was in my underwear. I never slept in my underwear. I always changed into a T-shirt. Actually, how had I even got into bed?

The last thing I remembered was Carlos saying he was going to make dinner and then… I must've passed out. Which meant he'd undressed me and put me under the covers.

Did we…? *No*. He'd said he wouldn't when I was injured. And what time had he left? So many questions.

I went to move and my ankle throbbed, so I decided it was best to stay put. Instead I picked up my phone again and dialled Cassie's number.

'Hey, sis!' she answered after the second ring. 'How did your date with Carlos go? I hope I didn't interrupt any morning sex earlier. I waited as long as I could before calling! I've been dying to know what happened!'

'Even if something *did* happen yesterday, why would you think I'd jump into bed with him on the first night?' I teased.

'Because the sexual tension between you guys has been building like a pressure cooker since you arrived in Spain. And I know what it's like when you fancy the pants off someone. Sometimes as much as you want to, it's hard to wait.'

When Cassie had first told me she and Nico had got busy literally hours after they'd met, I'd been shocked. Not that there was anything wrong with it. Her body, her choice and all that, but when it came to men, Cassie was like me: suspicious and cautious. We didn't just throw caution to the wind. We'd been taught that if you gave up the goodies on the first night, the guy wouldn't respect you.

I had no doubt that was true in some cases, but Cassie and Nico proved that it didn't always have to be like that. Sometimes you just had a connection with someone that was too strong to deny.

And after spending time with Carlos, I could understand how easy it would be to fall into bed with him. That was exactly what I'd wanted to do last night. Anyway, it wasn't like he was a total stranger. Technically I'd known him for almost two decades, so…

'Something *did* happen, actually. We kissed.'

My eardrums nearly popped as Cassie screamed down the phone.

'That's *amazing*! I knew he liked you! Hold on a sec. Come in. I mean, *entrez*.' I heard the door open and a male voice speaking French before Cassie responded. 'I'm fine. Just speaking to Lily. She kissed Carlos!'

'Cass! Don't tell the whole world!'

'It's not the whole world, it's Nico!'

'*Bonjour*, Lily.' Nico came on the phone. 'I am very happy for you. I will leave you alone to continue your conversation.'

'*Merci!*'

'Sorry, Lil. Nico heard me scream and came to check if I was okay! So how was it? How did it happen and what happened next? Tell me *everything*!'

I filled her in on how mind-blowing the kiss was and how the intensity of his touch caused me to completely lose my shit, fall and twist my ankle.

'Yeah, so I've just woken up and I'm in my underwear.' I picked up the bottle of water resting on the bedside table and took a huge glug. 'And I wasn't even wearing my best set either. It's the comfy M&S bra and knickers that I've had for donkey's years which don't even match. I came here on a strict dating detox. If I'd known that things were going to happen with Carlos, I would've at least put on something decent!'

'I'm sure he wasn't even thinking about what underwear you were wearing, more like imagining how good it would be to see you *without* it!' Cassie laughed and I realised how much I'd missed her. I really should visit her soon.

'*Hardly!* I practically offered myself on a plate and he turned me down. Said it wouldn't be right because I was injured. It's not like I've broken my leg, but as frustrated as I am, I have to admit, it was really sweet. Fuck, sis. I like him *so* much!'

'I can see why. He acted like a true gent. Carrying you home, not taking advantage of you when you're not a hundred per cent and putting you to bed. He definitely sounds like a keeper.'

My stomach sank. Carlos could never be a *keeper*. If he was still interested, it could only ever be temporary. Anyway, now wasn't the time to think about that.

'I wish I knew what else happened last night. If I fell asleep with my mouth wide open and whether I snored. I was really tired and I *always* snore when I'm tired.'

I angled my phone towards the pillow. As the light shone down, I saw it was covered in make-up. A flash of fear raced through me, wondering if that was why he'd left. Whether he'd taken one look at my skin and run.

'When a guy's really into you, he doesn't care about all that shit. Trust me.'

'If you say so.' I crossed my legs. I couldn't believe I'd gone the whole night without going to the loo, but my bladder was about to burst. 'I'll call him in a bit to say thank you and see how he is towards me. Hopefully he hasn't changed his mind.'

'He won't!'

'Cass, I'm bursting for the loo, so can I call you later? I want to hear about how it's all going with Nico's hair academy.'

'Course! But text me as soon as you speak to Carlos. I can't wait to hear about the latest developments in your love life. Soooo exciting!'

'Yeah! It kinda is!' My heart swelled. It was rare that the word *exciting* was used to describe my romantic life, but it felt great. 'Speak later. Love you.'

'Love you too.'

I hung up, then swung my legs around to the edge of the bed. My ankle throbbed, but I didn't have a choice. I had to wee.

Putting my hands behind me, I pushed down and launched myself up off the bed.

I hopped on one foot across the bedroom area and towards the bathroom. It was difficult to see. Hopping over to the main windows to open the shutters or turning on the light switch by the front door straight away would make more sense, but I could only hold on for a few more seconds. I had to wee first.

Thankfully, I made it in time. After I finished, I hopped back towards the window, but accidentally tripped over a cushion that must've fallen off the sofa and landed on the floor.

Just as I struggled to get back on my feet, the whole room illuminated as the lights turned on.

'What are you doing?' A deep voice vibrated around the room. I turned and saw Carlos rushing over. 'You should be resting in bed. Did you not get my note?'

'Note? What note? How did you even get in?'

'With your keys. Remember I used them to open the door last night? Come.' He scooped me off the floor and carried me back to bed.

As much as I hated the fact that I'd fallen over twice in

two days like a clumsy idiot, I had to admit I kind of liked this whole caveman *let me rescue and carry you* routine that Carlos had going on. Nothing felt better than being in his arms and resting my head against his solid chest.

My nose twitched. As well as Carlos's gorgeous scent, I could smell something sweet, like sugary donuts. My stomach rumbled.

After putting me down, he walked to the window, pulled up the shutters, switched off the light and sat down beside me.

'Lie down and put your leg up, here: on the cushion.' He handed me one that was resting on the edge of the bed. 'Look!' He pointed to my ankle. 'It is swollen. It is important not to put weight on it. You need to keep your foot elevated. Wait here.'

Carlos went to a large bag resting on the floor by the door and pulled out a bag of ice.

'Keep this on your ankle. It will help the swelling go down.'

As he placed it on my ankle, I jumped. The cold sensation was a shock to the system. Not as intense as when Carlos had kissed me yesterday, though. I didn't know if I'd ever experienced something so powerful.

'It is cold at first, but you will get used to it. Do you have a towel?'

'Third shelf.' I pointed to the wardrobe. Carlos pulled out an orange towel and placed it over the cushion.

'So that the bed does not get wet.'

I wished we could make the bed wet in another way…

'Thanks for all this.' I quickly dragged my mind out of the gutter. 'You said you left me a note? What time did you come back this morning?'

'I did not leave. I stayed here last night.' My eyes widened. '*On the sofa*.' Carlos clarified. 'I am already breaking Nate's trust. If he finds out that I also left you alone when you are injured, he would kill me twice. I had to stay to make sure you were okay.'

Butterflies fluttered in my stomach. Then I breathed a sigh of relief. Imagine if Carlos hadn't gone out and was on the sofa listening to me talk to Cassie about him. It was so dark I'd never have known he was here. Phew.

'That was really kind, thanks.'

'And I left the note to tell you that I will go to get churros for breakfast and I will be back soon.'

'I didn't see it. Where did you leave it?'

'On the table next to the bed.'

I looked over at it and then glanced at the floor. There it was. I must've knocked it off when I was feeling around for my phone.

'Sorry. And thank you for staying and getting the churros and ice.'

'You did it again!' He grinned and shook his head.

'Did what?'

'You said sorry and you also said thank you—*twice*!'

'I can't help it! It's a polite and normal thing to do. You're the rude weird one if you don't think it's right to thank someone when they do something nice for you.'

'I have to tell you a secret.'

'What?'

'You know that to sleep here, I just lie on the sofa and closed my eyes and I did not make the churros myself, *sí*? I just go to the shop and buy them. Same for the ice. It is not a big deal.'

'Well, *I* think it is, so thank you, thank you, *thank you*!' I teased.

'*Madre mía*,' he sighed. 'I will get the plates before you say thank you again. And remember, do not move!'

As the bright sun shone through the window, I squinted. Then I realised—I didn't have my face on. Shit.

I'd *never* let a guy see my face so soon. Especially before we'd even slept together. I'd normally wait a few months to be sure that they would stick around. It was far too intimate. Even more intimate than sex. You could do that with the lights off, and under the covers, it was easier to hide. But showing my true self was much more personal.

I reached into my handbag, quickly pulled out my powder compact and swiped it over my cheeks and jaw, where the blemishes were the worst. Although Carlos hadn't stared at my complexion so far, I'd feel less self-conscious if I didn't have bare skin.

My heart rate slowed and now I had my mask on, I instantly felt better. I placed my pillow against the head-board and sat up straighter, then adjusted the cushion under my feet to try and make myself more comfortable. My ankle still throbbed. I took two painkillers, hoping that they'd start working soon.

A few minutes later, Carlos brought two cups of coffee and a plate of churros over to the bed. We wolfed it down. It was the first thing I'd eaten since the tapas last night. Carlos said that by the time he'd finished making dinner, I'd fallen asleep. Not surprised after all the walking we'd done.

'So how exactly did I get in the bed?'

Carlos was sat cross-legged at the edge of the mattress,

looking gorgeous as ever in a fresh blue vest and a pair of tan-coloured shorts. He must've gone home to shower and change before he got the churros. Which reminded me. I definitely needed to shower this morning too.

'I put you there.'

'So you took off my clothes?' I raised my eyebrow.

'*Sí*. I did not think that you would want to wear clothes from the day to bed. I hope that was okay? I did not look. I did it in the dark.'

'How the hell did you do that?'

'I turned off the light. It was not difficult. You wear just a skirt and T-shirt.'

'I suppose you've had a lot of practice at taking women's clothes off in the dark…' I left my words hanging.

'I must go to the gym now,' Carlos replied. 'I have massage clients this afternoon, so I need to go before then.'

So no confirmation or denial of his womaniser reputation, then. I supposed he didn't want to admit that he'd had more women than hot dinners. And if things were going to happen between us, I'd have to accept that. It was just some fun whilst I was on holiday. It wasn't that deep.

'Okay,' I muttered.

'I will come back at lunch to give you food. Until then, try not to move.'

'But what if I need the toilet?'

'That is what this is for.' He lifted a red bucket out of the large bag and placed it beside the bed. I guessed he'd bought it when he went out.

'*Seriously?* You want me to wee in a bucket? No way!'

At some point the bucket would need to be emptied

and I couldn't let him do that. *Hell no.* I'd hopped to the toilet earlier, so I'd do it again.

'Use the bucket.' He waved his hand as he walked to the door. '*Hasta luego.*'

Turned out using the bucket *was* a good idea.

Once Carlos had left after lunch, I'd tried hopping to the loo again and stubbed my bloody foot on the corner of the bed. The pain was horrible. So the next time, I'd parked my bum on the stupid bucket and weed there.

I told myself I'd just have a quick siesta, but when I'd woken up, it was after seven in the evening and the bucket was empty. Gasp.

Carlos had emptied my piss. I was mortified.

As always, he shrugged it off and said it was no big deal. But it was to me. When we'd kissed yesterday, we'd both thought we were about to indulge in a steamy, no-strings night of passion. But twenty-four hours later, here he was dealing with my dehydrated, smelly wee. *Ugh.* It was even worse than farting on a first date. Hardly romantic. Everything had gone in a completely different direction, and our chances of hooking up after this were looking unlikely.

My head was doing a victory dance because that meant I could stick to my no-men vow, but my body prayed that somehow, it could still happen.

Monday was my day off, so I hadn't had to worry about work. But by the evening, it was obvious that I wasn't going to be able to stand on a twisted ankle for several hours to do my shift tomorrow, so I had to do the thing I rarely did: call in sick.

Everyone else I knew didn't think twice about calling in when they didn't feel like going to work, but I'd always felt too guilty. Like I was letting someone down. But this time, I didn't have a choice. I needed to give my ankle time to heal. Hopefully it'd be better in a few days. A girl could only wee in a bucket for so long.

CHAPTER TWENTY-FIVE

A sharp pain shot through my ankle, which, two days on from our trip to Alhambra, still wasn't much better. If it didn't improve by tomorrow, I'd have to think about going to the doctor's.

Carlos had stayed over again and was currently sleeping on the sofa, so I wanted to hop to the bathroom to put my face on before he woke up.

I'd gasped when I'd caught sight of my skin last night. Because I'd only used powder, it looked all cakey. Foundation would give a more natural appearance, but it was in the bathroom. I could make it. I knew I could.

Whilst Carlos was at work last night, I'd crawled there to wash. Sitting down in the shower wasn't comfortable, but I'd managed. I'd done a number two on the toilet too. He may have emptied my piss from the bucket yesterday, but if I took a dump in there, romance would definitely be off the cards.

I swung my legs out of the bed and tried hopping

quietly. I'd almost reached the bathroom door when I hit something solid.

I held my hands out to steady myself and then the room lit up.

'Carlos! Sorry!' I stuttered, realising my hands were resting on his bare chest. It felt just as toned and smooth as I'd imagined. With the bathroom light on, I had a prime view of its gorgeousness.

I swallowed hard. The right thing to do would be to remove my hands immediately, but it felt so good I couldn't quite bring myself to follow through.

'What are you doing?' Carlos frowned.

'Sorry!' Heat flooded my cheeks. 'I didn't mean to…' I quickly stepped back, causing my hands to fall.

'No, I mean, why did you get up? Is the bucket full?'

'I don't need the toilet. I had to—I had to… get, I mean *do* something important.'

'What?'

I wracked my brain, trying to think of what I could say. Nothing plausible came to mind and I hated lying.

'My make-up,' I said quietly, hanging my head.

Now he'd think I was so vain. I should've said I had to brush my teeth. That was a point. Yesterday I'd drunk some water before I'd spoken to him in the morning, which had at least washed my mouth out a little. But now, he had a triple whammy: morning breath, messy hair *and* bare skin. *Jesus*. This was all too much.

'Why would you need make-up? Where are you going? Your ankle still needs to heal.'

'I'm not going anywhere. I just… I need it. This is embarrassing.' I winced.

'Tell me.' He lifted my chin. 'You do not need to be embarrassed.'

Now he was looking me in the eyes, it was even worse. I didn't want him to see me like this. Exposed. Flawed. Imperfect. My stomach twisted. I might as well tell him and get it over with. Hopefully then he'd leave me alone and I could go back to bed, pull the covers over my head and stay there for the rest of the day dying of embarrassment. I took a deep breath.

'To cover my skin.'

'Why?' His brow furrowed. 'What is wrong with your skin?'

'*Come on!*' I scoffed. 'You have eyes! You can see what's wrong with it! It's covered in spots and ugly marks.'

'I do not see why you feel you need to cover this.'

'Don't lie!' I didn't know what was worse. Hearing Carlos claim he didn't see anything wrong or the way River had winced whenever he'd touched it.

Carlos leant forward and stroked my bare cheek. This time I flinched. When he'd done that before at Alhambra, I was wearing foundation, so at least I had a barrier of protection. But now I was completely exposed.

'I am not telling lies, Lilita. To me, you are beautiful.'

My eyes widened and my stomach did a weird flip-floppy thing. There was no way he could really think that.

'But how can that be true?' I frowned. The reason Carlos had kissed me before was because my flaws were covered. Normally when I showed how I really looked, men shied away. 'Look at your skin and everyone else's my age. It's smooth and clear. But mine has bumps and scars. I'm thirty-two and still have teenage fucking spots!'

'It happens sometimes. The skin produces too much oil and the pores become clogged.' Carlos took my hand, opened the shutters a little and led me to the sofa. He pushed away his blanket and pillow to make room for us to sit down. 'But having marks or scars does not define your beauty. Does that mean that people with freckles are not beautiful? I have moles on my arms and back. Does this mean that I am ugly?'

'No, but…' I hung my head and Carlos lifted my chin again.

'It is the same thing. I do not judge people by their skin. It is shallow. You are much more than that. If you are wearing make-up because you feel you need to hide your skin from me, then it is not necessary. Let me show you something.' He picked up his phone from the coffee table and scrolled through hundreds of photos. 'Look. This is me when I was sixteen.'

I glanced at the screen. It was an awkward-looking young Carlos flashing his trademark smile. He looked so cute. It was only when he put his fingers over the screen and zoomed in that I noticed he had acne all over his face. *Oh.* I would've never have thought that he'd suffered from it. His skin had been so flawless when I'd met him a few years later, and it still was now.

'I didn't know you had it too. But that's the thing: you were sixteen. It's *normal*. But not in your thirties. I've had this since I was twelve. That's twenty years of having a pizza face. Two decades of trying different products and treatments and always being disappointed. Having to cover up my skin because people would stare if I didn't. It went away for a while when I took the strong medication, but since then, there's always been something.'

I knew wearing make-up wasn't good for my acne, but it helped my confidence. I always tried to buy brands that were oil-free and kinder to the skin. And I made sure I removed it properly at night.

Over the years I'd also spent a small fortune on professional treatment courses, and although my skin looked better straight afterwards, the results wouldn't last. I even used the aftercare products the beauty therapists at the salon recommended, but the angry spots and scars never went away permanently.

'My sister was the same. The medication and treatments that worked for me did not work for her, and so in her twenties, she still had acne. Things changed when she finally listened to my aunt, who had been telling her that other things like diet can affect the skin, so to try not to eat cheese or drink milk from the cow. When she cut out dairy products, she saw a big difference.'

'Really?'

'*Sí.* Of course, everyone is different and many people drink milk and are okay.'

'I *do* drink a lot of milk.' I'd experimented with eliminating loads of things over the years—fried food, sweets, chocolates, all the unhealthy stuff—but never really noticed a major improvement. But I hadn't tried cutting out milk or dairy.

'If you want, you can speak to my aunt about it. Or Elena, the manager at the hotel spa. If you think it will be helpful.'

'Can I think about it?' I didn't want my first introduction to his aunt to be about how terrible my skin was.

'Of course.' He leant forward and kissed me on the cheek. I tensed a little. I was always nervous about being kissed without having make-up to mask my skin. Maybe he really didn't mind. 'Now that you are awake, would you like breakfast?'

'Yes, but you've been working all night, let me—'

'The only thing I want you to do today is rest. I will take care of you.'

'Thank you.' My heart fluttered. 'I suppose I won't have any milk in my coffee today, then. Cutting out dairy products won't be easy, but it's worth a try to see if it makes a difference. No more *leche* or *queso* for your Quesito.'

'It does not matter if you drink milk or eat cheese. You will always be my Quesito.' Carlos kissed me softly on the forehead and walked to the kitchen.

My shoulders loosened as something told me that he really meant it.

CHAPTER TWENTY-SIX

I t was now Saturday and I'd returned to work. My ankle still wasn't a hundred per cent, but it was good enough.

Carlos had been an absolute angel. Insisting I rest whilst he took care of me. Doing the shopping, cooking and checking I was okay. He'd even bought some oat milk so I could have it in my coffee.

I'd never lived with a guy before and even though he was out at work most of the day and night, the moments when he was in the flat were lovely.

When he woke up in the mornings, he'd make us coffee and breakfast, then come and sit on the bed and tell me about how his night was at work. Or he'd played me some new songs he planned to add to the playlist for that night.

It wasn't just our chats that I enjoyed. It was him just being there. Might sound weird, but just hearing him in the shower or looking up and seeing him standing in the kitchen made me smile. Somehow I found his presence so calming. I loved having him close by.

And I felt like I could be myself around Carlos. Since that heart-to-heart on Tuesday, I hadn't worried about putting on my usual mask of make-up, and yet he still acted exactly the same around me. It was like a tonne of bricks had been lifted from my shoulders.

I had no idea how I'd ever be able to repay Carlos for his help. I'd given up saying thank you after he'd threatened to leave if I said it again.

'Quesito,' he'd said. 'I have counted. It is only eleven in the morning and you have already said thank you *six* times. *Seis veces! Madre mía!*'

'That's impossible,' I'd scoffed.

'And today is a good day. Sometimes you have said it more than ten times in one hour.'

'Rubbish!' I'd folded my arms. 'When did I say it this morning?'

'You said thank you when I opened the shutters, again when I bring you toast, once more when I give you coffee, again when I take your plate and cup and now when I say that I will go to get fresh fruit from the market. It is not necessary.'

'Ah,' I'd said, realising he had a point.

I wasn't used to people—well, *men*—doing things for me. I still felt guilty. Carlos had thought he was going to get sex, but instead he'd ended up being my temporary carer. I hadn't earned the right for him to do all of these kind things for me.

Now I knew that saying those words to Carlos didn't have value, I had to find another way to thank him.

The lunchtime rush was over, so I'd just filled Zach in

on how helpful Carlos had been and asked if he could help brainstorm alternative ways to show my gratitude.

'Just offer him a BJ!'

I spat out my water.

'Zach!'

'What?' He grinned mischievously. 'It's a good idea! Show me a guy who doesn't like getting sucked off and I'll show you a dinosaur with pink hair. *Exactly.* All men love blowies. I'd kill for one right now.'

My eyes widened. 'I hope that wasn't a request!'

'Don't worry, honey. It wasn't!' he chuckled.

'Oh yeah, how did your date go last weekend?'

'It didn't. Wanker didn't even turn up. I think I'm going to die alone!'

'Course you won't! And you're still so young. Enjoy your twenties.'

'Yes, Mum!' Zach cackled.

'Enough of the mum jokes. So do you have any more sensible suggestions on how to repay Carlos? I don't think he's motivated by sex. If he was, we would've got busy this week or he would've at least tried it on.'

Since I'd started working here, he'd also taken me home every night and stayed with me all week to help out whilst I was injured, so I was starting to question whether he really was the womaniser I'd thought he was.

'Fair point. I reckon you need to think about his love language.'

'I've heard of love languages, but never really looked into it.'

'It's the way people give and receive love. I read an article on it the other day. I think there are about five of them. Well, I went down a bit of a rabbit hole and found articles that said there were seven or eight, but there seemed to be five basic ones. One of them was receiving gifts.'

'I'm not sure.' I frowned. 'Carlos doesn't seem that materialistic.'

'I don't think it has to be something expensive. It's more about giving something you know they'll love, like what you did the other day when you gave him those palmeras. Or, y'know, how he brings you fresh churros.'

'Oh, okay. That sounds cool.'

'Another one was quality time—when they focus just on you, so not sitting at a table for two scrolling on their phone or watching TV like my ex used to.' I nodded. I knew the feeling. 'Then there's physical touch. Stuff like holding hands, hugging and kissing.'

I thought about it and Carlos was very tactile. At Alhambra he'd liked holding hands. We hadn't kissed since that evening, so I wasn't sure if he enjoyed that a lot too.

'Hold on a sec.' Zach reached for his phone. 'I can't remember the others, so I need to google it. Here we go… the next one is *words of affirmation*. Where I guess you tell the person how amazing you think they are and praise them and stuff.'

'That's definitely *not* his love language!' I laughed, thinking about how much he hated when I said thank you too much or paid him compliments.

'And then the last one is *acts of service*, which is where they do stuff to make your life easier. Like when you're busy, so they offer to do the washing up. Or in your case, tip your bucket of piss down the toilet!' Zach threw his head back and cackled.

'Stop!'

'I couldn't resist. Actually, I meant to ask, what happened when you needed to do a number two? Don't tell me you shat in the bucket too!'

'Course not! I didn't use the bucket to wee in for long, and when I needed to poo, I crawled to the loo.'

'Thank fuck for that! So what do you reckon? Which are his top love languages? The article said most people have one or two main ones.'

'Mmm.' I rested my finger on my chin, turning the options over in my head. 'Hard to say. Like I said earlier, words of affirmation are a definite no-no, and although I'm sure he likes physical touch to a degree, it's not a key motivator. He seems really independent, so that's acts of service out of the window. When I'm around him, I'm never distracted. I'd spend every minute of the day with him if I could and I'm pretty sure he knows that.'

'Which just leaves receiving gifts.'

'Yeah, I like the idea of a thoughtful gift that means something to him rather than anything too flashy.'

'So what does he like or value?'

'He loves music, obviously, and food. I know!' A flash of inspiration flew into my head.

I needed to do something for him that required effort. He liked food, so maybe I could cook him a meal?

My culinary skills were about as good as my talents behind the bar. In other words, crap. There was as much chance of me being invited to compete on *MasterChef* as me getting a call from Beyoncé asking me to be one of her backup dancers. But maybe that was all the more reason to try. It'd show Carlos how much I cared.

And instead of inviting him for lunch or dinner at my

place (after five days of staying there, he was probably sick of those four walls), I could cook and pack it into a picnic basket and we could have it on the beach.

Yes. I liked the idea.

Now I just had to work out what to make and, more importantly, how.

CHAPTER TWENTY-SEVEN

I t was Monday evening and I was at my flat, waiting for Carlos to meet me after finishing his massage shift.

I'd spent most of the afternoon whipping up a feast. Not on my own, obviously. After I'd had the idea, I'd asked Eva if she'd help.

Dinners in Spain were lighter than what I was used to eating in England, so Eva said it was best to just do little dishes. Especially as we were going to the beach.

As well as the food, I had wine, extra-cold bottles of both alcoholic and alcohol-free beer, plates and cutlery. Yep. I was good to go.

My readiness wasn't just related to the food. I'd tidied the flat and also put on some nice underwear, you know, just in case.

Bella and Cassie were always harping on about *the universe*, so I'd put in several requests saying that I'd be eternally grateful if the manifestation lords could kindly arrange for Carlos's lips to be magically planted on mine at some point today. Fingers crossed.

The phone buzzed. Carlos had messaged to say he was downstairs. I smoothed down my sleeveless knee-length red dress, grabbed the picnic basket and cool box Eva had leant me and headed downstairs.

'Hey,' I said, walking towards him. Carlos was leaning against the car, dressed all in white, wearing his cool sunglasses and looking gorgeous as ever. He had his hands casually in his shorts pockets, allowing me to see the beautiful curl of his biceps. *Damn.* Somebody hose me down.

'*Qué guapa!*' Carlos's eyes widened. He kissed me gently on the first cheek. I was tempted to turn my face so that rather than kissing the other side of my face, he'd get my lips instead. It'd been eight days since I'd last felt his mouth on mine, and my body ached for him.

Too late.

'What did you say?' I asked as he lifted his lips from my other cheek.

'I said that you look very beautiful.' He flashed his smile and my body temperature rose another few degrees. *Carlos just called me beautiful again*—when I was wearing less make-up than usual and was showing my bare shoulders in this dress. I couldn't deny it. Words of affirmation were one of my love languages. When he complimented me, it meant so much.

'Th—' I paused. 'Oops! I almost said the dreaded T-word.'

'Ah! *Sí.*' He nodded.

'If I say *gracias* instead of *thank you*, does that count?' Carlos's face broke into a smile.

'I think that is allowed. You are practising your Spanish. But a hundred times a day is the limit, *vale*?'

'*Vale.*' I grinned.

'Where do you want it?' Carlos touched my hand, lifting the basket from it. 'Is the back seat okay?'

'You can put it anywhere you want,' I said. Carlos's eyes darkened and I realised what I'd just said. 'I um, yeah, the back seat is good. I mean, I'm fine with that if you want to…' I stuttered.

'You are still talking about the basket, Quesito?' His mouth twitched.

'Course!' I said quickly.

'Okay, I will put it here. Perhaps on the floor.'

'The floor could work too.'

Carlos held my gaze and I swallowed hard. We both stood there in silence, but the air felt charged with an electric force, pulling us together.

Carlos opened the back seat door and put the basket in the footwell along with the cool box, then placed my large beach bag on the back seat.

We got into the car and he started the engine.

'So, we will go to my beach. That is okay for you?'

'The one you told me about when we went to Alhambra?'

'*Sí.*'

'Sounds great!'

'You want to listen to your playlist?' Carlos pointed to his phone.

'Actually, I made one myself. For *you*.'

'*Qué?*' His brow furrowed.

'I'm no DJ, so it might not be great, but when I was resting at home, I had time to listen to a lot of music and decided to check out *your* favourite artists, and some of the songs were quite good, so I added them. That way we can listen to songs that we both love. Kind of like our own playlist.'

Carlos was silent. His Adam's apple bobbed as he swallowed hard.

I wasn't sure if I'd said something wrong. Maybe creating playlists was his thing, so he preferred to do them. 'Or we could just listen to Britney,' I said to fill the silence. 'I know you secretly love her!'

'Nobody has done this for me before, so I am just surprised, that is all.' He reached over and touched my hand. 'I would really like to hear the playlist that you made.'

I blew out a breath and my heart swelled. I was glad he appreciated the gesture. I hoped he'd feel the same once he heard my selection.

I pulled out my phone and plugged the lead into the port.

'This Is What You Came For', by Calvin Harris and Rihanna, vibrated from the speakers. Carlos's face lit up.

'Nice choice, Quesito!'

My cheeks warmed with pride. We were off to a great start. I couldn't lie. It was a catchy song. I started singing the lyrics at the top of my voice.

'And you learnt the words too?'

'It's not difficult!' I laughed. 'Dance music is basically just repeating the same thing over and over again.'

'The simplicity is the beauty of it. And the beat. When you hear it, tell me that it does not make you want to get up and dance?'

'True. Well, I would if I could.'

'But you *can*. We will practise again tonight. I have my

travel speaker, so we will have our own private beach party. With your excellent playlist.'

'You've only heard one song from it!'

'I know it will be good. You made it with love and that is what is important. *Gracias*.'

My stomach flipped at the mention of the L-word. Obviously it was a turn of phrase. Clearly I didn't *love* him, but yes, I cared a lot and made the playlist wanting him to know that.

'Er, hold on. Did you just say thank you? I thought that word was banned.'

'You know that I am only joking when I tease you after you say thank you and sorry. It is nice. Sometimes people say sorry and they do not mean it…' He hung his head for a few moments, then raised it again. 'But I know you are genuine. And being polite is part of who you are, so I do not want to change that.'

This man.

Just sitting beside him already made me melt and then he had to go and say those sweet words.

Right now, all I wanted to do was take his face in my hands and kiss him. Hopefully if all went well, I'd get my wish later tonight.

Carlos parked up and led me down a narrow walkway. We turned the corner and my eyes were treated to a gorgeous stretch of beach.

I could tell it was a quiet place just by looking at the sand. At the hotel, there were always loads of footprints from the many people walking along the beach. But this white sand was fresh, as if no one had been here for days. I almost felt guilty for stepping in it. I closed my eyes and inhaled the salty sea air. No wonder Carlos loved coming here. It was so peaceful.

Now that it was early evening, the weather was much cooler. Although the heat from the sun warmed my skin, there was a gentle breeze, making it the perfect temperature. Not too hot, not too cold. Just right.

'This is okay for you?' Carlos stopped. 'It is my favourite part.'

'Looks good to me!'

I pulled out a large beach blanket from my bag, laid it on the sand and put some stones I'd collected at each corner so it didn't blow away. Carlos put the cool box and picnic basket down and we sat at opposite ends of the blanket facing the sea.

'It's beautiful.'

'It is. So'—he put his hand on the basket—'this is very heavy. Do you have more rocks inside?'

'No! It's just dinner. Like I said, I wanted to do something to thank you for all your help. With my ankle and, y'know, everything.'

'It is not necessary, I helped because I want to.'

'Well, whatever the reason, I'm grateful. Are you hungry?'

'A bit.'

'Great!'

Carlos connected his travel speaker to the phone, and as Calvin Harris and Rihanna's 'We've Found Love' played, I started pulling out multiple dishes. Eva had been a star, lending me several different pretty containers to put everything in. 'So we have *jamón, queso* for you, *croquettas*, *pimiento verde, tortilla…*'

'Wait. You made all of this?'

'Well, not the cheese and ham, obvs, but the *croquettas*, fried green peppers, Spanish omelette and other cooked stuff, *sí*!'

'You told me before that you do not cook.' It was true. Usually everything I attempted, even rice or pasta, ended up burnt or overcooked.

'I had help. From Eva, the chef at the hotel. We made it together this afternoon. I know you like good food, so I wanted to do this for you.'

Carlos's eyes were now like saucers.

'I-I… do not know what to say.'

'You don't have to say anything. Just eat. And pray that it tastes okay and that you don't get food poisoning!'

'Okay,' he laughed. 'I can do that. *Gracias*.'

'Hold up! I've been counting and that's already *two* thank-yous in one evening. If you're not careful, my over-politeness might rub off on you, permanently.'

'Perhaps this is a good thing.' He squeezed my hand, causing goose bumps to erupt across my skin.

Once I'd ordered my heart rate to calm down, I opened the containers and handed Carlos a plate. He cut the Spanish omelette into slices and, after offering it to me, picked up one for himself and took a bite.

'*Qué buena!* It is not easy to make this well, but this is delicious.'

I did a mental fist pump. Eva had done all the hard work, but I'd helped cut up the potatoes, chop the onions and mix the egg, so maybe I could take at least ten per cent of the credit.

Carlos tucked into the rest of the food with enthusiasm, cooing over how tasty everything was. I couldn't wait to tell Eva how it all went.

'That was incredible.' Carlos patted his belly. He took my hands in his and looked me deep in the eyes. 'Seriously, I really appreciate this, Quesito. You are so kind. It is one of the many things I have always liked about you.'

'*Always* liked?' I frowned, trying to process my thoughts. 'You mean… like as in fancy me, *like*? So you— how long have you…?'

'I have *always* liked you. Why do you think I gave you that maths book and always wanted to talk to you?'

'I just, I…'

My head span. I'd thought Carlos had just started liking me because of my new cool clothes and make-up. I remembered thinking it was kind of him to get me the book knowing how much I loved maths and studying, but the concept of him thinking about me *romantically* when I was an awkward-looking teenager was mind-blowing.

'I-I had no idea.' My cheeks heated.

'I could sit here all night and list the things I like about you. But I think your head would be so big, it would not fit through your front door.'

'Yeah, *right*!' I scoffed.

'It is true. You are so smart, funny, caring, loyal, hardworking, fun to be around and… *very* sexy.' His eyes darkened.

I couldn't remember anyone ever calling me *sexy* before, but my body wasn't complaining. Tingles erupted between my legs.

'You're pretty amazing yourself.' I edged towards him on the blanket.

'Not really.' He shook his head.

'You've *got* to be joking! If I told *you* all of the things I adored about you, never mind a door: your head wouldn't fit on this beach!'

Carlos hung his head. That wasn't the reaction I'd been expecting to my compliment. Then again, knowing that words weren't his love language, I shouldn't be surprised.

Maybe a different approach was needed. If I couldn't tell him how I felt, I'd use another way to *show* him.

Screw waiting for the universe. I was making my own shit happen. I closed the gap between us, leant forward and planted my lips on his. Carlos's body stiffened.

Oh. I pulled away, my stomach crashing beneath the sand.

'Sorry. I thought… my bad. It's just—you just said you liked me.' My shoulders slumped. Maybe the time we'd spent together at my flat had been too much for him after all. Then again, he'd just called me sexy. I didn't understand.

I went to get up, but Carlos grabbed my arms and pulled me back.

'I *do*.' He squeezed his eyes shut. 'You have no idea how much. Quesito, I like you so much it hurts. When I am with you, it is like I have swallowed fire. Every part of me burns. My heart, my skin, my dick… that is why I had to end our first dance lesson and then the massage.'

'Oh. *Ohhhh…*'

Shut the front door.

My eyes widened as I realised what he was saying. So it *wasn't* a stray boner when I'd rubbed up against him. And he'd been just as turned on as me during that massage. *Mind. Blown.*

'Every time I see you, outside of work, I tell myself it will be the last time. But I cannot keep away.'

'So don't.' I leant forward and kissed him again. He groaned. 'Fuck what Nate thinks. We both want this. That's all that matters.'

'It is not just because of Nate. I am not good for you. I cannot give you what you want.'

'What?' I ran my hand down his arm. 'You can't give me multiple orgasms that make my toes curl and make me scream your name?'

'No. I am certain that I can do that to you. And so much more…' He growled, his eyes the colour of charcoal.

'*Promises, promises.*' I inched closer. 'As the saying goes, "actions speak louder than words", so instead of *talking*, you should *show* me your moves and let *me* be the judge of that.' Decades of wanting him and hearing the feeling was mutual had given me some sort of super sexual confidence.

'You do not know how much I would love to do that, but I am serious. I cannot give you a relationship.'

'Who said anything about a relationship?' I jumped in. 'Let's just enjoy each other's *company* tonight.'

'For just one night? You are sure you can handle it?' Carlos raised an eyebrow.

'Absolutely!'

The word flew out of my mouth before I could stop it. The truth was, I absolutely *wasn't* sure. On paper, it was a terrible idea. Before I'd arrived in Marbella, I'd vowed to steer clear of guys completely, especially ladies' men. I'd told myself that my heart needed more time to heal.

But thinking about it, this was different. *I* was in control of the situation. It'd just be a one-off—to get this crush out of my system once and for all.

And because it was just a one-time thing, I wouldn't be

able to get hurt. Carlos and I wouldn't be together, so there would be no expectations after today. Which meant there couldn't be any cheating or heartbreak.

Yeah. I'd been sensible my whole life. A one-night stand wasn't something I'd normally do. But it was time for a change. Time for a new Lily. This trip was about stepping out of my comfort zone and enjoying myself, right? When would I get a chance to do something exciting like this again?

I wanted Carlos. I'd *always* wanted him. No. Right now, I *needed* him. I knew he'd give me the best sex I've ever had. So even if he rocked my world just for tonight, I'd take it. Like Doris said, life is for living.

'You're asking if I'm sure that I can handle having a steamy night of passion with you taking me over the edge over and over again?' My body vibrated with excitement. 'I've never been more sure of anything in my life.'

Carlos closed the final few inches between us, crushing his lips onto mine. His mouth was hot, hungry and impatient. As if he'd stored every desire and urge to kiss me into a pressure cooker and after building and building and building, all of those emotions were finally released.

As he slipped his tongue into my mouth, I moaned, climbing onto his lap and wrapping my legs around him.

Our kisses grew more intense and he released one hand from my waist. Carlos pushed the dishes to one side, clearing a path on the blanket. Then he laid me down and straddled me.

'Is this okay?' he asked.

'Yes,' I said breathlessly.

Carlos didn't need to be told twice.

He pushed his hot, firm body on top of me and I moaned again as I felt his hard-on between my thighs.

'I want you so badly, Quesito. Tell me you feel the same.'

'I do,' I panted.

He planted soft kisses across my cheek and along my neck before pulling down the straps of my dress. My body sparked uncontrollably and I couldn't resist gripping on to his solid arse.

Carlos's mouth skimmed over the fabric of my bra and I bucked into him. I was torn between wanting to continue feeling his lips roam over my skin and wanting him inside me.

His hands travelled behind my back and I raised it slightly to give him easier access. He unclipped my bra in one swift move and as he tossed it onto the blanket, warm air hit my nipples.

'*Madre mía.*' He licked his lips. 'You are spectacular.'

Before I'd even had a chance for the compliment to register, he cupped a breast and took my nipple in his mouth, then started circling it with his hot, wet tongue.

'Fuck!' I screamed. It was a good thing I was lying down. The sensation of his mouth on me was electrifying.

As I heard the waves crash against the sand, it suddenly registered that we were outside: on the beach. Although we hadn't seen a single soul for hours and it would be dark soon, anyone could walk past at any minute. This was so risky. But…

Oh God.

After pushing up the bottom of my dress, Carlos's mouth travelled past my belly button. As he tugged at my knickers, I bucked against him again.

'I want to taste you. Is that okay?'

'Mmm-hmmm.' I nodded. I didn't care if we got caught. The anticipation of what was about to come rendered me speechless and every thought about what was right and wrong evaporated like a puff of smoke.

Carlos slowly peeled off my knickers, spread my legs, then buried his face between them.

'Jesus!' I gasped sharply.

His tongue flicked gently over my throbbing clit and my hips jerked up. *Holy shit.* My body had been hot before, but now I felt like I'd been dropped into a volcano that was seconds away from erupting. I'd never experienced anything so mind-blowing.

'Mmm,' he moaned, licking me like I was his first meal in years. I gripped his hair, pushing him deeper.

Never mind the waves from the sea. I could feel a giant wave of pleasure building inside me already. This was incredible.

'*Yes*,' I whimpered as he continued sucking and licking, with every stroke of his tongue sending me closer to the edge. '*Sí*… right there…'

Carlos picked up the pace, this time circling my clit as he plunged two fingers inside me. As he slid them in and out, back and forth, intense pleasure ripped through me.

Game over.

I rocked my body against him as I climbed higher and higher and higher until…

'Oh my Goddddd!!' I screamed again. 'Carlos! I can't, I can't…'

My body stilled as I came back down to earth.

'Did you enjoy?' He lifted his head, my wetness covering his chin.

'Do you even need to ask?' I panted.

'I like to be sure.' He licked his lips.

'Thank you,' I said.

Our eyes locked and we burst out laughing.

'Sorry! I couldn't help it!' I slapped my palm against my face, realising I'd apologised again.

Although I needed some time to recover from the incredible high, I wanted Carlos to experience the same feelings of ecstasy.

'I can see you're a man of actions, rather than words, so instead of *saying* thank you, maybe it's better if I use my mouth for something else…'

I pushed him off me so that he was lying on his back. Now it was my turn to straddle him.

I tugged at his belt buckle. Whilst I undid it, I glanced around the beach. I'd never done anything like this in a public place before, so wasn't sure what the protocol was. Take his shorts off fully to see him in all of his glory, or be more discreet and leave them on to make it easier to conceal the 'crime' if we got busted?

Screw it. This blanket was big. I could throw it over us if I needed to. Right now I was too excited to hold back. I slid down his shorts, oh-so-slowly, giving Carlos the opportunity to object if he didn't feel comfortable, but when I glanced at him, his eyes were fixated on my every movement.

He lifted his bum, making it easier for me to get them down.

My God.

I paused, taking a moment to appreciate the finery beneath me. Even though he still had his vest and boxer shorts on, I didn't think I'd ever seen a more beautiful human being. Not in real life. Not even in the pages of a magazine. Carlos was a god, and every other man was just a mere mortal.

I looked at the bulge in his boxers and swallowed hard. Holy shit. He was *big*. I wondered if that was even going to fit in my mouth. But I'd dreamt about this moment for decades, so I'd give it a go or die trying.

'It's time to get rid of this.' I rolled his vest up his body and he lifted his arms as I pulled it over his head and tossed it on the blanket.

For the love of all that is holy.

I'd said before that Carlos was a god, but even that word didn't describe what I was seeing in front of me. *His chest.* I swear that he couldn't be human. It was like a team of the world's most skilled masons had taken the finest piece of marble and sculpted the most magnificent torso, then planted it on his body.

I ran my hands down it, starting from his shoulders, moving towards his chest, along his eight-pack (seriously, he couldn't just have a six-pack), then followed the dark trail of hair below his belly button to the top of his boxers. I started peeling them down. I'd barely moved the fabric a few inches before his cock sprung free.

Jesus Christ.

My eyes grew so wide they almost flew from their sockets.

Never mind if he was going to fit in my mouth. If he put *that* inside me, it was so long it might come up and out of my throat. Okay, slight exaggeration, but he had the biggest cock I'd ever seen.

How could one man be blessed with a body that every

woman would want to touch and most guys dreamt of having?

I was one lucky lady.

I continued rolling his boxers down. Carlos was now naked and I was torn between just sitting here and staring in awe or going down on him. I decided that making him feel good was more important. Like Zach had suggested, a blow job was sure to make him happy.

I moved my body down, positioned my head between his legs, opened my mouth, then slid him inside.

After just a few seconds, Carlos squeezed his eyes shut and lifted his hips, pushing himself to the back of my throat. 'Lily,' he moaned. '*Madre mía! Para.* Stop.'

I paused, looked up and took him out of my mouth.

'Did you say stop?'

'*Sí.*'

'Did I do something wrong?' My stomach plummeted. Maybe my teeth had scratched him? I thought I'd covered them with my lips, but I must be out of practice. I knew I wasn't an expert, but I'd hoped that I at least knew how to give a decent BJ.

Carlos had probably had millions of them done by women much more experienced than me and he must've been able to tell from that first suck that, well, my skills *sucked*.

'No.' He sat up quickly and stroked my cheek. 'It is the opposite. I-I do not want to feel like I am taking advantage. If we do something together, it has to give you pleasure. I want to be inside you now, *vale*?'

I nodded. He rolled me onto my back, pushing my dress up beneath my bare breasts again, and started kissing me from my feet up along my calves and inner thighs, then between my legs. As his tongue slid over my clit, I wasn't sure if I'd last long enough for him to enter me.

Carlos lifted his head. His browny green eyes had turned black again.

'Quesito, you taste so good,' he growled.

My body bucked beneath him and I dug my nails into his back.

'I need you, Carlos. *Now.*'

He grabbed his shorts, pulled out his wallet and then a condom. Once Carlos had ripped the packet, he rolled it down his throbbing rod. The condom was bright pink and such a contrast to his deep olive skin. It could be bright yellow for all I cared. All I wanted was him, inside me.

Carlos climbed on top, rubbing his hard cock against my opening. I went to grab it, but he intercepted my hand, pinning it above my head.

'Not yet. I want you to be ready for me.'

'I *am* ready!' I protested. 'Can't you feel how wet I am for you?'

'*Sí.* But I want to take you to the place where you want it so much that if you do not have it, you feel like you will die.'

'But I already do!'

Carlos shook his head, continuing to rub against me, teasing me, slowly. First, he brushed it against my clit, then at my opening, all whilst flicking his tongue against my rock-solid nipple. Whoever said men couldn't multi-task hadn't experienced the magic of his touch.

His tip entered me, then retreated. Carlos did this repeatedly until I felt like I was going to pass out.

'Oh God!' I cried out. 'It's too much! I can't take it. *Please!*' I begged.

Just as I contemplated grabbing my phone to dial 112, the Spanish emergency number, Carlos thrust inside.

Fuck.

I literally felt him in my stomach. But then the initial sharp, stabbing pain transformed into pleasure as I looked up into his eyes and realised what was happening. Carlos, the man of my dreams, the subject of every deep and delicious fantasy I'd ever had, was inside me. He felt approximately a hundred trillion times better than I'd ever imagined. And he was only just getting started.

We quickly found our rhythm, my hips rising in perfect harmony with his. Watching him slide in and out of me was the most delicious thing I'd ever seen. He leant forward, sucking on my breasts.

'Oh God,' I groaned, raking my nails down his back.

This felt like heaven. If I died now, I'd be happy. But experiencing this level of pleasure just made me greedy. I wanted more. I wanted to feel every one of those precious inches he'd been blessed with. I clamped my legs around his waist and pushed him deeper.

'Harder,' I commanded.

Carlos lifted his head and smirked. Without saying a word, he slammed in to me with full force.

A loud cry shot from my lips. I'd bitten off more than I could chew, but I was determined to enjoy every second.

He slammed into me again. And again. And again.

'I'm going to… I… I'm so close,' I said through a ragged breath.

'Not yet,' he growled. 'I want you on top. I want to see all of you. And *then* I will take you over the edge, *vale?*'

'*Vale,*' I panted like I'd just run a marathon.

He gripped my waist tightly and rolled over, still inside

me. I straddled him, then wasted no time rocking on top as he squeezed my bum. As I picked up the pace, his eyes rolled into the back of his head with ecstasy.

'*Sí,* Quesito,' he called out, rubbing his fingers against my clit and sending me out of my mind.

My nails sunk into his solid chest and I tried and failed to steady my erratic breathing. There was no way I could hold on for much longer.

I bounced up and down on him, harder, faster, the sea air causing my nipples to harden even more.

'I-I-I can't…'

The sensations rose from my toes through every millimetre of my body as the wave built and built and built until…

'Oh God!' I let out a loud scream, shuddering, then collapsing on top of him. Carlos continued rocking beneath me for several seconds before finally letting himself go and groaning into my hair.

He wrapped his arms around my back and we lay there, chests heaving.

Once I'd finally caught my breath, I knew I could move, but I didn't want to. I could feel his heart beating under mine and it was the most comforting sound.

Normally to hear this kind of calmness, I'd have to select a playlist, but not tonight. It was right here in real life.

'I do not know how you feel, but for me, that was more than worth waiting all of those years.' Carlos brushed a curl from my cheek.

'Definitely.' I kissed his chest. 'Although I wish we'd done it sooner.'

'If it happened sooner, it would not be the same. It

feels like this because of the people we are now and the experiences we have.'

'True.'

But now that it'd happened, I wanted to make up for lost time.

Like I said earlier, I was feeling greedy.

If I only had Carlos for this evening, I had to make the most of it. I was already counting down the seconds until I could experience these blissful feelings all over again.

CHAPTER TWENTY-EIGHT

I stroked Carlos's chest, wondering how long I could stay here. I'd happily lie on top of him, wrapped up in this blanket, for hours.

'Want to go for a swim?' Carlos stroked my back.

'I don't think I have the energy.'

'Come. It will be nice. It will help us to cool down.'

'Okay. I'll just put on my swimming costume.'

'That is not necessary. There is no one here. I will go like this.' He gestured towards his naked body. I swallowed hard as I thought about how delicious it was and how much I wanted to feel him inside me again. 'This trip is all about moving from your comfort zone, *si*?'

'Er, yeah, but *skinny dipping*?'

'It is fun.'

'But I'm shy!'

'*En serio?*' Carlos frowned. 'Shy to show yourself? But I have already seen you naked. The image of your beautiful body will be burned into my brain for the rest of my life. If it was a song, I would put it on repeat so I could experience the sight of it over and over again. If you decide to take your clothes off or do not, it is already here.' He tapped the side of his head.

English wasn't even his first language, but the words he used to describe me were more beautiful than anything a guy from my home country had ever said. My heart was so full it could burst.

'And we just have sex on the beach—if you can do that, being naked in the sea is not so scary. You have the water to cover you. But *tranquila*, if you do not feel comfortable, it is okay. You can stay here and watch!'

I rolled off his chest, wondering whether I wanted to give it a go. Carlos sat up, removed the condom and put it on top of the dirty plates.

After kissing me quickly on the lips, he ran to the sea. Thankfully the sun hadn't fully set, so I was still able to get a glorious view of his sculpted bum.

He sank beneath the waves for a second, then his head popped back up again. 'So refreshing!' he cried out.

I debated whether or not to join him. Just a couple of weeks ago I'd been shocked to see people on a nudist beach. Was I really ready to throw caution to the wind and join them? Well, it wasn't really the same. There was no one else around. Just Carlos, and like he'd said, I'd just had my arse and boobs out on show whilst we had sex, so being in the water naked was much more PG.

Screw it. Tonight was all about letting loose. I pulled my dress off completely, tossed it onto the blanket and headed towards the sea.

The fresh sea air caressed every inch of my skin and my body came alive again. There was something so free-ing, knowing that I wasn't restricted by clothes. No

MY SPANISH ROMANCE 223

covering up. No worrying about my scars. It was just me at one with nature.

He was right, the cool water was refreshing. After taking a few more steps, I sunk into Carlos's arms. As he pulled me into him, his hardness pressed against my belly.

'You walked too quickly. I wanted to take another picture of you.'

'Picture?' My eyes widened. 'Nobody else needs to see me naked!'

'No!' he laughed. 'Here!' He pointed to the side of his head again.

'You don't need a mental picture. I'm right here.'

'You are…'

His mouth crushed onto mine and his hands wandered over my body. Along the curve of my breasts, down my stomach, then in between my legs.

OMG.

The combination of Carlos's touch and the ripples of the water made the feelings even more intense. This was pleasure on a whole different level.

He slid two fingers inside me whilst stroking my clit. It was a good thing that Carlos was strong, because at this rate he'd have to carry me from the sea after I passed out.

'You like?'

'*Sí*…' My breath hitched.

'Show me how much. Come for me, Quesito.'

Just hearing his sexy, deep accent was probably enough on its own to get me off. But as he picked up the pace, thrusting his fingers harder, deeper and giving stronger, firm strokes, I knew I was past the point of no return.

I threw my head back as the wave gripped me, before collapsing against his chest.

'Wow,' I gasped. 'You really know what you're doing, don't you?'

'I try.' He smirked.

'But what about you? I want to do something for you.'

'You being here, allowing me to touch you, is doing more for me than you can ever know. I do not need anything else.'

My heart melted like ice cream over hot apple pie. As another gentle wave hit our backs, I shivered a little.

'Cold?'

'A bit.'

'Okay, let us go back.'

We walked a few steps forward and then Carlos stopped and put his arm out in front of me.

'Wait,' he whispered. 'There is somebody here.'

'Where?'

'There.' He nodded to the left.

I looked over and saw a woman with a dog.

'Oh shit!' I gasped.

'*Tranquila*.' Carlos stroked my bum beneath the water. 'She does not know that we are naked. The sea covers us. Just relax. When they are gone, we will leave.'

Except when I saw the owner release the dog from its leash, something told me it wouldn't be so simple.

It shot off through the sand and at first, I thought we were in the clear when it ran past our blanket, but then the dog circled back, making a beeline for the plates.

I remembered there wasn't much food left as Carlos and I had literally devoured everything. There were maybe just a few bits of ham and…

'*Madre mía!*' Carlos shouted.

'What?'

'The condom! I think the dog has it.' He dived out of the water.

'Carlos! Your clothes! You're naked!'

I couldn't let him run out of the water alone—especially with his giant beast of a dick swinging around. He'd probably give the poor woman a heart attack.

I squeezed my boobs together and tried to shield them with one hand, then put my other hand between my legs, trying to catch up with him. I was in danger of fucking up my ankle again, but this was an emergency.

As Carlos got closer to the woman, he slowed his pace and called out something to her in Spanish. The dog was running around the beach with the condom hanging out of his mouth. *Please don't let him or her swallow it.*

Now both Carlos and the woman were chasing after the dog, who thought it was a fun game, so ran faster every time they got closer. It went back and forth and in circles, clearly chuffed to be getting so much attention.

As I reached the blanket, I quickly pulled a sarong from my bag, tied it around me, then grabbed a towel for Carlos and did my best to join the chase.

'*Miguel! Ven aquí!*' the woman called out.

I hobbled after it, but Carlos whizzed past me, still clutching his dick with both hands. He was now just a few steps away from little Miguel. He leapt forward and grabbed him. Carlos then started talking to the dog, holding him with one hand whilst trying to coax the condom out of Miguel's mouth with the other.

Eventually the dog dropped it on the sand and Carlos scooped it up.

The woman and I caught up to them at the same time.

'*Lo siento*,' Carlos said as he handed the dog back to its owner. But she didn't reply. Her eyes were fixated on Carlos's body. More specifically, her gaze was firmly focused on his dick.

'Carlos.' I raised my eyebrow, then handed him a towel, my head tilted in *that* direction.

'*Perdón!*' he apologised, launching into more Spanish.

'*No pasa nada!*' The woman licked her lips, still ogling him. I knew she'd just said *no worries* in Spanish. Clearly she enjoyed every moment of the Carlos Dick-Swinging Show.

'I think we'd better go, don't you?' I linked my arm in his and pulled him along the beach.

'*Madre mía!*' Carlos slapped his head. 'I forgot to get a towel when I came out of the water. I hope she does not think that I am a pervert—or, how do you call it when man show themselves to a woman in public?'

'A flasher.'

'*Sí*. I apologised and explained that I was trying to get the plastic from the dog, but…'

'I think she realised that it wasn't just a piece of *plastic*, Carlos!' I giggled. 'She knew *exactly* what we'd been doing.'

'You are right.' He smirked.

'But I wouldn't worry. From the look on her face, I think she was *very* happy that you *didn't* get a towel. That was probably the highlight of her week,' I chuckled. 'In fact, I reckon her only complaint would be that you didn't stay naked for longer!'

As we packed up our stuff, we couldn't stop laughing about what had happened.

'Where did you get those condoms from?' I asked, tossing my bag on the back seat of the car.

'From a club.' He winced. 'They gave them out for free.'

'Do you have another one?'

'What? You want to…? *Now?*'

'No! I mean, I wouldn't say no, but I wanted to see the packet. It didn't look like an ordinary brand.'

He reached into his wallet and pulled out another one.

'Oh my God,' I burst out laughing again.

'*Qué?*'

'These are bloody glow-in-the-dark, flavoured condoms! This one is *feeling fruity* flavour. The scent must be what attracted the dog to it!'

'Oh!' Carlos's face cracked into a smile. 'I did not know!'

'I've heard of flavoured condoms, obviously, but never used a glow-in-the-dark one before. Maybe we should've waited until after sunset to see how it looked!'

'Well, I have two more, so perhaps we can try later.'

'Deal!'

CHAPTER TWENTY-NINE

'*B*uenas!' I stepped onto the bus and greeted the driver. I grinned at all of the passengers, alternating between *hola!* and *buenas!*, which I'd also heard Spaniards use.

I sat down and started whistling 'We Found Love'. I wasn't a good whistler and it was probably a bit weird to do it on a bus, but I didn't care. It reminded me of my amazing evening on the beach yesterday and nothing was going to kill my high. That was the best one-night stand ever. Okay, it was my *only* one-night stand, but I didn't see how anything could top that.

Definitely no regrets. I'd realised this morning that I'd got a mosquito bite on my bum, but not even the fact that it'd leave a scar bothered me. My heart was fine and my body felt fantastic. Yep. Life was good. I'd never been so excited to go to work.

Full disclosure: it was less about going to work and more about the fact that I'd be seeing lovely Carlos.

It was like Prosecco bubbles were popping in my

stomach as I pictured his gorgeous smile, which was like sunshine personified, and of course his amazing body. *God, that body.*

After we'd left the beach, Carlos had come back to my flat and, using the two other condoms, we'd conducted some very in-depth *research*. The results of our study concluded that they did glow in the dark as advertised. It was weird watching what looked like a *Star Wars* lightsaber or giant highlighter pen thrusting in and out of me, but it was fun.

I didn't get to check whether they tasted of strawberry or summer berries because when I tried to go down on him again, just like on the beach, Carlos stopped me and said he'd like to give me pleasure instead. And boy did he do that and then some.

A zing of excitement rippled through me again. It hadn't even been twenty-four hours since we'd got together, but I already knew that what happened between us was a night I'd remember forever.

It wasn't just the sex, which of course was off the charts. I loved the fact that Carlos focused so much on wanting to make sure *I* was satisfied. That had never happened before. My exes had only ever cared about whether they'd come. And when they did, they'd roll over and go to sleep without giving my needs a second thought.

But not Carlos. It was like he was some kind of special sex agent and the sole purpose of his mission was to take me to pleasure world.

He'd stayed the whole night, with his arms wrapped around me. The sensation of his warm skin pressed against mine and feeling his heart beat against my back was heavenly. So much so that I must've held my wee for two hours because I didn't want to leave the bed.

I forced myself to go eventually, though, because if I stayed any longer, I'd wet myself and that would definitely be a passion killer. Where was that bloody bucket when I needed it?

Yeah, so he'd left this morning to go home and get changed before his massage shift and now I was on my way to the hotel for my evening shift.

Once I'd locked away my bag, I headed to the bar. My eyes immediately went to the massage area to see if I could spot him. As if sensing I was there, he looked over and smiled. My stomach exploded with joy. *Every. Single. Time.* I swear Carlos's smile should be available on the NHS. It would make anyone feel better. But right now, I was glad that smile was just for me.

I walked behind the bar wondering how the hell I was going to concentrate on pouring drinks. I'd rather sit and stare at Carlos all night.

'What's up with you?' Zach frowned. 'Did you win the lottery or something?'

I just smiled. My mouth didn't have the power to speak at the same time.

'Oooh! If you did, that would be mint. There's a brand-new laptop I saw online yesterday that I'd love to get, but it's out of my price range. But I'm sure you'd like to buy it for your bar bestie, wouldn't you? As a thank-you for saving your backside when you couldn't even pour a can of Coke in a glass without making a mess.'

Nope. Still couldn't talk. Carlos had just looked over again and my stomach was doing an acrobatic routine worthy of an Olympic gold medal while my grin was so wide you could park a hundred artic lorries in my mouth and still have room for several cruise liners.

'Earth to Lily!' Zach shouted. He followed my gaze. 'Oh! *Ohhhh!* OMG! I forgot! It was yesterday, wasn't it? The big thank-you gesture thingy! How did it go? Did you, you know, *thank him*?!' He gasped. 'You did, didn't you? For God's sake, woman! Spill the tea!' Zach stood in front of me, arms folded.

'What are you doing!' I shouted. 'You're blocking my view!'

'Oh my days! You totally did! You two got busy last night!'

'*Maybe…*' My mouth twitched.

'You *totally* did! It's written all over your face!' Zach jumped up and down on the spot like an excited puppy who'd just been given a new toy to play with *and* a month's supply of doggy treats. 'Tell me *everything*!'

'No! That's tacky!'

'Er, *hello*? Do you not know me? I can totally do tacky! Spill!'

'It was *amazing…*' My mind wandered again, playing a reel of highlights from last night on repeat.

'I want details! Was he hung like a donkey? Did he rock your world? How many times did you do it and where? Come on, honey. My love life is a crapfest right now. Give a guy some hope.'

I desperately wanted to tell someone. Cassie had a big event today, so I didn't want to disturb her when she had a million things on her plate. I'd fill her in tomorrow once it was over.

On the one hand, Zach had been here since the beginning. Well, since Carlos and I were first reunited, and it was his advice that helped steer me in the right direction to organise the stuff yesterday. But on the other, he was my work colleague and technically Carlos and I were breaking the rules by hooking up together, so I didn't want to risk getting found out. It was tricky.

'We're at work and, you know, there's ears everywhere, so all I'll say is, we had a nice evening at the beach, things happened, *multiple times*, and I'm a very lucky and *extremely* happy lady.'

'I knew it!' he shouted. 'I knew he'd be a rock star in the sheets. You lucky cow!'

'Sssh.' I pressed my finger against my lips. 'Remember, it's supposed to be a secret.'

'Course, hon. Don't worry. I'll keep it on the DL.'

'The DL?'

'The down-low.'

'When did you become American?' I laughed. 'Wait! I think he's coming over. Don't act weird, okay?'

'*Moi?*' Zach spun around dramatically. 'Carlos! Hi! So nice to see you! How was last night?' I kicked his foot. 'I mean, how was your Monday night?'

'It was excellent, *gracias*.' He looked at me, smiled, then licked his lips.

Sweet Jesus.

I swear my heart just stopped for several seconds.

'Brilliant…' Zach's voice trailed off as he saw Carlos's eyes locked with mine. 'Lily.' He handed me a serviette and whispered, 'You're dribbling.'

Shit.

I quickly wiped my mouth. The serviette was as dry as a bone. Bloody Zach and his practical jokes.

'Are you busy now?' Carlos asked me.

'I was about to get some ice, but after that, I should be able to take a break, right, Zach?' The bar was always quiet at the beginning of my shift. Most guests probably went to shower and prepare for dinner or an evening of partying.

'Yeah, that's cool.' Zach nodded.

'Great! See you in a bit!' My heart flipped like a fish on steroids. I couldn't wait for my shift to end so we could be together.

I knew I shouldn't wish away my life, but every second felt like it was crawling across my watch at a snail's pace.

But then I remembered.

There would be no being together *later*. We'd agreed. Last night was just a one-time thing. I was just supposed to be having that hook-up to get Carlos out of my system.

Who was I kidding?

As my mind replayed a video of Carlos with his head between my legs and the way he'd fucked me so good multiple times that I saw stars and was transported to another universe, I kicked myself.

What the hell was I thinking? I knew Carlos would give me the time of my life, so I should've also realised there was no way that one night would ever be enough.

Before, I'd just wanted him. But now my body *craved* him. I'd never taken drugs before, but after last night, I imagined that this was how it felt to be addicted.

I *needed* to feel his hands roam across my naked skin.

I *needed* to feel his tongue all over me.

I *needed* him inside me again.

Fuck. I had it bad.

I dragged myself to the stockroom, wondering how to suppress my feelings.

After unlocking the heavy door and turning on the lights, I went to the freezer and pulled out a bag of ice. Just as I was about to leave, the door flew open. My eyes almost popped out of their sockets.

'Carlos, what are you do—'

Before I'd had a chance to finish my sentence, he pulled me around the corner, pushed me against the wall and planted his lips on mine.

My mouth parted instantly and he thrust his tongue inside. The kiss was frenzied and passionate like we hadn't locked lips for years instead of hours. Without even realising it, I dropped the bag on the floor.

Our hands roamed everywhere. Whilst mine went from his head, along his back and stopped at his firm bum, his travelled down my side, skimming the edge of my breasts and then between my legs.

'Quesito,' he moaned. 'I want you. I have been going crazy all day.'

'Me too,' I panted. 'But we're at work. We shouldn't. And we said it was only for one night…'

'I know.'

'Anyone could come in. A-and the ice,' I stuttered as Carlos kissed my neck. I loved when he did that. 'It'll… it will—it's g-going to melt.'

The truth was I didn't give a toss about the ice. Feeling Carlos's lips on mine was like heaven and I didn't want him to stop. But I didn't want to get him into trouble either.

'You are right about everything. This is very dangerous. And the ice. It will melt quickly. So maybe we should use it before it does…'

Carlos bent down and ripped open the bag. My eyes

widened as most of the cubes scattered across the floor. He scooped one out of the plastic, stood up, looked me straight in the eyes, then started trailing the cube from my wrists and up my inner elbow. I'd never thought those areas would stimulate me, but my whole body tingled.

Next he put the ice cube between his teeth. After slowly unbuttoning my shirt, he reached behind my back, unclipped my bra, slid the straps down, whipped it off and placed it on a shelf. My body sparked with anticipation. I couldn't wait to feel what he was going to do next.

He leant forward, then started trailing the ice cube down my chest. I cried out. The cold sensation in such a sensitive area was a shock to the system. Not to mention the fact that he had me up against a wall in the stockroom. I thought the beach sex was the most outrageous thing I'd ever done, but I had a feeling that this was going to be on the same level.

Carlos drew circles around my breasts with the ice, slowly working his way towards my nipples. When he finally reached one, I gasped at the sensation.

'You like?'

'*Sí.*' A breathy moan escaped my lips.

Carlos continued trailing the cube downwards, past my belly button. He paused, kneeled in front of me, then took the cube out of his mouth.

'It is hot in here, no? This will help to cool you down.'

After putting the ice back in his mouth, he pulled my leg forward, then swiped the cube behind my knees. I swallowed hard. That felt so… *wow*. How did he know touching me *there* would do *that*?

He continued swiping it upwards inside my inner thigh as the icy water trickled down my skin. Carlos had said he wanted to cool me down, but my body temperature had just risen by fifty degrees.

Using his hands, he pushed my skirt up around my waist, then teased the cube over my knickers.

I was already wet, but the coolness and the sight of Carlos's head moving up and down between my legs heightened my pleasure.

He pulled my knickers to one side, then gently rubbed the ice directly over my clit.

'Fuck!' I cried out, gripping the wall. The sensation of the ice and his warm breath against me was driving me insane.

He pulled back and popped the ice out of his mouth again.

'Open your legs,' he commanded. 'Wider. I am going to make you come.'

I wasted no time doing what I was told. My body craved him. I needed him to continue.

Once the ice was back between his teeth, he rubbed it over me, starting slowly and then picking up the pace. Every inch of my body sparked and my head became all fuzzy and light.

I gripped Carlos's hair, pushing him deeper into me. I didn't know how much more pleasure I could handle, but I needed to come before I collapsed. As he sped up, I knew I was hurtling towards the edge. He'd lit my inner fuse and the bomb inside me was seconds away from detonating.

The temperature between my legs suddenly went from cold to hot. The ice must've melted completely and now it was just Carlos's mouth on me. As I felt his hot tongue licking, my clit throbbed and my body shook.

After I squeezed my eyes shut, a loud cry escaped my

lips. I quickly bit down on my wrist to stifle the screams of ecstasy as the explosion happened.

Wow. Just. Wow.

When I managed to open my eyes and looked down, Carlos was staring up at me, his eyes bright. He licked his wet lips like he wanted to savour every last drop of me.

My legs were too weak to stand anymore. I slid down the wall and onto the floor. *Ooops.* I'd forgotten about the ice. Now my bum was damp. Didn't matter. Thanks to Carlos's skilled mouth, I was already soaked down there.

'That was good for you?' he asked.

'Good? It was more than *good*. How do you say spectacular in Spanish?'

'*Espectacular.*'

'It was *muy, muy espectacular*!' I leant forward and kissed him.

He smiled, then his face froze. I went to speak and he held his finger up to his mouth.

'I hear steps,' he whispered. 'I will hide.'

As Carlos crept away, I quickly jumped up, pulled my skirt down and buttoned up my shirt just before I heard the door open.

'Hello?' a female voice called out. I'd just done up the last of my buttons before Pandora turned the corner. 'Lily? What are you doing here?'

'I, I—er, I came to get ice.'

'Why is your skirt so wet? And the floor, it's covered in ice! What happened?'

'I…' *Think Lily, think!* 'I, well, I went to get the first bag of ice and I think the bag was damaged and I held it the wrong way and it started to fall out and I slipped and fell. I think I hit my head. I can't be sure.'

'For God's sake,' she tutted. 'How do you feel?'

'Okay, I think.'

'Good. You'll need to fill out an accident report. And find a change of clothes. You're wet everywhere. Even your shirt! You can't work like that.'

'Okay, will do.' I nodded, my heart thundering against my chest. I *think* I'd convinced her, but I wasn't counting my chickens just yet.

'Right.' She turned her back and started walking towards the door. My knickers were still wedged to one side, how Carlos had left them, so I used the opportunity to pull them across so everything was covered down there.

Talking of underwear, oh my God. I'd left my bra on the shelf. I hoped Pandora hadn't seen it when she was talking to me. Shit.

'Get this cleaned up, and in future, check the ice bags before you start to carry them.'

'I'll do that right now.' I stood still, waiting for her to leave. 'Thanks.'

'What are you doing?' She frowned.

'I'm staying to clean up.'

'How will you do that without a mop?'

I opened my mouth, then closed it again. She was right. But if we left, she'd double-lock the door and I wasn't sure if Carlos would be able to leave. And my bra would be on the shelf. Someone would see it—then it could get reported to HR, who'd probably call a meeting reminding us that we weren't supposed to get involved with colleagues, and then all the managers would be on high alert, looking for the culprits.

I'll admit, we'd been completely irresponsible. But the way Carlos had just made me feel really *was* spectacular.

When his head was between my legs, he could've asked me to rob the Bank of England and I would've agreed. Whenever he touched me, logic flew out the window.

But if I was going to be bad and lose my self-control, I had to accept that there'd be consequences.

'Of course!' I slapped my forehead. 'You're right. I wasn't thinking. I must still be in shock from the fall. I'll get a mop, then bring it straight back to clean up.' I raised my voice, hoping Carlos would hear me.

As I stepped out, Pandora flicked off all of the lights, pulled the heavy door shut and locked up.

Now Carlos was stuck inside. I just hoped I could get back to let him out before someone else came to the stock-room and found him.

CHAPTER THIRTY

I t'd been two hours since I'd left the stockroom. Pandora gave me a lecture on health and safety and the importance of being dressed appropriately for work.

When I'd explained again that my skirt had got wet in the stockroom and I hadn't arrived at work like that (which was true), her eyes dropped to my chest. In my haste to do up my shirt, I'd buttoned it up the wrong way.

I glanced down and winced. It looked like it had been done up by a three-year-old and I couldn't exactly explain that it was because minutes before she'd come in, Carlos had been running an ice cube over my nipples. I'd be sacked on the spot.

And she'd recommended that I wear a bra so I didn't 'distract' any male guests. I wanted to point out that they shouldn't be looking at my chest in the first place, but again, I had to avoid drawing attention to myself.

Anyway, after I'd changed, she'd pulled me in to help out with drinks in the restaurant. I tried everything to get away. When I told her I needed to mop up the mess, she said she'd send a cleaner to do it. I tried saying that Zach would be expecting me, but she said the beach bar was quiet and they needed me here.

The thing was, though, Carlos was due to start his DJ set any minute now and he was still stuck in the stockroom. We might've got away with our sexual shenanigans, but if he wasn't ready to start playing in the next three minutes, he'd be in big trouble.

I told the restaurant manager I had to go to the toilet, then crept to the stockroom.

'Carlos?' I whispered. No answer. I moved to the drinks aisle. Nothing. After checking three more aisles, I scratched my head. Where could he be? I didn't have my phone, because when I'd finished changing, Pandora had seen me holding it and reminded me that they were supposed to be kept in our lockers. So I couldn't call him.

After searching every nook and cranny, I admitted defeat and locked up. My heart raced, worrying about the possibilities. I wondered whether the cleaner had found Carlos and reported him to another manager, who was interrogating him about why a DJ was in the drinks stockroom…

Shit.

Once I returned to the restaurant, Pandora sent me back to the beach bar.

'Where the hell have you been!' Zach shouted. 'I've been rushed off my feet here.'

'I'm so sorry! Have you seen Carlos?'

'Yeah, he's there!'

I looked over at the box just as Carlos walked towards it.

Thank God. Relief washed over me. *That was close.*

~

We were so busy tonight that I hadn't even got a chance to speak to Carlos. And as much as I wanted to, it was better that we didn't. I still had no idea how he'd got out of that room, who'd seen him or what had been said, so it was best to keep my distance.

Once we'd cleared up the bar, I got my bag and phone, then texted Carlos to check he was still okay to meet me in the car park.

He didn't reply, but I could see why. He was swarmed with women. *As usual*. A flash of jealousy gripped me as I looked at how beautiful they were. Legs up to the sky, big perky boobs, flawless skin—everything that was desirable to a man and everything I didn't have.

But as Carlos nodded and smiled at them, I noticed something I hadn't before.

Yes, he was smiling, but it was different. When Carlos smiled at me, his whole face lit up like a firework display. It was so wide it reached the corner of his eyes and he had those little crinkles around them. It was etched in my brain so clearly that if I had pen and paper, I could sketch it now.

But the smile he gave these women wasn't the same. Although it was nice, his face was only lit up about ten per cent. It was the equivalent of just having one street lamp to light up the whole of London's Oxford Street. He was being polite. Doing his job. That was all.

It was clear. He liked me and I liked him. So why limit things to just one night (and our epic stockroom session) when the attraction was this strong?

Carlos broke away from the crowd. He reached for his

phone, and seconds later my mobile pinged with confirmation that he wanted to meet in the car park as usual.

I hung back for a few minutes, then followed him. Before I got in the car, I looked around to check the coast was clear.

'Hey.'

'Hey.' My cheeks warmed. I wanted to kiss him but held back, just in case. After I put my seat belt on, Carlos reversed out of the space, then drove towards the exit. 'What happened earlier?'

'The cleaner came about an hour after you had left. I tried to call to let you know and to tell you I have your bra, but there was no answer.'

'Yeah, Pandora made me put my phone in my locker. I was wondering about my bra, so that's a relief. How did you get out?'

'I acted like I belonged there. Said I did not find what I was looking for and that I would put in another order. She just smiled and I left.'

She was probably too busy drooling to pay any attention.

'Thank God for that. I was worried you were going to miss your set.'

'I was sure I would be fine. And anyway, it was worth it.' He stroked my leg.

'So… does that mean that our one-night thing is out the window?' I held my breath, hoping he'd say yes.

'Well…' He turned to face me and my stomach flipped. 'It is difficult. I still cannot give you a relationship, and I know that we should stop this and just be friends, but I am finding it very hard to resist the need to have you again.'

'Then don't.' I repeated what I'd said on the beach.

If he didn't want a relationship, we could just have a fun holiday fling. It could never be a long-term thing anyway, seeing as we lived in different countries.

There was no point depriving myself. I'd prefer to enjoy the rest of my time here with Carlos, instead of yearning for him and feeling sexually frustrated day after day. I was stronger now. I'd be fine.

'*Vale*. If you are sure.'

'I am…' My body sparked with anticipation.

Carlos stopped at the traffic lights and our eyes locked. After checking that there were no cars either side of us, he ran his hand up my thigh, before moving it between my legs. As he slipped his fingers beneath my knickers and they made contact with my clit, I groaned. I was already wet for him.

'Oh God.' I opened my legs wider, savouring his gentle strokes. 'I can't wait for you to continue this when we get back to my flat.'

'Me too.' The light turned green and he slid his fingers out of my underwear, licked them slowly, then put his hand back on the steering wheel. 'I like to give you pleasure, Quesito. It is now my favourite thing to do.'

I was glad to hear it, because I hoped Carlos planned to spend the two weeks we had left together doing exactly that.

CHAPTER THIRTY-ONE

The past few days had been a whirlwind. Like a dream, fresh out of a sizzling romance novel.

Carlos and I had spent every moment we could together. After work, he'd come back to my flat and we'd crash through the door and onto the bed. We couldn't get enough of each other. He'd then hold me all night, go to his massage shift, and then I'd see him again in the evenings when I went to work.

We hadn't had any more stockroom sessions. It was too risky. And in a way, it only built up the anticipation for later. Watching him all night and knowing he'd be coming home with me later was such a turn-on.

In between our sex sessions, Carlos had been helping me with my dancing. My ankle was much better, so I'd had more lessons with him this week and I felt like I was really improving. I could move in time to the beat and if he danced with me, I didn't end up stepping on his feet like I did that first time.

I'd even started watching YouTube videos so I could practise on my own. And I was really starting to enjoy it.

That wasn't the only thing I was getting into. Carlos's taste in music had grown on me. Don't get me wrong, I was still a cheesy pop lover, but when he showered in the mornings, he'd played some songs that I really liked.

I'd been Shazaming like crazy, searching for the names of the tracks and adding them to *our* playlist. I liked that I was broadening my taste.

Talking of dance, that was where we were going this morning. It was Saturday and Carlos was giving another dance lesson to the kids, so I'd asked if I could come too. Carlos had beamed like a child on Christmas Day.

'That would make me very happy,' he'd said.

The key went in the door and Carlos stepped into my flat clutching multiple bags.

I jumped out of bed and rushed over to greet him. He put the bags on the floor, wrapped his arms around my waist and pulled me in for a long, slow kiss.

'I missed you,' I said once we'd come up for air.

'I have only been gone for one hour.' He smiled.

'I know. But it felt like five.' I probably would've never said something like that to any of my exes for fear of sounding too clingy, but with Carlos it was different. Even though I knew what we had was temporary, I felt like I could say anything.

'I missed you too. That is why I came up with an idea to persuade you to let me spend a few more hours together after the dance class.'

'No persuasion necessary, but what did you have in mind?'

'You have been in Spain for four weeks now, *sí*? But I have not made you my paella. I must fix this immediately.'

'Oooh! That sounds amazing!'

'*Muy bien*. Now let us have breakfast.'

After we'd eaten and showered together, we headed to the lesson.

I loved watching Carlos teach the children. He was so patient and sweet with them. They were doing a run-through for a performance that was coming up soon. There was one little girl in the back row, I think her name was Renata, who was having trouble following the steps. She looked like she was seconds away from tears.

Carlos stopped the music and I think must've told the children to take a break as some headed off to the toilets. He went to Renata and bent down to talk at her level. I didn't know what he was saying, but she nodded. After a minute or two her shoulders lifted and her face broke into a smile.

He held her hands as they did the steps together. After a few tries, she got it and jumped up and down with excitement and I swear I felt my ovaries explode. Carlos would make such a great father. If I could choose anyone to have babies with, it would definitely be him.

Er, hello?! my mind screamed. *Remember this is a fling. Don't start catching feelings. In just over a week you'll be going back to London! And if he doesn't do relationships, the last thing he'd want is to settle down and have kids!*

My stomach twisted. I knew that was what I'd signed up for, but I loved living in this beautiful, happy bubble and I didn't want anything to take me away from that.

I'd spent so much of my life planning and worrying, so

I reminded myself that for once, I was going to just have fun and live in the moment.

There was no point thinking about the future now. I'd worry about what would happen in nine days' time.

When the children returned, Renata rejoined the group. She still missed some steps but was more confident than before. Carlos's pep talk had clearly helped. He was so good at everything he did. Being a DJ, massages, teaching dance, giving me pleasure... his face should be listed in the dictionary under the definition of multitalented.

The lesson finished, and once the parents collected their kids, Carlos came and kissed me softly on the lips.

'Ready for your lesson now?'

'Yep!' I said enthusiastically.

'*Muy bien*.' He pressed play on his laptop.

The chords sounded familiar. I was sure I knew this song. It was a pop track, but it sounded different. It had a dance vibe.

'What's this? Have you played it before?'

'No.' He looked over at me. 'It is a remix I am working on.'

'You remix songs?' My eyes widened.

'*Sí*.' He nodded. 'I have not had much time lately, but I love doing this. I wish I could do it more.'

'It sounds amazing! Much better than the original.'

'*Gracias*. I still have some work to do, but maybe I will play it at the hotel. See what the crowd thinks.'

'You really should!' I bobbed my head and swung my hips a little.

'You feel the beat, *sí*?' Carlos started dancing behind me and rested his hands on my hips. 'Today, just close your eyes and dance with me. That is all. Just do what you feel. Listen to the beat and move, *vale*?'

'*Vale*.'

I did exactly what he said. Feeling Carlos's heartbeat and his hard body behind me definitely helped. I danced all the way through without missing a step. And did the same for the next few songs.

'You are doing so well,' Carlos whispered into my ear, his warm breath tickling my skin. My heart swelled. I span around and wrapped my arms around his neck.

'I know you hate me saying it, but *thank you*. Seriously, *gracias* a hundred times. Without you, I wouldn't be able to dance.'

'No.' Carlos shook his head, brushing a curl from my cheek. '*You* did this. All you needed was somebody to show you, but you did the hard work.'

I knew that even if I spent the rest of the day trying to dispute that fact and tell him what a difference he'd made, he'd never accept the compliment, so I just hugged him again.

'Maybe one day, I'll feel confident enough to dance in a club or in public again without feeling like a plonker.'

'Plonker? I do not know this word.'

'Sorry, I mean without feeling like a fool.'

'You are no fool, Quesito. You are the smartest woman I know.'

'Hardly!' Now it was my turn to scoff.

'It is true. You have a great job, you own your own home, you are clever and responsible and successful.'

'So are you! What you did with the children today was incredible. And you're the best DJ and masseur ever!' I added. It was what I was thinking earlier, and I meant every word.

'Anyway, that is good for today.' He pulled away and turned off the music. 'I am getting hungry. We should go so I can make the paella.'

I knew I was bad at taking compliments, but Carlos took it to the next level. Normally he seemed like such a confident guy, but somehow, in the last sixty seconds, it felt like his mood had shifted.

He had something on his mind, and I hoped that maybe when he was making paella, he'd open up and tell me what.

CHAPTER THIRTY-TWO

During the journey back, Carlos was quiet. He occasionally moved his head to the music, but he definitely wasn't his usual happy self.

'Are you tired?' I turned to face him.

'A little.'

'I honestly don't know how you do all of this. Massage shifts in the day, DJing all night, then teaching dance, plus rolling around in bed with me…' I tried to lighten the mood. 'Don't you ever want to take a break?'

'I cannot,' he said sharply. 'I need to work. The summer is the most important time of the year for me. I cannot afford to take breaks.'

'Oh, okay,' I said softly. I was sure he knew what he was doing. I was just worried about him.

We pulled up outside my flat. Once we were inside, Carlos headed straight for the kitchen.

'Want some help?' I came up beside him. His eyes widened.

'You do not want to relax?'

'No. I'd love to watch you and learn.'

Carlos's smile returned as he started taking out the ingredients. I was glad that he seemed a bit happier.

There was a special pack of rice, green beans, some herbs and two packs of meat that looked like chicken. Carlos started chopping some garlic.

'Why do you have two packs of chicken?'

'One is chicken.' He pointed to the pack of meat. 'The other is rabbit.'

'Rabbit?' I gasped with horror. 'We're going to eat a cute little bunny?'

'You eat chickens and lambs, no? Are they not also *cute*? It is very traditional to include rabbit in paella.'

'I'm going to pretend it's chicken. Where's the chorizo?'

'*Qué?*' Carlos stopped chopping and glared at me. 'Did you just say *chorizo*?'

'Yeah…' I hesitated. He stared at me like I was a chicken with four heads.

'*Madre mía!*' He shook his head. 'You *never* put chorizo in paella!'

'Course you do. I saw it on a cookery show.'

'A *Spanish* cooking show?'

'Er, no. I don't think so.'

'*Exacto.*' His shoulders relaxed. 'Chorizo has no place in traditional paella. You can put whatever you want with rice, of course, but you *cannot* call it *paella*. One day we will go to Valencia to taste a real paella.'

One day. I liked the sound of that.

Carlos continued chopping, then he paused again.

'What are you doing tomorrow?'

'Nothing. I'm off tomorrow and Monday. Shall we go somewhere?'

'*Sí*. We should go to Madrid. I will show you around my city.'

I let out a squeal of excitement. I'd always wanted to go. And I wasn't going to lie. I'd been hoping for ages that he'd invite me.

'I'd love to!'

Carlos nodded. 'We will leave early in the morning and we should be there by lunch.'

I heard my phone ping from my bag. I went to the living room to check who it was. Nate. Shit.

He'd messaged last night whilst I was at work. God knows what time it must have been in Canada. I meant to reply this morning, but I'd got kind of distracted with Carlos.

If I messaged now, he might call, and knowing his best friend was here, I'd get all jittery. I'd respond later. It was safer that way.

'Will we get to see your mum?'

Maybe it was forward for me to ask, seeing as we weren't serious.

'No,' he said flatly. *Okay, then…*

'And your dad?' I asked. I thought I remembered Nate saying his parents were divorced. Carlos's face fell.

'My father, he… died four years ago.'

'Oh God, I'm so sorry. I didn't know.'

Carlos waved his hand away like it was nothing, but of course, that couldn't be true. I wanted to ask what had happened, but I sensed he didn't want to talk about it.

'It is getting late. We should continue with lunch.' He avoided my gaze.

'Course, sure. Just let me know what you need me to do to help.'

'Perhaps it is better if you relax. I will cook faster on my own.'

'Oh.' My stomach sank. 'Okay.'

'We can cook together another time, *vale*?' He rubbed my shoulder to reassure me. Me mentioning his dad must've upset him, and I kicked myself for bringing it up. I wasn't to know, because Nate hadn't told me, but I still felt bad about making him sad.

'*Vale*.' I returned to the living room.

Not knowing about Carlos's dad reminded me that there was so much I still didn't know about him. His family was just one element of his life that he kept under wraps.

Even though Carlos had said from the start that he couldn't give me a relationship, and even though I knew I shouldn't, I wanted to get to know him better and was praying that he'd change his mind.

But if he didn't feel close enough to tell me more about his personal life, then it wasn't realistic to hope that we could ever have a real future together.

CHAPTER THIRTY-THREE

Kylie Minogue's 'Can't Get You Out of My Head' blared from Carlos's car speakers and I placed my hands on the side of my head, mimicking the move Kylie did in the video whilst singing at full blast.

The song lyrics were accurate. Carlos had well and truly wormed his way into my head and I definitely thought about his *lovin'* a lot.

Despite his quietness on the way back from the dance lesson yesterday and when I put my foot in it asking about his dad, we ended up having a good day together.

He'd cooked the most amazing paella I'd ever tasted. Okay, I hadn't tasted many, but even if I had, I was sure it would rank as one of the best.

We'd had a little siesta on the sofa before work, then I'd spent most of my shift gazing at him from the bar, counting down the hours until we could be together again. Yep. I had it bad. That was why I was so excited that we'd get to spend the next forty-eight hours together. No work, no interruptions. Just the two of us.

I turned to face Carlos and swore I saw his mouth moving along to the words.

'Hold on. Were you just singing along to Kylie?' I raised my eyebrow.

'No!' he smirked. 'Maybe…'

'Oh my God. You like Kylie! I *knew* it!'

'It is catchy!' he protested. 'And the lyrics are very simple.'

'You don't have to justify yourself to me.' I rested my hand on his shoulder. 'It's okay to like pop. I won't tell anyone.'

'Promise?' he said with mock concern.

'Your secret's safe with me.'

'Well, now that I know this, I can sing it properly!'

Carlos started singing the *la-la-la* part of the song at the top of his voice, doing cheesy dance moves and shimmying around in his seat. I couldn't stop laughing. His deep voice wasn't remotely in tune and he knew it, but didn't care. He saw his enthusiasm for my favourite music was making me happy and that seemed to be all that mattered.

After he'd finished his performance, he took a bow and I clapped enthusiastically.

'That was excellent!' I shouted over the dance track that was now playing. 'How do I say *more* or *encore*?'

'You can say *más* or *otra vez*.'

'*Más!*'

'That was an exclusive performance for one morning only.'

'*Spoilsport!* How far away are we now?'

'Just a couple of hours.'

'*Toro!*' I shouted the Spanish for *bull*.

'*Sí!*' He nodded.

As well as singing throughout the journey, we'd also been playing spot the bull. Not real bulls, obviously. Along the motorway to Madrid, every so often, there would be a huge black bull silhouette (with massive balls or *cojones* to match). So every time we saw one, we'd call out *toro!*

'I don't know how you're not tired. You can't have slept for more than five or six hours.'

'I am fine. I will sleep tonight.'

'Where are we staying?' I'd been so excited that I'd be spending time with Carlos that I hadn't even thought about our accommodation plans.

'At the house of my aunt. She is on holiday in the mountains, escaping the heat.'

Carlos had warned me about the heat in Madrid and said that many people tried to get out of the city during the summer because it was often over forty degrees. I still couldn't wait to see it, though.

'Is that the same aunt that works in a beauty salon?'

'*Sí.* My aunt is very special to me. After my mother left, she used to visit and help a lot.'

'Oh.' I paused. 'I didn't know about your mum. Sorry.' Carlos winced.

'That word: *sorry*. She—my "mother"—said that a lot when she left us. I was only twelve years old. My sister was just nine.' He shook his head. 'What kind of mother chooses to leave her children because she wants to run away with another man? That woman said anything to make herself look good. She thinks that she can just say *sorry* and everyone will forget the bad things that she did. And that she did not give a fuck about us.' He clenched his jaw.

I rubbed his shoulder. That must be why he didn't like me saying sorry so often. It reminded him of his mother. I hadn't realised.

'Do you still speak to her?'

'No. My aunt is more like a mother to me than that woman will ever be. Anyway…' He paused. I gathered he didn't want to speak about her anymore. 'I want to talk to you about our conversation before.'

'Which conversation?'

'Your skin.'

I held my breath, wondering what he was going to say about it. I'd been trying to wear less make-up to give it a chance to breathe, especially as it was so hot. But now I was thinking I should've covered it up more.

'Um, yeah?' I lifted my hand to cover my cheek.

'I know how much it worries you, so I spoke to my aunt. I did not say your name. She said it is better to analyse your skin face to face, but if I send some photos, she can give suggestions. She said that she can normally tell what causes the breakouts by seeing where they are. So if they are on the cheek, sometimes it can be because of too much dairy, meat or sugar, or from using a mobile phone. On the chin it can be hormones. On the forehead it may be hair products or alcohol. She is the expert, though, so it is best to see what she says when she sees the pictures.'

'Photos?' My eyes widened. Although Carlos had seen my bare skin many times now and never flinched, I didn't like the idea of taking pictures.

'The photos can just be of your forehead and another just showing your face but no eyes. That way no one can know it is you. Then I can send it to my aunt and ask for her advice?'

'Okay.' I'd already been to dozens of salons and I supposed it was no different than any other beauty therapist seeing my face. It was worth a try. 'Thanks.' I rested my hand on his. 'I appreciate you asking.'

'*No pasa nada.*'

'So your aunt—did she teach you how to do massage?'

'*Sí*. She lived in America a lot, but when she returned to Spain and opened a salon, sometimes I worked there. I also did some courses when I came to London to study. That is why I do it at the hotel. When the lady left suddenly, they needed someone, and when I told them about my experience and showed the manager what I can do, they gave me the job.'

I wasn't surprised. Carlos had magic hands.

'And your love for music? Where did that come from?'

Carlos paused, processing his response.

'It—it was my father…' His voice cracked. I was about to say that he didn't need to speak about him if it was too painful when he continued. 'We were very close. He used to play the guitar, the drums and the keyboard. He was in a rock band when he was younger. They had some successful songs in the charts. That is how he met my mother. At one of their concerts.'

'Your dad was a rock star? Oh my God, that's amazing!'

'Well, mainly before I was born, but even when he had to get a normal job, he still played at home and liked to write songs. After my mum left, he suffered for many years. He wanted to start performing again, in small bars and clubs, but then…'

Carlos's body tensed and his eyes watered. He didn't need to finish his sentence. I could fill in the blanks for myself.

I rested my hand on his shoulder, stroking it gently.

'I'm so sorry,' I said softly. He swallowed the lump in his throat. 'If ever you want to talk about it, I'm here, okay?' I leant forward and pecked him gently on the cheek. Carlos exhaled and he nodded again.

I sensed that he wasn't ready to elaborate, so I changed the subject.

'Looks like there's a service station in a few kilometres.' I glanced at the blue sign. I might not understand the words, but the petrol icon was explanation enough. 'Do you want to stop, stretch your legs and maybe get a bottle of water? You've been driving for hours.'

'*Sí.*' He nodded. 'That sounds good.'

CHAPTER THIRTY-FOUR

I t was early afternoon and we were at the Plaza Mayor in Madrid city centre. I'd seen this beautiful square loads of times when I'd researched places to visit in Spain, and now I was here.

I blinked several times, taking in the red-hued three-storey building, the multiple arches at the bottom and the swarm of tourists taking photos or sitting outside the many cafés, enjoying an ice-cold drink.

Carlos wasn't joking when he said Madrid would be hot. I blotted my forehead with a tissue, then took a gulp of water. *That's better.*

After stealing a quick look at Carlos, my heart flipped as the realisation hit me again that we were here. *Together.*

I know that he couldn't offer me anything serious, but I still had a week here. Maybe he'd change his mind?

'*Qué?*' Carlos asked. I looked at him again.

'What?' I said innocently.

'I saw you look at me. Do I have something on my face?' He rubbed the back of his hand over his cheek.

'No. I'm just happy, that's all.'

Carlos's face broke out into his full smile, the one I loved so much, where his eyes lit up and crinkled in the corners. The one that made his whole face come alive.

'I am glad. I am very happy too and it is all because of you, Quesito.'

He leant down and kissed me softly on the lips and my heart fluttered again.

I didn't remember ever hearing a guy saying I made them happy before unless I'd bought them a gift or done something in the bedroom to please him. So for him to say those words for no particular reason meant a lot to me.

'So do you like the Plaza Mayor?'

'Yeah, it's really pretty.'

'*Sí*. There are lots of places to see in Madrid. We will not be able to see everything this time, but I will show you as many places as possible. *Vale?*'

'*Vale.*'

Carlos took my hand and led me to another square called Puerta del Sol, where there was a bear and tree statue that was apparently very famous.

'Do you see the clock?' He pointed to the top of a building in the square. I nodded.

'This is where they count down for New Year's Eve. Every time the clock chimes, you must eat a grape to bring you good luck.'

'What? Twelve grapes in twelve seconds? That's impossible, right?'

'It is not easy, no. But you will have to try. Come. I want to show you the Royal Palace.'

As Carlos wrapped his arm around my waist, for a second I wished we'd be able to try popping twelve grapes, together. But I quickly shook my crazy thoughts out of my head. That was months away, and as I reminded myself for the millionth time, he didn't want a relationship.

The best thing I could do was just live in the moment and enjoy my time with Carlos. For however long it lasted.

Carlos really packed in the sightseeing. As well as the Royal Palace, we'd visited multiple famous squares, including the Plaza de Oriente, where the Royal Theatre was based, and Plaza de Cibeles, which had beautiful marble sculptures and a fountain. Then we went down the busy Gran Vía, which from what I could see was like Madrid's version of Oxford Street.

There were more restaurants, some theatres showing well-known musicals and high-street shops including the biggest Primark I'd ever seen.

After taking my hand, Carlos led me up some back-streets to find a place that he liked.

The sounds of loud chatter and laughter filled the air. Despite being a Sunday evening, it was buzzing with people strolling leisurely through the streets or sitting outside bars and restaurants enjoying a refreshing round of drinks. It was a lot cooler now, so it was a good time to be out.

As I walked down the streets, I turned my neck from left to right and from right to left, taking in everything around me.

'That chicken shop looks pretty.' I pointed to a shop on the corner with a pink sign that instantly caught my attention. There was a long queue, so the food must be good. 'Maybe we can take a look?'

I was still full from the late lunch we'd had when Carlos had taken us to the place that created the original sauce for *patatas bravas* and we'd eaten a huge plate of them, plus Spanish omelette and *bocadillo de calamares*— a sandwich with fried squid rings.

Carlos burst out laughing.

'Quesito: you will not find any chicken in that shop!'

'Why?' I frowned. 'I know my Spanish is crap, but I'm pretty sure *pollería* means chicken shop, right? So why would they call it that if it doesn't sell chicken?'

'You are right: normally *pollería does* mean chicken shop, but that is not what they sell there. Come,' he laughed again. 'Perhaps I should not use that word. Let me show you and you will see why.' He smirked.

As we approached the store, a couple were leaving, clutching large… WTF?

They were running their tongues up and down a dick on a stick. My jaw dropped. Especially when I saw the posters outside of the shop, which showed *exactly* what they sold here, and Carlos was right. It definitely was *not* chicken.

'What are they eating?'

'Waffles.'

'No way!'

'Yes, way.'

When we eventually got inside, I realised he was right. The smell of sweet batter flooded my nostrils and behind the counter was a menu for cock-shaped waffles (complete with very authentic-looking veins), which you could choose to have dipped in your choice of chocolate.

'Oh my God!' I giggled. 'No wonder you questioned your use of the word *come* when you took me inside!'

I could hear the guy serving behind the counter speaking English and asking the customers in front whether they wanted a dick waffle or ice lolly.

'You want one?' Carlos asked. I was kind of curious to know how it tasted, but wondered whether I was brave enough to walk down the street licking and biting a 'penis' in public.

'Go on, then!' I said enthusiastically. 'I can never say no to dessert.'

Carlos fumbled in his wallet to get the cash.

'I can pay!' I said.

'No. I am sure I had five euros in change.'

All day I'd offered to pay for things, but he'd refused. Carlos eventually pulled out a ten-euro note and handed it over.

'Oooh, cash!' the server said. 'I see this is not the first time you have paid for sex,' he teased. Carlos blushed.

'How do you like it?' The server turned to me.

'White chocolate, please,' I chuckled. I usually ate milk chocolate, so thought it would be good to try something different. Even though I was supposed to be cutting back on dairy, I could allow myself one treat.

'And you want a happy ending?'

'Who doesn't?' I said coyly. 'I'll have the strawberry sauce, please.'

I smirked as the server stuck a stick into the base of the dick-shaped waffle, dipped it into the white chocolate sauce, then drizzled the strawberry chocolate down the centre of its head so it looked like cum.

As I carried it out of the shop in its little pink tray, I couldn't stop laughing.

'That was hilarious!' I picked up the stick. 'Before I get stuck in, you have to take a picture so I can send it to Cassie!' I handed Carlos my mobile and he snapped away, all smiles. 'So, what do you think is the best way to eat it? Lick it from the base first or concentrate on the head?'

I ran my finger around the chocolate dripping towards the bottom, then sucked it off slowly in a way that I hoped looked seductive.

'Maybe a little bit of both is good.' Carlos smirked.

'Like this?' I trailed my tongue slowly upwards to the tip. 'Is that how *you'd* like it?'

'Are we still talking about the waffle, Quesito?' Carlos raised his eyebrow.

'Yeah…' I swallowed hard. As embarrassing as it was, I had to admit that now could actually be a good time to ask him something I'd wanted to know since we'd got together. After all, what better time to ask a guy how he liked his BJs than when you had a phallic-shaped waffle in your mouth?

Part of me said it would be better to pose that question when my head was actually between his legs, but I'd been worried about killing the mood. At least this way, I could keep it more light-hearted.

'Actually, *no*. I've been wanting to ask…' God, this was awkward. 'Never mind.'

'Lily.' Carlos stood in front of me and rested his hand on my shoulder. The warmth from his palm sent shock-waves through me. 'Tell me. What do you want to know?'

'It's just that every time I try to go down on you, you stop me.' I didn't get it. I mean, like Zach said, guys love

BJs, right? So it must be my technique. 'I know you always say you want to focus on me, but is it because you don't like blowies, or did I do something wrong when I started doing it that first time on the beach, or—'

'No!' Carlos jumped in. 'You did nothing wrong. It is not about you. Well, it is. But not how you think. *Sí*, I like to have BJ, but, I—' He sucked in a breath. 'When my father passed, I found it difficult. I went a little crazy. No. A *lot*. I drink a lot. I party a lot. I...' Carlos paused again. 'When you are a DJ, there are a lot of women. A lot of women who are happy to do things to you... and during this time, I let them. I am not proud of this.' He hung his head. 'And so, when you try to... I didn't want you to do *that*.'

Oh.

'When you say *a lot* of women...' I paused, not sure if I wanted to know how many. I didn't. 'So what, they would just ask if they could...'

'*Sí*. They offered and I took it. After I broke up with my ex, I tried to avoid getting involved with women I met when I was working.'

'Why?' I wanted to hear more about his ex, so made a mental note to ask about that later.

We turned right and started walking down another street.

'Some of them think a DJ is a trophy. Someone they can fuck on holiday for fun and brag to their friends before they go back home to their normal lives and find someone good enough to really be with. I know DJs who think women are a benefit of the job. But I never did it for that. I do it for the music. Every time I do a set, I cannot believe people pay me to play my favourite songs. Music for me is like therapy. It helped me through many difficult times.'

'Like with your parents?'

'*Sí*. When I was a child and they argued, I would stay in my room, put on headphones and listen to music. If I am sad, I listen to music or I dance and it is like medicine. It makes me feel better. Music brings joy. That is why I became a DJ. To make other people feel that happiness.'

'I get that. Music makes me happy too.'

'I always thought that when I returned from London a few years after I graduated, I would continue with physio-therapy and massage work. But one weekend, the DJ who was supposed to be playing at my friend's party could not make it. I used to play music and DJ for fun with my dad, so I said I would help. It went well and someone else asked me to play, then I got asked to play at a small club and slowly it grew bigger and bigger.'

'That must've been exciting.'

'*Sí*. So back to your question. I always focused on doing a good job. Playing good music. And when I became single, I was careful not to get distracted too much by the women. But when my father died, everything changed. The music did not help like it used to. It reminded me of him. Of what I had lost. I started not to care anymore. I did not care if women wanted me as a trophy, if they wanted to "have fun with the DJ with the big muscles" or if they wanted more. I did not want to talk or have a relationship. I just wanted to release. To not feel my emotions. To feel better for a few seconds. A BJ was a quick solution. It gave me a high. Sometimes we fucked. It meant nothing. It was just like the alcohol: something I used to try and forget the pain. But then I started to lose control and it affected my work…' He rubbed the back of his neck. 'It became a bit of… a-an addiction.'

'Oh…'

I didn't know what to say. I'd always thought Carlos had a lot of women, which was why getting involved with him wasn't the smartest thing to do. But I hadn't realised it had developed into something that caused him to spiral. I sensed that was in the past, though. I didn't believe he was the same person now.

'That is why now I am careful not to sleep around or get into relationships. Relationships are messy and always lead to problems. They are a distraction. If I stay by myself, nobody can get hurt. I cannot use people and they cannot use me.'

I swallowed the lump in my throat. Carlos had clearly experienced a lot of pain, so I could understand why he felt that way. I'd also sworn off relationships before this trip. But spending time with Carlos had changed my views. I liked him a lot and kind of hoped he felt the same…

'So that's your plan? To be on your own for the rest of your life?'

Carlos shrugged.

'It is best not to think too far ahead. My dad made plans for his retirement and he died before then.'

I wondered whether what had happened with his mum leaving also had something to do with his aversion to relationships, because of how much she'd hurt his dad. I also wanted to know whether Carlos had been in a serious relationship with the ex he'd mentioned earlier, but I resisted the temptation to ask. He'd opened up to me a lot today, so I trusted that he'd share more when he was ready.

'I get where you're coming from, but surely that's all

the more reason to enjoy the time we have whilst we're still alive?'

'Maybe this is true.'

'That's why I'm in Spain. To have fun. And you promised to help me do that, right?'

'*Sí.*'

'So where's this place you wanted to take me? I'm sure you didn't originally plan to go to the waffle shop!'

I chuckled and Carlos smiled too, his shoulders loosening a little. I could tell he was still feeling bad about his past and I wanted to make him feel better. Show him that even if he wasn't happy with the person he was before, I believed that he was a good person now.

'Come.' He led me down another street. 'I have an idea. If fun is what you want, I know exactly where to take you.'

CHAPTER THIRTY-FIVE

C arlos stopped outside a doorway. I looked up at the sign.

'Is this a nightclub?'

'*Sí.*'

'Oh, I don't know…'

'You will enjoy!'

'Okay,' I gulped. He led me down some stairs, then through a door. The sound of a heavy bassline boomed through the small dark room. There were only a few lights illuminating the bar, which had several people sat on the stools in front of it, and I could just about make out the silhouettes of a small crowd on the dance floor in the centre.

'What do you want to drink?'

'Um, surprise me.'

Carlos signalled to the barman and ordered our drinks. After swiftly putting two large glasses on the counter, the barman filled them with ice, then started pouring the rum.

Whoa. Talk about heavy-handed. Wasn't he going to measure it? That was what we did at our bar. The glass was getting close to being half-full with rum. At this rate, there'd be no room for any Coke.

'Did you ask him for a quadruple or something?' I laughed. 'That's a *lot* of rum.'

'This is how we serve drinks here. It is not like at the hotel or in London. In real Spanish bars they are generous.' Carlos paid with cash, then handed me a glass.

'Bloody hell!' I coughed after taking a sip. 'This is *so* strong.'

'Once the ice has melted it will be weaker. But if it is too much, I can get you something else or just water?'

'No, no, it's fine. I haven't had a rum and Coke for ages. Think the last time was with Nate.' Which reminded me that I still hadn't replied to his text. Must do that tomorrow.

'It is his favourite. He just called. I must call him back. It has been a week since we spoke and he has called many times. I have to tell him. That you and me have been together.'

I took a large glug of my drink. I'd enjoyed living in this bubble with just the two of us. I wasn't ready to invite any negativity into our lives.

'Let's not think about it tonight. It's late and you can't call him from a club. It's too loud. Anyway, I thought we were supposed to be having fun?'

Carlos dragged his hand over his face. I knew he felt guilty about keeping this from Nate, but right now, it was for the best.

'Okay. But I must call him tomorrow. And you are

right. We are here to have fun, so come.' He took my hand and led me to the dance floor.'

'Noooo! I can't!'

'*Sí, tu puedes!* Yes, you can! Stand in front of me.'

I sighed, my heart pounding, and then did as he asked. Carlos wrapped one arm around my waist and pulled me back into him. The heat from his body set my skin on fire. I took another swig of rum, hoping it would cool me down.

'Feel the beat,' he moved closer. The warmth of his breath tickled my ear, sending more shockwaves through me. I started to sway gently. I could feel Carlos's heart beating and that wasn't the only thing I could feel.

I pushed myself back onto him, feeling his hardness against me. He was turned on and so was I. He started showering my neck with gentle kisses as he moved behind me.

The reggaeton beat vibrated through the room and my body. I didn't know if it was the music, the rum, feeling Carlos's dick pressed against me, or a combination of all three, but I was buzzing. I didn't remember ever feeling so free and comfortable on a dance floor. Not to mention horny. I started rotating and grinding my hips into him. And this time, I knew for sure that he liked it.

Fuck. I was dancing. And nobody was laughing.

Yeah, the dancing was probably a little X-rated. The way we were grinding wasn't too far off having vertical sex, but I didn't care. Like Carlos had said during that first lesson, the most important thing was to have fun and I was certainly doing that.

We continued dancing for a few more tracks. By this time, Carlos had finished his drink and had both arms wrapped around my waist, although his hands did occasionally roam elsewhere, skimming my thighs and the sides of my breasts, and I didn't stop him. I was sure no one could see, and even if they could, they were too busy enjoying themselves to care.

I took the last sip of my drink, then turned to face him. After placing the glass on the table nearby, I put my arms around his neck.

Our bodies instantly pressed together, as if a magnetic force was drawing us closer. I rested my head on his chest and inhaled his intoxicating scent. His skin was slick with sweat, but he still smelt delicious. Like gorgeous, hot man. I was overcome with the desire to trail my tongue across every inch of him.

Carlos slid his leg between mine, rested his hands just above my bum and ground his body into me. He was as hard as steel. My knees buckled.

Fuck. What was he doing to me?

Carlos didn't speak, he just pulled me in and held me tight. I'd lost my flow. I know Carlos had told me to feel the beat when I was dancing, but I couldn't focus on that right now. All I could think about was how it would feel to have him inside me again.

No wonder so many dancers on that *Strictly Coming Dancing* show ended up falling prey to the 'curse' where they hooked up with their dancing partners. There was something so intimate about it. Pressing your body up against someone, bumping and grinding and getting sweaty. It was basically like having sex with your clothes on. And I was here for it.

I ran my palms across Carlos's bum and looked up at him. He took my face in his hands and pressed his lips on mine, kissing me passionately. I moaned, pushing him into me. I wanted him so much.

He pulled away.

'Perhaps it is better if we leave, no?' he growled, licking his lips.

'Good idea.'

CHAPTER THIRTY-SIX

We were on the motorway, back to Marbella. It'd been a fun forty-eight hours in Madrid.

After leaving the club, we got back to his aunt's flat around two a.m., horny as hell. We'd made love—I mean, had sex (this was a holiday romance, not *love*)—twice. And this time, when I unzipped Carlos's shorts, pulled down his boxers and wrapped my lips around him, he didn't stop me. He fisted my hair and groaned with pleasure as I licked him from base to tip and brought him to the edge until he exploded.

Yesterday, as tempting as it was to stay in bed, because it was our last full day in Madrid, Carlos had taken me to more of his favourite places.

Once we'd eaten lunch in the centre, we queued up for the Madrid Teleférico—the cable cars. I was absolutely terrified at first, but I'd squeezed up beside Carlos, and when he put his arm around me, my heart rate slowed and I was able to relax enough to enjoy the views of the city and the huge Casa de Campo park beneath us.

We'd strolled hand in hand through Oeste Park, then within Jardines de la Rosaleda—a beautiful, peaceful garden in the heart of the city with hundreds of different types of roses, plus pretty statues, fountains and ponds. It was lovely to just walk around and hug and kiss so freely.

In the evening, Carlos had cooked dinner and we'd got an early night, ready to set off this morning.

We were both working tonight. There were about two hours of our journey left, so even though we'd have to shower and get ready, we'd still make it back in plenty of time.

The song switched to NSYNC, and just like all of our road trips, I sang loudly. From the corner of my eye, I saw Carlos frown before turning the volume right down.

'Either my singing is so bad that you want me to stop completely, or you want me to sing a solo just for you,' I joked.

'No.' He frowned again. 'Do you hear something?'

I listened. It was hard to tell, because the cars were driving past us so quickly. Ah. Hold on.

'Yeah, like a rattling noise?'

'*Sí.*'

The sound grew louder. It now sounded like banging. Shit.

'I will pull over.'

Luckily we were able to make it to the slip road leading to a service station before the car stopped. A chill ran through me as I thought about what could've happened if it had broken down on the motorway.

'Do you have the AA or RAC—you know, the roadside breakdown service?'

Carlos shook his head.

'I did, but… not anymore. And it is not included in my insurance.'

'Oh.' My heart sank. I looked at the time on my phone. There was almost three and a half hours until we were due to start work. We could still make it. That all depended on how long it took to get a mechanic out here. 'We'll just have to call around, then.'

'It will cost a lot and…' Carlos rubbed the back of his neck. 'I-I do not have enough money.'

'I'm sure they'll take credit cards. They have those little portable machine things.'

'I do not have credit cards, and I spent all of my money.' He dragged his hand over his face. Carlos's shoulders were hunched like he had a thousand rocks resting on top of them.

'Oh no! I wish you'd let me pay for things!'

'I wanted to treat you. Make you feel special.'

'I appreciate that. But you don't have to spend money on me to make me happy. You make me feel special in so many other ways. I'll cover the cost for calling out the breakdown people. If it wasn't for me, you wouldn't be driving so much. You took me to Granada and to Madrid and you've taken me to all of these places without ever accepting any money I've offered for petrol. It's the least I can do.'

'No. I cannot take your money.'

'Well, how else are we going to get back and make it to work?'

Carlos hung his head.

'Okay. But I will pay you back. I will have more money this weekend.'

'Is that when you get paid for doing the dance classes?'

'No. I do not take money for that. The parents pay for the hire of the room, but I do the lessons for free.'

So he gave up time that he could be working at the hotel and earning cash to help the children? From an accounting perspective, that was crazy, but on a human level, I loved that he did that. Not everything was about money. Carlos's phone rang.

'It is Nate again. *Mierda.* Lily, this is why I told you that I am no good for you. When Nate discovers what we have been doing, our friendship will be over. I do not want to betray him like the best friend of my dad.'

'Huh? What did he do?'

Carlos squeezed his eyes shut as if he was relieving something painful.

'I told you before that my mum left us. For a man. She ran away with my father's best friend. My dad never recovered. He suffered so much from that betrayal. I would not wish that pain on my worst enemy.'

'That's awful, I'm so, so—' I stopped before I used the word *sorry* again. 'I can't even begin to imagine how that must have felt. But it's different. Nate is my brother, not my husband.'

'I know it is not the same, but it is still dishonest. Betrayal from someone close to you. Putting desire before loyalty to your family, like my mother and my dad's friend did. Nate is like a brother to me. He trusts me and I have broken that. Nate will not approve of us and he is right. You can do better than me. I have nothing to offer you. You should be with someone who can provide for you. Give you the best things in life. That is not me.'

'Erm, hello? This is the twenty-first century. I don't need a man to *provide* for me. I can take care of myself.'

'I know you can, but you should not have to. Like I said already. I am not good for you. My life is a mess.'

'Why?'

'I have problems with money.' Carlos's eyes fell to his feet.

I sighed inside. I told myself that if I ever got involved with a man again he'd have to *not* be a woman-iser and know how to manage his finances. The point of coming on this trip was to learn from my mistakes. Instead I'd just repeated them by getting attached to a man who was popular with women *and* had money troubles.

But there was an explanation for Carlos's Casanova reputation, so there must be one for his financial situation too. Maybe this was just a one-off. A month where his expenses were super high. We all had them. And paying for everything during our trips to Alhambra and Madrid couldn't have helped. I wanted to hear the full story before I jumped to conclusions.

'We all have tough months financially. January is always the worst for me. Paying for Christmas shopping, the heating bills are extra expensive, and then my car and house insurance are also due. Hopefully next month will be better for you?'

'No.' He shook his head. 'It will be the same next month. And the one after that. I have big debts. Like I told you, when my father died, I went crazy. Not just with women. Also with money. Before, I was sensible, like him. I used to spend carefully. But when he had the stroke and died, I thought what is the point? He spent his whole life trying to save and plan for the future and he never got to enjoy it. Life can be taken from you at any moment. So I decided I was not going to waste time being sensible. That is why I blew all my money.'

'What did you spend it on?'

'Parties, buying drinks for strangers… and one night when I was working, I was so drunk, I was sick over the crowd. The bosses warned me already about getting involved with women at the club, so after that, of course, they fired me. So I lost my job too.'

'Shit.' Admittedly, this sounded much worse than I'd thought, but my gut told me that Carlos wasn't the same person anymore. 'But that was in the past. You must have done something to get yourself out of that hole. You seem to be doing really well now.'

'It was Nate. He helped get me cleaned up and I stopped drinking. That helped a lot. I started to think more clearly and stopped fooling around with women. It has taken years to get better and I still must be careful. That is why I do not drink when I work. Only alcohol-free beer. And I only drink alcohol on special occasions, like when we go out. It is only in the past eighteen months that I started to get good gigs again. *Sí*, I am doing better. But everything that I earn now has to pay my debts. That is why I have to work so many jobs. Just to survive. And I pay with cash to control what I spend. If I do not have the cash, I cannot buy things. So you see, this is why I told you from the beginning that I am no good for you. I cannot buy my own home or pursue my dreams. Even before my problems with money, I wasn't enough.'

'Why do you say that?'

'My ex. My last serious relationship, she…'

'It's okay.' I squeezed his hand. 'Take your time.'

'Even though we first met at a club, I believed that I

had found someone who liked me for who I am inside. Not because she wants to be with a DJ or because she thinks I am "cute". Looks are temporary. So I want someone to like me for more than that. I thought I had a good woman like my married friends have. Genuine and kind—like my aunt and my sister. Not the party women that usually like me. But one day, after two years together, which was around four months before my dad died, she told me it was not working between us. I did not understand why. Then one week later I found out that she was dating another DJ—a famous one.'

'So she cheated?'

'I think so. But I cannot be sure. It does not matter now. By moving on so quickly, she made it clear that I was not important to her.'

No wonder the poor guy was anti-relationships. His mother had walked out on his dad and caused him to spiral. His last serious girlfriend had probably cheated on him. And then there was all the stuff with him going off the rails a few months later after his dad died. Shit.

'I'm sorry all of this happened to you.' I winced, realising I'd just used the S-word again when it was such a trigger for him.

'It is not your fault. You can see that things are not good for me right now. And I know that if I am ever going to commit to someone properly, I need to know that I can provide for my family. I like women who are independent and have a career that they love. But if my wife chooses not to work and wants to stay at home and raise the children for a few years, she should be able to do this and know that I can earn enough to support all of us.'

'So you *do* want to settle down one day?' My eyes widened. 'To get married? And have children?'

Because Carlos had said he didn't do relationships, I'd just assumed he'd be an eternal playboy and had no interest in having a family.

'It is one of my biggest dreams.'

'Oh, wow.' My heart fluttered and I told it to calm down. Just because he might want those things, it didn't mean he wanted them with me.

'But I do not know if it will ever happen for me. I am a mess.' Carlos's eyes watered.

He really believed he had nothing to offer and looked so broken that my heart wanted to shatter into a million pieces, because as far as I was concerned, nothing was further from the truth.

'Come here.' I took him in my arms. 'You are *not* a mess. You are someone who made some mistakes when they were grieving and in a dark place. And do you know what that makes you?' He looked me in the eyes, then shook his head. 'That makes you human. We *all* make mistakes. The important thing is that we learn from them and try and do our best not to make them again. And you've been working your arse off to fix things and get your life back on track. A lot of people would've given up, but you, you work night and day, running yourself into the ground. That's not what someone does if they don't care. You think you're a mess, but I think you're amazing!'

He looked at me again, his eyes wide with shock.

'It's true!' I added. He needed to know exactly what I thought of him.

Carlos wasn't like River. He may have squandered his money when he was grieving, but I knew he wouldn't do it again. He hadn't just spoken about wanting to change. He was doing it. Making it happen. There wasn't a single doubt in my mind that he was genuine.

'You're a brilliant DJ. You're a brilliant dance teacher. What you do with those kids is fantastic, and you taught me to dance, which was nothing short of a miracle. And you're kind and caring and smart and funny. Yep. Like I said. You're amazing. And in my eyes a man like you with a kind heart is worth a billion times more than some rich guy who just throws his money around but doesn't give a fuck about anyone.'

Carlos took my face in his hands and kissed me. It was slow and gentle but filled with emotions.

They say a picture tells a thousand words, but this kiss told a million. Without even speaking, when his lips were on mine, I could tell how grateful he was that I'd said what I had. This kiss said thank you for accepting him and making him feel better.

When we came up for air, he looked me in the eyes again.

'*Gracias*, Lily. Your kindness, it means a lot to me.'

'I'm only telling you what I believe. Are you okay?'

He nodded.

'Sorry. I just… sometimes my situation, it can over-whelm me.'

'It's okay.' I rubbed his back. 'I know it must be a lot to handle. If you feel comfortable, maybe you can show me some of your bills and things and I can see if I can help you? I also have a killer budgeting spreadsheet that I created to keep track of my spending. There's a load of apps and other stuff I can recommend too… I'll shut up now and take my accountant hat off!' The corner of Carlos's mouth twitched.

'I would like to hear your advice, *gracias*. Anyone who can add up a bill without a calculator must know what they are talking about!'

Carlos had been amazed when we'd eaten out in Madrid and I'd calculated the total before the waiter had even produced the bill.

'It wasn't difficult. There were only eleven items!'

'You are the smartest woman I know, Quesito.'

'*Gracias*, Carlitos.'

Carlos cracked a smile and his shoulders loosened. Must have been so hard to keep all of that bottled up for so long.

'You okay?' I squeezed his hand again.

'*Sí*. Much better. Thank you for listening to me.' Carlos stroked my cheek.

'No worries. I know it wasn't easy, but I appreciate you trusting me enough to talk about it.' Carlos nodded. 'Shall we call a rescue service? Get us back on the road?'

'*Sí*.' He took out his phone. '*Mierda*. There is another missed call from Nate and my battery is at three per cent. I must charge it.' He reached over to the back seat and rummaged around in his overnight bag. 'I think I left my charger in Madrid,' he groaned.

'What phone do you have? iPhone?'

'No. Samsung.'

'Oh. You can't use my charger, then. Let's call the car rescue service with my phone.'

After ringing around, eventually we found one who could come out within the hour. Even then, there'd be no way either of us could make it to work in time, so we had to phone in.

Zach said he could handle the bar until I arrived if I wasn't going to be too late. Carlos's boss sounded hurried during their conversation, which was in Spanish, so I didn't know what was said, but I assumed she'd told him he needed to get in asap.

Whilst we sat on a nearby hill waiting for the rescue service to arrive, Carlos suggested that he should return Nate's call, but we couldn't exactly do that with my phone. That would definitely set alarm bells ringing. Nate wouldn't answer if the number was withheld, and if he did, he'd definitely ask why Carlos was calling from an unknown number. We both agreed it was best to wait until Carlos could charge his phone. He could then send a quick text to say he'd phone Nate back in the morning. I'd reply to his message then too.

A few hours wouldn't make any difference. Right now, focusing on getting back to Marbella and to work was a much bigger priority.

'Look at you!' Zach grinned. 'Dancing behind the bar. I thought you said you had two left feet?'

'I did... until I got some private lessons.' I smiled.

'I don't have to be a genius to know who gave you those! Be honest, was that really why you were late? Were you two busy doing the horizontal dance in the car and you lost track of time?'

'No! I told you, we broke down.'

We'd managed to make it to work just forty-five

minutes late. Luckily, the mechanic guy was able to fix the problem pretty quickly and get us back on the road.

Once we'd got to my flat, we'd dumped our bags, showered, changed in record time, then literally flew out the door.

The beach wasn't that busy when we'd arrived, but Carlos's boss wasn't happy about him being late. According to Zach, Pandora was pissed off too and said she'd be coming to have words with me later. Great.

'Yeah, yeah. I believe you! Steamy sex and dance lessons with the hottest guy in Spain. Seriously, sweetie, you are living my fantasy right now.'

'I have to admit, I do feel *hashtag blessed.*' I smirked.

'Although…' Zach's voice trailed off. 'Maybe my fortunes are about to change. I spy with my eagle eyes a hottie that might just give your BF a run for his money.'

'He's not my boyfriend!' I protested, wishing he was. 'It's just casual, and trust me, there's not a man on this planet that is hotter than Carlos.'

'Oh yeah? Think again. Check out the tall guy with the big muscles, short curly hair and immaculate beard. Yum.' He licked his lips. 'Over there. With the bag slung over his shoulder.'

I followed Zach's gaze and then froze.

'Fuck!' I shouted.

'I know, right? Told you he was hot.'

I swallowed hard like I was trying to squeeze a block of concrete down my throat.

'No! You don't understand, Zach. That man isn't just some random guy. That's Nate. My brother.'

CHAPTER THIRTY-SEVEN

I ducked behind the bar, my heart thundering against my chest.

What the hell was Nate doing here? He was supposed to be in Canada. Thousands of miles away.

'Lily!' Zach whispered. 'Get up! Pandora's coming!'

'I can't! Didn't you just hear what I said? My brother's here!'

'Well, you're going to have to choose. You're skating on thin ice with her. You've only been working here just over a month and you've had almost a week off sick, you were late today, and let's face it, honey, you're not that great at your job, so unless you want to get the boot four days early, you'd better get your butt off that floor right now and show your face.'

Shit. If I got up, I'd keep my job for the agreed length of time and wouldn't let Nico and Cassie down, but it would set off World War Three when Nate saw me. But realistically, there was no way I could avoid him. If he'd just arrived, the first place he'd head was the bar. Or to see Carlos.

Fuck.

Carlos!

No. It was fine. He didn't know anything about us. *Yet*. Everything was okay. He'd be pissed that I hadn't told him I was working here, but *whatever*. It was my life. I was a grown woman. I could do what I wanted.

Screw it.

I grabbed a couple of glasses and stood up like everything was normal, just as Pandora arrived.

'*Hola!*' I put on my best smiley nothing-to-see-here face.

'Good of you to join us, Lily,' she hissed sarcastically.

'I'm so sorry about earlier. I broke down on the motorway.'

'Yes, you said. It's funny, because I wasn't even aware that you had a car to drive here?'

'Um…' What was she? MI5? Was I under surveillance or something? As far as I knew, whether I had a car or not wasn't a crime.

'And it is a big coincidence because I was speaking to Louisa earlier and she said one of her staff, the DJ, had also broken down on his way to work.' She raised an eyebrow.

Dammit. Louisa was Carlos's boss. I knew exactly what she was implying. I couldn't let her know that she was right about us being together.

'Rental!' I shouted as the brainwave entered my head. 'It was a rental. I'll definitely be complaining. But I was only forty-five minutes late. I mean, it's a lot, I know, but I was worried it'd be more and… I'd be happy to come in an hour earlier tomorrow to make up for it.'

'Yes. That would be best.'

Just as the words fell out of her mouth, Nate locked eyes with me. He frowned, blinked, then blinked again.

'Lily?' he shouted.

'Er, Lily, could you be a love and go and help that customer? The tall guy with the bag. He came by earlier. I think he liked a cocktail you made for his friend last week or something.'

God bless Zach for trying to get me out of a sticky situation. I didn't know if Pandora would believe that my cocktails would send the tourists flocking, but the customer was king around here, so I doubt she'd risk it.

'Is that okay?' I looked at her for approval. 'Sorry again.'

'See you tomorrow an hour early,' she snapped before walking away.

I came out from behind the bar and headed over to Nate.

'Hi, bro!' I threw my arms around him like it was completely normal that we'd both found ourselves here on a Spanish beach.

His body tensed and he pulled away.

'What the hell are you doing here, Lil?'

'I could ask *you* the same thing. I thought you were supposed to be in Canada?'

'I left. You didn't reply to my text. And you said you were travelling. Around Europe. What are you doing working here? Behind a *bar*. At the same hotel as Carlos?'

'Don't start! I wanted to do something different, okay? And don't worry, I've been careful, and as you can see,

I'm fine, so no lectures. Like you said, I'm working, so I better get back. Let's talk later, yeah?'

He narrowed his eyes and I returned to the bar. I quickly grabbed my phone and texted Carlos.

Me

Nate's here! I repeat, Nate is here!

Me

I've spoken to him briefly. Just told him I'm working behind the bar. That's all…

I looked over to the DJ box. Carlos was bopping his head to the music. I saw him pause and pick up his phone, then he froze. A group of rowdy guys blocked my view before I got to see his facial expression, but I imagined it would be shock and horror.

Nate weaved his way through the crowd, getting closer and closer to Carlos. At least I'd given him the heads-up.

I came out from the bar to get a better look. When Nate reached the DJ box, Carlos took off his headphones, jumped off the stage and gave Nate a big bear hug. *That's good. At least they're still friends.* For now, at least.

How long that friendship would last once Nate found out that Carlos and I had hooked up was anyone's guess.

CHAPTER THIRTY-EIGHT

W e were so busy tonight that I barely got time to scratch my head, never mind keep an eye on what Nate and Carlos were up to.

The last thing I saw was Nate talking to Carlos, but Nate's back was to me, so I couldn't see if he was angry. I thought he'd at least come over and get a drink, even if he didn't sit at the bar, but nope. I couldn't see him anywhere. Not in the crowd or on the beach.

My heart raced and my brain whirled, wondering what had been said between Carlos and Nate. At least Carlos was still in one piece, so our secret must be safe.

Now my shift was over, I could check my phone. I touched the screen. There was just one message.

Carlos
Meet at the car.

He'd only sent it eight minutes ago, so that was a relief.

'Ready for me to escort you to your ride?' Zach

smirked. 'And in case you didn't guess, I'm using the word *ride* deliberately.' He jerked his hips back and forth and then cackled.

'Now's not the time, Zach. A fight could be about to break out.'

'Oh, sweetie, I know. Why do you think I'm so eager to get you there? Well, that and to get a better look at your hot brother.' He threw his head back with laughter.

'I'm glad you find the drama in my life so entertaining.'

'Gotta get my kicks somehow.' He squeezed my shoulder. 'Don't worry, darling. If the shit hits the fan, I've got your back.'

Zach teased me a lot, but I knew he had a good heart. We linked arms and headed to the car park. When we arrived, Carlos was leaning against the car. My body tingled. He always looked so sexy when he did that. I told my libido to pipe down. Now Nate was here, I didn't know when we'd have sexy time again, but I could guarantee it wouldn't be tonight.

'Hey,' I whispered. 'What happened? Where's Nate?'

'In the bathroom. He does not know yet, but I will tell him.'

'What? *Nooo!* He's already pissed at me. At least wait a couple of days until he's cooled down. How long is he staying?'

'I do not know, we did not get to speak a lot…' Carlos paused and looked over my shoulder. 'He is coming.'

'Hey, bro!' I span around with a grin plastered on my face.

'I'm still mad at you for lying to me.' Nate ground his jaw.

'Oh, come on! I didn't lie exactly...'

'You told me you were travelling, not working at a bar. How long have you been here? The whole time you've been away?' He turned to face Carlos, his eyes like lasers. 'How come you didn't tell me she was here, bro?'

'Because I asked him not to!' I jumped in before Carlos could respond. I didn't want to land him in hot water. 'Can you blame me? Look at how you're reacting. This is *exactly* why I didn't want you to know. As you can see, I'm totally fine. I'm happy, I'm healthy and I'm still in one piece. Carlos has been taking good care of me.'

Carlos's eyes widened with horror before he suppressed his expression.

'I take Lily home every night.' Now it was my turn to glare at him. 'To make sure she gets back safely,' he added quickly. 'I-I drive her home.' I didn't think I'd ever heard him stutter so much. He clearly realised that, given his track record, saying he took me home every night didn't sound good.

'And he does the same for me!' Zach piped up. 'He's such a good guy. Dropping us home.'

Carlos looked like a deer stuck in the headlights. He gave a small nod.

'I'm Zach, by the way.' He held out his hand for Nate. 'I'm Lily's work bestie.'

'Nice to meet you, Zach.' Nate gave him one of his firm handshakes. Zach probably wouldn't be able to use that hand for twenty-four hours now. Sometimes Nate forgot his strength.

There was an awkward silence. Nate looked at Carlos, then at me, then at Zach and back at me, still grinding his jaw.

I could tell he was trying to figure everything out. I wasn't convinced that he bought the whole Carlos colleague home drop-off service story.

'*Vamos?*' Carlos said.

'Yeah, let's go,' Nate replied.

I walked towards the passenger seat at the front but caught myself just in time. It would be less suspicious if I sat in the back with Zach and let Nate sit next to Carlos.

Once we'd all put on our seat belts, Carlos plugged in his phone and started the engine. Britney's 'Toxic' blared from the speaker.

'Whoa!' Nate shouted. '*You're* playing *Britney*?'

Shit. That was from our playlist. We'd listened to it on the way here.

'Yeah…' Carlos's voice trailed off. 'Thinking about doing a remix of some of her songs and giving them a dance vibe.'

'Ah, cool. For a minute it was like being back at home when Lily used to play her cheesy pop. How are the remixes going? You haven't sent me any for a while.'

'I know. It has been busy with the massage work in the day and doing my set at night.'

'Yeah, man, I get it. I was worried when I hadn't heard from you. That's why I came straight here instead of going back to London. I wanted to make sure you were okay.'

'So what happened in Canada?' I interrupted.

'Let's just say I didn't see eye to eye with the client. It got awkward, so I decided it was better to bounce. Thought I'd come and spend a few days with Carlitos. I was *not* expecting to see you here.'

'Yeah, you've mentioned that once or twice. Give it a rest.' I rolled my eyes. 'Where are you staying anyway?'

'Crashing at Carlitos's. I have to say, man, I wasn't even sure if it'd be cool because I thought you'd have *company*...' He slapped him on the back. 'The ladies are still swarming round you.'

'*Hombre*.' Carlos's tone was serious. 'I do not do that anymore.'

'*Purlease*,' Nate scoffed. 'You're not as wild as before, that's true. But you're only human, so I know you've still gotta have fun sometimes. The day you give up women completely is the day I settle down or take a vow of life-long celibacy. Never gonna happen, bro.'

I swallowed hard. Zach took my hand and gave it a little squeeze.

'Just by that red car will be fine,' Zach said, breaking the silence.

'I thought you said Carlitos dropped you off every night?' Nate asked. 'So wouldn't he know where you lived?'

'Um, yeah, but,' Zach stuttered. 'Tonight I'm not going *home*, if you know what I mean,' he laughed.

'Cool, cool. I hear you.' Nate nodded.

Excellent save, Zach.

Carlos pulled over and Zach opened the door. 'See you tomorrow, sweethearts. Nice to meet you, Nate.'

'Likewise. And thanks for looking out for my little sis. Means a lot.'

'She's a grown woman, so she does just fine on her own, but thanks anyway, darling.' I could hug Zach for saying that.

It didn't take us long to get to mine. Carlos pulled up in front of my building.

'Well, this is me.'

'Actually, Lil, I'll come up with you. I need the toilet.'

'But didn't you just go before we left?'

'Yeah, but I drank a lot tonight. It's gone straight through me.'

'You didn't even come to the bar.' I frowned.

'I was at the other bar. Inside the hotel.'

'Can't you wait until you get to Carlos's?'

My flat was a tip and I knew he'd have something to say about it if I invited him up.

'*And?* What's the big deal?' He spun around to face me. 'Is that any way to treat your big brother? I just need to piss.'

If I said no or kicked up any more of a fuss, he'd get suspicious.

'Okay. But no comments on how messy the place is. I left in a hurry.'

As I put the key in the door, I remembered that Carlos's stuff was here. His overnight bag and clothes were probably still on the bed from when we'd quickly got changed.

I couldn't let Nate see that. For all I knew, he might recognise Carlos's bag because they often travelled together.

Think, think, think.

I opened the door, then reached for my phone and turned on the torch.

'Come on.' I grabbed his arm. 'It's this way to the bathroom.'

'Why don't you just turn on the light?'

'Because, like I said, it's a tip, so I don't want you to see it.'

'Trying to keep your tidy rep in check!' he laughed.

'You were always the neat one. It would be nice to see your idea of mess. Proves you're just like the rest of us!'

'Yeah, something like that.' I chuckled. As much as Nate's visit had taken me by surprise and I was frustrated that his presence meant it'd be harder for me and Carlos to see each other, at the same time, I'd missed him. He was fun to be around when he wasn't in overprotective mode. 'Here it is.' I opened the bathroom door and turned on the light. 'And make sure you put the seat down when you've finished. I know what you're like!'

Once Nate shut the door, I quickly turned on the main light, then shoved Carlos's bag in my wardrobe. I scanned the room and saw his boxer shorts and vest on the floor right next the bed, so tossed them in the wardrobe too.

That was close.

I gave the room another once-over and ran to the sofa to see if there was anything incriminating.

The toilet flushed and the tap turned on.

I returned to the bedroom area. There was a glass on each of the bedside tables. I took them both to the kitchen. There was nothing suspicious about having two glasses in the sink. *All good.*

After smoothing out the crumpled sheet to make the bed look neater, I rushed to sit on the sofa.

The bathroom door opened.

'I didn't hear the toilet seat get put back down!' I spun around to face him with a cheeky smile on my face.

But Nate wasn't smiling. He had a face like thunder and was holding a bottle in his hand.

'What's this doing in your bathroom, Lil?'

I swallowed hard and my heart started thudding.

Keep calm. He doesn't know anything. Play it cool.

'What? It's shower gel. It's a bathroom with a shower in it, so obviously you need to have shower gel, duh!'

'But this is a *man's* shower gel.'

'*And?*' I folded my arms. 'What? Am I not allowed to have a man in my flat? For God's sake, Nate!'

I heard footsteps coming up the stairs and Carlos burst into the flat.

Nate looked at him, then at me, then back at Carlos. Nate's eyes widened with horror.

He knew.

Shit.

'What the fuck!' he shouted. 'Tell me you haven't been fucking my little sister.'

'Why would you think that?' I jumped up and stood in front of Nate, hoping that he wouldn't charge at Carlos. His eyes were on fire and I was worried about what he might do to him.

'This is his favourite shower gel. His aunt brings a load of it over every time she comes back from visiting the States. They don't even sell it over here. I know it's his. Fuck! Tell me the truth, Carlitos!'

He moved me to one side, stormed over to Carlos and stood right in front of him. 'Look me in the eye right now and tell me you haven't laid a finger on her.'

Carlos closed his eyes in defeat.

'Nate, I am sorry.'

'No, no, no! This can't be happening!' Nate dragged his hand over his face and shook his head. 'We're supposed to be brothers, man! You promised me! I fucking trusted you!'

Nate swung his fist in Carlos's direction. Luckily he ducked and I rushed in between them.

'Stop! Stop it!' I screamed, trying to hold him back. 'Nate! Calm down!'

Nate stepped back, nostrils flaring.

'Lily, you promised to never get involved with my friends!'

'That was years ago! We were kids back then. I'm thirty-fucking-two now! Stop being a dick!'

'Carlitos!' He shook his head. 'What the hell have you done? You know why this is so important to me. What the fuck?'

Carlos stepped over to Nate and put his hand on his shoulder. Nate shrugged it off.

'I know how it looks, but I can explain.'

'There's nothing to explain. You both betrayed my trust. And then you lied to me. You coincidentally end up working at the same place for over a month and neither of you mention it? Then all that bullshit in the car about just driving her home every night. I *knew* it. I *knew* something was wrong. I know you can't keep your dick in your pants, man, but you could have any woman you wanted. Why did you have to fuck with my little sister? After everything we've been through and after what happened, you knew what this would do.'

My heart almost snapped in two when I saw the pained expression on Nate's face. There was something they hadn't told me. This seemed like it was about more than just breaking the bro code. More than breaking a simple promise. More than being there for each other over the years. I'd known Nate would be upset, but he seemed physically wounded.

'I know, I wanted to tell you. I was going to do it tonight, but…'

'I don't wanna hear it. We are *done*. And you better let her down gently, because if you hurt her, I'll fucking cut your dick off.'

Nate stormed out, slamming the door so hard the room shook.

Fuck.

CHAPTER THIRTY-NINE

'Lily.' Carlos held my shoulders. 'You understand that I must go after him, *sí*?'

'Isn't it better to leave him to calm down?'

'No. We need to sort this out now.'

'But he's so mad!'

'He will not hurt me. He is upset. And it is late.'

'What did Nate mean when he said "after what happened"? What was he talking about?'

'It is not my story to tell. It is better that you ask him. I must go now. You will be fine?'

'Yeah. Message or call me later, though, so I know you're both okay.'

He ran out the door and I heard his footsteps as he raced down the stairs.

I dragged myself over to the bed and collapsed on the mattress. My head spun. Wondering whether Carlos had caught up with Nate, if they were rolling around on the pavement punching each other's lights out right now.

What if the police saw them and they were arrested?

Oh God. My stomach twisted. I was so torn. On the one hand I adored Carlos. And when I was with him, everything felt so right and I didn't care about anything or anyone else in the world.

But on the other, Nate's face tonight. *Damn.* The look of betrayal and hurt was something that would be etched in my brain forever. Yeah, he could be overprotective, and yeah, I should be able to date whoever I wanted, but he'd also done so much for me. No, for *us*. He was Carlos's best friend. The one person he'd thought he could trust. And now he'd discovered we'd both lied to him.

I couldn't help feeling guilty.

I grabbed my phone from my bag and put it beside me. I didn't want to miss any calls or texts. I wouldn't even be able to think about sleeping until I knew they were both okay.

The sound of a loud motorbike engine woke me out of my sleep. I had no idea what time I'd dozed off. I remembered checking my phone after five thirty in the morning to see if there were any messages.

I'd then called both Carlos and Nate a few times, but there was no answer.

The only messages I'd had were from Zach checking I was okay. I tried calling Carlos again, but his phone was switched off.

My chest tightened. What if he was in hospital? I couldn't bear it. All because I didn't want to burst our bubble of happiness. It was selfish of me to make Carlos keep a secret from Nate. He wanted to be honest and I'd discouraged it, because I wanted him to myself. I knew it would ruin their friendship and I'd ignored his concerns.

Well, I was going to pay the ultimate price. I'd finally found a man I truly loved and now I was going to lose him.

I swallowed hard as the realisation hit me. I'd just said I loved him.

I didn't know why I was so surprised. Anyone who ever spent more than a few seconds around me when I was with him would know that was true.

It was more than just the physical attraction and the mind-blowing sex. It was our connection. The way I felt comfortable around him. Even with bare skin.

The way we laughed together when we danced or listened to music in the car.

The way he looked at me, like I was the most amazing woman who'd walked the earth. And the way I felt. It was like I'd spent years trying to complete a jigsaw puzzle, but never could because the final piece never seemed to fit. Until now. Everything seemed so right. Things just felt so easy around him.

Shit. I really loved him.

My phone rang, snapping me out of my thoughts.

'Hello?' I answered within the first ring.

'I am calling to update you.' It was Carlos. His voice was low and croaky like he'd just woken up.

'Are you hurt? Where's Nate? Did you find him?'

'No. I could not find him. He knows my address, but he did not come. I tried calling. He did not answer and now his phone is off. I drove around the city looking for him. I do not know where he is.'

'Fuck. Okay. I'll make some calls. See if Cassie or Flo have heard from him. Maybe when he turns his phone on, he's more likely to take their calls rather than ours. But are *you* okay?'

'I am fine. Just tired. I only went to sleep about two hours ago. I was hoping that Nate would come back so that I would not have to worry you.'

'Thanks.'

'I am sure he is okay—just angry. Once he has calmed down, I will try to talk to him again.'

'Okay. I'll call Cassie now.'

I spoke to both Cassie and Flo, explaining what had happened. They both agreed that, like Carlos had said, Nate just needed time to cool off. I hoped that was true.

Nate was big enough to look after himself, but that didn't stop me from worrying. But worrying wouldn't change anything or make Nate magically reappear. We just had to try to continue as normal and wait for him to get in touch when he was ready.

How long that would take was a question neither of us could answer.

CHAPTER FORTY

I t was hard to believe that I only had two and a half days left in Spain. The saying that time flies was definitely true. The last five weeks felt like they were over in the blink of an eye. So the next sixty hours would probably feel like a millisecond.

It was now the early hours of Saturday morning and neither Carlos nor I had heard from Nate personally. Flo had texted yesterday to say that Dad had spoken to him briefly the day before, so at least we knew he was alive, although no one knew where he was.

I wound down the window. I was in Carlos's car coming back from our Friday night shift.

'I need some air,' I said.

'*Si*' was his only response.

Carlos had been a bit distant. Since Nate had left, he hadn't stayed over at mine and the only time we'd really exchanged more than a few words was when he dropped me home.

Even though he didn't say it out loud, I knew that he

was upset about Nate. I supposed I would be too if I'd just lost my best friend. But I hoped that at least I could help him through it. So far, though, it felt like I was just a reminder of what had caused him to lose his friendship. At least it made me realise that, despite the fact that I loved him, Carlos still saw us as just something temporary. In a couple of days I'd be gone and now that he and Nate were no longer friends, I'd never see Carlos again.

My stomach jolted. Just the thought of it made me feel sick.

Maybe that was why Carlos was being distant. He was getting ready to break things off nicely. Just like Nate had told him to that night. I still remembered his words: *"And you better let her down gently, because if you hurt her, I'll fucking cut your dick off."*

Yeah, Carlos was probably in self-preservation mode. He needed to keep his dick intact so that he could start using it again once I'd left.

I wanted to believe that wasn't true, that he really did care for me, but how could I when he was pulling away?

Anyway, what did I expect? It was only supposed to be for one night. Then one night became almost two weeks. It was silly to wish for more.

Carlos parked up outside my building.

He turned to face me. His face was solemn. My heart thudded, worrying about what was coming next.

'Thank you for the spreadsheets. They will be very helpful.'

'No worries.' I'd sent them to him earlier along with a list of apps to help with his budgeting. 'Remember, if you want, the offer still stands to go through your accounts and stuff and make some suggestions?'

'*Gracias.*' He fidgeted with the hem of his shorts. 'I will let you know.'

There was a long pause. I didn't know whether to stay or leave. I was just about to say goodnight when Carlos's mouth opened.

'What are your plans for Sunday?'

'Packing, I suppose.'

Carlos swallowed hard and nodded.

'I cannot believe it will be your last day here.'

'Me neither.'

'Well, I know you will be busy, but it will be the dance performance for the children and I wondered if you would like to come and watch? And then maybe we can have lunch or a drink together.'

'To say goodbye…' My voice cracked. Carlos nodded again.

'Okay,' I said. 'I'd like that.' There was a long silence. I didn't know whether or not to invite him upstairs.

I wanted him there, of course I did. Not even for the sex. I'd be happy to just be in his arms all night.

'Thanks for the lift.' I opened the car door, hoping that he'd say something to stop me. He didn't. 'Goodnight.'

'Goodnight, Lily,' he said. I closed the door and didn't look back.

I wiped down the bar, washed my hands and then stood back, taking in my surroundings. As it was a Saturday night, the beach was packed with tourists and guests who'd come to party.

Their bodies swayed and rocked as they danced.

Although the music drowned out the sound of the waves, thanks to the sparkling lights that dressed the beach, I could see them crashing against the sand and smell the seaweed and salty water.

Although I didn't love the job, I was going to miss being here. It had been hard. Especially in the beginning when I'd had no clue what I was doing. And standing on my feet for several hours was no picnic. But I'd enjoyed meeting new people. And when I managed to make a drink correctly, it was satisfying to know that the customer liked it. If I ever hosted a dinner party at home, I'd know how to whip up a mean mojito.

'Sad about leaving?' Zach rested his hand on my back. 'Let me know so I can get another packet of napkins to wipe up your tears when you start crying your eyes out!' he cackled.

'*As if!*' I protested. 'I'll be fine. Obviously I'll miss this'—I gestured at the beach—'and, you know, a few other things, but I had to go home at some point. This couldn't last forever.'

I wasn't in a hurry to return to work and stare at the cloudy London skyline. And I *definitely* wasn't looking forward to seeing bloody River every day at the office and worrying about whether he'd blab to Ruth. But I'd deal with it.

'Are we talking about your job, this trip or something else? Or should I say, *someone* else?'

'Do you mean working here with *you*?' I teased, the corner of my mouth turning up into a smile.

'Well, *obvs*, it goes without saying that you're going to miss working with me. But you're not getting rid of me that easily. Don't be surprised when I turn up on your doorstep in London asking for a place to crash.'

I laughed. 'You'll always be welcome. I couldn't have got through this without you. Well, I could, but it wouldn't have been as fun. Thanks for everything.'

'Awww.' Zach pulled me in for a hug. 'Sweetie, you're *so* welcome.'

I closed my eyes, resting my head on his shoulder. I heard someone clear their throat loudly behind us.

'I hope I'm not interrupting…'

I span around.

'Nate!' I ran from around the bar and threw my arms around him. 'You're okay!'

'Yeah.' He rubbed my back. 'Matt, was it?' He looked over at Zach.

'Zach.'

'Ah, that's it. Zach, I'd like to steal my sister away for ten minutes. Can you cover for her? If that's okay, Lil?'

'Depends.' I stepped back and folded my arms. Now that I knew he was safe, my defences shot up again. 'If it's to lecture me and act like an overbearing, overprotective arsehole of a big brother, then no.'

'No. I-I want to apologise.'

'You want to *what* now?'

'You heard. I want to apologise. And explain.'

'*This* I have to hear.' My eyes widened. 'Can I take my break now?' I turned to Zach.

'Course, hon.' Zach winked and mouthed *Good luck.*

'Let's walk.' I gestured to the beach.

I looked over at Carlos, who was deep in thought as he focused on changing the song. I wasn't even sure if he knew Nate was here. I was still trying to take it all in. I thought he'd gone travelling somewhere else or would be making his way back to London.

'So…' His voice trailed off. 'I'm sorry, Lil. I shouldn't have blown up like that. But it was a shock. Seeing you here and then discovering that you and my best friend had been, *you know…*'

'Having sex,' I clarified. Nate winced. I knew it was petty, but I had to say it out loud. He needed to get it through his head that I wasn't some sweet little innocent virgin baby sister anymore.

'Yeah… *that*. Like I said that night, I trusted you both. I know it was a long time ago, but you swore you wouldn't get involved with my friends and Carlos did the same. He promised he wouldn't touch you and… knowing that he had, it… it wasn't just about breaking the bro code or his promise to me. It—it also brought back all the memories of before.'

'Before?' I frowned.

'The time when another close friend of mine let me down.' Nate dragged his hand over his face.

'What friend? Who? What happened?'

Nate went silent. He inhaled a breath, then swallowed hard.

'Do you remember Jack?'

'Course!' Even though Nate had had so many friends that came to the house and it was hard to keep track, I did remember Jack. He was one of the few nice ones. If he came round and Nate wasn't there, he used to sit and chat with me. 'He was the tall, funny one. His dad worked for the council or was an MP or something? He used to come round a lot and then he moved?'

'Yeah.' Nate ground his jaw. 'That's him.'

'But what does he have to do with me and Carlos?'

'We used to all go out a lot, remember? Clubbing, drinking and stuff. And you know what it's like. We used to chat up girls. Even though he was a funny guy, he didn't —let's just say that looks-wise, he wasn't what the women were into. We tried to help him out, asking the women we were with if their friends were interested, but they never were. And that frustrated him.'

'I bet.'

That didn't surprise me. Nate was like a woman magnet. Wherever he went, he attracted the ladies. Carlos was no doubt the same, so their friends probably didn't stand much chance of pulling with them around.

'One night, he was trying to get this girl's attention. It was obvious she wasn't interested, but she was being polite. He kept trying to turn on the charm and said he'd get her a drink. I went over to tell him to read the signs and move on, but as I got closer to the bar, I saw him reach in his pocket, pull out something and drop it in her drink.'

'What?' I gasped. 'How did you know it was her drink and not his?'

'Because he was already drinking beer—from a bottle. She must've asked for a vodka and orange or something and that's what he dropped it into.'

'Fuck!'

'Exactly. I was going to jump in straight away, but I was shocked, y'know? I couldn't believe he'd do some-thing like that. He was my friend. A good guy. Came from a decent family. But I stood back and watched as he shook the glass and took it to her.'

'Oh my God! But she didn't drink it, did she?'

'Almost. I got there just in time. She was about to take a sip when I snatched it away. I told her what I saw and of course, she was horrified. He denied it, a big argument broke out and I was so close to knocking him out, but luckily one of the other guys stopped me. It wouldn't have ended well otherwise. Even though I'd seen what he did, who would security or the police believe? Someone like me—or a blonde, blue-eyed boy with a dad who's a local MP? It'd be a no-brainer.'

'So what happened?'

'We took him outside. I demanded answers, asked him how the fuck he could do something like that. He said it was nothing. Just something to relax her. I wanted to fucking kill him. The way the bastard smirked. When I threatened to grass him up, he said I wouldn't be able to prove anything. Can you believe the cunt even said he'd say it was me? That I was jealous? I saw a completely different side of him. I checked on the woman to make sure she was okay. She was shaken and I gave her my number and said I'd talk to the police if she wanted. Tell her what I saw, but I never heard from her again. I reported it myself on the Monday, but they said that without the victim coming forward, there was nothing they could do. I was so pissed.'

'You did what you could.'

'Maybe. But I was also angry because I missed the signs. I thought he was a good guy. I trusted him. I brought him into our family home. He was around you, Cassie and Flo so many times. I knew he liked you all, most of my friends did, but I didn't realise he was a predator. Someone dangerous. I had no idea. I was supposed to protect you, but I let you down.'

'Some people are good at lying and covering up their true selves.'

'That's right. And that's why I stopped having so many friends come to the house. And the ones that did, I made them swear never to touch you and I never left them alone with you.'

Now that I thought about it, the timeline was similar to when Nate had also made us promise to stay away from his friends. It all started to make sense.

'I understand better now, but you can't judge all of your friends by Jack's fucked-up standards. Carlos is a good guy. He's your best friend. You should know that.'

We turned around and started heading back to the hotel. My break was already over, and even though it was my last night, I didn't want to take the piss and leave Zach on his own for too long.

'I know, I know, but Jack was a good friend too. And I never saw that coming. It would kill me if I let one of my friends hurt you. So I just thought it was easier if you stayed away from them. That way you'd be safe.'

'I know you only did it to protect us, but as much as I know you want to, you can't be around all of the time to keep us away from all the bad people in the world. And you can't control who we fall in love with.'

'Wait, *what*?' Nate paused and stood in front of me. 'Did you just say the L-word? You *love* Carlos?'

Oops. That kind of slipped out. I hadn't even told Carlos how I felt, so telling Nate was definitely premature.

'Yeah. I do.'

'Fuuuuck!' He squeezed his eyes shut. 'But, Lil! Have you thought this through? You might be having fun now, but what happens when you go back to London? What are you seriously hoping is gonna happen? That you'll ride off into the sunset together and settle down?'

'No,' I lied. Deep down I knew that was what I was hoping for. The likelihood of getting that, though, was probably about the same as me winning the EuroMillions jackpot, but my heart wasn't logical. 'Maybe…' I confessed.

'Listen, first up, you know I love you, right?'

'Yeah.'

'And I know sometimes you think I'm an overprotective arsehole…'

'Sometimes?' I laughed.

'Okay, okay.' He held his hands up in surrender. 'I know I can come down hard maybe more often than you'd like, but I tell it how I see it because I want the best for you. And you know I love Carlos. He's been my best friend for what? Something like twenty years. But this isn't some romcom film. He's not going to drop this gig and follow you. Carlos doesn't do relationships. Not since that ex fucked him over a few years ago. And you've worked at your job for too long to just give it up and come here. It's not just that. Has he told you about his situation?'

'You mean the money and how he spiralled after his dad's death?'

'Yeah. So you know that he's broke, then. He can't give you the life you deserve, sis. You deserve someone to love you. To worship you. My sisters are fucking awesome. And all of you deserve the best.'

'I know.'

'And even putting that money shit to one side, he's a DJ. You might be fine with him staying out until three a.m. every night now because you're working similar hours at the same place. But what about when you're back doing your nine-to-five in London and he's still working here in Spain? Are you gonna be happy knowing that women are crawling all over him when you're asleep? And even if you moved and tried to find a way to work in an office over here, would you be cool knowing that when you get home, he's just leaving for work? And when you're leaving for work in the morning that he's fast asleep? I know you think I'm harsh, but I'm just trying to stop you from getting hurt.'

It was tricky. Nate had an almost perfect record of predicting whether our boyfriends were treasure or trash. He'd had reservations about all the men we'd dated, including River, and he was right. So it was possible he was right about Carlos too. But I wasn't going to give up so easily. His accuracy levels were good, but they weren't *always* correct.

'You said similar things to Cassie.' I remembered my birthday dinner, when Cassie had told the family about Nico for the first time and Nate had said it wouldn't work because Nico was a billionaire and they came from different worlds. 'And you were wrong about Nico.'

'Yeah, I was and I admitted that. I judged Nico before I'd even met him and that was wrong. But I *know* Carlos. Better than anyone else, and I'm telling you, Lil, it will be difficult to make this work.'

'Difficult, but not *impossible*.'

'Look'—he held his hands up in surrender—'I've said my piece. I've told you my concerns. Now, as hard as it is, I'll leave you to it. Like you've been telling me, you're grown up now and it's your life, so I'll butt out. But before you get any deeper, just think about what I said, carefully, *without* thinking about how hot you think Carlos is or however good things are with him in the sack.' Nate winced. 'Just take care of yourself, okay?' He leant forward and kissed me gently on the head. 'Love you, sis.'

'Love you too.' I squeezed his arm. 'Wait, are you leaving?'

'Yeah. Got a new booking in London, starting on Monday.'

'Aren't you going to speak to Carlos?'

'Dunno.' Nate blew out a breath. 'I haven't decided yet. I needed to fix things with you first. Come on.' We walked towards the beach bar. 'Let's get you back to work.'

CHAPTER FORTY-ONE

I t was early afternoon on Sunday, my last full day in Spain, and I was at the hall where Carlos taught his dance classes.

The seats had filled up quickly with parents eager to see their children perform. After spotting an empty chair in the middle row, I sat down.

A few minutes later, the room plunged into darkness before a spotlight shone on the stage.

I gasped as Renata, the little girl who was always so nervous, stepped to the front. She was dressed in a long, frilly red skirt and black T-shirt with her hair in a bun and a red flower in her hair. *So cute.*

Everything fell silent. Suddenly she stamped her foot on the floor, announcing the start of the show, and as the sound vibrated around the room, everyone knew Renata meant business.

Flamenco music boomed from the speaker and Renata stamped and tapped her feet in a mini dance routine. She moved her hips, twirled her arms and swished the frills of her skirt in time to the music, before the rest of the group, who were also dressed in red and black, joined her on stage and danced in unison.

Loud claps, cheers and cries of '*Olé!*' from the audience filled the hall and I couldn't resist joining in.

My chest expanded with joy. She'd done so well. I remembered how close to tears she'd been at the beginning and how Carlos had guided her. I thought my dancing had improved. But Renata's transformation was incredible.

After a few other short performances, the children took a bow. Everyone jumped to their feet and applauded. What a show.

I made my way through the crowd, then waited at the side of the stage. I watched on as the parents flocked to Carlos to express their gratitude and collected their children who beamed with pride. They weren't the only ones who were proud. The nervous-looking children I'd first seen had been replaced by a bunch of brilliant dancers. I was proud of each and every one of them and of Carlos too.

My stomach sank for the millionth time today. I couldn't believe that this was our last day together. This time tomorrow, I'd be back in London, and then a few days after that, back at work. *Ugh.* My shoulders slumped. I really wasn't looking forward to leaving Spain and facing reality back home. I was glad I'd factored in some time to readjust rather than returning to the office straight away.

Carlos looked over at me. Our eyes locked and his face broke out into the smile that I loved so much. My heart raced. God, I was going to miss that smile so much. It always struck me like a lightning bolt. It had the power to light up the entire room. To take my mood from zero to a thousand in a second. I *could* video it, but it wouldn't be the same. It was like when Carlos smiled it transmitted some sort of electromagnetic waves that penetrated your entire body. Like a triple shot of dopamine and adrenaline all in one. You could only feel the full effects by actually being in the same place as him.

As the children and the parents dispersed, Carlos walked over.

'What did you think? You like?'

'It was bloody brilliant! You did such an amazing job with them.'

'The children did the hard work.' He shrugged modestly.

'Well, it was *you* who taught them. You're a fantastic teacher. You should be so proud of them and yourself.'

'*Gracias.*' He shuffled his feet nervously. I knew Carlos wasn't good at taking compliments. Somehow he didn't believe that they could be true. But he needed to know that I meant every word. The man was amazing.

'You should give yourself more credit, you know. I wish you could really see what I see and how incredible you are.'

'You are very kind.' His cheeks flushed. '*Gracias,* Quesito.'

'Well, if you remember me for anything when I leave, I hope it will be that I was the woman who made you say thank you twice in one minute!'

Carlos flashed his grin again.

'There will be many things that I will remember about you.' He reached up to my face and stroked my cheek gently.

My body sparked and I felt a crack in my heart.

God, I really didn't want to leave him. I looked up into his eyes and we just gazed at each other in silence.

I wondered what he was thinking. If he was feeling the same. If his heart also felt that when we said goodbye in a few hours, it would shatter into a million pieces.

'Perhaps we should stay at home today.' Carlos took my hand. 'I will cook for you.'

'Like the Last Supper!' I joked. It was the only way I knew how to deal with this. As every minute ticked by, it felt like a knife was being slowly twisted in my stomach.

'I think it will be nicer to spend it alone, somewhere we are comfortable, instead of in a restaurant. And I like to cook for you.'

'Okay.' The old me would have asked if he was sure and worried about whether he was tired, but by now I knew Carlos and that he wouldn't have suggested it unless he really wanted to do it. Cooking for me was part of his love language, so it was important to let him express himself.

And when I used the word *love*, it was because of the saying, not because I believed that he loved me. But it was fine. We'd agreed from the start that this would be temporary. Love was never part of that agreement. I was the stupid one who couldn't control my emotions.

After going to the supermarket, we made a quick stop at Carlos's flat to pick up the big paella pan.

'Would you like to come inside?' he asked. 'It is not as nice as your apartment. That is why I have not invited you before. But it is cheap, and with my situation, I—'

'I'd love to!' I interjected.

When we reached the second floor, Carlos opened the

door. It was a modest one-bed flat with beige walls. The paint was peeling a little, but it wasn't terrible.

In the living room there were rows of records and DJ equipment neatly stacked in the corner, along with several large weights and a sit-up bench.

The bedroom had a double bed and a single bedside table with candles and a photo of a man I guessed was Carlos's dad in a white picture frame.

Freshly washed dishes were stacked in the drainer, resting against the old-fashioned brown tiles in the kitchen, which was a little bigger than mine.

'It's nice,' I said. Carlos shook his head.

'You are being kind. We both know that this is not the kind of place you are used to.'

'It's not super modern, but it's clean and comfortable, which is the important thing. And with the hours you work, it wouldn't make sense to spend a fortune renting a place when you're barely even here. Thank you for bringing me to see it.'

Carlos nodded in acknowledgement and picked up the paella pan and then we left.

Once we were back at my flat, I continued packing whilst Carlos started lunch.

The scent of fragrant rice and chicken filled the air, and my mouth watered. Carlos called me to the table, where the paella dish rested in the centre.

'This is my absolute favourite!' I gushed.

I'd have to savour every mouthful seeing as this was the last time I'd be eating it. I'd have to remind him to take the pan with him later. When he left. Sigh.

'I know.' He smiled gently. It wasn't his full smile. It was more subdued. Carlos opened his mouth to speak and then closed it again. I wondered what he'd wanted to say and whether it was about us.

There was so much I wanted to ask him, but I didn't have the courage. I knew it would upset me. Silly, really. I was all for equality, yet right now, I wanted *him* to be the one to say something. For him to ask if I wanted to change our agreement and have a future together somehow.

We'd changed the plan before, extending things from one night to two weeks, so why not change it again? Maybe I could work remotely? We could find a way.

But instead of raising the subject, I made a joke about the fact that he loved the burnt bits at the bottom of the paella pan. In England we'd throw those bits away, but apparently in Spain they thought the crusty parts were delicious.

After we'd eaten and cleaned up the kitchen, Carlos forwarded a message he'd received from his aunt.

Earlier in the week, I'd given him some photos of my face to send her and she'd replied with some really good advice, including different vitamins to take and a lot of natural remedies that I hadn't heard of, which I was looking forward to trying out.

We curled up on the sofa and fell asleep in each other's arms.

The sound of someone's front door slamming jolted me out of my sleep.

'Good siesta?' I looked up at Carlos and rubbed my eyes.

'Not bad.' He lifted his wrist to look at his watch. 'You have finished packing?'

'Yep.' I swallowed hard as the cloud of my ever-closer departure loomed.

'Would you like to come for a walk? On the beach?'

'Course!'

Just as I was about to get up, my phone pinged.

Cassie

I have something exciting to tell you! I know you'll be stacked with packing etc. today, so call me when you're free.

I was itching to know what her news was, but I only had hours left with Carlos, so I'd have to speak to her later. After locking up and heading down to the car, I typed out my reply.

Me

Oooh! Can't wait to hear more. Just going for a walk with Carlos and then we'll come back here to enjoy our last night together, but will buzz you in a few hours/before dinner or something.

Cassie

Great! Enjoy your time together xxx

Carlos put on our playlist and the Spice Girls' 'Wannabe' blared from the speakers.

'No singing?' He frowned.

'Not today,' I said solemnly. I loved this song and normally I'd sing at the top of my voice, but I didn't even feel like humming. My stomach was hollow and there was a burning sensation in my chest.

When we pulled up to Carlos's favourite stretch of beach, memories of our last time here flooded my brain. A burst of oxygen flowed into my heart and it began to flutter.

This was the place where Carlos had told me that he'd always liked me and the place we'd made love, well, had sex, for the first time. As sad as I was about leaving, I reminded myself that I'd come to Spain to create memories and that was definitely one I'd never forget.

'Let us hope that we do not see that woman with her dog again.' Carlos grinned as he shut the car door. My face broke into a smile.

'Yeah! At least we have all of our clothes on this time and no fruity-flavoured pink condoms!' We both burst out laughing.

'That night was wonderful.' Carlos took my hand and led me onto the beach. 'Every moment I have spent with you has been wonderful, Lily.' He stood in front of me and kissed me gently on the lips. 'I am really going to miss you. More than you can ever know.'

'I-I'm going to miss you too.' I swallowed a lump in my throat. I could feel the emotions building inside me and I was about two seconds away from bawling like a hungry baby.

As we continued walking and the sound of the waves crashing against the sand filled the air, the questions that had swirled around my head for days rose to the surface again. I knew that if I didn't ask them, if I didn't express myself and tell Carlos what I was feeling, I'd regret it. As hard as it was to risk rejection and hurt, I had to do the logical thing and ask him outright. No matter how hard it would be.

I'd been brave coming to Spain, trying a new job,

living somewhere new, and I was stronger for it. Now I had to be brave again.

'Does this really have to be the end?'

There. I said it.

I felt lighter for a few seconds before my stomach tightened and I was gripped with fear all over again.

Carlos stopped, sat down on the sand, took my hand and gently pulled me down to join him.

Several seconds passed and I swear it felt like hours. I guessed I had my answer. I was hoping that he'd leap up and say, *No, it doesn't! I can't possibly live my life without you. Stay here with me and let's make a go of things, together.* But he didn't.

'Lily.' He took my hand. 'You have no idea how much I would like that. I want to be with you so much. So much that the thought of being away from you, the thought of you leaving tomorrow, hurts. The pain I feel.' He squeezed his eyes shut. 'Sometimes, it is too much to bear.'

'I feel the same.' I gripped his hand tighter. If he felt the same, then maybe there was hope.

'But...' He paused, and I knew that he wasn't going to say something I wanted to hear. 'But, right now, I know that even if we both want it, it could not work.'

'Why?' I pleaded. 'If we want to make it happen, if we want to be together, we can find a way.'

'I would like to believe that. But right now, I must organise my life. And I cannot do that if I am in a relationship.'

'But I told you. I can help you. To organise your finances and stuff. That's what I do.'

'I appreciate your offer, and the advice you have given me has already been very helpful, but this is something I have to do myself. I must focus. This is not about not wanting to be with you. It is about me becoming the man I need to be before I can even consider being ready for a relationship. Does this make sense?'

My heart snapped in two.

'In theory, yes, but if I'm honest, I just find it difficult to believe that the only option is to end things completely.' My stomach twisted. Partly from the pain of what was happening, but also because I hated feeling so vulnerable and like I was practically begging him not to dump me.

I didn't want to feel desperate, but at the same time, I didn't want to leave with regrets. I needed to know I'd tried everything.

'Quesito.' He squeezed my hands. 'I do not want this to be over. I thought a lot about how we can make it work. I had an idea, but I do not think it will be fair for you, so as much as it hurts me, I have to let you go.'

'What was your idea?' I sat up straighter.

'I need time to clear my debts, sort out my life. If you agree, we can press pause. Take a break and speak again in six months. If you find someone else during this time, who deserves you more, then I will not contact you again. But if we still feel the same for each other in six months, we can meet to talk and see if we can find a way to make this work. Like I told you before, relationships, they… if I am honest, they scare me because of my past, but things feel different with you and if we can survive this separation, we will know that this is real. Not just holiday fun. We will know we can survive anything together. What do you think?'

Six months?

I paused.

That was a long time.

Although I was happy that there was an option not to close the door completely, whether I was up for it or not all depended on what the arrangement would be during that period.

'So what would happen in those six months? Would we video call or visit each other for the weekend, say in London or Madrid?'

'No.' He shook his head. 'No contact. I think staying in touch will make it more difficult.'

That I didn't agree with. It didn't make sense.

'Why do you have to be alone to pay off your debts? Surely *not* seeing each other would be worse than meeting up in person at least once a month and speaking every night on the phone?'

'That will not work for me.' He shook his head. 'If we stay in touch, I will want to see you and I will not be able to focus. This is still the peak season and I will need to work night and day to pay my debts. I cannot be distracted. If I do not make enough progress in the next six months, the interest will increase a lot and things will become much harder. I know this will sound selfish. That is why I said that I did not think you would be happy with this idea. I know that it is not a nice thing for me to ask of you.'

I looked out at the sea, hoping that somehow an answer would magically wash up on the beach. Unsurprisingly it didn't. This was a decision that only I could make.

Did I agree and then spend half a year yearning for him in the hope that he'd still feel the same way about me?

What if at the end of that time he didn't, or he found someone else? Then I would've wasted six months of my life. And not only that, I'd have to start the relationship grieving process, so I'd lose several more months as I struggled to get over him.

Or I could make a clean break now, put the last five weeks down to experience and move on with my life? Hopefully within six months I would've got over Carlos and I could avoid more heartbreak.

My head was spinning. It was an impossible decision to make right now, and somehow being here, on this beach where everything started, made it harder.

'Can we go back home, please? I can't think clearly here.'

'Sure.' Carlos stood up.

We drove back to my flat in silence. Something we'd never done. The car was always filled with music. Whether it was one of Carlos's dance tracks or one of my pop tunes, there was always a lively, happy atmosphere. But not tonight. Maybe I'd feel more like talking once we got upstairs.

I undid my seat belt and went to get out of the car, but Carlos remained still.

'Aren't you coming?' I frowned.

'It is better if I do not. I can see that you need time to think.'

My stomach sank about five thousand feet.

'But it's my last night here. Don't you want to spend it together?'

'Of course I want to. But it would not be right. Knowing that…' He swallowed a lump in his throat. 'Knowing that this could be the end.'

I'd known that things would be a little strained, but never had I thought that he wouldn't at least want to come up with me. If he really felt as strongly for me as he claimed, surely he'd want us to savour every last minute and second together.

Well, I wasn't going to beg. I'd done enough of that already today. I'd made my feelings clear. I'd offered my heart, my body and my soul to him, and he didn't want it.

'Fine.' I opened the car door. 'Thanks for everything and good luck.' I went to get out.

'Lily!' Carlos grabbed my arm. '*Por favor*. Please. Do not leave like this!'

'Bye, Carlos.' I shook off his hand and raced to my front door. Warm salty tears rolled down my cheeks. I had to get inside quickly, before he had a chance to follow me. I heard him shout something else, but it was drowned out by the sound of my sobbing.

So much for a romantic evening together and enjoying my last few hours in Spain.

My Spanish romance had come to an end. And my heart was utterly broken.

CHAPTER FORTY-TWO

I must have cried myself to sleep, because when I opened my eyes, the room was pitch black.

I checked the time on my phone. It was almost eleven. I went to the bathroom and jumped back when I caught myself in the mirror. My eyes were swollen and bloodshot. Jeez. How much had I sobbed? From the look of my puffy face, I was surprised my tears hadn't flooded my flat.

When I returned to the bedroom I suddenly remembered: *Cassie*. I'd promised to call her back.

Talking was the last thing I felt like doing now, but she'd said she had exciting news and I wanted her to share it with me. I loved hearing about all the amazing things she was doing with the charity foundation she'd set up with Nico, and some good news might help cheer me up. For a few minutes anyway. After what had happened with Carlos earlier, even if someone delivered a truckload of churros and chocolate, I wouldn't feel any better.

'Lily!' Cassie screamed like a child that had just gobbled down a truckload of sweets.

'Wow!' I attempted to mirror her enthusiasm. This must be *really* good news.'

'It's the best! Can we switch to a video call?'

'Um…' It was hard enough to pretend to have an upbeat conversation, but she'd take one look at my face and know something was wrong. 'I'm a bit tired, sis, so I'm not looking my best.' I hoped that would be enough to dissuade her.

'I bet you are! You and Carlos have probably been at it all day with your goodbye screwing!' She cackled. My stomach plummeted. *If only.* 'C'mon, Lil! You know I don't give a toss about how you look. It really will be better to FaceTime!'

I groaned internally before pressing the video call button. When I did, I wasn't greeted by Cassie's face. Instead her hand took up the entirety of the screen with… wait. Was that…?

'I'm engaged!' she screamed. 'Nico proposed!'

I swallowed hard. As I attempted to take in what Cassie had just said and focus on the pretty diamond ring in front of me, my mind raced so fast that I felt light-headed. I tried to snap myself out of my dizziness. This was Cassie's big moment. Even though my own heart had just been crushed, I couldn't let my crappy love life get in the way of my happiness for my sister.

'Oh my God! That's amazing! I'm so happy for you, Cass! You deserve this so much!'

As I digested the last few words that had flown out of my mouth, my body slumped. I'd said Cassie deserved this happiness. So did that mean my unhappiness right now was my fault?

'Thank you!' Her face now filled the screen.

Although her hair was thick and curly like mine, Cassie's looked like she'd just stepped out of a salon. Every ringlet was beautifully defined and shiny. One of the perks of having a celebrity hairdresser boyfriend. Correction: Nico was now her *fiancé*.

'As you can tell, I'm pretty chuffed. I had no idea he was going to do it. I mean, things are going so brilliantly, so I'd always *hoped*, but y'know, the way he proposed. It was such a surprise and sooo romantic. He…' Cassie paused and her face creased with concern. 'Lil, what's wrong?'

It was possible that I'd unintentionally zoned out for a few seconds. Wondering whether I'd ever find the kind of happiness that Cassie had. I'd thought I had with Carlos, but clearly I was wrong.

'Don't worry about me! This is your happy moment. I really am thrilled for you both.'

'Out with it!' Cassie crossed her arms. 'Did something happen with Carlos? Or are you just sad that you're going home tomorrow? Tell me!'

'No!' I shouted, wishing that I was a better actress. I hated that the conversation was going to turn to me when this was a time when it should be all about Cassie. 'I want to hear more about your engagement.'

'*Lily!*' Her tone was serious and insistent, like she wanted to reach through the phone and shake me until I told her what was up. That was the problem with being so close to her. Cassie could read me like a book.

'It's over.' Just saying those words out loud was like pummelling my heart with a sledgehammer. It hurt so much. 'It really was just a holiday fling.'

I filled Cassie in on what had happened and his whole

six-month suggestion. She said she thought it was a difficult decision. But talking about it out loud, I wasn't even
sure if the idea was legit.

I thought Carlos was different to all the other guys that
had let me down, but maybe he'd deliberately made a no-
contact suggestion so that I'd refuse and he wouldn't need
to feel like the bad guy. Bit like River cheating instead of
being man enough to say he didn't want to be with me.
Why did I keep attracting cowards?

'So now you know, can we go back to talking about
Nico's amazing proposal, please? I need cheering up. I
need to have some hope that one day I'll find the perfect
guy for me, just like you have.'

'Don't go home tomorrow,' Cassie said.

'What? I've told you. Carlos doesn't want a relationship. There's no point in staying. And I'm going back to
the office in a few days.'

'Yeah, I know. I don't mean stay in Spain. Come and
see me in Paris. You said you needed cheering up, so stay
for a couple of days. Melody's coming tomorrow too, so
we can spend some girly time together. I'll book your
ticket. What do you say?'

'Oh my God!' My eyes widened. 'That would be
amazing, but I don't want to be some weepy wet blanket
putting a dampener on your fun.'

'I'm your sister. I want you to be happy and I won't be
if I know you're at home alone, crying yourself to sleep.
You've had so many great experiences these past five
weeks. Don't end your sabbatical on a low. Come over.
The first few days of a break-up can be the hardest. Let us
help you through it.'

A flutter of hope filled my belly. I had to admit. I'd

much prefer to spend a couple of days in Paris than locked away in my house feeling sorry for myself. And I adored Melody. Like me, she'd been unlucky in love, so she'd understand what I was going through.

Cassie had been kind enough to invite me over, so I'd be crazy to refuse.

'Okay! I'd love to come, thanks, sis! Looks like I'll see you tomorrow in Paris!'

CHAPTER FORTY-THREE

I sank my teeth into the rich, buttery pastry and groaned with pleasure. I was sat outside a Parisian café with Cassie and Melody having breakfast, and this *chausson aux pommes* French apple turnover thingy that Cassie had recommended really did taste as good as she'd promised.

It was my second day in the city and despite the sad circumstances that had brought me here, I was enjoying spending time with Cassie. I'd really missed her.

Yesterday, once I'd arrived, I was shattered so I'd slept for most of the afternoon. My body clearly needed to catch up on the sleep it had missed on Sunday night, when I'd tossed and turned, thinking about my last conversation with Carlos and his suggestion.

Then, once Melody had arrived, we'd gone out and done some touristy things. Visiting the Eiffel Tower and walking down the tree-lined Champs-Elysées before returning to Cassie and Nico's ginormous penthouse apartment, where their chef cooked us a slap-up meal. Talk about how the other half live. It was a completely different world. Cassie had really hit the jackpot with Nico.

I hadn't felt like talking about Carlos yesterday. It was too raw. It still was. But Melody wanted to know what had happened, so I'd just finished explaining it all to her.

'Oh, love, I'm so sorry.' She rubbed my shoulder, causing the dozens of colourful bangles she had on her wrist to jangle loudly. Melody had a silky rainbow-coloured hairband at the front of her reddish-brown hair, which had been backcombed at the crown to give it a sixties vibe.

'Me too.' I hung my head.

'When Cass told me about how everything was going for you, I really thought you'd found *the one*. I remember meeting Carlos briefly at one of your family dos years ago, and he seemed really nice. We were having a good conversation until your dick of a brother stole him away.'

Melody was not a fan of Nate. They'd had their run-ins over the years and we all knew never to leave them alone together in case they ended up wrestling each other to the ground.

'You and Nate, honestly!' Cassie shook her head, then twirled one of her shiny highlighted curls around her finger. 'I've never understood why you guys hate each other so much.'

'Yeah!' I added. 'He's not so bad.'

'Anyway'—Melody rolled her eyes, clearly not wanting to devote another second to talking about Nate —'back to Carlos. So what do you reckon about this six-month thing? Do you think you could do it? Are you worried about going without sex for that long or whether he'll be able to keep it in his pants whilst he's doing all of his DJing?'

'It's not about me being celibate. I've gone much longer than six months without sex, although, yeah, I admit, now I've had a taste of what it's like to sleep with someone you have a deep emotional connection with, it'll be hard to go without it. If he is telling the truth and this suggestion isn't just a way to let me down gently, I *do* worry about whether he'd even be able to hack it. I know he said he isn't into the whole sleeping around thing anymore, but the ladies love him and with temptation around every night, it will be hard for him to resist.' I sighed and took a sip of coffee. 'I don't know.'

'But what about the *other* side of this?' Cassie piped up. 'You said yourself that you love him. So if he is serious about his suggestion and there's a chance of being together for a lifetime, is six months really that long to wait?'

When she put it that way, it didn't seem so bad. I'd been dating since my late teens, and nearly fifteen years later I'd never felt about anyone the way I felt about Carlos. But, if I waited six months and discovered he could live without me and wasn't interested, that would be devastating. It'd be much harder to deal with that than making a clean break now.

'Cass has a point.' Melody nodded. 'Six months isn't so long. And like he said, if you find someone amazing during that time, he won't stand in your way. It'll be tough, but you can do it, girl! And if you need to relieve yourself, I can send you the link to a great ethical porn website that your big sis recommended! The way my love life is going, I'll be single until my moody teenage daughter goes to uni, so this site has given me hours of pleasure!' She threw her head back and cackled.

'What!' My mouth dropped open. I turned to face Cassie. 'Do you watch that *with* or *without* Nico?'

'Nooooo!' Cassie shouted. 'I read about it, that's all. Not that there's anything wrong with watching ethical pornos, but I have plenty of fun in the bedroom, so I don't need anything else.'

'Pff!' Melody said. 'You two barely have nookie in the bedroom. They're the king and queen of al fresco fucking. You've done it on the Eiffel Tower, on top of the Arc de Triomphe, in the middle of the Champs-Elysées... Have I missed anywhere?'

'Seriously?' My eyes bulged out of my head.

'Of course not!' Cassie rolled her eyes. 'Mel's exaggerating. We haven't done it *any* of those places. Yeah, we've made love outdoors a few times, but not on iconic monuments. We'd be arrested faster than you could say *fromage*!'

My stomach twisted. Hearing Cassie mention the French word for cheese reminded me of the Spanish, *queso*, which then reminded me of Carlos's nickname for me.

It'd only been a couple of days since we'd last spoken, but I already missed the way he called me Quesito.

And hearing Cassie talk about getting it on outdoors made my mind race back to our first time, on the beach. The way Carlos had looked at me. The feeling of his lips crushing onto mine. God, I missed him so much.

'Well, I can safely say I won't be doing anything in or out of the bedroom for a long time. I think the best thing I can do when I go back to London tomorrow is to forget about Carlos and men completely and focus on me. Until then, I'd like to enjoy my last twenty-four hours here with you ladies.'

I didn't rate my chances of keeping Carlos off my mind all day, but I was going to give it a good try.

CHAPTER FORTY-FOUR

I took a deep breath and stepped through the large glass doors of the office building.

'Lily!' said my colleague Manu. 'How was your trip?'

'Great, thanks.' I smiled. It was true. *For the most part.* I'd gone to Spain to travel and have some memorable experiences, and I'd achieved that. So on paper, it was a success. Nursing a broken heart wasn't one of my objectives, but what was that saying? *It's better to have loved and lost than never to have loved at all.*

And it was true. Given the choice, I'd much rather have had those few precious weeks with Carlos than nothing at all. Without it, I might have spent more of my life thinking about him. Wondering and wishing.

Then again, that was exactly what I was doing now. In some ways, it was worse, because I'd had a taste of him and seen what it was like when we were together. And I wanted more.

I wanted *forever*.

'Glad to hear it! You'll have to tell me all about your

travels later.'

'Will do!' *The PG version, of course.* 'But now, back to reality!'

'Enjoy your first day back.'

'Thanks,' I replied, walking to the lift.

In many ways, everything was exactly the same. I slipped into my old role as if I'd never been away or I'd just been off on a weekend break. The office looked the same. The views of London were the same. Despite it supposedly being summer, it was cloudy and grey. Just like my mood.

After tackling my mountain of emails, I met with Ruth and some colleagues who brought me up to speed.

As everyone filtered out of the conference room, I hung back.

'Ruth,' I said softly as she plucked a pile of papers from the table. 'Do you have a minute?'

'Sure, what's up?' She smiled. 'Don't tell me. You had such a fabulous time in Spain that you've decided to up sticks and live on the beach, sipping sangria in a bikini every day?'

'No…' Although that did sound appealing. Now I'd had a taste of travelling, I couldn't wait to do it again. 'I don't think you'll like what I have to say, though.'

'Oh.' Ruth's face fell and she sat down.

'You see, the thing is'—deep breath—'it's about River.'

'Our client, River?'

'Yes.' I winced. Her reminding me that he was a client made it even worse. 'There's no easy way to say this, but basically, we dated. I'm sorry.' I really was. Sorry that I ever let a loser like him in my life.

Ruth's face was frozen. I couldn't read the expression in her eyes. The room was so silent, you could hear a pin drop.

Although I was sure she was pissed off, I didn't regret telling her. I couldn't go on with this secret hanging over my head. And I didn't want it to be something that River could blackmail me with either. It was better for me to control the situation and take the power he might think he still held over me away from him. If Ruth wanted to sack me, I'd find another job. I'd survive.

'Is that it?' Ruth raised her eyebrow.

'Erm, yeah, pretty much. Other than the fact that we're not together anymore.'

'Good for you!'

'What?' I frowned. 'You're not mad?'

'Mad? At you? No! Obviously, you know I'm not a fan of office relationships but, Lily, you're one of the sweetest, most genuine, hard-working people I've worked with. River on the other hand… well. He's a client, so I should be professional, but he's only been in the building a few weeks, and let's just say I can already see how he operates. Guys like him turn on the charm and it can be hard to resist. I can see how easily it could've happened. Let me guess: he was the man who cheated and the reason you had to get away?'

'Yeah.' I nodded.

'And that's also why you didn't want to work on his account?'

'Yep.'

'I *knew* there must've been a reason. Don't worry. Whilst you were away, I realised more than ever what a valuable part of the team you are, Lily, and I appreciate you coming to tell me. His account has already been assigned to Sadiq, so you shouldn't have to deal with River too much. And there'll be more opportunities for growth here for you in the near future. I'll make sure of it.'

'Thank you!' My eyes widened. That was not the response I'd expected, at all. I exhaled. I was so glad I'd told her. It felt good to have everything out in the open.

'Was there anything else?'

'No.' My stomach rumbled. I looked at my watch. It was almost two in the afternoon. 'Just going out for lunch.' I grabbed my jacket. There was no way I was getting caught in the rain again.

'Okay. And, Lily, I like your dress.'

'Thanks!' My cheeks warmed.

I was wearing a new orange dress I'd bought in Paris. I'd started wearing brighter colours in Marbella because I'd wanted people to think I was cool and fun. But actually, now it wasn't about how I was perceived. I liked that it lifted my mood. Now I was doing it for me. Those grey suits wouldn't be coming out of my wardrobe again anytime soon.

'Good to have you back.'

As I walked out of the building, I had a spring in my step. So far my first day hadn't been as bad as I'd feared.

Looked like I'd spoken too soon. My stomach sank as I saw River heading towards me.

Great.

It had to happen sooner or later. At least I'd get it out of the way now.

'Lily!' he said excitedly.

As always, River was dressed in a sharp suit, with his hair perfectly groomed. The kind of look that used to send me weak at the knees. But as I glared at him, I felt nothing. Not even a twinge of attraction.

He reached forward to kiss me on my cheek and I stepped back.

'No,' I said firmly. 'If you want to greet me, a simple hello is enough.'

'You never used to complain when I kissed you, or when I did a lot more… you couldn't get enough of me.' He smirked and bile rose in my throat. The thought that I was ever intimate with him and had stayed with such an arrogant, self-satisfied twat made me want to throw up.

'Well, what can I say? You live and you learn. It's amazing the things I used to believe. Like, I thought I'd had good sex before, but now? Pff! After the mind-blowing experiences I had in Spain, now I know better.' It was my turn to smirk. 'Those Spanish men, I tell you, they really know their way around a woman's body! They could teach British men a trick or two. Anyway, have a good day.'

As the blood drained from River's face and his jaw fell to the ground, I held my head up high and walked off. I knew River's ego was bigger than several continents, especially when it came to his prowess in the sack. So implying that I'd had someone better than him would rattle his cage.

I could've said a lot worse, and he deserved it after the way he'd cheated and how he used to make me feel about my skin, but I didn't want to stoop to his level.

Now I knew that running away to escape River had given him too much control over my life and delayed the inevitable rather than just facing the issue head-on. But I didn't regret going to Spain.

Before, I'd been afraid of change. I'd thought doing

something unfamiliar was bad. But now I realised that sometimes the opposite was true. Sometimes familiar things were bad because they kept you stuck. Sometimes, no matter how much you've been hurt, no matter how scary something feels, it's important to take a deep breath, take the leap and do those scary things anyway, because they move you forward in life.

That was what I'd done by travelling, and I felt much better for it.

When I'd first returned to the office earlier, I'd said everything was the same. But it wasn't. That was true for my surroundings, but *I* was different. Something had shifted in me. I never would've had the courage to say something like that to River six weeks ago, or to tell Ruth the truth. I felt stronger.

Even though things hadn't worked out how I'd hoped, being with Carlos had helped me find my confidence.

I'd always believed that if I showed a man my true self, especially so soon, he'd run a mile. That I could never be considered attractive without my mask of make-up. But during our time together, I didn't feel flawed or like I wasn't enough like I always did with River. I felt treasured. Special. Adored.

The sabbatical had done me good. Now I knew I could make it through work, whether it involved seeing or working with River or not. He'd already taken up too much of my life and brain bandwidth, so I wasn't going to waste another second thinking about him.

Yep. I could handle work. Now I just had to figure out how to mend my broken heart.

CHAPTER FORTY-FIVE

Six months later

'So, dear.' Doris took a sip of her tea. 'Is there any news?'

I'd started visiting her again the week I returned from Spain, and I'd been religiously coming to see her every weekend since.

'No.' I swallowed the lump in my throat and readjusted myself in the seat by the window. It's not quite six months yet, so…'

'It will be tomorrow.' She smiled.

'How do you know?'

'I wrote it in my diary. I know you said you didn't want to talk about it, dear, but it's time. Tomorrow will be exactly six months since Carlos's suggestion. So what are you going to do about it?'

Although I'd told Doris I didn't want to talk about Carlos, it didn't mean I hadn't thought about him. I had. Every. Single. Day. When I woke up, when I was at work, before I went to bed. It was probably easier to say when I *hadn't* thought about him.

These past six months had been hard. I'd deliberately avoided looking at his Instagram account. It would be too painful to see photos of him enjoying himself.

No matter how hard I tried, I couldn't seem to get him out of my head. See what I mean? When I hear 'Can't Get You Out of My Head', I think of Kylie Minogue, and that makes me think about my love for pop. Then I think about the playlists we both made and how we used to sing to them in the car on one of our road trips.

In fact, any time I thought about anything to do with music, I thought of Carlos. When I heard a dance track on the radio or in a shop, when I listened to Spotify, when I saw someone with headphones bopping their head on the Tube.

Or if I saw anything remotely related to Spain, or *queso*, or dancing, or beaches, or happiness or *love*. There were reminders of him. *Everywhere.*

I hadn't considered dating anyone else. I know that people suggest that to get over one man you should get under another, but I couldn't even contemplate that idea. No one else could ever measure up to him. It wasn't just how breathtakingly beautiful he was or how amazing he was in bed. Even without all that, there were so many things I loved about Carlos.

His kindness. Not just how he'd helped me when I'd arrived in Marbella, with the shopping and dancing and so many other things, but his selflessness. Even though he was struggling with money, he'd still paid for everything on our trips. He taught those dance classes for free. He'd given me a lift home every night to make sure I got home safely.

He'd taken care of me when I was injured. He'd emptied my piss, for God's sake. Something he wouldn't do if he just wanted a shag. And he always made me feel special. Comfortable and adored.

Even though he was embarrassed about where he lived, he'd still invited me to visit without me having to ask or practically beg like I had with my ex.

And he'd never cringed at my skin like River had. Carlos had supported me and helped me build my confidence.

God, I loved him.

If I had any doubts before, I definitely didn't have them anymore.

Carlos was the one for me.

I just had to hope and pray that he felt the same.

'I'm going to call him.' I blew out a breath. It was scary to say it out loud, but at the same time, kind of a relief.

I'd wanted to call him hundreds of times just to say hello or to hear his voice, but I'd resisted. An important part of being in a relationship is listening to your partner's needs. And Carlos had told me he needed six months to sort himself out, so calling before then would show I didn't respect his wishes. So I'd waited. And waited. And now, the wait was almost over.

'Great!' Doris clapped enthusiastically. 'When?'

'I was thinking I'd do it on Monday because then it's definitely six months. And I know he won't be working then. On a Sunday, it's possible that he might be tired from working on the Saturday night.'

'Are you sure you're not just putting it off?' Doris narrowed her eyes. 'Why wait? If tomorrow is the six-month mark, do it tomorrow.'

She was right on both counts. In a way, I was putting it off—I was scared of the rejection. I *should* do it tomorrow.

In fact, I wondered if I could do it *today*.

What difference did twenty-four or forty-eight hours make after waiting six months? If Carlos felt the same way I did, he'd be glad I called early.

And calling today was better. That way, if things didn't go the way I wanted them to, I'd have the rest of today and tomorrow to eat ice cream.

I'd found some vegan ice cream a few months ago, which meant I could still indulge in one of my favourite treats without breaking out. My skin had cleared up massively since I'd reduced my dairy intake, which was easy to do thanks to the alternatives available in the super-market. I'd started following a new nutrition and skincare regime too. I had Carlos and his aunt to thank for that.

If I saw him right now, I'd wrap my arms around him and shower him with thank-you kisses. He had no idea how life-changing it was to wake up and not have to glare at yet another blemish. I couldn't thank him enough.

I chuckled to myself as I thought about how much he'd hate it if I said thank you more than once.

Then I thought about his smile… my stomach flipped.

'That's it!' I stood up. 'Sorry, Doris, but I'm going home. To call him.'

'That's my girl!' She beamed. 'Go get your man. And don't forget to invite me to your wedding!'

'Hold your horses!' I slipped my scarf around my neck.

'We're not even officially together yet. Cassie's wedding will be the next one you go to.'

We were all excited about Cassie's upcoming wedding. The prep was in full swing and I couldn't wait to watch her tie the knot.

'Oooh, yes! I'm really looking forward to it. Let me know how you get on with young Carlos, dear.'

'*Lo haré!*' I said, remembering the Spanish for *will do*.

As I left the building, a flutter of excitement filled my stomach.

I was going to get my man. Well, at least call him anyway.

I wondered how I'd be feeling in an hour or two. On cloud nine after an amazing conversation with Carlos where we'd both declared our enduring and undying love for each other, or sobbing on the sofa after he told me he didn't feel the same way?

There was only one way to find out…

CHAPTER FORTY-SIX

This was it.

I sat on the edge of the bed and picked up my phone. I went to dial his number but paused. Maybe I'd be more comfortable on the sofa. Then I could sit up straighter. Feel more confident.

I walked to the living room and lifted my phone again. Was I sure that he hadn't said *he'd* call *me*? Maybe it was better for Carlos to make the first move. After all, he was the one who'd said he needed time. Calling him might be too pushy. Plus, we hadn't spoken or messaged since I'd stormed off that last night. So for all I knew, he might have thought that was it. That I never wanted to see or hear from him again.

Oh God. I should've been clearer. I should've told him plainly that I wanted to give the whole six-month thing a try instead of sulking like a baby. But I was upset.

I considered asking Nate if he'd heard from him, but no. On the few occasions I'd tried to probe him to see if they'd made up, he'd shut down the conversation. And anyway, this was a decision I had to make on my own. What was done was done. There was nothing I could do now except try and get back in touch. It was time to put on my big girl knickers.

Let's do this.

I took a deep breath and dialled his number.

The phone rang once.

Then twice.

My stomach tensed as it rang a third and fourth time.

After the ninth ring, my finger hovered over the end call button. I waited several more seconds and then hung up.

Carlos was clearly busy. Either that or he wasn't interested.

What we had had *seemed* genuine, but *who knows*? I wouldn't be the first woman to get the wrong end of the stick when it came to knowing where she stood with a guy.

One thing that was for sure, though, was that if I thought about this too much, I'd drive myself crazy.

My phone rang and I jumped with excitement.

'Hello?' I said without even looking at the screen.

'Hey, cousin!' It was Bella. My shoulders slumped. It wasn't that I didn't adore her, I really did. But I'd hoped the call was from someone else.

'Hey!' I perked up. 'How are you?'

'I'm good! Listen, what are you doing tomorrow night?'

I resisted the temptation to say I'd be at home drowning my sorrows in a pint of my special ice cream.

'Nothing, why?'

'Well, I've just heard about this throwback nineties and noughties pop night in town, and I know that's the kind of thing you like, so I wondered if you wanted to go?'

'Oh!' My eyes widened. 'I didn't know you were into that?'

'Yeah, not really…' I sensed her smiling down the phone. 'But Cassie told me that tomorrow is kind of a big day for you, and I thought maybe you'd like to do something to take your mind off things. Sometimes it's good to have a distraction and some company.'

Bella was such a sweetheart. She'd been checking on me a lot more since Cassie had moved. It was good to know I had someone I could lean on for support if I needed it.

'Okay, cool! If you're sure you can suffer the music, then yeah, I'd love to!'

'Great! Let's meet at London Bridge at six thirty tomorrow. I'm sure you're going to love it!'

'Thanks for calling, and see you there!'

My shoulders loosened. If all else failed on the Carlos front, at least I had something to look forward to.

Singing along to some nineties tunes wasn't on the same level as the man you love declaring he wanted to be with you, but at least it would take my mind off things for a few hours.

I pulled out my phone. Only to check the time. *Honest.* I wasn't looking to see if a certain person had returned my call from yesterday. Nope. Not at all.

As much as I'd wanted to call Carlos again, I'd resisted. He would've seen my missed call yesterday. I'd taken the first step. Now he had to meet me halfway. I had to be patient and wait for him to get back to me. Or not.

Anyway, I was going to try to avoid thinking about him tonight and focus on having a nice girly evening.

'Sorry!' Bella rushed over. 'Mike got back late from lunch with his friends, and obviously I couldn't leave Paul on his own.'

'No worries!' I gave her a hug.

'How are you doing?'

'Okay-ish. Well, trying to be. It just doesn't make sense. If you'd found the love of your life, hadn't spoken to them for six months and missed them like crazy, wouldn't you return their call quickly if they made the first move?'

So much for me not thinking about Carlos anymore, but I had to offload to someone.

'I hear what you're saying.' Bella nodded.

'I mean, surely no matter how busy you were, even if you didn't see the missed call until three in the morning, you'd at least text to say you'd call later or whatever, wouldn't you? Clearly he's not interested.' My stomach plummeted as the realisation that Carlos wasn't going to call, hit me.

'Don't give up hope.' Bella rubbed my shoulder. 'Let's forget about phone calls this evening. They'll be playing nineties and noughties pop all night and there'll be tribute acts too, so you're going to have a great time!'

'Yeah.' I tried to sound upbeat. 'Let's go and enjoy ourselves.'

We walked towards a pub about ten minutes away from the station. In the window was a poster for the event. I was excited.

As we climbed the stairs, Britney's 'I'm a Slave 4 U' blared. There was already a crowd of people in the function room at the top of the building. It was dark, so I couldn't see their faces, but looked like there was a mixture of men and women.

A Spice Girls tribute act came on first. Bella and I sang along to 'Spice Up Your Life'.

Next an MC came on stage.

'Ladies and gentlemen. For one night only, please welcome to the stage, the incredible, the incomparable, UNSYNC!'

'Yay!' I cheered. 'An NSYNC tribute band. My favourite!'

The lights went up and five men stood with their backs to the crowd. As the familiar intro to 'Bye Bye Bye' came on, each of them span around.

What the…

My mouth dropped open.

On the stage were Carlos, Nate and three other friends I recognised.

'Oh my God! Bella! Look, it's…' I turned to face her and when I did, I saw a huge grin spread across her face. 'You knew?'

She nodded.

I whipped my head back to the stage. Carlos was now in the front, miming to the song whilst doing some impressive dance moves. In fact, they *all* were. They were doing the whole routine. The bounces, steps, kicks, shoulder shrugs, head movements, arm pumps, waves and jumps were perfectly *in sync*. Pardon the pun. I'd watched that video and their performance at the American Music Awards a million times when I was younger and they had the choreography down to a T.

My mouth dropped open again. I couldn't believe this was happening.

Carlos wiped his face with a towel quickly, then threw it out to me. I caught it and screamed with excitement like a teenage groupie.

The track switched to 'Girlfriend'.

Nate started rapping the intro from the Nelly remix of the song. I burst out laughing. He was *good*. Carlos walked to the edge of the stage and called me over. The backing track lowered just as the chorus came on and Carlos sang, 'Would you be my girlfriend?' Just like in the song.

My eyes widened and my whole body fizzed with happiness.

I nodded and my face broke into a huge smile.

Carlos jumped down from the stage, lifted me in the air and spun me around. I threw my arms around his neck. God, he smelt so good. I'd missed his scent so much.

He lowered me to the ground, wrapped his arms around my waist and pulled me in for a passionate kiss, which instantly set my blood on fire.

It was as if we'd been apart for years rather than six months. Carlos's lips were just as soft and delicious as I remembered.

As he gently slipped his hot tongue inside my mouth, I pulled him closer into me. Every atom in my body buzzed and my mind turned to mush. The only thing I could think about was how amazing this felt and whether supergluing his lips to mine was an option so I could feel his mouth on me permanently.

When we finally came up for air, I opened my eyes. I

hadn't even realised that the music had stopped. As soon as Carlos's lips were on mine, he was the only thing that existed. Everything else just faded away.

I noticed that the lights were on and everyone on stage was staring at us, their eyes wide with joy. Well, everyone except Nate, who had his hand covering his eyes like a child who wasn't supposed to be watching an X-rated film.

'So I guess you guys made up, then?' I tilted my head in Nate's direction.

'*Sí*. He came to Spain and we had a good talk. When he saw how serious I was about sorting out my life so that I could be with you properly, he realised that you were not just something casual for me. And when I told him my idea for tonight, Nate said he would help me to organise everything.'

'Well, it's genius! You must *really* like me to learn the dance routine to not one but *two* pop songs!'

'I do not *like* you, Quesito: *te quiero mucho*.'

'What does that mean?'

'That I love you. A lot.'

My eyes almost popped out of their sockets and a million butterflies filled my stomach.

Carlos said he loves me.

I'd dreamt about hearing those words so many times and now it had happened. I quickly pinched myself to check this was real. *Ouch.* That was a bit too hard. But, yep. I was fully awake.

'In case you didn't already know, I love you too.'

Carlos leant forward and kissed me again. The whole room cheered.

As I regained full consciousness, I noticed that the faces around me were very familiar. I saw more of Nate's friends and then, OMG! It was Cassie. She waved excitedly. And Melody and, wow, Zach was here too!

'I can't believe you organised all of this! For me!'

'Of course.' Carlos brushed a curl from my forehead. 'Lily, I need you to know that I would do anything for you. Before you came to Spain, I did not believe I would meet anyone who made me want to think about the future and settling down properly again. Who I could trust and give my heart to. You did not care that I did not have money and did not live in a nice place. You did not just want me for fun. You are the only woman who has seen the real me and liked me anyway. Being without you these past six months has felt impossible at times. But a woman like you deserves the world. So I had to become the best man I could be, to be worthy of you.'

'You were *always* worthy of me.' I kissed him gently on the cheek.

'*Gracias*. It is kind of you to say, but I was not happy with my life. I knew I could become more. And I could not ask you to love me until I was able to love myself.'

'And do you now?'

'*Sí*. I am in a better place. Especially now that I am with you. I have missed you so much.' He kissed me again.

'I've missed you so much too. The only reason my lips aren't fixed to your face is because I want to hear how you've been. I'm glad you're in a good place. So, how long do I have you for before you return to Spain?'

'For as long as you want.'

'What?' My eyes bulged. 'Seriously?'

'I thought I could stay in London for a while, if you are okay with this, and then we can talk about where we would like to be and discuss our future, *together*.'

'Oh my God!' I threw my arms around him and squeezed tight. I didn't want to let him go, but I needed to see his face. To check I hadn't misheard. 'That's the best news! But what about your gigs and stuff in Spain?'

'Do you know the artist called JC?'

'Yeah, course. He's huge. He's the one who sings "Rainbow" and "Make You Proud", right?'

'*Sí.* I have done the remix for some of his songs. We met before he became famous and when he decided that he would like some dance remixes, he remembered me and asked if I would do them. The money I will get will be enough to clear the rest of my debts.'

'Carlos! That's incredible! I'm so happy for you.'

'*Gracias, cariño.*'

'Wait. Was that two thank-yous? You really are a changed man!'

'And you? How are you, Lilita? Nate tells me that you are okay and doing well in your job?'

'Yeah, all good. I got promoted! My boss said that whilst I was in Spain, she realised what an asset I was. Finally!'

'*Genial!*' He picked me up and spun me around again. 'I am so proud of you.'

'Now it's my turn to say *gracias*. And I went to a family party a couple of weeks ago and I actually danced. Everyone almost fell off their chairs.'

'That is fantastic! The dancing part, not the people falling off their chairs!'

I let out a giggle and Carlos's face broke into his adorable smile. The smile I'd missed so much. For the last six months, I'd wondered if I'd ever see it again, but now here it was. And even brighter and wider than I remembered. Now I'd get to see that smile every day for the rest of my life.

'You did the playlist for tonight, didn't you?' I jigged around to the "I'm Too Sexy" track by Right Said Fred that had just come on.

'*Sí.*'

'It's amazing! Almost as good as your dance routine. Seeing as you've gone to the trouble to include all of my favourite songs, we shouldn't let them go to waste. Carlitos, would you like to dance to some cheesy pop music with me?'

'Quesito.' He took my hand. 'I will *always* want to dance with you. I want us to laugh and love together. Tonight and always.'

My stomach flipped.

And as Carlos led me through the crowds to the centre of the dance floor, I knew he meant every word.

EPILOGUE

LA: Three months later

'So? Did you like?' Carlos jumped down from the stage.

We were in a huge nightclub in LA, where Carlos had finished yet another sell-out headline show. One of his biggest sets to date.

When his remixes of multi-award-winning musician JC had come out, Carlos's popularity had exploded. Not only had every singer and his dog been asking him to put a dance spin on their tracks, he'd also had so many requests to play all over the world. To say that his career had exploded was like saying that the Spice Girls had sold *a few* records.

'*Like*? You were brilliant! As always!' I pulled a tissue out of my jean shorts and wiped my forehead. I'd been dancing all night, and despite the air con, I was still hot.

'*Gracias!*' Carlos flashed his gorgeous smile, then threw his arms around me.

'I'm all sweaty!' I winced before resting my head on his shoulder and breathing in his intoxicating woody scent. We'd lived together in London for three months, and I still hadn't worked out how Carlos always smelt so good. Even after he'd finished a set or had come from the gym, somehow he just had the aroma of hot, sexy man.

'Hot and sweaty is exactly how I like you, Quesito!' He licked his lips. 'It makes me happy to see you dance so much.'

'Me too! If someone had told me a year ago that I'd be in a nightclub in LA, shaking my tail feather all night in a club where my gorgeous boyfriend was DJing, I would've laughed in their face.'

It was true. Now dancing was one of my favourite things to do. Music was always playing in our house, and I'd shimmy around every room.

I loved those moments when Carlos and I were cooking his delicious paella together in the kitchen and he'd come up behind me and hold my waist, then I'd swing my hips and grind against him. It often led to us bumping and grinding later in the bedroom, which I didn't mind one bit. We still had to make up for the six months that we were apart.

I thought the sex we'd had in Spain was amazing, but now making love was even better. Knowing that we were together, properly and fully committed, just made the connection even more intense.

Our dancing wasn't just limited to the house. As well as getting lost in the music at Carlos's gigs, if he wasn't working at the weekend, we'd also find somewhere to go and shake a leg. Not always at a club. We'd often just find a low-key bar that played salsa or flamenco and hang out there. I still had a long way to go until I mastered all the moves, but I was having fun trying.

'You were awesome, man!' Chad, the promoter, slapped Carlos on the shoulder. 'We'd sure like to have you back! My buddy Shawn who works with the best clubs in New York was here earlier and he'd like to get you into some of his places too. Okay if I set something up?'

'*Sí!*' Carlos's eyes widened before he quickly composed himself like it was no big deal. 'If you call Jonah, he will discuss it with him.'

Jonah was Carlos's agent. They hadn't worked together long, but he'd already set him up with gigs in Ibiza, Amsterdam, and of course London.

'New York, eh?' I said once Chad had left. 'That'd be so cool!'

'It would!' Carlos finished packing up his laptop. 'We will see what happens. And if you have organised things with work by then, perhaps we can stay there longer—for a holiday?'

'Yes!' I jumped up and down.

Workwise, things had changed for me. Although I'd started a new director role soon after I'd returned from Spain, something hadn't felt right.

It was weird. For so long, I'd wanted more responsibility and to rise up the corporate ranks. But after those five weeks away, I wasn't the same person. My dreams and desires were different.

Spain and getting together with Carlos showed me that there was so much more to life and that I'd missed out by not travelling more and sooner.

I knew I couldn't do anything about the past, but I could change my future. That was why, two weeks ago, I'd spoken to Ruth about going freelance from next month, so I had more time to globe-trot.

Carlos had invited me on his international trips and if he was doing a set on the Saturday night, we always tried to arrive on the Friday and leave on the Monday to give us time to explore the city. Which meant I'd exhausted my holiday allowance in record time.

Ruth didn't want me to leave, so tried her best to accommodate my requests, but she was running a business, so she could only do so much. And I didn't want to be tied down to traditional working days and hours anymore. My work could be done remotely, and now that there were two of us sharing the bills, I could afford to work and earn less.

Although Carlos's income was now enough to support us both, work was an important part of my identity, so I didn't want to give it up completely. But as Doris wisely said, nobody went to their grave wishing they'd worked more. Life was for living, and I wanted to do more of that, with Carlos.

As we slid into the back seat of the taxi, Carlos pulled me in for a long, slow kiss.

'I have wanted to do that all night.' He stroked my bare cheek.

'Me too.'

His phone buzzed and he pulled it out of his pocket.

'Do you have plans for the end of next week?' he asked, reading a text message.

'I'm out on Thursday evening with Melody and I was thinking me and you could go to that new salsa night in Soho on Saturday, but apart from that, I'm free.'

'Would you like to come to Madrid again? My sister will be there and I would like you to meet her.'

I'd met his aunt, Carmina, in Madrid a month after Carlos and I were reunited and she was lovely. She'd cooked up a feast and whilst Carlos had gone to the bathroom, she'd pulled out a load of old photo albums. Carlos cringed at the pictures when he came back, but I thought they were adorable.

Carmina had also invited me to her salon the next day, where she analysed my skin properly before giving me the best facial I'd ever had and a handful of natural skincare products. My complexion had already improved a lot thanks to following the advice she'd given to me whilst I was in Spain, but these helped even more.

My confidence had grown massively. Now I only wore a very light foundation to work if I felt like it. But most of the time, if I went to the supermarket or out dancing with Carlos, I'd just go out with my bare skin.

He loved me just the way I was, and more importantly I was finally happy with how I looked too.

I'd realised that I was never going to have completely clear, flawless skin and having a few blemishes was okay. Accepting that had brought me a lot of peace. Plus it'd saved me extra time in the mornings, which meant more time in bed with Carlos.

'Count me in! I can't wait to meet your sister and hear all about her adventures in Australia.'

'She will love you. Almost as much as I do.'

'I was hoping she might like me just as much!'

'That is impossible.' Carlos stroked my cheek again. 'I love you more than you love churros.'

'Wow, that's a lot!' I smiled. 'More than you love

palmeras?'

'Hmmm.' He scratched the back of his neck and I gasped with mock horror. 'I am joking! I love you more than palmeras, *queso* and music.'

'Three of your favourite things! I'm honoured!'

'I would give up palmeras forever if it meant I could spend the rest of my life with you.' He took my face in his hands and kissed me.

'That means a lot.' I wrapped my arm around him and gave him a squeeze. 'Luckily you don't have to choose. And you'll be able to get some when we're in Madrid. Talking of travel, I've just realised that in the next few months we'll be going to at least four countries: your gig in Greece, Spain, possibly here in America again and the South of France for Cassie and Nico's wedding. And who knows? Maybe we'll love one of those places so much we'll end up living there one day. So exciting!'

'*Sí!* And this is only the beginning, Quesito.' Carlos kissed me gently on the forehead. I cannot wait to travel all around the world with you. And I know that wherever we go, if you are with me, I will always be home.'

Want More?

Want to find out what happens when Carlos takes Lily on an a dreamy surprise date? Join the Olivia Spring VIP Club and **receive the *My Spanish Romance* Bonus Chapters for FREE:** https://bookhip.com/TRCFBQL

Ready For Book 5? As Melody and Nate travel to France for Cassie and Nico's wedding, will hate blossom into romance? **Order the enemies-to-lovers romcom *My French Wedding Date* from Amazon now!**

ENJOYED THIS BOOK? YOU CAN MAKE A BIG DIFFERENCE.

If you've enjoyed *My Spanish Romance*, **I'd be so very grateful if you could spare two minutes to leave a review on Amazon, Goodreads and BookBub**. It doesn't have to be long (unless you'd like it to be!). Every review – even if it's just a sentence – would make a *huge* difference.

By leaving an honest review, you'll be helping to bring my books to the attention of other readers and hearing your thoughts will make them more likely to give my novels a try. As a result, it will help me to build my career, which means I'll get to write more books!

Thank you SO much. As well as making a big difference, you've also just made my day!

Olivia x

ALL BOOKS BY OLIVIA SPRING:
AVAILABLE ON AMAZON

The Middle-Aged Virgin Series
The Middle-Aged Virgin
The Middle-Aged Virgin in Italy

Only When it's Love Series
Only When it's Love
When's the Wedding?

My Ten-Year Crush Series
My Ten-Year Crush
My Lucky Night
My Paris Romance
My Spanish Romance
My French Wedding Date

Other Books
Losing My Inhibitions
Love Offline

ALSO BY OLIVIA SPRING

Only When It's Love: Holding Out For Mr Right

Have you read my second novel ***Only When It's Love?*** Here's what it's about:

Alex's love life is a disaster. Will accepting a crazy seven-step dating challenge lead to more heartbreak or help her find Mr Right?

Alex is tired of being single. After years of disastrous hook-ups and relationships that lead to the bedroom but nowhere else, Alex is convinced she'll never find her Mr Right. Then her newly married friend Stacey recommends what worked for her: a self-help book that guarantees Alex will find true love in just seven steps. Sounds simple, right?

Except Alex soon discovers that each step is more difficult than the last, and one of the rules involves dating, but not sleeping with a guy for six months. Absolutely no intimate contact whatsoever. *Zero. Nada. Rien.* A big challenge for Alex, who has never been one to hold back from jumping straight into the sack, hoping it will help a man fall for her.

Will any guys be willing to wait? Will Alex find her Mr Right? And if she does, will she be strong enough to resist temptation and hold out for true love?

Join Alex on her roller coaster romantic journey as she tries to cope with the emotional and physical ups and downs of dating whilst following a lengthy list of rigid rules.

Only When It's Love **is a standalone, fun, feel-good, romantic comedy about self-acceptance, determination, love and the challenge of finding *the one*.**

AN EXTRACT FROM ONLY WHEN IT'S LOVE

Chapter One

Never again.

Why, why, *why* did I keep on doing this?

I felt great for a few minutes, or if I was lucky, hours, but then, when it was all over, I ended up feeling like shit for days. Sometimes weeks.

I must stop torturing myself.

Repeat after me:

I, Alexandra Adams, will *not* answer Connor Matthew's WhatsApp messages, texts or phone calls for the rest of my life.

I firmly declare that even if Connor says his whole world is falling apart, that he's sorry, he's realised I'm *the one* and he's changed, I will positively, absolutely, unequivocally *not* reply.

Nor will I end up going to his flat because I caved in after he sent me five million messages saying he misses me and inviting me round just 'to talk'.

And I *definitely* do solemnly swear that I will *not* end up on my back with my legs wrapped around his neck within minutes of arriving, because I took one look at his body and couldn't resist.

No.

That's it.

No more.

I will be *strong*. I will be like iron. Titanium. Steel. All three welded into one.

I will block Connor once and for all and I will move on with my life.

Yes!

I exhaled.

Finally I'd found my inner strength.

This was the start of a new life for me. A new beginning. Where I wouldn't get screwed over by yet another fuckboy. Where I wouldn't get ghosted or dumped. Where I took control of my life and stuck my middle finger up at the men who treated me like shit. *Here's to the new me.*

My phone chimed.

It was Connor.

I bolted upright in bed and clicked on his message.

He couldn't stop thinking about me. He wanted to see me again.

Tonight.

To talk. About our future.

Together.

This could be it!

Things *had* felt kind of different last time. Like there was a deeper connection.

Maybe he was right. Maybe he *had* changed…

I excitedly typed out a reply.

My fingers hovered over the blue button, ready to send.

Hello?

What the hell was I doing?

It was like the entire contents of my pep talk two seconds ago had just evaporated from my brain.

Remember *being strong like iron, titanium and steel* and resisting the temptations of Connor?

Shit.

This was going to be much harder than I'd thought.

Want to find out what happens next? Buy *Only When It's Love* by Olivia Spring on Amazon now!

ACKNOWLEDGEMENTS

My tenth acknowledgements page!

Usually I try to keep this page as short as possible. But ten books is a huge achievement and it's the perfect opportunity to thank the many people who've helped me along the way. Grab a cuppa and a biscuit because there's a long list…

Firstly, thank you, my dear friend Alain. Although you're no longer here, I truly believe that you sent the inspiration for my first book when I really needed it.

Jas: you were the first person to read my debut, which was *very* different to the version that was eventually published! Since then, you've continued to read and champion all of my books. Thanks for being there from day one and for letting me stay at your place whilst I researched key locations for *My Spanish Romance*.

Mum, I remember being so nervous giving you my debut to read, because you always tell it like it is, which I love. Thankfully, your feedback was constructive and I appreciate you continuing to read everything I write and being my amazing unofficial editor.

Loz, thanks for all of the millions of messages you've sent over the years with invaluable feedback. Since book one, I've always valued your input and you never fail to find something that I would've missed.

To my husband! When I first started writing, you were a figment of my imagination. I hadn't even met you yet, but you're the manifestation of all of the wonderful heroes I've created in my novels. *Gracias* for your continued love and support, for giving me romantic inspiration every day and for helping with the Spanish for this novel.

Cams, J & J, Dad, Mich, big sis and Neresa, thank you all for your unwavering support, whether it's reading or buying my books, giving feedback or motivating me with words of encouragement. I appreciate the love you've given since I first announced I'd written a novel!

To my OG author friends: Clare and Mike, thank you for recommending the independent route and showing me what was possible! Thanks also to Brad and Kay for your encouragement and help with the blurbs!

I have so much gratitude for the three amazing ladies who I've worked with since my first book: my editor, Eliza, web designer, Dawn, and book cover designer, Rachel.

It's impossible to name every blogger who's supported my books, but there are some special ladies who've read most if not all of them: Emma aka Mrs LJ Gibbs (thanks also for beta reading *My Spanish Romance*), Hannah (Love Books Actually), Jo (BookMadJo), Stacy (Stacy Is Reading), Oriana (Head In A Book 18), Leane (Reading in

Lipstick), Angela (Angela's Bookshelf), Kira (Books and The Brummie) and Vik (Little Miss Book Lover).

Thanks also to bloggers who've supported several of my books over the years: Heidi Lynn Book Reviews, Ems Books and Tea, Jo Reads Romance, Tangents & Tissues, This Hannah Reads, Burrow into a Book, As Read By Danielle, Wendy Reads Books, Nic Reeves Writes, Girl Well Read, Love Books Group, ATG Reads, The Mum Who Read4 and read.athon2021.

To: Holly Martin, LJ Ross and Lucy Score. Thanks for your support, advice and inspiration.

And the biggest thank-you goes to my fantastic readers. Thanks for buying and reading my books, telling your friends about them, leaving lovely reviews, sending kind messages and giving me the career I've dreamt of having since I was a child. I appreciate you *so* much and look forward to writing many more books to entertain you!

Here's to the next ten novels!

Lots of love,

Olivia x

ABOUT THE AUTHOR

Olivia Spring lives in London, England. When she's not making regular trips to Spain and Italy to indulge in paella, pasta, pizza and gelato, she can be found at her desk, writing new sexy romantic comedies.

If you'd like to say hi, email olivia@oliviaspring.com or connect on social media.

TikTok: www.tiktok.com/@oliviaspringauthor

facebook.com/ospringauthor
twitter.com/ospringauthor
instagram.com/ospringauthor